# EVERYBODY LOVES STELLA CAMERON!

"Shifting genres is difficult—often disastrous—for many authors, but Stella Cameron, who writes contemporary as well as historical romances, seems to accomplish this feat with little effort. Her narrative is rich, her style distinct, and her characters wonderfully wicked."

—*Publishers Weekly*

"Stunning!"

—*Romantic Times*

"Dazzling and refreshing!"

—*Affaire de Coeur*

"Stella Cameron leaves you breathless, satisfied . . . and hungry for the next time!"
—*NYT* bestselling author Elizabeth Lowell

"Sizzling, sexy, and sensational!"
—*NYT* bestselling author Jayne Ann Krentz

"Stella Cameron writes an exciting, fast-paced and very sensual novel—just the kind of book I love!"
—*NYT* bestselling author Linda Lael Miller

"Stella Cameron works magic with our hearts and casts a seductive spell!"
—Bestselling author Katherine Stone

"Stella Cameron's books are filled with wit, grace and sizzling sensuality!"
—Bestselling author Ann Stuart

**Turn the page and see why. . . .**

# IT WAS A VERY UNUSUAL JOB INTERVIEW. . . .

Phoenix wasn't filling in any strategic gaps in the interrogation. Roman could almost feel Vanessa's irritation.

"How about men?" Vanessa asked.

Roman smiled and crossed his ankles. He could script the rest of this exchange.

"I like them."

That wasn't in his script.

"You like them?" Vanessa repeated tonelessly.

"A lot." Phoenix nodded her red head vigorously. "Actually, it's been my salvation to be a masseuse."

Roman leaned farther forward.

"Perhaps you'd care to expand on that?" Vanessa suggested.

"Well . . . I'm not shocking you, am I?"

Roman chuckled and shook his head. For once he wished he could see Vanessa's face.

"You're intriguing me. Do go on."

Phoenix drew her fine red brows together and lowered her voice to a confidential pitch. "It gives me an outlet for some of my excess, er, drive. I find that putting all of my energy into bringing pleasure to male bodies takes my mind off . . . Well, you know."

"I'm not sure I do. Why don't you tell me?"

"Yeah," Roman muttered. "Why don't you tell us?"

**It was the beginning of an extraordinary relationship. . . .**

# SHEER PLEASURES

## STELLA CAMERON

**ZEBRA BOOKS**
**KENSINGTON PUBLISHING CORP.**

ZEBRA BOOKS are published by

Kensington Publishing Corp.
850 Third Avenue
New York, NY 10022

Second Printing: October, 1995

Printed in the United States of America

*For Phyllis Board Lloyd-Worth,*
*who let her hair down and walked in the wind—*
*and dreamed.*

# PROLOGUE

Men like Roman Wilde welcomed the night.

This was the best kind of night: seamless. Mexican sky spliced to Mexican land with no traitor moon to backlight a figure in dark camouflage.

Roman used his night glasses to scan the area. The only thing that moved was an insomniac desert iguana seeking shelter. Absolute stillness settled in. Not even a breeze. His stocking cap felt like a mini-sauna.

Then he heard an engine. Low, powerful, deliberately slow.

He brought his mouth close to the tiny mike on his tiger-striped shirt collar. "Yo, Nasty?"

"Hear him," came the cryptic response into his earpiece.

Nasty Ferrito and Roman didn't need many words. They'd racked up enough two-man missions in their eight years with the same Navy SEAL team to read each other's brains across blazing Kuwaiti oil fields, a Panamanian airfield—or several miles of Mexican desert.

Settling a hundred pounds of equipment more comfortably on his back, Roman inched forward on his belly, while easing out the Beretta strapped to his thigh.

With the toes of his boots dug into sand and rock and the glasses in place, he took up a position at the edge of a shallow escarpment, extended his arms, and braced the Beretta in both hands. Below lay the track where the mark—if no wires had been crossed—intended to take possession of a certain gentleman the United States would be very sorry to lose. So Nasty and Roman would just have to become the gentleman's new reception party and make their country happy by escorting him home.

The engine drew nearer.

Roman peered to his right and frowned. Full headlights rocked into view. Fools. Or was this their idea of cute? Who'd suspect a . . . He adjusted the glasses to bring the vehicle in closer. *Shit.* Some idiot in an old pickup with cab-over camper.

*Shit!* Roman lowered his face to the warm sand and dust. If the mark saw activity he'd do his damndest to abort the mission.

"Nasty," Roman said into his mike. "Relax. Not our man."

"Gotcha."

The engine noise changed. Roman looked down onto the track again. Immediately below, the camper idled. He grimaced. Time for a little route analysis, maybe? *"You sure this is the way, Mabel?" "Of course, Artie. See, there's that cute cactus, the one they drew on the map."*

The headlights went out.

Roman closed his eyes. Next would come the campfire and marshmallows. He started to use the mike again—and froze.

A new sound reached him. A muffled scream.

Dim light showed where the back door of the camper had been opened. A figure, doubled over, hauled something from inside and slung it over one shoulder.

The next scream was more like an animal shriek. It sank to a moan and went on and on.

With a shrug, the pickup driver deposited his burden at the edge of a ditch and used his foot to kick the bundle over.

That bundle had a body in it. And the body wasn't dead—yet.

Within moments the pickup engine burst to full life and the headlights cut the darkness again. Backing up. The bastard backed up, turned and set off—spewing sand and pebbles—in the direction from which he'd come, heading straight for the mark. Only the mark would already have picked up the unexpected vehicle on a scanner and changed his mind about coming.

"Not tonight," Roman told Nasty. Explanations would come

later. "Time for beddy-byes. Tell 'em to stand by to pick us up."

Whatever was in the ditch was none of his business. Doing what he was told to do—by whatever means he had to—was his business, and he'd better never forget it.

Several more seconds and the pickup's engine became a distant rumble.

Roman hesitated before instinct took over and he sheathed the Beretta. Crouching, he moved backward.

The next sound was neither scream nor shriek—nor moan. A keening sob hit him somewhere in the region of his stomach. Roman knew a woman's sob when he heard one.

"Shee-it," he hissed under his breath.

Those who said he was the fastest big man alive were probably right. Fast and very, very, quiet. For those blessings he spared fleeting thanks. He made it to the track in seconds. With the Beretta once more in his hands, he approached the ditch and dropped to his haunches. More like a big foxhole than a ditch. Deep and narrow. And at the bottom lay a dark, shifting mass.

If this was an attempt to outmaneuver his team it was stylish. He glanced all around but saw nothing approaching. With the gun trained on his target, he dropped into the hole and stood, feet braced apart. "Identify yourself," he said through his teeth.

The responding howl made him flinch. A black tarp covered whoever made that noise, and the tarp writhed.

Holding the weapon in his right hand, Roman stooped to yank open one of two ropes tied around the bundle. He undid it and pulled a corner of heavy oiled cloth aside.

His lenses made a green halo around long blond hair matted with blood.

A woman's battered face tossed from side to side. Her eyes were swollen almost shut.

Roman shoved his glasses on top of his head, holstered the gun again, and tore the tarp away. "It's okay," he said into the woman's ear. "You're okay." With the aid of a pencil-slim hooded flashlight he looked at her. She wasn't okay.

The abrupt bucking of her body distracted his attention from her face. Whatever color her torn dress had once been didn't matter. It was the color of blood now. Blood everywhere.

With a practiced hand, he found a rapid, thready pulse at her throat. Breathing, shallow. He had to find out the major source of blood loss and stop it.

A sweep of the light showed fresh red welling over her lower body. Roman narrowed his eyes and lifted the long, sodden skirt—and opened his mouth to breathe.

"Bill!"

"I'm not Bill." He glanced from knife wounds in her naked stomach to her parted, colorless lips. "Who are you? What's your name?"

She convulsed again and he spread his fingers over the wounds.

He felt the power of a contraction rippling through her swollen belly.

The baby's head was already visible.

Bile rose in his throat, and hatred. He was no stranger to disgust or to deep, shattering horror at the bestiality some men enjoyed practicing, but he'd never become quite tough enough to bury his anger, or the need to avenge the weak.

"You're doing just fine," he murmured. "We'll have you feeling better soon."

She grew still and slits opened between puffy eyelids. The touch of her fingers on his bare forearm shocked him. "April," she said clearly. More blood trickled from a deep cut at the corner of her mouth.

"You're called April?" He smiled and prayed the darkness disguised the burnt cork smeared on his face.

"April," she whispered again and her chest arched off the ground. "Help me. Help my baby. Please?"

Roman tore his attention from the agony on her features and cradled the infant's head. With the next contraction, tiny shoulders slithered into sight.

"Go with it," he said. "You're doing great. The baby's doing great."

The next sound he heard was, miraculously, a bubble of laughter from the woman's throat.

"That's right," Roman said, swallowing his own urge to curse aloud. The wounds on her belly bled freely. "Get ready to push and we'll have this guy all set to walk away."

He felt the woman hold her breath.

"That's the girl. Good girl." Vaguely, he remembered general instructions for moments like this. Very vaguely. Maybe some things were just instinct. He hoped to God they were. "Now. *Push.*"

She pushed, and the baby shot into his hands. And blood gushed in its wake.

"You did it," he remembered to whisper. She was going to bleed to death.

She didn't answer.

"April?"

"Yes. Baby?"

Placenta. What the hell was he supposed to do about the placenta? A gasping cry erupted in bursts from the child.

"Girl," he said, on automatic pilot now. "A beautiful baby girl."

Fumbling, he set the baby, facedown, on her mother's chest, found a length of thin twine and tied off the cord.

So much blood.

"The baby's fine," he said, rapidly bundling the tarp into a roll beneath April's hips. "Got to get your tail up here, kid. Hang in with me. Please hang in with me."

The flutter he saw was a pale hand settling on the tiny, protesting infant's back. He thought April crooned something.

It came back to him—what he'd been told to do for excessive vaginal bleeding after an abortion. Or a birth, he supposed.

For an instant he turned his head away and swallowed. She'd had enough pain. Was still having enough pain.

"Past Peak."

He looked closely into her face. "What did you say?" Her eyes were turquoise blue.

"Town. Past Peak. In Washington."

His earpiece crackled and Nasty's voice demanded, "Where the hell are you?"

Roman turned his head and said, "Wait for me. Do *not* leave without me. I'm gonna need special help."

"What—"

"Out," he snapped, breaking the connection.

"I've got to stop the bleeding," he said. "It won't be easy. Trust me, April."

"Look after my baby."

"You'll look after your own baby." Gritting his teeth, he lowered a knee to her belly and applied pressure.

Her jaw snapped upward. She clutched her baby to her breast with both hands.

"I'm sorry," Roman said, scarcely able to draw a breath.

"Look"—her mouth remained open—"look after my baby."

"Yes. Now just you hold onto that baby for me." He ground his knee down harder.

"He *lied!*"

"Who lied?" Please God let him do what was right. Please God let him save her. "Who lied, April?"

"Past Peak. The . . . club. Billy."

His pantleg grew warm and wet, and sticky. The bleeding wasn't stopping.

"Past Peak." Her throat clicked. "Club . . . Be . . . careful. *Billy!*" Her hands slipped away from the child.

Roman stopped the tiny girl from sliding to the ground. He undid his shirt and buttoned her inside. "Now," he told April. "I'm taking you for a ride."

Holding the tarp around her he began to lift. "Come on, Mom. You're strong, kid. And brave. I never met anyone braver than you." As carefully as he could, Roman got to his feet. "We're going to get you to the experts."

"Look after her."

His head cleared the top of the ditch. "We'll both look after her until you can go it alone." Once he got them all out of this hole. "I'm going to put you up there first. Okay, kid?"

Roman felt the slight weight in his arms grow almost imperceptibly heavier. She'd passed out on him. Just as well.

He glanced down. April's head hung back. Her mouth sagged open.

Roman moistened his lips. He couldn't risk moving her. She'd already lost too much blood. Very carefully, he set her down once more and trained the light on her face.

The place he'd once thought of as his heart clenched tight. He felt for her pulse, knowing what he'd find. Nothing.

Tipping up her chin, he breathed into her, then applied the heels of his hands between her breasts and pounded. He breathed, and pounded. Breathed and pounded, while the baby squirmed feebly.

Sweat poured from him.

*"Come on, April."*

"Roman?" Nasty's voice barked through the earpiece. "We've got to get out of here."

Roman sank back. "Yeah." She was dead. "Yeah, I'm coming."

Miniature arms and legs jerked inside his shirt. A small face, its seeking mouth open, bumped against his chest. The child whimpered.

"Roman! You're going to have to make it fast, buddy."

*"Yeah,* Nasty." He pulled the tarp over the limp body beside him. "I'm on my way."

# ONE

"My friends call me Phoenix." And if any of them could see her now they'd call her a fool with suicidal tendencies. She closed the office door softly and waited for a response from the room's lone occupant.

The woman rose majestically from a chair shaped like a creamy leather manta ray. Regarding Phoenix as she might a cottonmouth snake in a swimming pool, she walked slowly from behind the single sheet of heavy, pedestal-mounted glass that served as her desk.

Tall, very tall and definitely very female. The woman's black hair fell, smooth, glossy, and long, from a central part. Her eyes tilted up a little and seemed to have no pupils. Carefully applied red lipstick didn't completely disguise thin lips. It did lend a transparent cast to the woman's white skin.

Phoenix got a swift image of Morticia Addams and squelched a nervous grin as she glanced away.

"How did you get in here . . . *Phoenix?*"

This was it. She was about to be either thrown out, or, if she was really unlucky, chained up in a dungeon somewhere. "I heard about the club," Phoenix said cheerfully. "Sort of. Anyway, I'm . . . well, I really love this part of the country and I want to stay in Washington State. But there isn't a whole lot of work available for a masseuse in a backwater like Past Peak."

The woman's legs swished faintly inside the slim skirt of a gray silk suit. "Do you know who I am?" She made a leisurely circle around Phoenix.

Some things couldn't be faked. "No," Phoenix admitted.

"I didn't think so. I am Countess Von Leiden."

Phoenix looked at her with fresh interest. Did one say, hi, countess, nice pearls—or just curtsey? Or salute maybe? Phoenix straightened her back. "Pleasure to meet you, ma'am."

"Countess."

That answered one question. "Pleasure to meet you, Countess."

"I shall be much better pleased when I get to the bottom of your intrusion. We do not employ people who wander in off the streets."

"I heard about the club and tried to call. There isn't a listed number. I drove up the driveway and—"

"It isn't possible to simply drive up the driveway. There are security gates and dogs."

"I noticed. Isn't it a disgrace to have to go to such lengths to keep the riffraff out? Honestly, you can't trust anyone these days. In my last apartment—"

"How did you get past the gates?"

Phoenix shifted her weight from foot to foot on her small swatch of an acre or so of gray marble floor. Several miles of sheer gray draperies veiled the early spring splendor of the Cascade Mountain foothills. The countess had redefined minimalist in her "office."

"The gates?" she repeated, standing too close to Phoenix.

"Some guy happened along right in front of me." He'd happened along almost two hours after Phoenix had set up her vigil, waiting for someone to find a way through those electronic gates. "I just followed him in."

"You should have been stopped. Such carelessness is unacceptable."

Phoenix had counted on the possible success of dumb luck and it had worked. "I hope I haven't annoyed you, er, Countess. When I told the nice man at the front desk that I'd come for an interview he showed me in here." She smiled engagingly. "I guess he thought I meant I already had an interview. D'you think that's what he thought?" She was making herself sick with the ingenue act.

The opaque eyes didn't flicker. Neither did the red mouth. "Who told you about the Peak Club?"

Phoenix willed herself not to sweat. "Mort and Zelda, I guess."

The countess's smooth, rounded brow puckered. *"Mort and Zelda?"*

"They own Round the Bend. You know. Trendiest little bar and diner in the West?" She rolled her eyes and laughed. Maybe the dumb redhead approach wasn't such a good idea after all.

"In that row of dumps near the old train depot?"

The countess wasn't destined to become one of Phoenix's favorite people. "You can see the train depot from there. Mort and Zelda used to have a circus act. *Be* a circus act, I guess. Trapeze. They have all these circus posters—"

Countess Von Leiden interrupted. "And this Mort and Zelda talk about the Peak Club?"

Phoenix moistened her lips. "They've mentioned it. Their nephew—at least, I think that's what he is—he runs the truck stop out of town on the way to Fall City. Up the Creek. I expect you know it."

"Hardly."

"It's hard to miss. Len—that's the nephew—he used to be a jockey but he had a bad fall and he can't ride anymore."

"Fascinating."

"Len mentioned the club, too."

"How?" The countess's narrow nostrils flared. "What did all these people say?"

She should have listened to Mort. He'd begged her not to try this. So had Zelda and Len. "They said they'd heard it was really plush and exclusive. I've been doing some work for Mort and Zelda but I need more than they can pay me, so I decided to come and see if you needed anyone."

"We don't serve burgers and fries to truck drivers."

Phoenix felt her face flame. "I do. I like it—at the Bend. I'm here to see if you need a masseuse."

The countess's first smile wasn't a comforting sight. Her eyes narrowed and there was the faintest glimpse of pointed and overlapping eye teeth.

"You certainly fit the redhead stereotype. Quick temper. Some men are titillated by that. Where did you train?"

Phoenix absorbed the rapid-fire non sequiturs and responded to the question. "Sweden." She'd kept house for a masseur in Stockholm for three months and very nearly learned more than she cared to about massage.

"Really?" Permanently surprised brows rose even higher. "What on earth are you doing in Past Peak?"

Lying didn't come easily. "Looking for a place to settle down. A quiet place to live. But not at the expense of some excitement." She cast a meaningful glance at Countess Von Leiden. "I guess I'm saying I want to use my talents where they'll be appreciated—in a place *I* appreciate. And I'm into keeping business, the kind of business I'm very good at, separate from the rest of my life."

In the two years since she'd left Oklahoma City—and the law firm where she was the bright young trial lawyer supposedly destined for the stars—she'd done her darnedest to make sure she never forgot that business was supposed to support life, not the reverse. She had been burned by the business she'd chosen— by the law—and the blisters still stung.

The countess's cold fingers, settling on her cheek, startled Phoenix violently. "Hmm," the woman said, tilting her head to one side. "Perhaps . . ." Her lips remained parted and she stroked Phoenix from temple to chin.

There wasn't enough air left in the world. "Perhaps?"

"We are very selective here at the Peak Club. Our members are influential—extremely influential. All of them. They pay a great deal and they expect a great deal. We cannot afford any mistakes. We certainly cannot afford to make mistakes in the people we hire. Every one of them is a member of an elite team."

*Don't let her smell my fear.* Phoenix looked steadily back into the countess's black eyes. "Do you need a very good masseuse? The very best of masseuses?"

"Are you the very best?" This time it was the backs of the cold fingers that followed the lines of Phoenix's face.

"I'm good."

"Hmm. I wonder if you are. We usually go to great lengths to recruit our staff. But . . . Hmm. We wouldn't want to miss an opportunity if it simply presented itself."

Phoenix endured the stroking in silence.

"Of course, we would have to thoroughly investigate your credentials."

"Of course." And, as they spoke, an old friend in Oklahoma City was unwillingly but industriously at work gathering those "credentials."

"Where are you from?"

"New York originally. In recent years I'm from all over."

"You find it difficult to settle down?" A pucker attacked the smooth brow again.

"Let's say I reached a point when I knew I needed to see the world or risk never seeing it at all. I've done it now. In the future I intend to travel differently."

"And what does that mean?"

"Maybe nothing. Maybe that I'm tired of paying my own way? Does that sound unreasonable?"

"It sounds"—the fingers descended Phoenix's throat—"it sounds as if we may have more to discuss. Yes. Yes, I think you and I could just find ourselves talking a great deal. Is your family still in New York?"

If Phoenix put her teeth together, the muscles in her jaw would flex—and the depth of her distaste and apprehension wouldn't need any further discussion.

"Your family?" the countess persisted.

"I'm afraid I'm the black sheep." Almost true. "We don't keep in touch anymore." Absolutely the truth.

Phoenix was honored with another pointy-toothed smile. "On your own, then?"

"Yes. I like it that way."

"Strong women appeal to me, Phoenix."

"I'm glad."

"Soft skin. And so many freckles."

Phoenix couldn't stop herself from blushing. "Another trait of the redhead, I'm afraid."

"Fascinating." The countess brought her Shalimar-scented face in for a microscopic examination of Phoenix's fascinating freckles. "So fine. Such fine skin. Where else are they?"

Phoenix swallowed. "Where else?"

"The freckles. Where else do you have them? On your breasts?"

Roman had been too engrossed in searching rapidly through file drawers to do more than listen absently to Vanessa grilling some light-brained female.

The good countess's last question grabbed his attention.

He eased shut the file drawer he'd just searched and looked at a bank of television screens, speakers, and recording reels ranged above a long table littered with sundry electronic debris. The table ran the length of one wall in a room otherwise devoted to file cabinets and locked cupboards—and a flight of steps leading to an overhead trap door. Finding that trap door had eaten up two tedious, endless months. It had eluded him because he'd taken that long to figure out that either there was a wall about twelve feet thick between two other rooms, or there was a room in this fabulously expensive piece of real estate with no apparent entrance.

"I've embarrassed you." Vanessa's humorless laugh had its predictable effect on Roman. His toes curled. "Forget I asked you that. Where do you live?"

Roman dropped into a chair before the speaker that emitted sound. With one practiced finger he flipped on the closest screen. A clear picture of the inside of the mausoleum Vanessa called her office brought a satisfied grin to his lips. He'd been convinced this setup existed somewhere at the club. Finding both a nastily efficient voyeur's paradise, and what was obviously information he was never supposed to see—in the same

night—might make a man believe there really was a Santa
Claus.

"Rose Smothers?" Vanessa was saying. "I almost think I
remember hearing that name before."

Geoffrey Fullerton—*Sir* Geoffrey Fullerton, late of the Welsh
Guards, probably wouldn't relish being likened to Santa Claus,
but Geoffrey had unwittingly led Roman to this Aladdin's cave.
And evidently Geoffrey had been spying on Vanessa before he
left, carelessly failing to turn one speaker all the way off.

The redhead wasn't a kid—except in the IQ department.
Thirty, maybe. Maybe younger.

"Rose Smothers is a sweetie," she said. "A weirdo, but a
sweetie."

Roman trained his flashlight on the monitor controls and
zoomed in on the woman's face.

He slipped down in the chair and rested his head against the
back. She was scared. Scared green eyes. Shit, Vanessa Von
Leiden was a vampire. What the hell satisfaction could she be
getting out of playing around with a hash-pusher who'd wandered into the wrong crypt?

"Where would we find this Rose Smothers?"

"She doesn't like strangers." Something else hovered in those
wide-set eyes. The woman's red-gold lashes flickered, casting
a moving shadow in green depths. "But she'd talk to someone
if I was with her. It's amazing really, but she trusts me. I've
only lived there a month. Mort and Zelda suggested I go and
see if she could rent me something. I've got the sweetest little
apartment over the garage. She's got a car in there that's never
been driven. Can you imagine that?"

Roman waggled his head. Scared, and running in place to
keep up. She wanted something and he'd bet all his next winter's
acorns a job wasn't it—not all of it.

He jerked forward to bring Vanessa back into the frame. A
view of her hourglass back, the ample bottom propped on her
desk, was his reward. Then she held out a hand, palm up, and
wiggled her fingers.

The other woman, Phoenix she'd called herself, swallowed loud enough to make a click in the speaker.

"I want to see your hands," Vanessa said, with more wiggling until she got what she wanted. "Good. Strong. I like strong hands. Capable. Capable of such lovely things, hmm?"

Roman experienced a dual reaction. The sexual jolt was okay. The acid taste of bile wasn't okay. Von Leiden sickened him. Not that her little hobbies, or how she found ways to feed them, were any of his business.

"It's an Aston Martin. A DB2. Can you imagine that? A robin's egg blue DB2 and it hasn't been out of the garage since it was delivered. She orders everything she wears from catalogues. Everything in the picture, right down to the shoes and jewelry. Anything else she needs is delivered. She never goes out, but she loves to talk. Weird, but—"

"Sweet?" Vanessa finished for Phoenix. "I can imagine. Are you her first—er—tenant?"

"Oh, no. No, I know I'm not."

Roman came in for another closeup of those green eyes, and the full, unpainted mouth that trembled ever so slightly. He narrowed his own eyes. Vanessa might be entranced by the act, but he wasn't buying whatever Phoenix thought she was selling.

She smiled.

It was Roman's turn to swallow. An angel's smile. Wide and tip-tilty cornered and framed by twin dimples in softly rounded cheeks. She shouldn't be here. She shouldn't be anywhere near the kind of evil and danger that soaked every inch of the Peak Club.

"Rose told me her old tenant will be coming back eventually, but that might not be for some time. I'll worry about it when I have to."

"Very wise. My partners and I make it a rule never to hire a new employee without a taste test." Vanessa gave her short, humorless laugh. "This has been a disturbingly tense day. Why don't we see if you can relax me."

Phoenix's hands were still wrapped in Vanessa's claws. "You mean you want me to give you a massage?"

"Possibly. I should go a little further into your living arrangements first. We don't encourage too many people to live on the premises, but if we particularly value an employee, and if they don't have satisfactory accommodations, well . . ."

In the pause that followed, Roman made a more complete tour of Phoenix. From what he'd learned, the shape wasn't exactly the countess's style. Slim, but curved in the right spots, the redhead didn't appear tall or athletically boyish enough for Vanessa's tastes.

Phoenix wasn't filling in any strategic gaps in the interrogation. Roman could almost feel Vanessa's irritation and he didn't have to see her flat, black eyes to know how they would be barely concealing venom right now.

"How about men?"

Roman smiled and crossed his ankles. He could script the rest of this exchange.

"I like them."

He braced his weight on the chair arms and scooted more upright. That comment wouldn't have been in his script.

Vanessa's shoulders flexed inside the jacket of her gray Givenchy suit. "You like them," she stated tonelessly.

"A lot." The red head nodded vigorously. "Actually it's been my salvation to be a masseuse."

Roman leaned farther forward.

"Perhaps you'd care to expand on that?" Vanessa suggested.

"Well . . . I'm not shocking you, am I?"

Roman chuckled and shook his head. For once he wished he could see Vanessa's face.

"You're intriguing me, Phoenix. Do go on."

Phoenix drew her fine red brows close together and lowered her voice to a confidential pitch. "It gives me an outlet for some of my, er, excess sex drive. I find that putting all my energy into bringing pleasure to male bodies takes my mind off . . . Well, you know."

"I'm not sure I do. Why don't you tell me?"

"Yeah," Roman muttered. "Why don't you tell us?"

Phoenix withdrew her hands from Vanessa's and pushed at

her wildly curly hair. Her breasts rose inside a loose, dark green T-shirt. No bra. Nice breasts.

She laughed a little, a little awkwardly, Roman thought, and said, "I think sex is healthy, don't you?"

"Yeah," Roman said, echoing Vanessa's affirmative response.

"Some people need more of it than others," Phoenix continued, her fingers still buried in her hair. "They need and enjoy more of it. I've been reading a lot about sexual addiction and I guess that's what I may have."

Roman mouthed, "Welcome to your kind of place," and allowed himself a few seconds of fantasy about helping Phoenix out with her addiction.

Evidently Vanessa was, unbelievably, at a loss for words.

"Seriously," Phoenix said, her eyes round with sincerity. "Seriously, you would find me the perfect employee. I know how to make people feel good—very, very good. And they don't know I'm, well, that I'm getting off on feeling them, if you know what I mean. Not unless I can tell they'd want to know."

This lady was a piece of work.

Vanessa's slowly exhaled breath whistled in the speakers. "How about women?"

"Oh, I don't mind massaging women."

Roman smothered a laugh before he remembered he didn't need to be silent. He'd already checked the area for bugs.

"Does it . . ." Vanessa stood up and turned—directly toward the camera. "Do you get any sexual satisfaction from working with women?"

Vanessa's eyes narrowed. She held her tongue between her teeth and the avid light Roman had come to detest shone in her eyes.

He turned his attention to Phoenix. Her hands slowly descended from her hair, hands folded into tight fists. He frowned. Either she was struggling to hide revulsion, or she'd just caught a passing flu virus and was about to lose her cookies. The woman looked sick and shaken.

"Women?" Vanessa repeated.

Phoenix wiped her palms on her jean-clad hips. "I like women."

Not as bed partners, Roman thought.

"What does that mean? Like?"

"I appreciate a beautiful female body. And I don't have anything against working on them, of course. But they don't help me with my—problem."

Keeping her back to Phoenix, Vanessa smiled thinly. "Have you ever been made love to by a woman?"

"No!"

"Too quick, my love," Roman whispered.

Vanessa's smile became predatory. "Good. As I told you, we have to be very careful here at the Peak Club."

Roman knew what Vanessa meant by being "careful." And he could almost hear her contemplating the broadening of Phoenix's sexual education. Vanessa took her pleasures with both men and women but never hid her preference for the latter, particularly if they'd never been with a woman before.

"Maybe I should just make a proper appointment and check back with you when it's more convenient?"

Phoenix the nymphomaniac was losing her nerve. Roman studied her face again. Intelligent eyes. Something didn't fit. Years spent reacting to instinct, backed up by the most rigorous training in the world, had left him with an overdeveloped knack for sensing a setup. Phoenix wasn't for real. This was all an act.

And he'd been cooped up in this place too long. He was turning to fiction for entertainment.

"I think we can make a little more progress than that," Vanessa said, finally facing her visitor again. "I pride myself on having good people-instincts and my instincts tell me you could be exactly what we're looking for."

Roman felt a foreign uneasiness stiffen his spine.

"Yes," Vanessa went on. "Yes, you might just be what we're looking for. Of course, I'll have to get final approval from my four partners, but I believe in grabbing opportunities."

Roman bared his teeth and muttered, "Run, babe, run." With the aid of some very persuasive incentives, he'd contrived to graduate from club member, to Geoffrey and Vanessa's most recent partnership acquisition. The Hon. Miles Wilberton, former captain in the English Horse Guards, and Pierre Borges, ex-officer in the select Swiss Alpine Corps and son of the Swiss-French banking Borges, rounded out the company of five partners, but Geoffrey and Vanessa reigned supreme. Roman had already witnessed one employee "approval ceremony." The lucky—and successful—candidate was an ex-dealer from Las Vegas who proved herself willing and very able to perform some interestingly lucrative games of chance. Phoenix, whoever she might be, was cut from very different cloth.

"How serious are you about working for us, Phoenix?"

"Very serious."

Roman saw how Phoenix's throat moved.

"Good. Will anyone miss you if you don't go back into town this afternoon?"

A beat passed, and another before Phoenix said, "No."

"That'll make everything go more smoothly," Vanessa said, all business now. "In fact, I'd like you to consider spending the night here. That would give us a chance to complete our interviewing procedures."

The prospect of owning a self-declared female sex addict had made Vanessa too eager. She wanted this one, and she was moving fast to make sure she got her.

"This sounds great," Phoenix said. The downward jerk at the corners of her mouth suggested she lied. "But I will have to go back to Rose's tonight. She'd worry if I didn't."

"I thought you said she was some loony-tunes old bat you hardly know." Vanessa's too-perfect diction tended to slip if she was rattled.

"Weird, is all," Phoenix said quickly. "But very kind."

"This is more important." Vanessa went to the wall behind a black marble statue of two headless, sexless, but intimately entwined figures, and swung open a panel. She glanced back at Phoenix and selected one of the ankle-length sarong skirts and backless cross-over halter tops the female members of the club staff wore. "Green suits you," she said, closing the panel and walking back to Phoenix.

"Rose would get upset if I didn't show up."

"Why? And why does it matter to you?"

Phoenix almost dropped the uniform Vanessa thrust into her hands. She crumpled it into a bundle and held it before her like a shield. "It doesn't really matter except my stuff's all there—and my cat—and I don't like scenes."

"So collect your things in the morning. You don't even have to see her, do you?"

Phoenix appeared to consider. "I'm flattered. And I do want this job. But I think I'm going to keep the apartment. Mel—he's my cat—Mel doesn't eat unless I feed him myself. And Rose reminds me of my only aunt. She was really good to me. She died."

Vanessa made an impatient sound.

"Rose says she's sure her other boarder will come back eventually, but there's something funny about it."

"Funny?"

"Uh huh. I don't think she could have taken a thing with her when she left. I had to clear out drawers and make room in closets for my clothes. She left all her toiletries and makeup in the bathroom. And there's jewelry most people would lock away."

Roman found his attention wandering back to the rows of file cabinets. With the scanty clues he'd been given he had no alternative but to search each one. The task would be tedious, but he was a patient man—could be a patient man when something mattered as much as his present self-assigned project mattered.

"Rose is pretending. I'm sure of it."

He only half-concentrated on the conversation now. If Geoffrey decided to come back the explanations would have to be fancy.

"Pretending about what?" Vanessa asked.

"That she's sure the tenant she had before me will come back. She's been gone a year and a half."

Roman turned slowly back to the screen.

Vanessa sat on the edge of her desk once more. "Eighteen months? Has she heard from her?"

Phoenix hesitated before saying, "I don't think so. I think Rose has just made up her mind this tenant will come back when she's ready."

Vanessa reached back to prop her weight on splayed and whitened fingers. "But you don't believe it?"

"I'm not sure," Phoenix said. "Rose talks about her all the time. A very beautiful blonde, she says. But she doesn't really seem to know anything about her, except that she comes from a rich family and doesn't need to work except to pass the time. And that her name's April Clark."

# TWO

She was out of her depth. Nothing else could have caused her to toss April's name out like that. Out of her depth and desperate for any scrap of information that might help her find her oldest friend.

The smile Phoenix kept on her face felt like a Halloween mask. "The main thing," she said, looking steadily into the countess's unreadable eyes, "is Mel. He goes everywhere with me. I take the care of animals very seriously. I've always thought you could judge a person by the way she—or he—takes care of animals. That's one of the things I admire about the English. They really—"

"I'm glad you took a chance and dropped by," Countess Von Leiden said as if she hadn't heard Phoenix babbling. "This is going to be very fortunate for all concerned."

Phoenix's smile wobbled. Either she was even more desperate for a lead than she'd thought, or the countess's manner had undergone an extravagant reversal. The woman positively oozed charm.

"Of course you must take care of domestic matters in whatever way affords you the most satisfaction. We'll work around those things. What you say about this former tenant—this April—certainly is a puzzle. Did your landlady happen to mention anything else about her?"

Charm didn't suit the countess. The wider she smiled, the more gum she showed and the more she reminded Phoenix of a snarling feline. But there was no doubt that April's name had pressed a button.

"Not really," Phoenix said. "And it isn't my place to ask questions. But I do wonder if someone shouldn't alert the police or something." Her heart did odd, thunderous things.

"Oh, I shouldn't think so. If there was anything to be concerned about, this rich family of hers would already have taken any necessary steps."

The invented rich family April didn't have. Foster child in a home where the state's fees had bought her safety but no love, April had ducked out the minute she could. Phoenix was the one constant in her life, the one person she clung to, even if the grip slipped for long periods. At least, Phoenix had been the anchor until April's last excited call when she'd been so happy and so certain she'd met the love of her life, the man who would finally give her everything she'd ever wanted.

That call had come from Past Peak around the time when April had last been seen there.

Then silence.

Phoenix held up the skirt and top the countess had given her. Her insides trembled. Mort and Zelda were worried about April. So was Len. They all thought she'd met someone here at the Peak Club, someone she'd been reluctant to discuss and who might have something to do with her disappearance. Apparent disappearance. Whatever she did, Phoenix knew she mustn't forget that this wasn't the first time April had dropped out of sight. Only she'd never been gone this long and never without some word. If Phoenix hadn't been rushing from country to country, then from state to state, trying to forget she'd been fired for honesty, she'd have come looking for April months ago.

"I almost forgot!" The heavy beating of her heart became deafening. She'd promised to move cautiously. "April Clark used to stop by the Bend for coffee sometimes. Zelda says she remembers her because she was so pretty."

The countess made an interested sound.

"Did I say that's what gave me the idea to come and see if

you might be able to use me?" Mort knew where she was. If she didn't show up tonight he'd come looking for her, she knew he would.

The door swung open and a big, dark-haired man entered the office.

"I didn't hear you knock," the countess snapped. "I'm busy."

If the newcomer was shaken by the reprimand he didn't show it. He closed the door behind him and strolled confidently to stand beside the countess. "Bob said you were interviewing." He smiled engagingly at Phoenix. "I thought I'd come and have a look."

And he most certainly did look. He crossed tanned, muscular forearms, settled his weight on one leg and studied Phoenix from head to toe and back again. And he smiled.

Good-looking men couldn't be trusted. That had been a lesson Phoenix had learned early and painfully. This man would stand out in any crowd of knock-em-dead males.

"Bob didn't mention the position you wanted," he said to Phoenix.

"Masseuse," the countess said shortly. "Bob wouldn't know. This is Phoenix. She may prove useful to the club. In fact I'm almost certain she will."

"Is that a fact?" His eyes were the same color as those of Phoenix's cat, but a whole lot more disturbing. Her cat Mel was a rangy black tom whose unwavering blue stare spoke of a Siamese relative in the woodpile. Mel had come along shortly after Phoenix had seen a Lethal Weapon movie. She'd left the theater with visions of unforgettable curly lashed, blue eyes lingering in her brain.

"A masseuse, huh?" Strong, straight teeth and a wide mouth. A firm, full but not too full mouth. The guy had lived a lot and all of the living hadn't been easy. The lines of his face were hard, all the way to the cleft in his chin and the deep grooves that slashed downward from dimples beneath definite cheekbones.

He must be six and a half feet tall with shoulders that might not fit through some doors. A dark blue polo shirt, open at the neck, revealed curling hair as dark as the hair he wore short and brushed back from a straight hairline. Teamed with well-washed, well-worn jeans and scuffed sneakers, the polo shirt would give some men a relaxed appearance. What Phoenix felt in this man's presence was anything but relaxed. This one would be ready to pounce in a split second. That's what she felt.

"Quiet," he remarked, still smiling at her. "That might be useful in some situations, Vanessa."

Phoenix stirred. She'd started down a path she might as well pursue, at least until she was convinced she'd gone almost too far. "I'm pretty new in the area," she said. "I've been doing some casual work at a place in town and they suggested I might be able to use my training here."

"This is Roman Wilde," the countess said. She straightened her jacket and threaded her fingers together at her waist. A not-so-subtle crack had appeared in her commanding air. "Roman is one of my partners. A junior partner. You'll see more of him later." She emphasized "later."

Not an entirely unpleasant thought, Phoenix decided. Evidently her bizarre inspiration to plead sexual addiction was rubbing off on her naturally reserved nature where men were concerned. She shuffled her feet and realized she'd been standing long enough to make her back ache with tension.

"The people who own the diner told me they knew someone else who worked here and enjoyed it."

"You didn't mention that."

Phoenix made herself regard the countess with startled realization. "Good grief, I didn't, did I." She gave an embarrassed little chuckle and covered her mouth. "It was April. The woman who stayed at Rose Smothers's house before me. Gosh, I guess I'm more overwhelmed by all this than I thought." She spread her arms, indicating the room.

Roman Wilde rubbed the back of his neck and arched his back. "Who are we talking about, Vanessa?" The expansion of his chest was an event not to be missed.

The countess's brows had snapped together. "As far as I'm

concerned we're talking about a myth," she told Wilde. "A woman Phoenix knows. She certainly never worked here."

"But—"

"No." The countess cut Phoenix off. "I assure you no April Clark ever worked here. She sounds highly unreliable to me. We don't employ unreliable people."

The smile left Roman Wilde's tough face. "We don't even consider employing anyone without being damned certain they are reliable." His intensely blue stare bored into Phoenix. "Were you invited to interview with us?"

Muscles in her thighs contracted at the quiet menace in his tone. "No." But she wasn't about to be intimidated by someone big enough not to need to victimize little people. "I have no idea how one would go about trying to get an invitation to interview here. But I'm darn good at what I do and you'll be darn lucky if you get me. And all I know about April Clark is that she rented the rooms where I live now, and that she knew a bunch of people in Past Peak."

The corners of his mouth flickered and the lines in his cheeks reappeared. "Spirited," he told the countess, who continued to hold her hands in a scrunched knot. "Have you discussed what a job at the club would entail?"

"Not entirely. I did mention the need for a consensus among us—the partners, that is—before a final hiring decision can be made." The countess went to the cold black marble statue and stroked its curves. "Miles and Pierre are in Paris so we'll have to wait a few days to finalize things. I'm going to spend a little time with Phoenix myself now. Then we'll make arrangements for her to come back."

This could all be straightforward.

If straightforward included asking a woman if she'd made love with other women.

Wilde's next glance in Phoenix's direction was impersonal. "Don't you and Geoffrey have a meeting? I thought I heard him say there was something special on tonight."

The countess frowned and crossed to study an open book on

her desk. She tutted irritably. "It's not like me to forget. Leave your telephone number, Phoenix. I'll be in touch."

"I don't have a phone," Phoenix lied. "Rose doesn't like modern inventions."

"Modern inventions?" Countess Von Leiden wrinkled her nose. "Ridiculous. In that case we'll have to arrange for you to come back—" She broke off abruptly and turned to Roman Wilde. "Unless you've got time to take over for me, Roman."

He wandered past wall-mounted glass shelves, blowing at nonexistent dust on soapstone sculptures of nothing identifiable to Phoenix.

"Roman?" the countess pressed.

"What did you have in mind?"

"I'm sure you can figure it out," his partner said, snapping her pointed teeth together. "A preliminary evaluation is all we need. Do you understand?"

He smiled faintly and bowed. "Absolutely. The pleasure will be mine."

Phoenix knew a moment of fear. She ought to run, but she wouldn't get far if they decided they didn't want her to.

Countess Von Leiden smoothed her skirt, then her hair. "I'd better make sure everything's ready." She beckoned Wilde nearer, threaded an arm through his and drew him some distance from Phoenix. "There's something I ought to warn you about." Rising to the toes of her gray suede pumps, she whispered in the man's ear.

Looking at Phoenix over Von Leiden's sleek head, he raised straight, dark brows and said, "Really?"

"Yes. And I don't have to remind you that there must never be any question of unprofessional behavior on our part."

"You most certainly don't."

The glitter in those blue eyes brought heat to Phoenix's cheeks. She didn't need an explanation of what the countess had whispered. This man had actually been warned to be prepared for a sexual attack! From Phoenix!

His laugh turned her embarrassment to annoyance. He looked her over with amused curiosity.

The countess followed his gaze. "You can't tell much from appearances," she said. "If you don't think you can—"

"Don't give it another thought," he told her. "There's nothing here I can't handle."

Too easy, Roman thought. Too pat. He walked ahead of Phoenix along corridors lined with lemon-yellow watered silk. Soft ivory carpet absorbed the faintest sound.

Geoffrey hadn't looked back when he let himself out of the concealed room. For the first time, Roman questioned why Geoffrey hadn't checked around to make sure he wasn't seen. Was it perhaps because Roman was supposed to come upon him, and the entrance to the room, and to believe Geoffrey wouldn't know Roman had gone into that room? And had the carelessly live speaker been pure chance? Or had the entire scenario been a setup? Was Roman's seeming stroke of luck an elaborate trap?

"Where are we going?"

"To one of the treatment rooms," he told Phoenix shortly.

She could be a plant. A test to see if he'd hear April's name and would now bite. If that was the idea then someone had reason to think he wasn't what he pretended to be. Someone knew he'd sought out membership in the club, then insinuated himself into its ownership purely to further his efforts to catch a murderer. He believed that the murderer, or at the very least whoever had arranged April's murder, was very near at hand here.

A flight of steps led downward past windows overlooking the Snoqualmie River. At this point it swept past massive gray rocks etched with spring moss and topped with crowds of straight-spined Douglas fir. Snow on mountain peaks still gleamed against an afternoon sky turned to lavender with the approach of evening.

At the bottom of the steps he stopped and stood aside, motioning for her to go ahead of him. With a quick, apprehensive glance, she did so. And she didn't turn around when he continued on behind her. That control must be costing her.

What if Geoffrey had just been in a hurry? The important "meeting" was real enough. Roman had seen the chopper coming in for a landing. He'd watched a portly figure hurry, his head bent, toward the entrance to the underground hideaway known only to the very few members of the Insiders, a club within the Peak Club.

Sir Geoffrey Fullerton and widow Vanessa, Countess Von Leiden had created the Peak Club to cater to wealthy Americans with a yen to rub shoulders with sophisticates who could offer exciting diversions—and absolute discretion.

Months of covert enquiries had finally led Roman to the club. An introduction from a grateful Middle Eastern acquaintance had brought about a membership. He'd quickly figured the only way to continue his investigation was from the other side of the operation.

Analyzing the makeup of the partnership—a countess, two aristocratic ex-members of prestigious British military divisions, and a Swiss with both banking and military connections, had pointed Roman in the right direction to achieve his goal. At first his approaches had been rebuffed. The "management" wasn't looking for another partner. He'd continued to chip away until they were convinced that in the role of a highly decorated, mysterious ex-member of the select Navy SEALs, he could draw in both men and women fascinated by the illusion of covert power attached to the corps.

So far, so good. Mustering out of the navy had taken time and been the toughest decision he'd ever made, but when it was all over he'd been at peace—possibly for the first time in his life. His new life was fulfilling in ways that the old life had never been. There were as many battles to fight in the private sector as in a military capacity.

"Here we go," he said, reaching past Phoenix to open a door. This he pushed wide. "We work very hard to make sure our members have every comfort, and then some."

She entered cautiously, looking around as if she expected

someone or something to leap from behind the door or under a massage bed covered with sable—genuine sable.

Roman closed the door and locked it.

Her arms tightened over the bundle of silk knit Vanessa had given her.

"We always run through things exactly as they'll be if you come to work for us," he said. If he had to guess, he'd place the camera immediately above the bed. "Unless a member indicates otherwise, we lock all doors during sessions. Privacy is paramount for these people. They're important. From different worlds, but all important. And unless they choose to talk about themselves we don't ask questions."

"They come to keep fit," Phoenix said, surveying gilt-framed mirrors set in recessed panels around a room plastered in a rosy hue.

Roman regarded her closely. If this was an act, she was good. "They come to be entertained," he told her. "To get away from what they're supposed to be—what the public thinks they are. They come to use their bodies, to have them used. And their minds. They want them used in ways they can only indulge inside the safety of this building. I think you know what I mean."

Phoenix had the fair skin of the red-haired—fair and dusted with the freckles Vanessa had found so interesting. Right now a bright flush was spreading over as much of that skin as he could see. She didn't answer him.

"You aren't going to pretend you thought this was just some sort of fancy health spa?"

Her shoulders met her ears. "Of course not." She laughed.

He wasn't convinced, but he'd go along. "People come here to live out their fantasies." Be careful, he reminded himself. Don't be in such a rush that you give yourself away on tape. "They pay a great deal. Our job is to make sure they get what they pay for. And my job with you is to see if you'll fit into our program. How old are you?"

"Thirty. How old are you?"

He grinned. "Who's the interviewer here?"

"Asking an applicant's age is against the law."

"I was asking off the record. I'm thirty-six. Are you married?"

"Hardly."

"Ever been married?"

"No. You?"

"Do you want a job here?"

"Yes."

"How badly?"

She moistened her lips before saying. "I really want a job here."

"Good. That means I do the asking and you do the answering." Geoffrey and Vanessa would like that. "Where was your last job? As a masseuse?"

"In Stockholm. I've been back in the States about fourteen months and I haven't settled anywhere long enough to do anything but casual work."

"I understand you like being a masseuse."

Her fey green eyes shifted quickly away and back again. She knew what Vanessa had told him about her.

"The countess said you'd assured her you could keep your— appetites under control?"

The blush deepened. "I've never had difficulty keeping myself under control at all times."

"Really? I rather thought that was an area you did have difficulty with."

She turned away, her eyes downcast, evidently forgetting he could see her from every angle in the mirrors. Once her back was to him, she placed a fist over her mouth and squeezed her eyes shut.

On the other hand, if this was a setup, she knew he could see her in the mirrors and the nervousness was entirely for his benefit.

"If you're comfortable," Roman said, feeling anything but comfortable himself, "why don't we see how you work. I'm not a small man, but neither are some of our members. And I'm uptight. Think you can do something about that?"

The fist slipped down to her throat and she nodded. "Absolutely. Have you had cross-fiber massage before?"

Pulling his shirt over his head he said, "I've had every kind of massage, Phoenix. I like it hard and deep. Lots of pressure. Can you give me what I like?"

"Where are the sheets?"

"We don't use sheets."

"Fair enough," she said without missing a beat. Straightening her shoulders, she set her bundle on a shelf beside pots of massage oil. "Do you like music?"

Rather than respond, he swung open a mirror and dealt with the sound system hidden in the cabinet behind. Whitney Houston's lush voice sobbed out her need for the love of her life. He closed the panel. "The countess is good at gauging size. The clothes should fit."

Phoenix looked from him to the discarded outfit. Then set her pointed jaw. He saw her make up her mind. When she began pulling the T-shirt over her head, he made himself concentrate on taking off his jeans. He was only a man. A man who hadn't been with a woman he wanted to be with for far too long.

When he looked up she was yanking the halter into place. Her nipples prodded at the soft fabric, a fact she had to be aware of. Still keeping her gaze averted from his, she wrapped the sarong around her waist, fastened it, and stepped out of her jeans, showing glimpses of long, white, slender legs all the way up to high-cut black panties.

"Nice legs," he said.

She examined labels on jars. "Thanks."

"Is this going to be a new method?"

"New?"

"Massage by feel?"

One jar satisfied her. She unscrewed the top. "Massage is always by feel."

"True. But the therapist usually has to look at the client eventually." Facedown, he stretched himself out on the bed and propped his chin on crossed hands. He didn't like what he'd decided to do, but what choice did he have? Attack was the only defense here. He'd goad her, invite her to get her jollies from touching him. He'd push her and see if she'd crack. If she held up, the least they'd both have was a good time. And for the benefit of the cameras the little masseuse would look good, and he would be doing the job he was supposed to do—and keeping his cover.

If Phoenix did crack, he'd just have to make sure she got out safely—and didn't come back. Either way, he was about to become this lady's second skin. The trick was to make sure she didn't know she'd grown one. But that was Roman's specialty and he was very, very good at it.

Phoenix replaced the lid on the jar, set it down, and picked up another jar.

Stalling.

"What's up? Don't we have your brand?"

"I always familiarize myself with my equipment."

Sure. All six jars of it.

The club hiring system was sickeningly foolproof. By the time any hopeful employee had been drawn into whatever game Geoffrey and Vanessa devised, the promised rewards were so high, and the threats of damning public exposure so horrific, that no further persuasion was needed. As far as Roman knew there had never been a defection.

Except for April.

With every passing moment he became more convinced April had worked at the club and turned into a threat to its owners. The result of that threat would live in his memory forever.

Phoenix was taking too long. "Come here," he told her.

"I think we'll use this." She set aside yet another lid.

"Just come here and give me your hands. I want to make sure they're warm."

"They'll warm up soon enough."

"Yeah, I'll make sure of that. But not on my bare ass, thanks. Come here."

She turned toward him and this time the color left her face. Her eyes stayed on his, then traveled his length. Her lips parted and remained parted. The sound of her swallowing drowned out Whitney.

Roman rose up onto his elbows and offered her his right hand. "Not so fast, lady," he said. "Patience. You only get yours if I get mine. Would it help if we covered the strategic parts?"

She closed her mouth at last and took a deep breath. Great little breasts, but trembling. The whole package was trembling and he could only hope it was with arousal.

"There are towels in the bathroom. Push the second panel from the corner behind you. To the right of the corner. Cover up any distractions. Should help keep you focused."

She shook her head. Her eyes retraced a path down his spine to his bare backside and on to his legs. "I've got great powers of recall, Mr. Wilde. And anything that makes a real impression stays with me forever. The towel wouldn't help a thing. Why don't we get on with this?"

"You've got it," he told her, grateful he was lying on his erection. "We'll get right on with this."

# THREE

He was naked.

He was beautiful.

He was dangerous with a great big capital *D*.

Phoenix looked from his outstretched hand to his watchful eyes. *I dare you* was the unspoken taunt.

Well, she dared. For April, who'd never had another champion, Phoenix dared.

"Are you sure you aren't up to taking it like a man?" She moved to scoop balm from the jar she still held. "Cold hands included? Grit your teeth and bear it?"

"I've already bared it," he said, deadpan. "Put that down and come here. The first lesson you have to learn is to do whatever the member wants. Whatever he or she wants. You never question, never argue, never try to persuade them out of what they want. What they want is what you want. Do you understand?"

Phoenix replaced the jar on its shelf.

"What's your other name?" he asked.

"I don't have one."

"Everyone has another name."

She took a step toward him. "I don't have one I care to share. My parents were sadists."

That didn't make him smile either. "Phoenix is your last name?"

She raised a hand slowly toward him. "W. G. Phoenix. Thirty. Single. Native of New York. More recently from all over and looking for a place to settle down."

Cool, callused, strong fingers curled around hers and pulled her close. "The other one, W. G. Phoenix." Rather than wait for her to obey, he brought her palms together between his two hands and rubbed.

Starting at her neck, a shudder traveled the length of her spine and onward to bury itself behind her knees. Mr. Wilde was a puzzle. He was also sexy, the sexiest man she ever remembered being this close to.

"Cold," he murmured. His thumbs made little circles on her forefingers. "You know what cold hands can do to a man. We wouldn't want that."

Another flash of heat hit her at breast level and spread. This day had brought more blushes than she'd suffered in years.

"Are they warm enough now?" She tried to pull away.

He kept her trapped. "Not quite." With her hands still clamped between his, he brought them close to his lips and blew softly. "Did someone do this for you when you were a kid coming in out of the snow?"

Phoenix couldn't speak. Her scalp tingled. And her face—and the tips of her breasts.

Shifting his grip to her wrists he sent another tickling, warm breath over her fingertips, and smiled when she curled them into fists.

Fortunately he couldn't see inside her shoes.

"You'll have to use your elbows," he told her. "To get deep enough."

Swedish Goran had been a big believer in elbows. He'd been a believer in things that kept a stream of happy female clients paying for several sessions a week. "Naturally, elbows," Phoenix said. With any luck she sounded nonchalant. She added, "Knees, too, if necessary," without thinking.

"Yes, indeed, ma'am. I do believe I'm ready for you to go through your paces."

He took a long, long look at her breasts, at the effect his little game was having on her nipples. If he could see inside her body he'd really know how lethal he could be. Phoenix-the-cool, as she'd been dubbed by her colleagues in Oklahoma City, had gone through a rapid thaw all the way to total meltdown. Her insides were liquid. So were parts of her outsides.

Another darn blush started.

He released her wrists, rested his face on the table and lowered his arms to his sides. "Go," he mumbled indistinctly.

Phoenix glanced at the locked door. She flexed her numb fingers and dug a pile of waxy balm from the jar she'd left open. Very tentatively, she smoothed his left shoulder, a passage over hard, defined muscles that didn't give a fraction even when she deliberately increased pressure.

Warm and unyielding. She smoothed both shoulders and upper arms and he turned his face until she saw that his eyes were closed.

*Forget the man.* She must forget the man and remember April. April had said she'd met someone wonderful, someone who could hardly wait to marry her. The man had been something to do with the club. And Phoenix was never to try to contact April there because employees weren't allowed personal calls. Phoenix hadn't felt good about that at the time but April laughed it off and insisted there was nothing to worry about.

The music changed, grew slower. A lone horn echoing.

His skin shone. Shadows on smooth gold.

With two fingers Phoenix traced his spine as far as his waist and followed the same line with her knuckles, using her weight. "Mm," was her reward.

*A man who was something to do with the club.* He hadn't shown any reaction to the mention of April's name. But these weren't ordinary people with ordinary reactions. Perhaps they were people with extraordinary reactions—the kind so finely honed and controlled they were hidden before they appeared.

She smoothed outward from his spine. A wide, graceful, incredibly powerful back.

The countess alluded to four partners. How many of them were male? And which one of them had been involved with April? She'd spoken of this man having found her in the health club in San Francisco where she'd worked as a personal trainer.

He'd persuaded her to come to work here. Surely that meant one of the owners—one of the partners.

Roman Wilde could be the one, the man whose name April said she couldn't give—yet. April did have a history of fantasizing where men were concerned. Phoenix mustn't forget that. But there'd been something different about April during their conversation, something excited and young—and hopeful. Phoenix had never heard her so full of hope before.

Gripping Wilde's sides beneath his arms, she worked, repeatedly pressing with her thumbs, all the way to his hips.

He'd been naked in the sun.

"I'm not sure I've ever known a nymphomaniac."

Phoenix jumped and jerked her hands away.

His mouth curved in a satisfied smile. "Does that mean you were quietly getting it on and I caught you?"

"Don't flatter yourself."

"Tell me about being a sex addict."

"I'm . . ." Setting her lips firmly together, she attacked his muscles with renewed energy. Making fists, she pummeled as she'd seen Goran pummel. With grim satisfaction, she saw Roman Wilde flinch.

"Some people, like you, get a kick out of pain. Inflicting pain—and taking it. Isn't that true?"

Phoenix applied an elbow to his right trapezius and ground down toward the shoulder blade.

"Ooh, lady. You have some elbow. It almost hurts. A good hurt. A give-me-more hurt. Does that make you happy?"

Her response was to repeat the process on the left side.

He moved so quickly that his arm folded around her waist before she could react. "Just helping," he said, smiling, his eyes still closed. "Feel good?"

"Let me go."

"Ah, ah. Member is always right, remember? Member always calls the shots."

If this got really sticky there probably wouldn't be a thing she could do about it. "The member calls the shots," she agreed, with another glance toward the door.

He tucked his fingers under the waist of her skirt.

She breathed in through her mouth.

"You feel nice."

There was no way she could be his type—unless any woman was his type. "You feel nice, too." She could play his game.

His eyes opened. "Tell me what this does to you. Blow by blow."

"What do you mean?"

"I want to know what happens. While you massage me. I'm the member and I want to know what happens to a sex addict who gets her jollies from massaging men—and women? I think we've got members who'll get a charge out of knowing they turn you on. In fact, I know we have."

*Oh, joy.* Her stomach turned. "Women don't do a thing for me, friend."

"Hostile," he said. "Not good. You'd better learn to be nice, very nice."

"Nice," she muttered. "I'm very nice."

He slipped his fingers back and forth underneath her waistband, moved up to her bare back and kneaded. "You certainly are very nice, Phoenix. In fact, I'm beginning to get some really clear ideas about what I want you to do. Do I frighten you?"

*To death.* "I'm not a kid, Mr. Wilde. Neither am I new to this sort of thing."

"Work on the obliques."

She made to move to his side but he stopped her. "I like you where you are. You can reach."

The instant she bent over his back he gripped her arms just below her shoulders and made butterfly-light passes on the soft, exquisitely sensitive undersides.

Phoenix froze.

"What does that do to you?" he asked.

She could handle him. "It tickles. What does it do to you?"

"It makes me want to find out if you're just as soft all over."

*"You* aren't."

"Tell me about it."

This was more than she'd bargained for. "Your neck is tense."

She demonstrated how tense. "Soft hair. Surprisingly soft." It curled slightly. Phoenix touched the curls absently, combed and dug in a little under his occiput. "You aren't relaxed, Mr. Wilde. Relax. Go limp. Breathe from your stomach."

"Yes, ma'am."

She didn't know if he was breathing from his stomach, but he shifted his mesmerizing strokes from her arms to her sides, passing with dragging, unbearable slowness over the edges of her breasts, flicking his thumbs briefly over the fullness beneath her nipples, and slipping on to her waist.

"I'm relaxing," he said. "How about you?"

"Don't talk."

The inch of bare skin between the top and the skirt fascinated him. He tested it with his very fingertips, with the backs of his fingers, with the heels of his palms, before spanning her waist and letting her know how ineffective her resistance was.

"Lower," he murmured.

Lower meant she stretched until her ribs rested on his shoulder. "This would be easier if I was beside you," she told him.

"Easier on whom?"

"Both—"

His grip, settling on her bottom, scrambled her brain. She would not say anything. He jerked a little when she dug around his hips to his belly.

"That's good, Phoenix. Very good. How do you feel?"

*On fire.* "It's how you feel that matters."

"I bet you're satin under this skirt and those black panties of yours."

"Go with your imagination." When she found April, she'd make her fry for this. "Let your mind float. You'll deepen the experience."

"Mm. I'd like to deepen the experience." He cupped her bottom, delved steadily, drew her even closer. "Does this make you ache?"

She closed her eyes. It made her ache. "I find my work very satisfying." These were sensations she remembered but hadn't felt for a very long time—and never in circumstances anything like these.

"Satisfying?" He contrived to bring his lips to that dangerous inch of skin. With each of a string of feathery kisses came the flicker of his tongue, the nip of those strong, straight teeth. "This would be a whole lot more fun if we were both naked."

Phoenix's legs all but gave out. She worked rapidly back to his nape. A mistake. He smiled up at her and placed his hand on one breast, over the green knitted-silk halter.

She stared straight back into his brilliant blue eyes.

His smile did nice things to his face. It did devastating things to Phoenix.

"What do you think?" he asked.

"What do *you* think?"

"That you're gutsy."

Whatever that meant. "Thanks, I think."

"And sexy as hell."

She looked away from his eyes. "Shall I work on your legs?"

"Shall I work on yours?"

Her next breath stuck in her throat. "How many people are employed here?"

"No fair changing the subject. Not many people. We're very, very selective."

"Do many apply?"

"Nobody applies. We recruit."

"I've applied."

He found the overlap in the sarong skirt and slipped inside. "You're one of a kind."

Phoenix stood absolutely still.

"Beautiful legs." To demonstrate the basis of his opinion he used touch to paint mind pictures for himself. "Do you dance?"

*Not on tables.* "Occasionally."

"I bet you move well."

The mire was getting thicker and deeper. "So I've been told."

"I won't know until I've had a demonstration, will I?"

Another of his delicate explorations followed a panty leg all the way up to her hip and down again, over her groin.

A startled little cry escaped her lips and she jumped. "Sensitive there?"

"Isn't everyone?"

"Answering questions with questions again. Naughty, naughty."

Under the lace edge.

Phoenix held her breath. Her fingernails punished him but didn't stop him from playing with the hair he'd found.

"Is it red, too?"

If she made it through this test, the rest would probably be a breeze. "Dark red."

"Mm. Nice thought. Do you ever climax while you're working?"

Anger unfurled. "All the time. I've climaxed twice while I've been working on you."

"Ooh, gutsy indeed." His fingers shifted. "I think you're lying, but I don't think it would take much to make your dreams come true."

She began to throb. The force of her need stole her breath. Purely physical, she told herself. Purely physical and this man might be the one April loved—not that casual sex was likely to be a habit Phoenix would suddenly adopt.

He took his hand from her and rose onto his elbows. His hair was tousled, his eyes darkened with the shadows of arousal. Muscles in his shoulders and chest flexed.

Holding her breath she said, "On your back. Let's see how tight you are in other places."

"I'm tight," he said, very low. "I'm so tight I may explode at any minute."

"That's what I'm here for. Over you go."

He smiled and the effect was devastating. "Either you are one naive woman, or you're exactly what this club can't do without."

She'd come this far and she wasn't turning back. "I'll see if I can make up your mind. Roll over, Mr. Wilde."

With one shove he did exactly as she asked. The result drained her blood to her feet. This was a day filled with new experiences—and shocks. And this man wasn't shy offering either one. Not that he had anything to be shy about.

Phoenix moved slowly to stand beside him. She settled one hand on his stomach and smoothed her fingers through the dark hair that narrowed to a soft line there.

He caught his tongue between his teeth. His nostrils flared. "Have you given a lot of erotic massage?"

She didn't even know what it was. "Lots." She did have a perfectly good imagination.

He narrowed his eyes. "Do you enjoy it?"

"It's an art. I'm an artist. When I perform well, I'm happy."

Wilde slid a hand around her neck and pulled her face down to his. She closed her eyes and braced for his kiss.

"How do you feel now?" he whispered against her lips. "You want me, don't you?"

She kept her eyes shut.

His tongue made a single, slow journey over her bottom lip and she felt herself sinking against him.

"Well," he murmured. "You've passed the test, W. G. Phoenix."

Her eyes snapped open and she focused on his face. The lines were harsh, tense. "Passed?" she said, her body heavy with longing.

"You're one hell of a masseuse." He lifted her upright, swung his legs over the edge of the table at the same time. "I'll tell Vanessa we'd be fools not to hire you."

Stunned, Phoenix stepped backward.

Wilde stood up, slipped on his jeans and shirt and pushed his feet into his sneakers. "I'll see you out. We'll be in touch. By the way, drop the Mr. Wilde. My name is Roman."

# FOUR

Rose Smothers's age was a secret she showed no sign of sharing. Her unlined skin was dewy, her pretty brown eyes clear and bright. Phoenix had moved into the apartment over the garage three weeks earlier but she had yet to see Rose's blond hair other than wound into a smooth, heavy chignon.

Tonight Rose sat in the overwhelmingly floral sitting room of her white mansion, three miles out of town, with a closed expression on her face. She held her soft lips firmly together and her equally soft hands tightly laced in her lap.

The sweet, summery scent of roses filled the room from the bouquets of hothouse blooms that were delivered weekly. This week the roses were white, with scarlet centers.

"You said you were sure April would be coming back soon," Phoenix said. Her previous two attempts to draw Rose out had produced no response. She'd arrived back from the Peak Club smarting from her experience with Roman Wilde, and determined to find April, then leave Washington as fast as her exhausted brown Chevy Nova would take her.

"She will come back. She said she would. You're her friend, you ought to know April always does what she says she'll do."

Rose stood up and gathered a catalogue from one of three stacks, as tall as the arm of the overstuffed couch where she'd been sitting. She thumbed through to the page she wanted and held it out to Phoenix. "Does the dress look like this on me?"

A confident-looking model, hands on hips, chin tilted defiantly upward, wore a clinging ankle-length beaded black dress with tight sleeves and a neckline that dipped recklessly between impressive breasts.

Phoenix looked from the picture to Rose. "The dress looks better on you," she said honestly. "You're absolutely stunning, Rose." And absolutely wasted.

A pleased smile flitted across Rose's features. "And the shoes?"

She wore the same shoes as the model—black satin with rhinestone-studded heels. On her ears were the crystal earrings featured, and a matching crystal collar flashed at her throat.

"The shoes are great. The whole outfit is great. Now we need to get someone to take you somewhere wonderful."

Predictably, Rose turned away and started turning pages in the catalogue. She went to sit on one end of the bench before a white grand piano crowded with silver-framed photos. She behaved as if Phoenix were no longer in the room.

Time had become much more important than Phoenix had thought it to be when she arrived in Past Peak. Not only did she have to find April, she had to decide what to do with the rest of her life. Drifting, feeling alone, had made her too vulnerable. This afternoon's disaster had proved that.

She got up from a deep armchair and went to stand behind Rose.

"Is it a pretty day?" Rose asked unexpectedly.

"Very pretty. Buds everywhere. And crocuses. I love crocuses."

"My. That time of year already."

"How long have you lived here?" Mort and Zelda had warned Phoenix not to press Rose for information about herself, but curiosity drove her to at least try for some answers.

"I was born in Georgia." Rose's voice hadn't lost its soft southern accent. "My daddy didn't want to stay after we lost Momma. We came here. That was a long time ago."

Zelda said that no one seemed to know anything about the Smotherses, except that Rose's father had been very rich and when he died, Rose became his sole heir.

"Were you still in school when you came to Washington?"

Rose ran her fingers along the closed keyboard cover. "My daddy bought me this piano when I was eight. Daddy couldn't do enough for me, but he worried so."

"About you?"

"There are so many evil forces in the world, so many ways for a good person to be turned bad. Daddy protected me from all that."

Phoenix's skin grew cold. "I saw someone checking your car over yesterday. It's beautiful." The mechanic from a garage in Past Peak had said plenty about changing the oil in a car that had never been driven since delivery.

"My sixteenth-birthday present from Daddy," Rose said with a dreamy smile.

Which meant the Smotherses had been here at least since Rose was sixteen, if not longer.

"Your father never considered marrying again."

Rose slapped the catalogue shut. "Evangeline cooked something that smells positively sinful. Will you share a bite of dinner with me? I do believe I'm a little peckish now."

In other words, there wouldn't be any more personal information for a while. "I promised to go and put in a few hours at the Bend. They'll expect me to eat there."

Rose inclined her head. "You don't talk to strangers at that place, do you?"

"Sometimes," Phoenix said, amused. "I'm a waitress."

"The next time Zelda stops by I must tell her to keep a careful eye out for you the way she did for April. You've always got to be careful with strangers. Sometimes a stranger will make you do things you'd never normally do."

Phoenix felt her smile slip. How right Rose was. A stranger had accomplished a remarkable feat today. He'd turned Phoenix into someone she'd never been before—a totally sexual creature. And then he'd told her to get lost until he beckoned for her to come running.

"Whatever you do," Rose continued. "Do not ever get into a stranger's car. People have done that, you know. People who were perfectly good and Christian. And then they were gone. Lost. Never to be found again."

"I won't get into any strangers' cars," Phoenix said absently. "What did you and April talk about?"

"Why?" Rose turned a bright stare upon Phoenix. "If she's your friend you already know all about her."

Phoenix shrugged but knew she'd been careless. "I haven't seen her for a long time. I'm interested in what's been happening to her." Mort and Zelda had suggested they'd all get farther if Rose didn't suspect that Phoenix was actively hunting for April or that she thought she might be missing. The owners of Round the Bend watched over Rose and made sure her groceries were delivered for Evangeline, Rose's live-in housekeeper, to prepare. They knew how fragile Rose was and how she'd come to rely on April to describe the outside world that both fascinated and terrified her.

"April's in the Midwest."

The statement electrified Phoenix. "The Midwest? How do you know?"

"She writes to me from there. I'm surprised she hasn't written to you."

"I've been moving around a lot." From experience, Phoenix knew that if she showed too much interest, Rose would change the subject.

When Phoenix had first gone to Mort and Zelda's diner, inquiring about April, they'd been cagey. Slowly, they'd opened up, admitting that April Clark had come into the bar looking for a lead on a place to live. They'd thought it might be good for Rose to have fresh company and they'd been right. She'd taken April in and quickly become very fond of her. April continued coming into the Bend until almost a year later, when, without advance warning, she'd stopped coming. They were afraid something unpleasant might have happened to her but could do nothing about an investigation because Rose insisted April had told her she was leaving for a while.

That was when the suggestion had been made that Phoenix—who had arrived in Past Peak armed with April's address at

Rose's—should ask Rose to rent her a place to live, but that she should not reveal her true concerns about April. Zelda's black eyes had clouded with anxiety when she'd spoken of April being unhappy, of being sure she only came into the Bend to find companions who didn't want anything from her, companions who would listen to her.

What did April talk about? Her dreams. Marriage and children and a home and how she would soon have them all—as long as she was patient.

Why didn't Rose know about April's job at the Peak Club? Because April was sensitive and very attached to Rose. Rose wasn't worldly enough to understand the concept of a club that catered to the whims of rich, jaded, influential people—a club literally on Rose's innocent doorstep. She'd have nagged April to quit.

"Would you like to see April's cards?" Rose sounded anxious. Sometimes Phoenix thought Rose was happy just as she was. On other occasions Phoenix was sure there was a lonely longing in the other woman, a longing to be part of the world that so frightened her.

"If you'd like to share the cards, I'd love to see them," Phoenix said, careful not to sound too eager.

Rose got up and went to a delicate white and gilt rolltop desk. She rolled up the lid, pulled out a drawer, and took out a small stack of postcards tied in a white ribbon. She untied the ribbon and brought the top card to Phoenix. "There," she said. Her hand shook a little. "That's from my April. She's such a dear girl. So thoughtful and kind. She'll be back, you just see if she isn't."

Wheat fields beneath a sky so blue it hurt. Phoenix itched to turn the card over and read.

"That's in Kansas," Rose said. "See what April wrote?"

Phoenix held her breath. "Are you sure you don't mind if I do?"

"Of course. I like you. You're good, like April. You don't judge me for what I am."

The statement surprised Phoenix. "What you are is lovely,

Rose. Generous and honest—and decent." She turned the card over. *Hi Rose: You'd enjoy it here. Simple, with simple people. I mean the people are what they seem to be. No airs or lies. Sometimes I think all the honest people in the world are gone, but they're not. Take care. Love, April.* Phoenix blinked back tears and glanced at the postmark. Kansas City in the spring of the previous year. Her heart grew tight.

"Are you cryin'?" Rose asked quietly.

Phoenix looked up at her. "Maybe. What she writes makes me feel sad. She sounds as if people haven't always been kind to her." And they hadn't.

Rose bit her bottom lip and nodded. "I've always felt that about April." She took back the card and made no attempt to share anymore. "Thank you for saying nice things about me."

"They're true."

"Are you sure you won't join me for dinner?"

"Not tonight, but thank you. I'll come by tomorrow. Can I bring you anything?"

Rose closed her desk and shook her head. "I have everything I need, dear."

Phoenix made to leave, but stopped. There was a risk that needed to be taken. "Rose, I haven't . . . In the past few years I haven't always been very happy myself."

Rose's bright brown eyes were instantly intent. "I know, dear. I felt that about you just the way I felt it about April, I expect that's what brought you together, isn't it? A mutual need to feel safe with someone?"

This woman didn't entirely fill her mind with catalogue pictures. "In a way. There are people I don't want to allow close to me. Don't worry, they aren't dangerous." Please God let that be true. "But I'm trying hard to find peace. If anyone comes here and asks questions about me—or about April, for that matter—I'd really like it if you just said you didn't know anything."

"Is someone going to come?" Rose stood stiffly, her arms crossed over her middle.

"No! No, probably not. It's just that I'm desperate—no, determined to have a private life now. I haven't always had that. Everything's fine."

"Are you in trouble, Phoenix?"

She hadn't expected that question. "Of course not."

Rose swayed a little. "I'm not as fragile as I seem, you know. I always told Daddy that. You can tell me if you're really worried about something. I'll help you."

For one crazy instant, Phoenix had the urge to hug the woman. Instead she said, "Thank you, but there's nothing to worry about."

"I see." Rose smoothed the beaded dress over slim hips. "Do you . . . April's fine, you know. Nothing's happened to her."

"No."

"Really. I know I'm right. You're not afraid she's in trouble, are you?"

Phoenix cleared her throat. "I want April to come back soon. I miss her."

"So do I, but I just know she's safe. Her heart is so good and good hearts are kept safe." And the longing to believe what she said laced Rose's every tightly spoken word.

Phoenix said, "I'm sure you're right."

"But you wouldn't want me to talk to anyone about you or April."

"Right." She wanted, but didn't dare to ask Rose not to men- tion any connection between Phoenix and April. "Don't think about it anymore. I'm just fussing. I'd better get off to the Bend. Have a lovely dinner."

She left Rose to silent but efficient Evangeline, and emerged from the mansion onto the wide veranda that fronted the build- ing. "Belle Rose." Rose's daddy hadn't held back in his efforts to make his little girl feel special, right down to building a beautiful Southern-style mansion on several remote acres of heavily wooded land, and naming that estate after his only child.

An estate that became the child's prison.

Phoenix shivered and ran quickly down crescent-shaped steps to a gravel driveway lined with dense but carefully trimmed shrubs. Rose employed a faithful staff dedicated to the upkeep of Belle Rose.

Darkness had slipped in around the shapes of trees and hedges. Phoenix had already come to love night skies so far from any major city. The blackness could seem absolute, the stars more dazzling and myriad than she'd ever known was possible.

Tonight the scents of wet pine, and winter not long past, clung to the air. A chill curled in stillness. An unmoving film of cloud shrouded the moon and obliterated the stars. The only sounds were the vague rustlings of unseen life in the underbrush beside the driveway.

Once away from the lights of the house, Phoenix peered at the pale shimmer of gravel to find her way. The garage, with her apartment beneath its sloping second-story eaves, stood in a clearing at the end of a wide path not far inside the front gates. Evidently the apartment had once been home to the Smotherses' chauffeur. An impeccable black Rolls Royce—also maintained in perfect condition—shared quarters with the incongruous Aston Martin. The Rolls, Phoenix had been informed, had been Mr. Smothers's vehicle and was kept ready in case Miss Rose chose to use it.

Phoenix had left her Chevy at the end of the path to the garage.

She began to run.

Where was April? Her clothes were still in the apartment. Perhaps not all of them, but enough to suggest that April had, indeed, intended to return.

Why had the truly spooky Countess Von Leiden behaved as if she'd never heard of April? Phoenix knew that April had worked at the club.

Phoenix stood still. She was running because she was scared. Fear always hindered sensible decisions for her. But this time she had no place or reason for fear. April had done crazy things before and this was just one more of her crazy things. She'd show up.

Something moved.

Phoenix drew in a breath and held it. Now she was getting really fanciful.

Something had moved. In the bushes on the far side of the driveway from where she stood.

A raccoon? A bear even?

The latter thought didn't appeal. She broke into a run again. *Snapping.*

Phoenix spun around, kept moving backward, and scanned the seething, textureless bands of shrubs.

Her heart pounded. Her pulse thudded in her throat. This was foolishness. She'd dealt with true evil—and suffered at its hands. There was no true evil here. Even the phony club was nothing more than an expensive play house for the self-indulgent.

All of the rationalization didn't stop her from dashing the last few yards to the Chevy. Looking all around, she unlocked the driver's door and peered into the backseat before getting in. The car had been home—the one constant—for longer than she cared to remember.

Phoenix switched on the ignition and drove onto the main driveway. Once the gates were in sight she had to stop and get out to open them. One of the unbreakable rules around here was that the gates were kept shut.

*April's car?* For some reason Phoenix hadn't given a thought to April's car until now. Surely she'd had one and she must have left in it—driven it to the Midwest or wherever, probably.

Why would April go to the Midwest when she was a big-city woman, a woman who gravitated to the coasts?

Phoenix swung the heavy white wrought-iron gates open and drove the stay bolts home before jumping back behind the wheel.

From habit, she checked in the rear-view mirror. Her cry was involuntary, so was jerking off the handbrake and slamming the accelerator to the floor.

The film had slipped from the moon. She hadn't heard a bear. It was no bear who stood in the middle of the driveway with what appeared to be field glasses trained on the car, on Phoenix . . .

# FIVE

"Len was already in his truck," Mort said. Deep frown wrinkles were rippling up from heavy gray brows toward a shaved and shiny scalp. "Got him on the cellular. He's gonna stop by Rose's and make sure she's all right."

"I should have gone back," Phoenix said, still shaking.

Zelda plunked a mug in front of Phoenix on the varnished knotty-pine counter in the darkened lounge at Round The Bend. "Black coffee with a good belt of brandy," Zelda announced. "Bottoms up." Her New York accent didn't match either her exotic name or face. Zelda willingly admitted to seventy years but her dark green leotard and narrow slacks showed off her slight, still-agile figure, and her black hair hung in a single shiny braid that swung below her waist.

Phoenix sipped her drink and grimaced. "You forgot the coffee."

"Drink." Zelda flapped her hands. "You're a wreck. Do as you're told. The younger generation has forgotten how to respect the advice of their elders."

The smell of smoke, laced with beer and fried everything, wrinkled Phoenix's nose. "I should have gone back," she said morosely.

"Yeah," Mort said, rolling his eyes. "That's what you should have done. There probably isn't anyone there, right? It's probably you just got kinda jumpy. Right? But let's suppose there was some crazed guy with murder on his mind. You gonna tackle him? You gonna wrestle the guy to the ground and disarm him?"

Phoenix shook her head, but she didn't feel any better.

"No," Mort agreed, pulling his square chin into a short powerful neck. "You're gonna come straight here and let us take care of things. We been taking care of Rose since she sold us this place after her pop died."

"I wondered how you met."

Zelda urged the mug to Phoenix's lips. "Then you shoulda asked. That makes you different from April. She asked everything. All the time, she asked questions."

The phone rang. Mort snatched it up, barked his name into the receiver and issued a series of grunts before hanging up again. "Len's with Rose now. Says she's fine. He's gonna take a turn around the outside of the house."

"What if there is someone there?" Phoenix liked Len Kelly, Mort and Zelda's nephew. "Len could end up getting hurt. Maybe we should ask the police to go out there after all."

"Uh uh." Mort waggled his glistening, domed head. "Rose would flip. Aren't I right, Zel?"

"She'd flip," Zelda agreed before moving down the counter to serve three regulars engaged in a noisy argument about the commercial potential in leading wilderness expeditions from Past Peak.

"Some guy was in earlier," Mort said to Phoenix, raising his voice over Garth Brooks's. "Looking for you."

She almost dropped the mug. "Looking for *me?*"

"Yeah." He glanced at her. "Chill out, as they say. Do they still say that? Anyway, cool it. He said he'd catch up with you later."

"No one knows I'm here."

He paused and considered, then shook his head slowly. "This guy was not the kind of guy you worry about. Take it from me. I know people. Nothing furtive about him. Said you'd forgotten to leave an address. Naturally, I wasn't about to give him one. Ring a bell?"

Phoenix blew at the hair that seemed determined to curl into her eyes. "Gotcha," she said, hoping she sounded nonchalant. She sure didn't feel nonchalant. She'd already wondered just how Roman Wilde intended to "be in touch," since he didn't know where she lived or have a phone number for her.

She looked over her shoulder. Another encounter with Wilde was more than she could bear to contemplate. On the other hand, the thought of never having another encounter with him . . .

Naked. He'd stretched out naked in front of her and invited her to massage his entire body. Darn, she'd made a pretty good job of doing just that. And he'd set his very capable hands on her in ways . . .

Phoenix blushed and sent up thanks for the gloom.

Why was she blushing? She was a cynical, washed-up lawyer, not an innocent kid. She was a thirty-year-old who'd been aced out of her lucrative job by a jealous junior prosecutor. He'd blown the whistle on her for giving the prosecution a lead on incriminating evidence against her own client. That client, a respected psychiatrist accused of repeatedly molesting a young female patient while she was under hypnosis, ended up in jail. The psychiatrist, a pillar of his community and stinking rich, had even made passes at Phoenix while she was questioning him. But she'd let her passion for justice get in the way of her client's rights. For that she'd been justly fired—justly as far as Justice was concerned.

"Okay if I sit with you, Phoenix?"

She jumped and looked up into Roman Wilde's serious face. He slid onto the brown vinyl stool next to hers. "Scotch," he said when Mort approached. "Straight. What about you, Phoenix?"

Mort raised his brows at her. "Is this okay with you?" he said. "Or—"

"It's okay," Phoenix told him rapidly. "Mr. . . . We know each other."

Roman grinned—too endearingly—and said, "We know each other very well. What'll you have, Phoenix, love?"

Her mind went blank.

"There she goes again," Roman said pleasantly. "Gets tongue-tied at the oddest moments. Bring her another of whatever she's drinking." He tossed bills on the counter.

Mort moved away and Phoenix felt Zelda studying her from the other end of the bar.

"I was looking for you," Roman remarked. His eyes met hers in the damp-speckled, yellowing mirror behind the bar.

Phoenix wasn't about to be the first to look away. "So I gathered."

"You didn't leave your phone number."

"I don't have one." The lie was getting easier.

"Everyone has one."

"No they don't."

"Have it your way, W. G. Phoenix. I've recommended that you be hired."

*Come into my parlor, said the spider* . . . "Thanks."

"You don't sound grateful."

"I'm grateful." And wary as hell.

Mort brought the scotch and poured more coffee into Phoenix's mug. She almost asked for another shot of brandy.

Roman picked up his glass and closed one eye while he swirled the scotch. "I understood you worked here."

"I do," she told him. "And I probably will be working here tonight. It's not busy yet." Standing up at all might be beyond her at the moment.

"What made you decide to walk into the club and ask for a job?"

"Already done this."

"I beg your pardon?"

Phoenix swiveled toward him. "Countess Von Leiden already asked me the standard questions and I answered them. But, for your records, I need more money than Mort and Zelda can pay me here. I heard about the club and thought you might be able to use a good masseuse, so I applied."

"You're better than good." He tipped his glass and took a long, slow sip. "You're great, W. G. Phoenix. Maybe the best. You did things for me no other masseuse ever did."

She choked on her coffee.

"Bone in there?" He slapped her back and bent close to her ear. "We want you at the club by ten in the morning. Orientation and a chance to meet some of the other employees. How does that sound?"

It sounded like a box getting smaller, with her inside. "Fine. I'll be there."

"The kind of personal attention you gave me doesn't come cheap—to our members. Mostly you'll be doing straightforward stuff."

"Mostly?" She looked at him squarely. "I don't expect my clients to touch me, Mr. Wilde . . . Roman."

The corners of his mouth turned down in a cynical grin. "Funny. I got the impression you enjoyed every second of it."

She didn't give him the satisfaction of hearing her protest— not that she had much right.

He swung toward her and rested a hand on the low back of her stool. "I might almost have thought you didn't want me to stop at all. But maybe you were caught off balance. Mm. I expect that was it. The whole experience was unexpected. Was that it?"

Phoenix couldn't look away from his mouth.

"I'd like to kiss you, too," he said softly. He touched a knuckle to her chin. "You're a very passionate woman, aren't you? We're going to have to do something about that."

He was hypnotic. Leaning toward her, propping one elbow on the bar, keeping his other hand behind her, he managed to close her off with him, to shut out everything but the space they occupied.

With her right thumbnail, she followed a side seam of her jeans over her crossed knee.

"What do you say?" Roman met her thumb with one long forefinger and made light strokes back and forth over her thigh. "You've got beautiful legs."

Phoenix remembered to breathe. "So do you."

He closed his eyes and smiled at that. "Tell me why a woman like you wants to press flesh for strangers."

"Money," she said, hating the way it sounded. "You switch your mind off and bodies become just so much meat—or bread dough, maybe."

He tilted his face in front of hers and waited until she looked at him again. His tongue made a pass along the straight edges of his teeth. "Was that what you did this afternoon? Switched off and pretended I was so much meat?"

What did he want, and why? "I guess that must have been the way it was."

"You guess?" His eyes centered on her mouth and he leaned a fraction closer. "Just so much meat, huh? Nothing more?"

Mr. Brooks sang about the weak not daring to take risks. Phoenix's gaze flickered away from Roman's steady stare.

"Listen to what the guy says," he told her. "Maybe he's talking to you."

"He's singing about something we're not dealing with here."

"Daring to get involved?"

Love. Nothing could be farther from what was happening in this bar. "Why are you here?" she asked. "Really?"

With drifting fingertips, he outlined the side of her face. "Just wanted to tell you we'll be expecting you in the morning."

"You've told me."

Her ear received the tickling touch. "I have, haven't I?"

"Uh-huh. Next excuse?"

He smiled and watched while he wound strands of her hair around his fingers. "Nothing better to do?"

"Thanks."

A broad grin did nothing to lessen the trapped-and-liking-it feeling Phoenix was choking on—choking on and nervously enjoying every gasp.

"Some hair. It is *red*."

"I'd already noticed."

"Are you for real?"

Her heart stopped. "What does that mean?"

"Something about you doesn't fit. The act isn't bad, but it still feels like an act."

In other words, she hadn't quite convinced him—or the sickening Countess Von Leiden. So why were they inviting her back—supposedly offering her a job?

"Have I touched a nerve?"

"You've touched more than a nerve." Surely she could play the game well enough to get by. "We've already discussed that, haven't we? At length."

"Not nearly in enough length, my love. Tell me what you think it'll mean to work at the Peak Club."

Phoenix felt the approach of Mort's short, powerful force. He crossed his massive forearms on the bar in front of them. "Everything okay here?" His fused cervical spine and the slight stiffness it caused was the only evidence of the accident that had ended his career as a trapeze artist.

"We're having a little discussion," Roman said, turning a fixed, jaw-flicking smile on Mort. "Phoenix and I go back a way, don't we, Phoenix?"

If she said no, Mort was likely to find his way onto her side of the counter without using the hatch. Then there would be no hope of going back to the club. Much as part of her wished she didn't have to, logic said she'd better not close off the best lead she had on April.

"Phoenix?" Mort repeated.

She beat a casual tattoo on the padded edge of the bar. "Roman and I have a lot of catching up to do. You don't need me yet, do you, Mort?" Looking around, she noted that the only newcomers were the squat man who ran a gun shop, and pawnbrokers out of Duvall, and Nellie, the blond, buxom, and good-natured proprietor of Cheap Cuts, Past Peak's lone beauty shop.

Mort followed Phoenix's glance. "Quiet night," he said. "We're managing fine." But his pursed mouth suggested he wasn't convinced that Phoenix didn't need rescuing from the big, dark man who dwarfed her.

"So, what do you think?" Roman said, affording Mort a view of the back of his head. "I really am interested in your opinions."

She waited, and Mort moved away. Anger stiffened her spine. "What kind of game are you playing? You came to tell me I've probably got a job. Fine. I don't see any reason to go through the rest of this performance."

"Don't you?"

"No!"

"Call it overtime—on my part. Or say we started something this afternoon and now it's time to finish it."

"Like hell." She wrapped her arms around her middle. "Say you're trying to bait me for some reason I can't figure out."

"Wrong. Listen to me, Phoenix. No games, no tricks, no bullshit. We take the club very seriously. I'm going out on a limb with you—"

"Why? You don't—"

"Hear me out." He gripped her wrist. "If you were going to say I don't know you, you're right. But there's something about you . . . Hell, I don't know. You felt good—good to me. And I don't just mean in the obvious way. That isn't so complicated, is it? I want you at the club. Okay, I'm laying it out. I think you'll be popular with a lot of members. You're different, fresh. They'll like that."

Her muscles drew so tight, they ached. She heard what he said, but knew there was much more he wasn't saying. "I'm not a prostitute." The word stuck in her throat.

"Think I haven't figured that out?"

She shook her head.

"Can we go somewhere else to talk?"

Somewhere he could be certain she had no one to save her from him? "We're talking just fine here."

"Have it your way. I'm offering you a deal. Come to the club as my friend. Do you understand what I'm saying?"

She pulled on the neck of her loose, black sweater.

"Do you understand?" he repeated.

"I don't think so. Why would you want me there as your friend?"

"Maybe I need you."

"You're a partner."

"Yeah."

"You can decide to bring someone in—as a friend?"

He chuckled. "I can decide to bring someone in as an employee with the understanding that the employee only performs in certain capacities for the members."

Phoenix narrowed her eyes. "You're going to have to go very slowly and make it very clear for those of us who aren't too quick, Mr. Wilde."

His mouth, descending softly but firmly on the corner of hers, almost knocked Phoenix off her stool. She grabbed handfuls of his denim jacket, but she wouldn't have fallen anyway. Roman all but pulled her onto his lap.

"Don't scream," he whispered, before kissing her again, in exactly the same spot. "If you don't like this, just say so and I'll stop."

Phoenix didn't say a thing.

"Hm." His clever lips slanted over hers, parted hers just enough to make sure she braced to feel his tongue.

Roman kissed her like an ardent, very promising, boy scout. No tongues. With his hands framing her face, he drew back enough to look at her. "I know what I feel in you, love. Enough pent-up good stuff to keep us both happy for a long time."

She jerked her head away and pushed back onto her stool. "You don't know what you feel," she told him through her teeth. "I need a job. I want a job. I don't want to live with my chin on my shoulder checking for you to creep up on me."

His straight brows raised. "Oh, what a puzzle you are, darlin'."

"Don't darlin' me. And don't call me 'love.' "

"Okay"—he held up his palms in submission—"I'll try to be absolutely clear. Tomorrow morning I'd like to tell my partners you're a masseuse. Nothing more and nothing less. Is that all right."

He confused her. "What's the catch?"

"No catch. I'll just tell the truth. Something happened between us today and I don't feel like sharing it."

Phoenix slid slowly to stand.

Promptly, Roman shifted to her stool and trapped her against the bar. "Would that be cramping your style? Vanessa told me you mentioned—"

"I can imagine what she told you."

"Surely you aren't suggesting it isn't true? If it isn't, you lied to her and that would mean we couldn't employ you. You like a lot of sex. I like a lot of sex. I don't like a lot of sex with a woman who's spreading it around. Is that clear enough?"

Words failed Phoenix.

"I think it is. You press flesh—spread a few jollies at a party when you're asked to. We'll pay you well. But the rest is mine. Do we have a deal?"

This had to be happening to someone else. If she blinked hard, he'd disappear.

He drew her between his thighs and nuzzled her neck. "Do we have a deal?"

Something. She had to say or do something to deal with this without blowing what she'd set out to do. "I've never been in . . . I've always been used to making my own choices. Taking my own time getting where I want to go. Do you understand?"

He was using his tongue now—on the tender skin beneath her ear. She breathed harder.

"Warming you up, am I?"

Phoenix averted her face sharply.

"Oh, yes, a warm lady. Have it your way. I can be very, very patient. I won't rush you. Just let me know when you're ready to pick up where we left off."

If he wasn't making her feel as if she was suffocating, and turning her warm, wet, and hot in hidden places, dealing with this logically would be a whole lot easier.

"Do we have a deal, W. G. Phoenix? I look out for you and keep you happy. And you keep me happy—when you're ready?"

They'd met that afternoon—if you could call what happened between them a meeting—and now he was asking her to have an affair.

"Of course, I'd understand if you'd rather strike a deal with the countess."

"Don't be disgusting!" She itched to slap him. "Okay, let's

see how this goes. But I still don't know why you've picked me."

When he stood up and settled his hands on her shoulders, Phoenix had to look up, way up, to see into his face. "Let's just say I think we'll suit each other nicely." He checked his watch and she saw his attention shift. "Tomorrow morning, okay?"

"Okay."

"Good. See you then." He gave her a purely wicked grin. "Don't feel you have to keep me waiting just for propriety's sake, sweet thing."

Before she could respond, he turned and made for the door. He'd remembered he had somewhere else he had to be.

"Mort," Phoenix said, hurrying along the bar. "Can you spare me tonight?"

"Why?" He shot a suspicious glare at Roman's departing back. "Who is that guy?"

"Old friend," Phoenix lied.

"The way he was plastered on you I'd have thought you were married."

She wrinkled her nose at him. "You're old-fashioned, but that's one of your strongest points. Roman and I need to catch up on a few things. You said it's quiet. I'll only be an hour or so. I'll check back before closing. Okay?"

"There's nothing wrong—nothing you're not telling me?"

She backed away. "Of course not, you worrywart." If she didn't go now it would be too late. "See you."

"Before closing, then."

Phoenix sped to the door into the adjoining, darkened diner. She pushed through in time to see the front door closing behind Roman.

Without being certain what she hoped to accomplish, she followed. Standing back a little, she watched him get into some sort of four-wheel drive vehicle and start from the parking strip in front of the Bend.

Within moments, Phoenix was outside and behind the wheel of the Nova. She turned the key in the ignition and sent up thanks when the engine instantly burst to life.

He headed along Highway 202 in the direction of the Peak Club. If he went straight there she'd wait a reasonable interval and return to the Bend. At the very least, she might discover a second entrance to the club. That could prove useful. But Roman might be going somewhere else and, if he was, Phoenix wanted to know where.

She kept well back.

April had described a man who could very well be Roman Wilde. He might be going to her now.

That was the only reason Phoenix was out here on a dark, deserted, winding mountain highway . . . wasn't it?

Tomorrow she'd start looking for someone to trust at the club, someone who might know something about April and be prepared to share that knowledge. But the more she could learn about all of these people, the better, and that included Roman.

On the other hand, it might be better for her health if she turned around right now and forgot the whole thing.

She wasn't a wimp. And she was perfectly safe if all she did was follow in her car and see where he went. Wherever that might be, she'd drive right on by and he'd be none the wiser. After all, he didn't know what kind of car she drove and it was too dark for him to notice her.

The wheels of the Nova scrunched over a recent fall of scree from the rock face that edged the road in many places. Phoenix slowed a little and ducked to look up at the pointed crowns of pine sentinels, blacker silhouettes against a black sky. The taillights ahead were the only sign of another life in the night.

Phoenix wiped at her forehead. Her fingers came away wet. When they'd been kids, April had been the leader. They'd been two against a world where those who'd been born luckier were automatically more important. Only, April wouldn't stand back and accept that law—not for herself, or for Phoenix, whose parents were rarely sober enough to care what happened to her. She'd done part-time jobs since she'd been thirteen, when a pharmacist hired her to clean his shop because she worked cheap. But as far as John and Hedda Phoenix were concerned, the sooner their only child got a full-time job and added more to the family income, the better. Schooling was a waste of time, a conspiracy to stop parents from getting their fair share out of kids who owed them.

The taillights disappeared around a bend.

Phoenix speeded up a little.

*"You want what?" Her father's red face turned even redder and he scrubbed a hand on the dirty T-shirt that stretched tight over his pendulous belly. "College? What the hell d'you think we are? Rich folks who get a kick out of slumming?"*

*"No, Dad." She'd offered him the first grade-sheet from her senior year in high school. "I'm carrying a four point. I can get financial aid. There's money—"*

*"We're not Goddamn charity cases!" His fist had knocked her backward over a chair. She'd slammed against the wall in the Phoenix's tiny kitchen in the Bronx. The last thing she remembered seeing before she fainted was a slimy glob of congealing ketchup on a wall that had once been pale green.*

The scar above her lip was faint now, but Phoenix could still feel it. Her fingers hovered over her mouth. When she'd crept from the apartment that night, leaving her father passed out over the kitchen table, April had been the one to comfort Phoenix and take her to an emergency room.

April had also been the one to nag Phoenix into applying to several of the best schools on the East Coast.

*"They'll take you." April's marvelous blue eyes were honest and sure. "You see if they don't. You're the smartest kid in the school. You'll get a scholarship."*

And Phoenix had got that scholarship—to Georgetown.

Phoenix smiled bitterly. Once more it had been April to the rescue when Phoenix's father had beaten her and refused to let her go. April showed up with a social worker and John Phoenix had skipped town to avoid arrest.

Georgetown, then Harvard. Then a major flub-up. But Phoenix owed April. She owed her just about everything, and payback time had been overdue a long time ago.

The red taillights were clearly in view, passing the Peak Club and sweeping right into another tight bend. Phoenix held the wheel tighter and closed out the old memories. All she needed to think of was finding April.

Double bends took the lights out of sight. Phoenix made the second turn and her stomach rolled. The vehicle was leaving the road, taking off on a track that seemed to close in behind it.

She drove on slowly, pulled over and killed her engine. With her arms crossed on the wheel, she rested her brow and tried to decide what to do.

Nothing.

Go back to the Bend.

Turn around, make sure she could find the spot again, then go back to the Bend.

Approaching the track from the opposite direction, she realized he'd driven not away from the road, but parallel to it for some distance. Her headlights picked up the shimmer of the vehicle's side panel.

Phoenix drove onto the opposite shoulder and stopped. This time she left her engine running.

He'd parked where only oncoming traffic might sight him. Not that anyone would take any notice—unless they had a reason to. Phoenix had a reason to take notice.

She should drive on.

With one fist ground against her chest as if it might slow her heart, she clicked open her door and slid out to stand on dirt and rubble.

A man didn't drive up a quiet mountain road and tuck his truck away in the darkness unless he had something to hide—something more than the truck.

Phoenix crossed the road. A wind had picked up and she held her hair out of her eyes. Her sweater flattened against her back. She reached the scrubby underbrush beneath trees that whined and swayed overhead.

Hunching over, she crept along, keeping a line of tall grass and bushes between her and the path Roman had taken. With each stealthy step she became more certain he'd looked at his watch at the Bend and remembered he had a visit to make. He could have April shut away somewhere in this wilderness.

Why?

Phoenix invented and discarded one reason after another. There was no end to the depths a human could reach; she'd faced enough of those depths to know.

She gained the tail of the truck and dropped to her haunches. Parting grasses, she got close enough to make out a Land Rover in some dark color.

Bent almost double, she edged forward until she could see the driver's seat. Empty. He'd left the Land Rover here because the trail went no further and it was easier to continue on foot to . . .

She needed help.

If she raised the alarm without being certain where Roman had gone and that April was with him—and in trouble—she might do more harm than good. She could either become cut off from any chance of finding her friend, or make a complete idiot of herself.

Whatever she did, it mustn't be alone. Mort and Len would come. She wouldn't have difficulty finding her way here again.

She straightened—and fell, pitched forward against the back of the Land Rover.

With her arms outflung, she collided with cold, solid metal and cried out.

A big, hard hand closed around each of her wrists and an even harder, very heavy body trapped her.

Phoenix opened her mouth to scream. Acid rose in her throat and she retched instead.

"You're going to have to learn the rules, love. *Fast.*"

"Please—" Faintness blurred her vision. "Please."

He ground his jaw against her neck. "Please what? Save it, W. G. You're about to find out it's a mistake to mess with people out of your league." His weight crushed her. "After tonight you're going to know how dangerous it is to pry."

# SIX

Parker Nash, investment banker, husband, father, civic leader, prominent crusader for civil rights and abused women, and rumored bright hope for the next Washington State governor's race.

Fifty something, silver-haired, portly but suave Parker Nash, the magician of mega-deals in faraway places, one of few men declared absolutely safe from the sly finger of scandal.

At this moment, suave Parker sweated and labored in a sexual frenzy. His sharp blue eyes were squeezed shut, his lips drawn back from perfectly capped teeth, the veins in his neck distended.

Naked but for a white satin robe loosely belted at her waist, Vanessa Von Leiden strolled past the heaving couple on the circular couch. She drew deeply on the joint Sir Geoffrey Fullerton had passed to her. Geoffrey observed their client's performance with his signature casual indifference.

Vanessa met Geoffrey's old, colorless eyes and glared. Geoffrey was going to find out who called the shots here and the answer wouldn't please him. She'd been too easy on him for too long.

"Jee-sus," Parker gasped. His pallid buttocks squeezed tight with every pumping thrust. In each hand he grasped a breast that testified to the miracles of augmentation.

The music was a single drum, beaten in slow, bass strokes. The drum wasn't keeping up with Parker.

*"Jesus-H-Christ!"* He was a happy man. He was always a

happy man when he got to fuck someone whose face he'd seen on a great big screen. That was Parker's weakness; fucking stars.

Geoffrey waited for Vanessa to pass close and took back the joint. Holding it between his teeth, he returned his attention to setting out pretty white lines on the mirrored surface of a cylindrical glass table that stood as high as his chest. Above the table, one of a row in descending heights, hung a crystal light in the shape of a naked woman, with her arms wound about a single, high-intensity bulb. The beam bounced off the lovely white lines.

On her next circuit of the subterranean room, Vanessa paused beside Geoffrey. "How much longer?" she murmured, indicating Parker.

Geoffrey raised a sandy brow. He ran a hand over straight, thinning fair hair brushed straight back from a high forehead. "Fancy a turn with Sabrina ourselves, do we?"

She snatched the joint from between his teeth. "In case you've forgotten, I've *had* my turn. So have you. You and I have to talk."

"Got our knickers in a twist over something have we, darling?" His tone infuriated her. He indicated the coke. "Break your rules for once and loosen up. Do you the world of good."

Running speculative eyes over him, Vanessa took another deep drag and tugged at the knotted belt on his red terry-cloth robe. "Parker seems to like big plastic tits," she said, releasing the belt and studying Geoffrey's smooth chest. "Do you?"

Geoffrey shrugged. "Not something a man notices in the throes, pet. All Parker cares about is sticking his dick into a hole millions of men dream of doing the same thing to."

Men. Weak. Good for one thing—to be used. "She's washed up. The last movie was a flop."

"All the better for our purposes, sweeting." He let the red robe fall to deep-piled white carpet.

The only interesting thing about Sir Geoffrey Fullerton, apart from his complete absence of conscience and an incredible ability to attract fabulously wealthy clients with expensive weaknesses, was his truly splendid body. But at the moment even

Geoffrey's body was somewhat lacking. When she finished studying his limp cock, she slowly raised her eyes to his once more.

He smiled crookedly and raised his palms in an almost apologetic gesture. "You'll just have to settle for the dope, partner. At least until this stuff wears off."

"Maybe we should feed some more to Parker."

"Already fed him enough to choke the bastard. He's not normal."

She laughed aloud. "You can thank whatever you pray to for that—and for a steady supply of similar animals. Help me convince him it's time to go home." Geoffrey had arrived late and there'd been no time to ask the questions that had plagued Vanessa since she'd left their succulent, would-be new employee in Roman Wilde's willing hands.

"Can't hurry the man," Geoffrey said. He bared one of Vanessa's breasts and bent to suck the nipple.

She watched the back of his head dispassionately. There were moments when she was grateful enough to react to him, but this wasn't one of those moments. His tongue curled around turgid flesh. She enjoyed the flare of sensation in her belly but tightened the damp flesh between her legs against his probing fingers.

"Geoffrey!" Parker's fulsome baritone boomed around the room. "Gimme some of that. C'mon. Gimme."

Geoffrey raised his head and Vanessa rolled her eyes. "Gives new meaning to the idea of getting better rather than older," she muttered, pushing Geoffrey aside. "Coming, Parker."

She reached the couch, carrying the customer's order on a sheet of stiff paper. He heaved himself off his famous playmate's sweat-slicked, fleshy body and stood, swaying over her.

Sabrina Lane pushed up onto her elbows and tossed back a couple of feet of gelled, strawberry-blond hair extensions. Her heavily lashed turquoise eyes were extraordinary, her full lips—swollen from Parker's attention—as sexy as ever. Vanessa returned the star's seductive smile and decided she'd arrange for her to spend the night at the club.

"Parker wants to find out more about making movies," Sabrina said in her light, breathy voice. "I'm going to help him, aren't I, Parker?"

"Oh, yes."

The randy bastard's equipment was at full attention again.

"Parker and I are going to make a film together, aren't we, Parker."

"Oh, yes. Gimme that."

Parker took what Vanessa carried. He pushed Sabrina back on the couch and hauled up her knees.

She squealed and protested, "Parker!" The complaint didn't ring true.

He propped her hips on his thigh, made a funnel of the paper, parted her, and tipped the white powder into her folds.

Geoffrey exclaimed, "I say," and chuckled. "You're quite the boy, Parker, old chap."

Parker inserted the straw where it needed to go and sniffed.

"Ohmygod," Sabrina panted. "Ohmygod. I'm coming!"

Geoffrey howled, pushed Parker aside and took his place.

The pace of the music picked up, faster and faster. Keeping her eyes on the cavorting trio, Vanessa strolled to raise the volume.

While she stretched out on a white damask couch to watch, Parker got what he liked the very best. He and Geoffrey sandwiched shrieking Sabrina and took her from both sides—not that one had to take what was freely given.

Another hour slid by before a still-dynamic Parker reluctantly left in the waiting chopper and Sabrina was safely tucked away in a room Vanessa intended to visit later.

"What the fuck's eating you," Geoffrey demanded, striding beside her through the tunnel leading to the main club buildings. "You've been behaving as if you've got a bee up your arse ever since I arrived."

"I find it hard to believe you gave *my* ass a thought. Now, shut up and stay that way until we get to the viewing room."

She led him to the trap door in the floor above her office and preceded him down the stairs. "Close us in," she said once the lights flooded on.

When they stood facing each other in front of the dark screens, she drew in a trembling breath and hit him. She hit his face with the flat of her hand, using all the force in her strong right arm.

"What the—" He caught her wrist and they stumbled against the file cabinets. "What the *fuck* do you think you're doing?"

She shook steadily now. "You had to have your fun, didn't you? You couldn't remember the rules long enough to make sure you protected what we've built."

He shook his head, a dazed expression in his eyes. "You don't make any sense, Vanessa. And you know I don't like violence, dammit."

"Violence?" She tilted up her jaw and laughed. "Violence? You don't like violence when it hurts your own precious body. Inflicting pain is something you do particularly well."

His fingers wound into her hair and tightened, tearing at her scalp. "And you don't like inflicting pain?"

"I don't pretend," she shouted.

He pushed his face close to hers. "What the hell's gotten into you? You want to play? Is that it? I'll play, darling. Just tell me the ways and where. Here? Right here?"

"No, goddamn you. You told me we'd never hear that girl's name again. You said everything was over. Taken care of. You *lied.*"

"Girl?" He blinked, and his grip on her hair slackened. "What girl?"

"You said she had no one. You said there wasn't a soul who would even remember her name."

"Oh, my, God." Slowly, he backed away.

She pushed him aside and started flipping switches and turning dials. A tape rewound and then the inside of her office appeared on a screen. "Listen, *Geoff.* Listen closely and be thinking very hard about what we might have to do."

The beginning of her interview with the woman, Phoenix, was of no particular interest. Vanessa fast forwarded the tape until she heard the start of the words she needed to have him hear.

"Listen," she hissed, aiming a long finger at Phoenix's image. "Listen closely."

"Rose talks about her all the time." Phoenix's wide green eyes were fringed with red gold lashes. Those eyes were innocent as they regarded Vanessa. "A very beautiful blonde, she says. But she doesn't really seem to know anything about her, except that she comes from a rich family and doesn't need to work except to pass the time. And that her name's April Clark."

From the edge of her vision, Vanessa saw Geoffrey grope for a chair and fall into it. She rewound the tape a little and pressed the play button again.

Vanessa watched her own back where she sat on the edge of her desk, and heard herself say, "Pretending about what?"

"That she's sure the tenant she had before me will come back. She's been gone a year and a half."

"Who is—"

Vanessa waved Geoffrey to silence while her taped voice said, "Eighteen months? Has she heard from her?"

"I don't think so. I think Rose has just made up her mind this tenant will come back when she's ready."

She turned off the sound and rounded on Geoffrey. "Did you get that?"

His jaw was slack. He shook his head slowly. "What does it mean? Who is that woman?"

"That woman," she told him, "is our new masseuse."

He gripped the arms of the chair.

"You never told me there was any *Rose* who might be flapping her mouth about April. And you told me April had cleared all her things out of wherever she lived."

"She did." When he started to rise, she pushed him back down and for an instant he looked close to tears.

"No. She did not. The redhead says she's living in the apartment where April left some of her things—a lot of her things. They're still there!"

Geoffrey said, "That was the first thing I asked her when she called me. About what she'd left behind and who knew about anything. And she said there was nothing left there and nobody knew. She *lied* to me. The bitch lied to me."

Vanessa ignored him. She selected another screen and worked the controls. This time she was rewarded with a view of the redhead working on Roman Wilde's commanding body. She'd already viewed the tape and listened carefully to every word that passed between Roman and Phoenix.

"So she happens to be living where April lived," Geoffrey said. "Coincidence."

"Coincidence?" Vanessa barely restrained herself from hitting him again. "Coincidence that she lives in the same place? Coincidence that she found out from some hicks in the town that April worked here? Coincidence that she came here pretending to be a masseuse and just managed to drop that little tart's name?"

"What did you say?"

"What do you think? I said I'd never heard of April Clark."

"Perhaps that wasn't a spectacular idea. Perhaps you should have admitted April worked here, and suggested we were also surprised when she ducked out."

"And risk some sort of official questioning if it ever comes to that?"

"Good God." He ground a finger and thumb into the corners of his eyes and indicated the screen. "She's giving a massage isn't she? And she isn't having trouble with anything else he wants her to do, either, is she?" His face snapped up. *"Pretending?* You said she was pretending to be a masseuse?"

"Look at her." She pointed at the screen again. "She's had a massage, all right. She may even have watched someone else getting a massage. But I know what I'm seeing. She's got guts, I'll grant you that, but she never gave a massage in her life before this afternoon."

"Who is she then?" Sir Geoffrey's voice rose to a semblance of a whine.

"If I had to guess, I'd say she's a plant. Whose plant, I don't know. We're going to move carefully and quickly and we're going to find out exactly who she is and where she came from."

"She could be nothing more—"

"No." Vanessa shook her head vehemently. "I don't believe this is chance and neither do you. It's all too calculated. The best we can hope for is that she's not a cop. I don't think she is. They'd have made sure she knew her stuff. I think she's either acting alone or with the freaks at that diner in Past Peak." She made a fist against her stomach. "Alone is my guess. I feel it here."

"How will we—"

She silenced him again. "Easy enough as long as we don't waste time."

"How can you say it's easy when you think there could be a chance she's working with someone else?"

"I think she may *not* be, I said." On the screen, Roman was on his back showing off his considerable assets. "I'm already on it. First we'll know who she really is. Then we'll make sure she loses interest in what goes on around here."

Geoffrey chewed the inside of his mouth and watched Roman and Phoenix. "The lady seems to like what she sees, Vanessa. She isn't hiding her eyes."

"Who would?" Vanessa told him grimly.

He pointed at their inconvenient interloper. "If she really is trying to find April—*if* I said, and I'm not convinced—but if she is, she isn't likely to lose interest just because you decide you want her to."

"Isn't she?" The tape ended and clicked off automatically. "Trust me. She'll lose interest."

# SEVEN

Either Phoenix was scared shitless, or she was one hell of an actress. "Who sent you to us?" He spun her around and trapped her against his Land Rover again. Every word from his mouth must be the right word. Nothing that could give him away.

She made a raw, gasping sound and hung her head forward.

Roman shook her. "Who?" Intimidating women wasn't his thing, but he'd sworn to accomplish something at Past Peak and this particular woman threatened to get in his way.

The wind gathered force, slapped straggling tree limbs against the sides of the Rover. Phoenix kept her head forward and her hair blew over her face.

"Look at me," he ordered. She felt insubstantial in her cheap black sweater. Her shoulders were small, the bones fragile. "Look at me, *dammit.*"

"I feel sick," she muttered, jerking her head to toss the hair aside. "I hit my stomach."

From what he could see she probably wasn't lying. Her face shone pale in the darkness. Sympathy was a luxury he wouldn't indulge in tonight. The folks she worked for were murderers. She might not know that fact, but he couldn't afford to educate her.

"I feel sick," she repeated.

"People who take on big, dangerous jobs usually know they might get hurt." He remembered another frail body, another suffering face. Who the hell was who in this deal? He'd have to continue to be very patient. He said, "Open your mouth."

Her eyes didn't even flicker a response.

"Breathe through your mouth. Big gulps. It'll help the nausea."

Her lips parted and she rested the back of her head against the Rover's rear window.

After several moments, he asked, "Better?"

"Uh huh. I think I cut my head." She sounded confused.

Roman leaned closer and peered. He spanned her neck with one hand to hold her in place and used the other to lift her hair. Blood trickled from a graze high on her forehead. "Probably did it on a molding," he said, cursing himself for not gauging the impact better. For some reason he'd thought she was more substantial. "Concentrate, W. G. The faster you answer the questions, the faster you go get your Minnie Mouse dressing."

"Nobody sent me."

"Sure. Let's start again. Who sent you and why?"

"Nobody."

*"Who?* What are they trying to prove? Is it a rival club?" He almost smiled at that. She'd report back that he was defending the home side and, with any luck, he might throw them off track for good.

"I was going to my place." The clarity of her voice surprised him.

Roman smiled thinly. "You'll have to do better than that. You followed me."

Her fingers curled over his and she tried to dislodge his hand from her throat.

"That's pointless," he told her. "I'll let go when I decide to. If I decide to."

"I overshot my turnoff."

"Save it." The first drops of rain found their way between the trees to drum on the car roof. "About a minute more and we're both going to be damn wet. I'd like to go home, how about you?"

"Yes." Her desperation raised the word to a squeak. "You're not in any trouble then? You don't need help?"

Inventive; he'd give her that. "As in I don't have a flat tire?

You're making me angry, Phoenix. You were told to follow me, weren't you? You were supposed to report back with anything you could find out about me."

"How could I hope to do that?" Her breath came fast and loud. "I didn't know you were coming to Mort and Zelda's tonight. I don't know anything about you. I never saw you before this afternoon."

At which point she'd seen plenty and seemed quite satisfied with the view. "What made you decide to leave the tavern right after me?"

"They weren't busy."

"So you said at the time. You also said you'd be working later. You told me you couldn't leave to talk to me somewhere else."

"And five minutes after you asked me if I could leave, you suddenly remembered you had somewhere else to be," she shot back at him, swiping at her tear-wet face.

He laughed, and tipped her chin up with the end of his thumb—a pointed, finely boned chin. "That annoyed you, did it? Or did it just make you decide to find out who I might be seeing? In case it interested whoever sent you?" The subtle, lemony perfume he'd noted that afternoon reached him again on a gust of sodden wind.

"You are going to feel so stupid." Now she clawed at his hand. "When I show up tomorrow you're going to wish we'd never had this little encounter."

"Do you expect me to believe you're still likely to show your face at the club again? You've blown it now, kid. Unless you give us something to make us think we ought to trust you. Why not cut your losses and tell me the whole thing. If you come over onto our side, I'm sure I can persuade my partners you'll make a useful addition to our team."

"I don't know what you're talking about! I've got an orientation tomorrow. You came to the Bend especially to tell me that. Or were you lying about that, too?"

"No." He watched with interest as she squirmed.

"Right after you left, Mort said I looked tired and I ought to go home. Let me go, darn it!"

Automatic reflexes brought his knee up to jam hers as she went for his crotch. "Keep still," he ground out. "Unless you want to get hurt."

She wasn't listening. *"Let me go!"* Both of her feet shot from beneath her. She clung to his forearm and scrambled for balance. "I'm going to scream!"

"Scream away," he told her calmly, gathering her against him with one arm. "Should be an owl or two around to enjoy the noise."

Her next attack aimed for his shins—and made contact. "You've got guts, W. G. Squelch them or they're going to make this a very bad night for you."

"It already is. I'll have you arrested!"

"For defending myself?"

She twisted until he hauled her feet off the ground. "I went past my turn, I tell you. I've only lived here a few weeks."

"A few weeks." He held her against him. His shins might never look the same again. "A few weeks in a wide-spot-in-the-road town and you still miss your turn on the way home?"

"I have no sense of direction. I realized I'd gone too far and turned back. That's when I saw your car. My headlights shone on the side."

She'd had time to start sounding logical. He hadn't had quite enough time to start believing her. "Your headlights picked up the side of a strange vehicle so you pulled right off the road and came to check."

"Y-yes." Her teeth were chattering.

"Is that a fact?" he asked her calmly. "I could have been anyone."

"Instead of someone who gets his kicks from pushing women around, d'you mean?"

"This is called self-defense."

The lady's loud snort suggested she was feeling much better. "Self-defense? Against someone half your size?"

"Oh, no. Not half. A third maybe. I like all the odds on my side."

"So, *get* your hands off me."

He loosened his grip, but promptly performed a very thorough, very pleasant body search, evading her plucking efforts to stop him.

"Unarmed," he pronounced, stepping back.

"How dare you!" Her attempted slap moved air in the region of his left ear.

"Ah, ah, ah." Moving out of range, he waggled a forefinger. "Can't blame me for expecting the obvious. If you're going to play games like this you ought to be armed, W. G."

"I hate guns," she fumed, taking a threatening step toward him. "I hate *all* violence."

"Oh, me too. Me, too, W. G."

"You could have fooled me," she told him.

"I do think we should have a little recap. Just to make sure I fully understand what happened here. You overshot your turn, doubled back, saw a car parked in the bushes beside this deserted highway and came to check it out?"

"That's right."

"Pretty stupid."

She yanked at the hem of her stretched sweater. "Thanks. I thought . . . Never mind what I thought."

"I do mind. And for the sake of our very successful business, I want to be sure you aren't something other than you pretend to be."

"Like what?"

"Some sort of spy for a rival outfit."

She was wet and getting wetter but her stance suggested her spirit had fully returned. "Maybe I'm a decent type," she suggested tartly. "Maybe I'm a good citizen who thought someone might be in trouble."

He regarded the place where the sky should be visible and squinted against the rain. "There is nothing you can say to change my mind. If you did what you keep suggesting you did, you're an idiot."

"I knew it was you."

Slowly, he lowered his jaw and looked at her eyes, glinting in the darkness. "What does that mean? Am I witnessing a confession here?"

"Not the kind you think. I'm not some secret agent for some enemy. But I did follow you. And I did pull off the road."

He whistled soundlessly.

"Why did you pull off?"

This about-face hadn't quite caught him flatfooted. "Why did you follow me?"

"I don't know."

"Aw, c'mon. You can do better than that."

He heard her escaping breath. "I'm impulsive sometimes."

"You can say that again."

"I'm impulsive sometimes."

It took him an instant to laugh. "Your mama never taught you when to be cautious, did she?"

"My mama never taught me anything. I followed you to see where you were going—in case it was to your home. You never know, I might decide to look you up sometime. I always say I'm self-sufficient, but even self-sufficient women get lonely."

"I have heard some lines in my time, W. G., but this takes the cake." The damnable thing was she might be telling the truth. Why else would she suddenly admit to following him?

"Why did you drive in here?"

"Call of nature, d'you think?"

She snorted again. "I asked you."

"I saw you following me, Phoenix. I pulled off to see what you'd do. Frankly, I didn't expect you to come back."

"Okay." She turned and started walking away. "I guess that's all straight then."

He caught up and fell into step beside her. "Yep. All straight. You want my body."

She broke into a run.

Roman loped along with her. "I hate to talk in clichés, but my place or yours?"

Phoenix reached the shoulder of the road and dashed across without looking in either direction.

"Drat you, woman!" Roman reached her car as she yanked open the driver's door. "Look where you're going, will you?"

"Don't waste time worrying about my neck, Mr. Wilde."

He stopped her from closing the door behind her. "Ten in the morning, W. G. In the meantime I'll think about your neck—and a few of your other parts. Obviously you'll be doing the same about me. Don't drive away until I'm behind you. I want to make sure you get home safely."

She ducked her head and cast him an incredulous stare. "Good night." Unfortunately she couldn't budge the door from his grasp. "Let go, please."

"I'm the man you followed into the wild, remember? Now you're kissing me off?"

"You've got it in one. I thought there was something special about you. That's what made me impetuous. I was wrong."

"I'm going to follow you home."

"No, you certainly are not." She paused in the act of reaching for the ignition. "The engine's not running."

"You have to turn it on."

"I didn't turn it off."

He layered his forearms on top of the door. "It died."

"What would I do without you?"

"Right now? Not much."

Bending over the wheel, she fiddled with the key. A flat click was her reward. And another, and another.

"Dead battery," he announced.

Phoenix rested her forehead on the wheel and drew it quickly back.

"Head hurt?" Roman pulled the door wide open. "Come on. I've got a first aid kit. I'll clean it for you."

"I'm staying here. I unloaded the darn cables with Mel's cage."

He vaguely remembered hearing her talking to Vanessa about a cat called Mel. "Mel?" he asked.

"My cat. The cables were inside his pet carrier. If you want to do something nice, give me a jump, would you?"

"Oh, I would indeed." He plotted the next move. "Unfortunately I lent my cables to a friend. Stay put. I'll get my car and take you home."

With his hair plastered to his head and his jean jacket and jeans soaked, he jogged away, leaped into the Rover and backed out to the road. He reached the Nova and came to a gravel-spewing halt.

Staring straight ahead, she sat where he'd left her. At least she knew when to give up. By his reckoning they were about even at this point. They'd both told a string of lies and neither had revealed a thing.

And now he was going to get inside April's apartment.

Watching Phoenix get slowly out of her car and lock the door Roman was painfully aware of the fiercely excited beat of his heart. For more than a year he'd been searching for some history on a woman named April. Just today he'd had his biggest break when he'd learned her last name: Clark. An argument could be made that he was jumping to conclusions in believing this was his April, but there were too many details that fitted the scenario.

He reached to push open the passenger door and offered Phoenix a hand. She hesitated only an instant before grasping it and letting him all but haul her into the high-riding vehicle.

"You're dripping," he said when she'd slammed the door.

"Sorry," she muttered, sounding subdued. "The seats are leather. They should be okay if they're wiped down."

He drove on. "I wasn't worrying about the seats."

She looked at him but didn't answer. In the glow of the dash her eyes shone like pale green tourmalines.

"What's your address?"

"I'll go back to the Bend. Mort will arrange for Len to help with my car."

Always one step ahead of the game. He made a production of tapping the clock and humming before he said, "My friend is going to start worrying about me."

Her arms crossed tightly.

"He always worries if I'm late."

"He?"

"The guy I share a place with."

"Where do you live?"

"Where do *you* live?"

"Leave me at the edge of town."

"I'm not going that far." The windshield wipers struggled to keep up with the deluge. He peered through the sheeting water. "Obviously you live this side of Past Peak. Can we stop playing games and give me an address?" Wind buffeted the vehicle.

She was silent.

"I didn't ask you to follow my car and scare the hell out of me."

"Scare you? I didn't scare you."

This had better sound good. "Wouldn't it scare you if you realized a car was following you up here? Particularly if you tried to get away and someone tracked you into the woods?"

"Not if I was being followed by—" She cleared her throat. "I give up. Turn on Mill Pond Road. I live above the garages at Belle Rose."

"Is that an apartment building?" Oh, he was quick tonight.

"An estate."

Roman thought he knew every inch of the area but he didn't remember an estate called Belle Rose. Or any estate. He did know Mill Pond Road, a left turn from 202 not far from the club. He made that turn.

"Follow this to the end," Phoenix said. "The estate isn't obvious from the road."

They traveled in silence until Phoenix tapped his arm. "The white gates up ahead," she said. "Thanks a lot. I'm sorry for all the trouble."

When he slowed, she made to open her door.

Roman snapped on the locks and shot through the open gates before she could figure out how to let herself out. "All the way to the house?"

"No! No, absolutely not. Rose goes to bed early. I'm fine here. The lane over there leads to the garage."

"I'll take you."

"No—"

"Yes. Please don't argue. I'm not leaving you alone out here, okay? I'm going to see you safely inside your apartment and, for the record, I'm too young to be Jack the Ripper."

"It's very late."

"You said it. Late and like the inside of an abandoned coal mine out here. You do not go in there alone, partner."

His attempt at levity was lost on her. "Okay. If you'd like to wait at the bottom of the steps, I'll wave as soon as I'm in."

*Like hell.* He grunted and saw a sprawling, white, three ve-hicle garage come into view. On the left side of the building, a flight of steep steps rose to a door leading directly into second-story quarters.

"Home-sweet-home," he said, drawing up at the bottom of the steps and hitting the door locks. "I suggest you get dry. Fast. You've got a big day ahead tomorrow."

"Yes." The anxiety in her tone was out of proportion to the moment. "I'll be there at ten."

"Hey." As she slipped out of the Land Rover, he leaned across the passenger seat. "Why don't I come by and get you in the morning?"

"I'll drive myself. But thanks."

"In what? What will you drive in?"

"My—"

"Exactly. You're not going to get it fixed tonight."

He saw her struggle for a response. "It'll be okay. My land-lady will help me out."

Funny, no woman had ever been quite so determined to avoid his company before. If the circumstances were different, his feelings might be hurt.

Phoenix slammed the car door and ran up the steps beside the garage. She let herself in without stopping to as much as give him a wave.

Smiling grimly, Roman swung an arc on the wide gravel area and drove back to the road. A hundred yards farther on, he cut his engine, got out and pocketed his keys.

Covering the distance back to the garage took only minutes.

The steps creaked under his weight. Roman gritted his teeth, waiting for Phoenix to shoot home the bolts and refuse to let him in.

A crack of light showed down the edge of the door. She hadn't bothered to close it?

Not a sound came from the interior.

Surely even reckless Phoenix wouldn't leave her front door open.

A familiar sense of danger traveled the small hairs on Roman's spine. He should have insisted upon seeing her all the way inside her apartment.

He scanned the area below him and flattened himself against the wall. Leaning forward, he raised a foot and tapped the door wide open. With his Beretta already braced in extended hands, he stepped in, swinging his arms and his gaze from one side of the room to the other.

"Phoenix!"

Nothing moved. She didn't respond.

He reached to grab the door and closed it softly behind him. He was in a large room with a sharply sloped, open-beamed ceiling. Comfortable, old-fashioned furnishings of no particular period stood on uneven varnished boards. Low, untidy bookshelves ran around the entire space with a gap where he could see an oversized alcove that served as a cramped kitchen.

Maybe Phoenix had gone straight into the shower and hadn't heard him.

He couldn't help running his eyes over the books and wondering if they'd belonged to April. Incongruous in the homespun setting was a glittering cut glass vase filled with graceful budding wands cut from a tree. Teddy bears in a line on the brown couch made him swallow. Phoenix's—or April's?

An old, blue-enamel stove stood in a terracotta-tiled corner with a willow basket of wood on one side. A big, multicolored rag rug covered the boards between the stove and the tweed couch with its facing two chairs.

"Phoenix!" He frowned and crossed the room toward a door

that was closed. Pausing, he brought an ear to a panel and listened. If water was running, he sure couldn't hear it.

Roman knocked and repeated, "Phoenix?" She could have slipped back out while he was returning to the highway, but he doubted it. Where would she go in the dark? Up to the house, he supposed. "Are you in there?"

Resting the Beretta on the opposite forearm, he turned the door handle and pushed, bracing to a ready stance as he did so.

He needn't have bothered.

The bedroom's two occupants represented no threat.

Cross-legged on the floor beside the bed, with its patchwork-quilt cover, Phoenix sat with her head in her hands.

In the center of the bed curled a small, black cat. That cat blinked its blue eyes slowly in Roman's direction, got up, turned around and rearranged itself facing the other direction.

Dismissed—by a cat.

"The front door was open," he said evenly. "Didn't anyone tell you that kind of thing can be dangerous?"

"My attention was elsewhere," she muttered. "Look at this place."

Roman looked. He clicked his tongue on the roof of his mouth and moved to lean on the wall just inside the door. "Looks like you had a visitor," he said gently.

Her eyes were closed. If she heard what he said she gave no sign.

"Hey." He spoke very quietly, settling the gun out of sight behind his hip. "Hey, look at me. I'm friend, not foe."

Her eyes opened and he experienced an unfamiliar jolt in a number of sensitive places. She resembled a beautiful, pale doll formed by an artist who knew how to pull all the right strings for a doll connoisseur. Her red hair shimmered about her face in a riot of tight, unruly curls. The freckles over her nose showed clearly.

Propped in her lap was a big yellow teddy bear, worn to shiny baldness in spots. All around her was strewn the contents of open drawers and two disemboweled closets. A scattering of glass suggested the intruder had swept everything from the top of a high dresser. Jewelry tangled with picture frames and broken perfume bottles. White powder coated several square yards, including twisted heaps of clothing. Spare bedding spewed from a cedar chest.

"The living room looks pretty good," Roman said, trying for a hopeful note. He did a rapid visual check for a remaining intruder before walking around Phoenix and into a bathroom no bigger than an average coat cupboard. Again he was confronted with broken glass. This batch—mixed with pills, dental floss and a squeezed-empty toothpaste tube—had come from a recessed medicine cabinet and half-filled the chipped enameled sink. The top of the toilet tank lay in three pieces on worn, pink ceramic tiles.

Roman tucked the gun in the waist of his jeans beneath his jacket. He returned to the bedroom and studied Phoenix. "Any idea who might do this to you?"

She shook her head.

"What did they take?"

She shook her head again.

He dropped to one knee beside her. "Look . . . Damn, I'm sorry. We'd better call the police."

"No."

"You'll have to. You'll have to make out a property—"

"I know all that," she said into the ancient bear's head. "If there's nothing missing, what am I supposed to report?"

"Hell, I don't know. Malicious . . . Nothing missing? How can you be sure?"

When she looked at him, tears swam in her eyes. "I don't have anything. Nothing to speak of." She nodded toward the heaps of clothes. "A few things mixed up with that. None of it's worth beans. Figures no one would bother to steal it."

He longed to pick things up and start looking for some clue to April, to find out who she'd been before she was a new mother dying in his arms in a Mexican ditch. "How about jewelry?"

"It's not mine, but the couple of good things she— The person who had this apartment before me left a lot of her things."

. . . *the couple of good things she,* what? He stared at Phoenix. Who was this woman? What exactly did she know about April? He wanted to know, dammit. And he wanted to find out she was for real and that she was decent.

Her face bowed to the bear's head once more.

Oh, great. Now—for the first time in who remembered when—he was going to decide he was interested in a woman, really interested. And he'd chosen a wild-haired, badly dressed, apparently impoverished masseuse who sometimes flipped burgers in a tawdry diner—when she wasn't probably trying to spy on him.

"Well, you did bring your bears." Roman felt awkward. "Are they all present and correct, too?"

"They aren't mine."

An unaccountable coldness slicked up his spine. "I see." He didn't see at all, except that he was looking at one more tiny piece of April Clark's personality. A collector of bears—evidently for a very long time.

"Phoenix, it is important to make a police report. They need to be on the lookout for the goon who did this."

"No, they don't"

She puzzled him. "Yes, they do," he told her patiently. "How will you feel if there's a series of break-ins and you haven't reported this one? You could help save someone else."

"Fine. I'll call them. When you've gone home." Turning an artificially bright smile on him, she pushed to her feet and arranged the bear carefully against the pillows. "Thank you for . . . Why did you come back?"

He could almost see her mind moving through the possibilities. "I got a funny feeling. I do that sometimes, so I followed the impulse to make sure you were all right." It was the best he could do since the truth was out of the question.

Phoenix pulled on the hem of the dreadful sweater and made a totally useless attempt to tame her hair with her hands.

Expecting rejection, Roman put an arm around her shoulders. "My impulse was right." She didn't try to shrug him off. "I wish it hadn't been," he added.

She said, "I can't do anything about this until the morning."

Firmly, he led her into the living room. "Did your predecessor leave all this, too?" He indicated the books and ornaments.

"Uh huh." She slipped from his arm and went to the crystal vase. "Waterford. She saved—"

He waited for her to finish. She didn't. He watched her narrowly, watched her throat contract and the corners of her soft mouth jerk downward. Good instincts had gotten him in and out of a lot of sticky spots. Good instincts were the reason he was still alive. Either his instincts had gone on the blink or there was a possibility W. G. Phoenix wasn't the enemy.

Moving as if he weren't in the room, she ran her fingers over the intricately faceted surface of the vase. The window stood open a crack and enough wind slipped in to shift the elegant spray of branches.

There was a possibility Phoenix knew more about April Clark than the fact that she'd lived in this apartment before her.

She'd know more if his beloved business partners were using her to check him out. Why would they be checking him out? There should be absolutely no way they could know he had any connection to April. He'd wormed his way into the club as a guest, then as a member, and, finally, as a partner by offering to provide the kind of rough thrills some people associated with elite American forces. And money. He'd come up with money— part of the inheritance he'd never had a reason to touch before. That was it. The whole story.

"Surely your landlady would want this reported. If you like, I'll take you up to the house to use the phone."

"Rose would only be upset." The vase kept her attention. Even the arrival of the black cat to rub around her legs didn't distract Phoenix.

"There's a cellular phone in the Rover," he said, uncomfortably aware that he was interrupting her thoughts. "I'll get it. After this you'd better have a phone put in."

In a sudden flurry of activity, she turned her back on the vase and hurried toward him. "Good idea." She took his arm. "I've caused you enough trouble tonight. If you don't mind, I think

I'll just go to bed and call in the morning. If you hadn't come back I'd have had to wait anyway."

"But I did come back."

She urged him toward the door.

Roman moved reluctantly.

"Really, I'm grateful for your concern, but this was probably the work of some malicious kid."

"A malicious kid who just wanted to look around? Didn't steal anything? You're sure of that?"

"I'm sure. I'll see you in the morning."

"And you'll do something about a phone?"

She got him as far as the door. "I will. I promise."

Roman opened the door himself. Then he saw it. On top of the bookshelf, not far from the wood stove, stood a black telephone.

He met Phoenix's eyes. She looked away.

Disengaging his arm from her grasp, he crossed to the instrument and tapped the receiver. "No phone, huh?"

Pink streaked her cheekbones. "I'm private. I mean, I like my privacy."

Roman picked up the receiver and passed it to her. "Fine. I won't ask for the number. 911 should get you the police. Then I'll leave with a clear conscience." Wanting to keep your phone number a secret wasn't a crime.

"Okay," she said, subdued.

He punched in the numbers for her and lifted the phone to move the cord that was trapped beneath.

"Police," Phoenix said into the receiver. "No, it's not an emergency."

Idly, Roman turned the base of the phone upside down. Before Phoenix could protest, he depressed the cradle, cutting her off.

"Why did you do that?"

He held the base toward her. "Know what this is?"

"What?"

He pointed to a small, round black object. "That. The phone you don't have is bugged."

# EIGHT

Bugged.

Phoenix rubbed sweating palms on her jeans. She ran a practiced eye over the top of the bookcase. She hadn't had much time for housekeeping since she'd moved in. Four distinct circles showed where the base of the instrument had rested—for some time. Unless someone had figured out a way to bug a phone without picking it up, the deed had been done before tonight—probably before she moved in, in fact.

"I've never used it," she muttered.

Roman had followed her gaze to the imprints in the layer of dust. "Are you sure of that?"

Trusting someone would feel so good. "I'm sure. I've never had a reason to." Why had he looked under the phone if not because he knew the bug was there? But why had he then pointed it out to her? "How do you know what it is?"

He shrugged. "I was in the service. One of the courses I took was in this sort of thing." The disc went into his pocket.

One of the many things she'd learned in the past two years was how to be versatile, how to be what didn't come naturally if being herself might get in the way. She took a deep breath and asked, "Did you know it was there?" Continuing to play the outspoken ingenue might serve her well for a while.

"Did I know it was there?" he echoed, his flaring brows rising. "Are you asking if I *put* it there?"

"I don't know, really. It seems weird how you picked up the phone and found it. Everything's been weird today. Maybe you

put it there while I was dialing, then showed it to me to make
me trust you."

His eyes rapidly darkened to inscrutable navy blue. "Trust
me for what purpose?"

Scooping up Mel, she held the cat before her and decided
his eyes didn't have a thing on Roman Wilde's. "Sometimes I
babble," she said lightly. "Usually I don't even know what I
mean. Really, don't give that mess in there another thought. I'll
clean it up as soon as you're gone." How long had the phone
been bugged? From April's time here?

He made fists on his hips. She could see him trying to figure
her out.

"When I come to the club in the morning will someone explain my duties to me?" She was making herself sick but she
plowed on. "I mean, my hours, and so on? And the type of
things I'll be expected to do?"

He studied his shoes and she had a feeling—no, she was
certain he couldn't decide what to say next.

"Is the club on the up and up?"

His face shot up at that. "What do you mean?"

She hugged Mel to her chest and drew her shoulders up to
her ears. "You *know.* Is it really just some expensive spa or
something? Or is it . . . Well, you know."

Keeping his eyes on hers, he shook his head deliberately from
side to side. "Nope. I don't know. But I do know you just pulled
a personality switch and I don't have the faintest idea why."

Phoenix opened her eyes wide. "What you see is what you
get." At least he seemed distracted from the fact that she'd lied
about the phone and, if she was lucky, he might start believing
she was nothing more than a bubble-headed masseuse with the
hots for his body.

The denim shirt he wore beneath his jean jacket clung damply
to his chest. Some chest. But she already knew that. She did
have the hots for his body . . .

Geez. Her timing stank, and so did her taste in candidates
for her attention.

Pounding footsteps sounded on the stairs outside and a male voice yelled, "Phoenix! Phoenix! You okay?"

She'd seen enough of the wrong side of the law to note the way Roman's hand slithered behind his hip. He was armed.

"Who's that?" he asked.

Before she could answer, the door banged open and Len Kelly's wiry, rain-soaked blond frame filled the space. His usually pleasant gray eyes glittered as he looked from Roman to Phoenix and back again.

He took a step into the room and focused on the bedroom; clearly visible through its open door. "Shee-it," he muttered. "Where did this bastard come from? Get out of the way, Phoenix."

She was still holding Mel, still standing exactly where she had been, while Len launched himself. For a man no taller than Phoenix and with a permanent limp, his flying tackle of Roman was an amazing feat.

"Sonuvabitch!" Len roared, wrapping his arms around his opponent's long, solid legs.

Mel yowled and scrabbled his way from Phoenix's grip to fly to the back of the couch.

"Len," Phoenix croaked. "For crying out loud. Len! Stop it."

"Picking on women," Len shouted. "Coward!"

She didn't see how it happened, but in the next instant, Roman held Len suspended upside down. "Roman. Don't. You'll kill him." She reconsidered. "You'll kill both of you."

Len's face turned purple. His arms flailed.

"Coward, huh?" Roman said, absolutely calm. He continued to suspend Len until a warbling groan erupted from his upside-down mouth.

Phoenix made a darting rush toward them but couldn't shift Roman's grip.

"Who the hell are you, clown?" he demanded. "Come on, who are you? Quick, or I see how deep a hole you make when you get to leave without using the steps."

"No!" Phoenix screamed. "It's Len. He's Mort and Zelda's nephew. He's my friend."

"In that case"—Roman dropped Len unceremoniously on his head—"he can stay. Maybe he's got some ideas about who might have enjoyed checking out your underwear."

Rubbing the back of his neck, staggering, Len scrambled to his feet. "What underwear? Who touched your underwear, Phoenix? This sick sonuvabitch?"

Phoenix regarded Roman with admiration, realized she should be horrified rather than impressed by what he'd done to poor Len, and clamped her open mouth shut. "The apartment was broken into while I was gone. Nothing's been stolen, just messed up."

Len turned his angular face a little to bring Roman into focus. "He was talking about your underwear. I don't like that."

"I don't like you," Roman remarked calmly. "If you like viewing the world this way up, I suggest you deal with your underwear fixation elsewhere. Were you here earlier? Did you do that?" He pointed toward the bedroom.

Len's face screwed up and turned red again. "What the fuck . . . Sorry, Phoenix," his upper lip curled with embarrassment. "Web called me. Said he saw lights on, but your car wasn't here."

"I asked you a question," Roman said. "Did you mess with the lady's things?"

"Who is he?" Len hooked a thumb in Roman's direction. "You known him a long time?"

Phoenix shook her head, then changed her mind and nodded. She'd told Mort she and Roman went back a long way. Lies always led to trouble.

"Shee-it." Len showed signs of advancing again. "Was he here when you got back?"

Phoenix shook her head again. Roman was sliding into his glazed-eye mode, a mode she no longer took as a reason to be unconcerned about his state of mind.

"Did Mort tell you I checked on Rose earlier?" Len asked.

"Uh-huh." This stillness in Roman unnerved Phoenix. "That was nice of you, Len." She could feel the tensed power in the man—as if he could spring and destroy in an instant.

"Mort told me about the guy in the driveway."

Books on a nearby shelf captured Roman's attention and he seemed to lose interest in the conversation. He pulled out a volume, made room for himself among the bears on the couch and started turning pages.

Apprehension rested in Phoenix's belly like cold, coiled lead. "You didn't find anything?"

"No sign of anyone. I looked good, though, Phoenix. Web went with me."

"Thank—"

"Yes," Roman said, cutting her off without raising his eyes from his book. "Thank you, Len. Make sure you don't trip on your way down again."

"Hey!" Len approached, but stopped before getting too close to the couch. "I go when Phoenix says I go. Okay?"

"Okay." Several more pages of *Alice In Wonderland* flipped through Roman's long, blunt fingers. "Phoenix says, thank you. Don't trip on the way down. Don't you, Phoenix?" He aimed a searchlight smile at her.

Len shoved his hands in his pants pockets and rested his weight first on one leg, then the other. "Who is this guy?"

She cleared her throat and pulled her gaze from Roman with reluctance. "Roman's, er, my new boss."

"Huh? You work for Mort and Zelda."

"Part time." Phoenix inclined her head, silently pleading for Len to back off. "Mr. Wilde and his partners are going to give me an opportunity that should work out just great for me."

"Mort know about this?"

"Mort knows."

"Mort knows," Roman echoed vaguely.

Phoenix scowled at him. She didn't need a beautiful man who braided her hormones every time she looked in his direction—particularly one who should be braiding her warning systems instead.

"You sure you don't want me to get rid of him?"

That awarded Len a tiny, amused slice of Roman's attention. "Do you want Len to get rid of me, Phoenix?"

"No. No, I don't want that." Why were men so thick-headed when they felt the need to impress a woman? Roman could pulverize Len—he'd already proved that. "In fact, Roman and I have just a few more things to discuss before he's got to head out. Would you do me a favor though, Len, and go by the Bend on your way?"

Len opened his mouth and she saw him forming arguments.

"Tell Mort I had car trouble but I'm fine. Tell him I won't be back tonight. Can you do that?"

"I don't like to leave you here with—"

"Can you do that, Len?" Roman said, with a smile that oozed sweetness. "We'd be ever so grateful."

Len set his jaw. "Are you okay, Phoenix? If not, just—"

"I'm okay. Really." As long as someone knew Roman was here with her, she would be okay. "You're a sweetheart for worrying about me."

He blushed with pleasure and backed away. "You'd let me know if—"

"I'd let you know. Tell Mort I'll be in tomorrow night. And if Nellie's there tell her I won't forget my appointment at Cheap Cuts in the afternoon."

Bobbing his head, Len made it through the door, before turning and clumping back down the way he'd come.

"You've got to be punchy by now."

Roman's comment startled Phoenix. She closed the door after Len. "I'm past being tired, if that's what you mean. You didn't have to treat him like that."

"The man wrapped himself around my legs. Come and sit with me."

Lightning, like a flash from a heavenly projection room beyond the window, momentarily distracted Phoenix. She said, "Len is kind and uncomplicated."

"And he wants you so badly he can taste it."

She glared at the top of his head. "You have a way of making everything sound dirty. There aren't enough people like Len."

"It's a mean world, Phoenix." He patted the couch beside

him. "Full of lascivious beasts, like me. Come on. I'll read you a story."

Braided hormones and braided nerves. He behaved as if they were old, comfortable buddies. "It's late. I appreciate you bringing me home."

"I appreciate bringing you home. You've got a lot of books."

"They aren't mine, remember?"

"Right. More stored treasures. Who's Web?"

"The handyman. He does repairs around the estate."

"And Rose is your landlady?"

Thunder grumbled in the distance. "Yes," Phoenix said. "She's a dear."

"Someone was watching you earlier?"

"I think so. In the driveway when I was leaving for the Bend. He had binoculars or something."

"Cute."

She didn't want to think about it. "I thought it was scary, not cute."

"Come here."

His tone made her grow still.

He extended a hand. "We might as well take advantage of the opportunity to cover a few points. After all, you did tell Len that's what we were going to do."

The unreadable expression in his eyes wasn't something a woman got used to, not this woman. She went to the couch and sat as far from him as possible.

A faint smile flickered about his mouth, and did nothing to make her more secure.

"What I said earlier stands. About looking after you."

In return for sleeping with him. Mel stalked to sit behind her head.

"The cat suits you."

She raised her brows in question.

"Graceful in a sinuous way. You're very sexy, Phoenix."

"You must meet sexy women every day. I've never been asked— No one ever came on to me the way you have." This was getting away from her. "Am I supposed to expect to be physically attacked at that place?"

His hand covered hers on the couch. He massaged her wrist with the tips of his fingers. "There are five partners in the club. We each bring something different to the business, something that appeals to certain types of people."

"What do you bring?" Dumb question.

"Vanessa is a bona fide countess. Widow of a European count. There are men—and women—who like to bask in the company of nobility of some kind—even if it's minor. And she has connections, of course."

"So people . . . They pay for her to introduce them to royalty?"

"Simply put, yes. Sir Geoffrey Fullerton, Miles Wilberton— the Hon. Miles Wilberton—and Pierre Borges, are the other partners. Rich women without partners will pay a fortune to go to big functions on the arm of a Sir, who's also ex-Welsh Guards, an Honorable who used to be a captain in the English Horse Guards or an ex-officer in the Swiss Alpine Corps, who is also the son of the Swiss-French banking Borges."

Phoenix took a while to digest what he'd said. Finally she said, "Nothing more than a high-class escort service?"

His smile was crooked this time. "Considerably more than a high-class escort service. We have special—packages? Yeah, I guess we'll call them packages. Some folks want to rub elbows with people out of their league. We can arrange that for them— and certain other things that are pretty specialized."

Things he clearly wasn't likely to outline even if she pushed. Where had April fitted into all this? "And what do you do? I mean"—she offered her best coquettish moue—"you must have a specialty, right?"

His back teeth met with enough force to jerk muscles in his jaw. The effort it took for him to relax was visible. "I was a Navy SEAL."

Phoenix frowned, hoping she looked suitably blank. Her insides turned to water. This was no effete, upper-crust Brit ready—for a price—to don his braid-encrusted bum-freezer jacket.

Roman laughed easily. "I can see you're impressed. We're commandos in a way. A crazy bunch prepared to be abused and used just to prove how tough we are." He set the book down on his lap and continued to explore her wrist. "We have our uses and a reputation some people blow out of proportion. They're the folks who like to keep company with men some think are little better than mercenaries."

"But you're not mercenaries?"

He slipped lower on the couch and his eyelids drooped. "Not unless mercenaries only work for their own countries."

Phoenix knew about his kind. Dangerous men. Men who came and went silently on sea, air, and land. Phoenix knew about the SEALs. Men taught to kill. Men used when conventional means would be useless.

She watched him covertly. His tough, handsome face wore his history in its hard lines. The relaxed posture wasn't real. To have become what he'd become, Roman Wilde would have learned to be constantly on alert—even in his sleep. Hours running on sand in combat boots, carrying in excess of a hundred pounds of equipment. Swimming fully clothed. Sit-ups with a man standing on his stomach. Phoenix didn't remember all she'd read, it hadn't mattered then. It did now. *If the pain got too bad you could always quit. You threw down your helmet and said, "I quit." And you walked away. No questions. But you never got to go back and you'd always know you weren't good enough.*

"How long were you with the SEALs?"

"Too long."

"And that's what people want to know about? When they want your, um, company?"

Disgust, the most naked expression she'd seen pass over his features, curled his lips. "That's what they want. Some of the men want to dress up and pack out with an IBS."

She touched the back of his hand and when he glanced at her she said, "IBS?"

Breath whistled out between his teeth. "Inflatable Boat

Small. They want me to take them out on Elliott Bay—down in Seattle—so they can slip around some of those old hulks parked out there and pretend they're on covert missions."

His disgust turned her stomach. "So where do I come in?" she said when she could speak again.

When he pulled her toward him she had no choice but to go. He turned and played with tendrils of her hair. "You," he said, looking down into her face with piercing concentration, "will be available for members who like to avail themselves of the club's other services. Usually before an event. Makeup. Wardrobe consultation. Some people come for minor plastic surgery and recuperation. We have several personal trainers on call. A psychic. And massage."

"Mostly women clients, then?"

"Just as many men. Maybe more."

She caught her bottom lip in her teeth.

"You don't have anything to worry about, Phoenix. You've got my word on it."

*Why?* "Why are you making me your business?"

"I think you already know."

"Why me?"

For an instant he rolled away. From his back pocket he took a card. This he set on a coffee table marred by dozens of pale rings. "That's the number of my condo in Seattle. If I'm not there, leave a message. I strip the machine regularly, but I'm usually there by late evening."

"How many club employees live in?"

"Almost no one lives in but Vanessa and Geoffrey. Any member can stay, and then the necessary staff are asked to be available."

Her jumping nerves became unbearable. She pulled her hand away from his and got up. "You didn't answer my question."

"Which was?" He rose fluidly to his feet.

Phoenix wondered just how terrible she looked. "Why do you think you want . . . Oh, forget it."

"Why do I want you?" With the unconscious, loping grace of a wild creature, he toured the room. Phoenix thought of a large cat pacing back and forth inside a cage. He stopped in front of April's vase and stared at the light shooting off its facets.

A sudden streak of lightning split the sky outside the window, casting a spear of white brilliance over Roman's features.

Phoenix held her breath, then found she couldn't breathe at all.

Thunder rolled in the distance.

He looked up, looked directly and unwaveringly at her. "I do want you. I've wanted you from the first moment I saw you. When you put your hands on me I thought I'd explode. I've never got that hard, that fast."

Phoenix went to turn away but found she couldn't take her eyes from his.

"Looking at you now hurts. Do you understand what I'm saying?"

She shook her head, keeping her lips parted to pull in little gulps of air.

"Let me spell it out for you." He approached until he was only inches from her. "I'm hard now. I want to open my jeans and sink into you, Phoenix. I want to push myself so deep inside you we don't know where you end and I begin. Then I don't care if I never come out again."

"Don't," she managed to gasp. She blazed, in her throat and her breasts and belly, and between her legs where she grew wet and aching—aching like the aching in her thighs.

"You asked and I'm telling you."

She walked backward.

Roman followed.

Phoenix collided with the front door.

Roman trapped her there, took her hands and pinned them— outstretched—above her head. His body, layered to hers, made sure she didn't try to move again.

"Can you feel what I mean now?" He ground into her with his hips. "Tell me."

The solid ridge of his most male flesh was an iron brand on her belly.

"*Tell* me."

"I feel it."

"And I feel you." He easily caught both of her hands in one of his. Her sweater, swept upward, revealed her naked breasts. "Tell me to stop and I will."

Phoenix pulsed. Everywhere he touched, and everywhere he didn't touch, pulsed.

He narrowed his beautiful eyes, bent over her and rubbed his rough jaw over first one nipple, then the other. Phoenix cried out and squirmed.

"Tell me to stop." His voice was jagged.

*Don't stop. Don't ever stop.* She arched her breasts and moaned when he applied the very tip of his tongue where his jaw had been.

Efficient fingers that probably loaded weapons in the dark dealt easily and swiftly with the snap and zipper on her jeans. A few competent motions and the cool air slipped around her bared hips and thighs.

"You don't say much, Phoenix," Roman told her, speaking softly into her parted lips before he bit and licked her mouth in a dozen ways. "Speak to me."

"You . . . Don't stop."

He chuckled deep in his throat. "I promised I wouldn't—unless you wanted me to."

He slipped a single finger into the hair at the juncture of her thighs. Probing, he added another finger, and another, working the slickness, working the swelling flesh.

"Why?" Phoenix sagged, shuddering in waves while tension gathered. "You didn't say why it's me. Or is it lots of women?" Was she mad? What would make her ask him a crazy question like that.

His breath sawed in her ear. "Do you want me to say yes— that this happens with lots of women?"

"We're strangers."

"Are we? If another woman ever made me feel like this, I don't remember."

*Believe him and you're the fool some people think you are.* "You don't know me."

"I'm going to. I'm going to know you as if your skin was mine, W. G. And I'm going to make you feel my skin sliding against yours even when we aren't in the same state."

*Why?*

The next sound she heard was the rasp of his own zipper. One second more and his penis pummeled her mound, seeking that endless deepness he'd both promised and threatened.

With his mouth open, his tongue thrusting far, he kissed her, using his hands to frame and hold her face still beneath the onslaught.

This could have been the bliss, the ecstasy April had said she'd found and never intended to let go.

"God, you're so sexy," Roman murmured when he drew back. "I want to lose myself in you. I want to make you forget who you are or where you are—and I want to go there with you. Open up for me."

As he asked, he sought to gain what he asked for, driving his smooth greedy penis between her legs, against her swollen, needy clitoris. Her heart batted like the wings of a trapped bird. That need at her core begged her to do as he asked, to kick away the jeans and wrap her legs around his slim waist, to impale herself and let him be the power for both of them.

He was pushing her jeans down, biting her lips again, squeezing one breast gently, but maddeningly.

Her seeking hands found his buttocks. Unyielding, contracted flesh.

"Come on," he muttered. "Help me."

Help him. Help him to bind her to him. Help him to make sure she would never be a foe.

Phoenix grew stiff.

Instantly, Roman was still. With one hand on her breast, the other on her thigh, he stood like a statue with the air in the room growing colder by the second. Once more lightning tore the sky apart. This time the thunder came almost at once.

She made herself absorb the coldness of the room and with that coldness, the part of her she'd never seen unleashed—not like this, never like this—grew quiet. The pulse pulsed on, but slower, less insistently.

Without a word, Roman dropped his hands. He shoved his shirt inside his jeans and fastened them.

Heat washed Phoenix's neck and face. Awkwardly, she pulled her sweater over her breasts and drew up her panties and jeans.

Roman picked up the gun she hadn't heard fall and tucked it into his waistband without comment before he looked her full in the face. "Excuse me," he said.

"It was my fault, too."

"Fault?" He slowly buttoned his shirt. "I said excuse me. You're standing in front of the door."

"Oh." She stepped aside quickly. "Sorry."

He let himself out and she heard him say, "Never let it be said I'm not a man of my word. Good night."

The next whiplash of lightning deadened his footsteps on the stairs outside.

# NINE

The red and brown checked bathrobe Dusty Miller wore had once belonged to his grandfather. Roman knew because Dusty had told him. Dusty was sixty-one.

"How old does that make the bathrobe?" Roman asked.

That earned him an expressionless stare from pale blue eyes that glittered beneath jutting white brows. The thick hair on Dusty's head was also white and stood up in an inch-long regulation military induction cut—the same cut Dusty had been wearing since he'd joined the navy when he was seventeen.

"The bathrobe?" Roman said, stretching out on the incongruously butter yellow carpet Dusty had chosen for the sitting room in his Issaquah house. "How old is that thing? Your grandpa was how old when he died?"

"They used to make things t'last."

"Hah." Roman shaded his eyes with the back of one wrist. "Used to? Back in the seventeen-hundreds, you mean?"

"Shut the fuck up," Dusty said succinctly. "You want to talk about the real issue now?"

Roman closed his eyes.

"Yeah," Dusty growled. "Either cut the shit and tell me why you're here waking me up at two in the morning, or drag your jumpy ass outa here. I got t'get my beauty sleep."

"Do I have to make an appointment to stop here now?"

"Cut the *shit,* I told ya."

"I'm tired. I need a nap before I make the drive to Seattle."

"The whole friggin' fifteen-minute drive to that nancy boy

114     *Stella Cameron*

condo of yours? Sure you need a nap. I'm givin' you one more chance. Speak in words that mean somethin'. Or you're walking. Ready or not."

"I'm muddled up, Dusty."

"No shit!" Dusty coughed and grumbled. "You'd think I smoked or somethin'."

"You smoked for forty-five years and gave it up a year ago. You've got a cold. Colds happen—whether you smoke or not. And didn't you tell me you'd given up swearing, too?"

"Yeah, I have. So I slip up sometimes. I'm human. It's this soft life I'm stuck in. Drivin' me petunias. I need some action."

Roman spread-eagled his arms and legs and moaned.

Instantly, Dusty shifted to the front of his chair. "What's the matter with you? You sick?"

"Maybe."

"You can't come in here sick. Germs fly around in the air. I told you that a million times. We gotta be careful."

Roman gave a beatific grin. "No germs would dare settle on all these frills and frou-frous. This has to be the yellowest room I've ever seen."

"I like yellow. I always said when I retired I'd have yellow. Yellow everything."

"And you do." He groaned and rubbed his stomach. Truth known, he did feel as if he'd been kicked all over. Sexual frustration of the magnitude he'd suffered could do that to a man.

"You sound sick," Dusty said, on his feet, his hairy ankles skinny between the antique bathrobe and impossibly fluffy slippers shaped like twin Tweetie Birds. "I'm gonna give you some aspirin, then I'm kickin' you out. No offense, but I got other things to consider here."

"I'm not sick. I'm deprived."

Dusty crossed one Tweetie over the other. "The last time I heard Nasty Ferrito call you that you tried to kill him."

"I would have if I hadn't had my pants round my ankles. And he called me depraved, not deprived."

"Are you upset about something, Roman?"

"You are so observant. I'm deprived. Sexually deprived. As

in going without something I've never wanted more than I want it now. Of course, you may not remember what that feels like but—"

A foot, hard despite Tweetie's padded bottom, knocked the wind out of Roman. "Don't you come into this house talkin' like that."

Roman held up his hands. "Sorry. I forgot you're reformed. I came for some sympathy, okay? I came because I knew I'd feel better if I did. I swear to you, Dusty, that I'm not giving up on what I set out to do because I can't. We both know why. But the deeper I get in, the dirtier I feel. And I think I may have met someone who could turn out to be the best thing that ever happened to me—if she hasn't already been turned into a piece of slime by the same disease that killed April."

The pressure of Dusty's foot increased. Wincing, Roman peered up and found his old friend suddenly looking wide awake.

"You met a woman?"

"Yeah. Get your big foot off my belly."

"A woman with an identity?"

"Get *off!*"

In slow motion, one fluffy Tweetie rose and descended to the floor. "You've met a female with an I.D."

"Everyone has an I.D., Dusty."

"Not one Roman Wilde remembers."

Testing his sore middle, he sat up. "You make me sound like a womanizer."

"Nice word for it." Dusty's lips stretched in a wide, straight line. "What I meant was you've never come home to ask my permission before."

Roman wrapped his arms around his shins. "Can you be serious? Would that be asking too much?"

"You're rattled. Some piece of skirt made a corkscrew out of your dick then made off with the bottle. Now you think you're in love with the bottle. It'll pass. Plenty more bottles."

"Not this vintage. I'm in a mess, Dusty. A royal, damn mess. I don't like myself. I don't like the way I'm behaving . . . *Hell.* I want you to listen to me. Then I want you to hold back on the wisecracks and think over what I say for a few hours after I go home."

"Wild Turkey?"

Roman shook his head. "You have some. A woman called Phoenix showed up at the club looking for a job as a masseuse."

Dusty carefully poured an inch of bourbon into the bottom of a glass and held it up to the light. "Isn't that like applying for a position in a brothel?"

*"No.* Not for this woman. Dammit, Dusty, listen, will you? Just listen and save the color commentary for later."

A loud slurping sound was Dusty's answer. The Wild Turkey disappeared in one gulp and he wiped the back of a gnarled, sun-spotted hand over his mouth.

"Good," Roman said. "Thank you. One of two things is going on here."

"In addition to you wanting to fuck her?"

*"Dusty,"* Roman roared. "Stow it."

"If you say so." Yellow chintz covered the plump country-style chair Dusty sank into. "Phoenix, huh? What kind of name is that?"

"Her name. I like it. Whatever she's doing here, she's lying about it."

"Perfect basis for a beautiful relationship."

Roman gritted his teeth. "She could be a setup designed to find out if I'm for real."

"Who for?"

Patience had never been Roman's long suit. "For my beloved partners, of course."

"I thought you said you had 'em snowed."

"I do. At least, I think I do. I thought I did."

"Make up your mind."

"April's last name was Clark."

Roman watched with satisfaction as Dusty used the arms of the chair to pull himself to ramrod-backed attention. "How'd you find that out?" he whispered.

"I got into a secret viewing room and heard Phoenix say the name April Clark as clear as you please. She talked about her casually, as if she didn't know her. But she told the countess April left the apartment she used to rent—Phoenix lives there now—but April Clark rented it, then left eighteen months ago and never showed up again. She was supposed to be coming back, but didn't. I think this is our April."

Dusty frowned.

"Now, I've got no reason to think I didn't just get lucky when I found that room. And the previous occupant probably forgot to turn all the equipment off properly. But, being the suspicious son-of-a-gun I am, I kind of wonder if I wasn't supposed to see Sir Geoffrey leave, then supposed to hear Phoenix mention April. If that's the case, then Phoenix—who subsequently gave me a massage to prove how competent she is—may very well be pretending to be a dumb redhead so she can find out if there's anything my partners don't know about me."

"Whoa!" Dusty held up a hand. "There's plenty they don't know about you. Like everything."

"Quick man. The point is, they're not supposed to as much as *wonder* if they don't know something about me."

"I thought you liked this woman."

His head began to ache. "I want to. I really want to, Dust."

"Dumb redheads wouldn't be the first thing I'd think of as turning you on—other than in the southern regions."

"She's pretending to be dumb—some of the time."

"This is too much for me." With his head pushed forward on his bull neck, Dusty made a return journey to the Wild Turkey. "Start at the beginning—when you first met Phoenix, the dumb redhead. Sorry, the sometimes-dumb redhead. Then give it to me slowly. I'm not too quick, y'know."

"I know."

Roman spelled out the day and the night, hour by hour, trying not to miss anything.

When Roman finished his story Dusty said, "And you're turned on by this broad?" and his amazement showed.

"Woman," Roman corrected. "Yeah, I am. And she's living in the middle of things that belonged to April. I was holding a copy of *Alice In Wonderland* in my hands. It belonged to April, Dusty. Can you imagine how that felt?"

"Oh, yeah." Dusty raised his chin and looked down upon Roman. "That must have been a transporting experience. Close to celestial or something, right?"

Roman bounced to his feet. "D'you know what I think could just possibly be true?"

"You'll tell me."

"It's my other theory. The other one I want you to think about. Phoenix could be doing what I'm doing. She could be trying to track April down." His blood seemed to stand still, then thunder as if a dam broke. "Geez, I'm sure that's it. She's trying to track down April, too."

"Hold it!" Dusty poured a fresh glass of Wild Turkey and pushed it into Roman's hands. "The southern regions are speaking. I'd know that accent anywhere. *Give it to me, give it to me, ugh, ugh, ugh.*"

The booze burned a trail all the way to Roman's gut. It didn't make what Dusty said any funnier. "It makes sense. If you saw her, you'd know she couldn't be one of them. She's unique. Biggest green eyes you ever saw. Honest eyes like clear green glass. Thoughtful. And she keeps trying to pretend she's brainless."

"Maybe she doesn't have to try hard."

"Red hair. Wild. Like she does it with an eggbeater."

"Be still my beating heart."

"This is not the kind of woman who could double as some sort of Mata Hari."

"Didn't Mata Hari have red hair?"

"I . . . For crying out loud, you can be difficult, Dust. She's okay, I tell you."

"She may be. You're not." Dusty sighed and removed the empty glass from Roman's fingers. "I want a promise out of you."

"About what. I don't—"

"I want a promise and I want it unconditionally. I want you to promise you'll do what I'm about to tell you to do without asking any questions. Because you know I'd never steer you wrong."

"Dusty—"

"Your word."

There would be no moving Dusty till he got what he wanted. "My word. I promise. Now, what did I promise?"

"Not to show one card in your hand to this red-haired spy until we know she's not waiting for a chance to slice off your balls."

Instinctively, Roman covered his crotch.

Dusty waggled an arthritic finger. "You got it, boy. Watch those family jewels. She's done a number on you. You're not thinking straight. Cast your memory past that poor kid in a tarp. The one in the ditch near Tijuana. She was mixed up with those hifalutin people who had Miss Thoughtful Perfection feel you up."

"I think of April every day," Roman said quietly. "How' could I forget her?"

"I wouldn't think you could. She was a hero. Didn't you say that?"

"Yeah." He wished he couldn't recall her battered face so clearly. "Yeah, she was a hero."

"Geesh. I never could figure out how women do that. Sammy used t'say we'd missed a bet. Figure out a way for men to get pregnant, she'd say. Make a pill t'do it and feed 'em to all the creeps in the world. Bammo. No more male creeps. They'd all die at the onset of labor." He smiled and his sharp eyes softened. "Sammy could always make you laugh."

Sadness, the kind that mixed a smile with the need to cry, pulled the corners of Roman's mouth down. "She could always make *you* laugh, you old badger. You've told me that enough times. I still can't figure out what she saw in you."

"My inner perfection"—Dusty raised his still-firm jaw— "my innate charm. We'd have had kids, y'know. They'd have been beautiful."

"Like Sammy." He'd seen the photos. "She was something,

wasn't she, Dust. Gentle and gorgeous to boot. And you had some good times together."

"Not enough good times. It wasn't long enough." The humor left Dusty's eyes and Roman knew he was seeing the delicate Vietnamese woman who'd loved him as he'd never been loved, before or since. "She's still with me, though. She talks to me sometimes. I guess you think that's a nutso thing to say."

"No, I don't."

"I wish—"

"Don't," Roman said quickly, cutting off the self-recrimination that was bound to come. "You couldn't have stopped it. And she didn't know what happened. The grenade blew the place to pieces, remember? There wasn't any time to know about it. You told me that." One more memory to make cold nights colder.

Dusty shook his grizzled head. "What's the matter with me? Getting maudlin in my old age. Thinking about you losin' your head, I guess. Don't close anything good off, but don't jump in where you'll get your toes burned—or your balls singed—either."

"Thanks for the warning. Will you think through what I've told you?"

"If I can find the time."

"Be open. Weigh it, Dust. You were always good at that."

Dusty ran a hand around his neck. "I'm already thinkin'. You should get yourself home—in case she calls."

Roman smiled. "Just got a stop to make first."

"Ah, ah," Dusty told him with no trace of humor left. "Not tonight."

"I need to." He went into the hall where a white-painted bannister curved upward beside stairs covered with the same butter yellow carpet as the sitting room.

"Keep it short and keep it quiet," Dusty said from behind him.

Roman climbed to a landing that led past a bathroom and a small bedroom to a master suite at the end.

At the small bedroom, he pushed the door open and stepped inside—onto yellow carpet with a two-inch deep pile. He trod silently across the room to a white crib bathed in a soft glow from a Winnie the Pooh nightlight.

Roman folded his arms on the side of the crib and turned his head to see the sleeping child's face. Lying on her back with her arms crooked so that her hands touched her ears, her gold eyelashes flickered on pink cheeks.

She sighed and one thumb searched for and found her mouth. Roman touched a wisp of almost white hair that clung moistly to her temple. Unable to resist, he put a finger into her tiny palm and grinned when she automatically squeezed and held on.

"Out," Dusty whispered from behind him. "Wake her up and I won't get any sleep tonight."

Reluctantly, Roman withdrew his hand. He leaned over the side of the crib and rested his mouth on her forehead. The child sighed again and wriggled. Roman straightened and trod quickly and silently from the room.

Dusty pulled the door to. He leaned against the wall and watched Roman's face. "Well?"

"Well what?"

"You never asked about the slippers."

Roman rubbed the space between his brows. "They're cute."

"She likes them and if she falls when we're horsing around she isn't going to bump her head on something hard."

"You're a good surrogate grandpa." Roman smiled wryly. "The best."

"I've got the best grandkid. I'd never have thought it, but she makes being a has-been bearable. It wouldn't hurt my feelings if I got to pick up and move her away from here without ever looking back. *Now.*"

They'd had this discussion too many times. "Every human being deserves to know where they came from. Who they are."

"She'll know who she is. She already does. Fourteen months old, remember. Secure in her own little world and nothing's going to change that. Nothing."

"It won't change."

"She's here because some hard-assed, hard-nosed sonuvabitch decided to save her one night."

"You think I should have left her there?"

"That's not funny."

"You wish I'd done what I said I was going to do and handed her over to the first American agency I could reach?"

Dusty scratched his head. "Quit the psychology. Doesn't cut anything with me. I'm makin' a point and you're not listening."

"Okay. Sorry. I'm listening now."

"Good." Dusty met Roman's eyes squarely. "Taking that little girl on. Giving her an identity, including a bunch of forged I.D. was an impulse."

"I don't regret it."

"Neither do I. She's the best part of you, boyo. Don't you ever forget it. And don't you ever do anything to jeopardize the life she's got a right to live."

Uneasiness made Roman shift his stance. "Where is this going?"

"Phoenix the lightbrained redhead with the eggbeater do. That's where it's going. Step into that one flat-footed and your reputation as a cold-minded bastard goes down the toilet. And our little girl's happy days could just go with it."

"It's not going to happen."

"Good. I don't have to think through what you told me. I'll give you my answer now. Don't trust this Phoenix, or anyone else, until there's too much proof to do anything else. Got it?"

Roman nodded slowly.

"Your last big impulse was the best. You got lucky. No more impulses allowed unless you're sure of the outcome. Got it?"

"Yes, Sir!" The damnable part of it all was that Dusty made sense. "You've got it. I wouldn't do a thing to upset your routine. It wasn't easy to get you to take on this nanny job in the first place."

"Never mind my routine," Dusty said, and anger edged his words. He pointed to the room they'd just left. "It's her routine that counts. Do what you've got to do here, but never forget you took on a little job for a dying woman. That little job became your daughter in every way that matters as far as the rest of the world's concerned. We're here to try to bring about a slice of justice. You're here to do that. I'm the support system and what you call the nanny. If I was a prayin' man I'd be askin' Himself to take care of the justice and let us get on with living."

"I know. I want it that way, too."

"Good, because little Miss Junior Wilde deserves the best and we're going to make sure she gets it."

# TEN

"Pierre Borges at your service, Phoenix."

The Swiss bowed sharply and came up smiling. Not a settling sight. His strange silver eyes contained a coldness that came from places Phoenix couldn't see.

He settled a hand lightly at her waist and ushered her down a tier of three steps surrounding an indoor pool on the lowest floor of the club. "We shall do very well," he told Countess Von Leiden, who had brought Phoenix to him. "I'll speak with you later, Vanessa."

"Yes, later, Pierre."

Phoenix felt the woman slip away but couldn't enjoy more than a moment of relief. Borges's light touch didn't fool her. Compact, of average height, with dark hair graying at the temples, he exuded the kind of force guaranteed to induce anxiety in gentle people.

"What have you been told about us so far?" he inquired, his perfect English accented in a manner that would doubtless reduce most females to bubbling puddles of wanting. "I understand Vanessa spoke with you at length?"

"Yes, yesterday."

"And Roman?"

"He showed me around. But not down here."

"Evidently you impressed them both, enough for them to hire you." His laugh was gratingly high. *That* impresses me, my dear. We employ carefully and never without a great deal of discussion. You must be extremely special."

"I'm a good masseuse." And a tired and scared masseuse. Only she wasn't a masseuse at all—which made her even more scared. "I enjoy my work."

"So Roman told me."

What else had Roman told him? Phoenix cast a sideways glance at her escort, found him looking back and turned her head away.

Movement caught her attention. Above the tier of blue-tiled steps an impressive array of exercise equipment—currently unused—stretched around the entire area. The only club member in evidence was a woman lifting weights. She wore a pink Spandex leotard and matching braided headband with lengths of blond hair carefully twined throughout to form a coronet. Pink socks slouched artfully about the ankles of her tan tights. The tights shone in lighter bands where they stretched over chunky thighs.

Even from a distance, Phoenix could see the perfection of the woman's makeup—and her smile, and the way she held the tip of her tongue between her teeth while she giggled. The giggle was for the benefit of a tall, tanned trainer who rested his hands far too low on her belly and back while he corrected her posture for a lift.

"The lady is preparing for a visit to Scotland," Pierre remarked. "Thanks to Miles Wilberton, one of my partners, she'll be the house guest of a lord with a crumbling castle."

"Really. Doesn't sound particularly appealing."

"If the Scottish lord needs a fortune to save his castle, and the very rich American lady wants to become . . . a *lady*"—he laughed again—"Well, a match made in heaven, wouldn't you say?"

"I suppose so," she said politely.

Behind the weight-lifting pair another presence moved. A dark, familiarly lithe man who strolled the perimeter of the workout gallery with loose-limbed grace.

And watched Phoenix.

She turned her back on Roman Wilde and trod determinedly

to the edge of the pool, tiled inside as well as out with bright blue tiles. "I take it there's a Jacuzzi?"

"On the other side of the glass." Pierre inclined his head to a smoky panel that formed a wall between the pool and an area Phoenix couldn't see. "Big enough to swim in. Big enough to do just about anything in." He snickered.

Phoenix felt her lip curl. Boys in high school had snickered—and girls. She didn't recall hearing the sound since.

Looking commanding, in a black turtleneck and jeans, Roman descended the steps. At the bottom, he kicked off boat shoes, pulled the sweater over his head and stepped out of his jeans.

Phoenix held her breath.

Roman's body rippled and flexed over muscle and sinew, moved in a thousand perfectly honed places.

He climbed to a low board and executed an economical, flawless dive. In the water, his buttocks showed only slightly paler than the rest of his naked body.

Applause and catcalls from the lady in pink brought a predictable snicker from Pierre. Phoenix swallowed a reaction she didn't want to feel, didn't want to own, didn't want to identify.

Jealousy.

Roman crawl-stroked the length of the pool with the kind of easy power associated with Olympic swimmers warming up. At the far end, he executed a smooth flip underwater and traveled half the return lap submerged.

Borges's next sound was more sneer than snicker. "Mr. Wilde's expertise isn't subtle, but it does please the crowd," he said. "All the discussion about brute force in swamps holds its fascination for certain types. Usually soft types. They want to be like him. Not an ambition I understand or share."

She wanted to ask if everyone around here swam naked, but didn't want to hear the answer. "I don't notice any massage beds in this area."

"No. All individual rooms." His touch at her waist became a fleeting caress. "So much more intimate that way."

Roman swam two more rapid laps and climbed from the pool.

Slicking back his hair, he walked with total confidence to pick up a blue towel.

He scrubbed at his face, then his hair, then draped the towel around his shoulders. With his feet planted apart and his hands on his hips, he twisted his torso and stretched his biceps.

More applause from the Miss Piggy gallery.

Phoenix gritted her teeth.

Roman looked at her and smiled—and waved. With a nonchalance she'd kill to acquire, he sauntered to meet them. "Showing her the ropes, Pierre?"

"From what I can gather, you already took her through some of the more interesting knots, my friend." Pierre sounded petulant.

If Roman noticed, he gave no sign. "Phoenix is a spectacular masseuse. You should take advantage of her the next time you're uptight."

Phoenix blushed at the implication and walked to the very edge of the pool. She wanted to tell him to dress, to stop letting anyone who walked by look at the body she didn't . . . The body she didn't want to share? Her mind must be failing.

"Let me have her, Pierre. I'll take her to meet Ilona. Or did she already do that?"

"No." Pierre didn't sound pleased. "But it could wait."

"I don't think so." Roman's manner was politely firm. "Ilona's only in for one of Geoffrey and Vanessa's clients. I just spoke with her. She'll be leaving in an hour or so and she'll be mostly tied up in the meantime. But she's taking a break shortly so we can catch her."

Pierre rotated very solid shoulders inside a blue and white striped shirt. "I think I'm getting uptight. Maybe you and I could get together this afternoon, Phoenix?"

She looked at Roman.

"I'll make sure you get her back," he said.

Walking behind him, incapable of looking away from his incredible body, she fumed. Arrogant male beast. He'd make sure slimy Pierre got her back? Like hell, if she could help it.

He reached his clothes, toweled down and proceeded to face her again while he dressed—slowly.

Phoenix couldn't stop her belly from contracting, or the thrill of sweet pain from darting between her legs. And she couldn't, wouldn't look away.

"Do you swim?"

"Not like you." Understatement elevated to an art form.

"I'll have to give you lessons."

"Not with an IBS in Elliott Bay, if you don't mind."

He tipped up his jaw and laughed, showing off his strong, even white teeth with the tiniest overlap in front. "Don't want to place dummy explosives on worn-out grain ships? Aw, where's your sense of adventure?"

Phoenix didn't feel like joking. "My sense of adventure is interested in other things." She also didn't believe she'd just said that.

Roman left the waist of his jeans unsnapped and swept up the black sweater. The powerful lines of his body were accentuated by damp lines of black hair, still beaded with moisture from the swim.

"Tell me about your sense of adventure. What interests it?"

"Where is this Ilona?"

"You're changing the subject."

"Talking to you is like making my way through a minefield in the dark."

"It can be done."

She glanced at him and realized he wasn't being funny. "By you, maybe. By me, never."

"Oh, good. Come into my minefield and be sure to wear boots. Big boots."

"Aren't you going to put your sweater on?"

"Do I have to?"

Sparring with this man shouldn't make her feel so good. "Not on my account. I thought we had to go somewhere."

"Ilona's seen me without a sweater."

"I bet most women have."

He pressed a long, hard finger to her lips. "Not nice. And

not true. Why don't you take your sweater off? Then we can be twins."

Her next blush was furious—and infuriating. "What a great idea. Who'd be able to tell us apart? What a pity I'm so chilly, otherwise I'd do just that."

"Take it off anyway. I'll warm you up."

She rubbed her green woolen sweater over her midriff.

"Your nipples believe me," he murmured, idly stroking his belly, low inside his jeans. "They're talking to me, Phoenix."

Crossing her arms only tightened the sweater over her breasts. "I don't understand you," she told him, suddenly angry. "Every word from your mouth is sexual."

"And I thought you were a woman of the world. Which words don't you understand?"

"What does Ilona do?"

Languidly, he pulled on his own sweater. "Ilona's a lovely woman. She's a psychic. We have a number of clients who don't get out of bed in the morning until they get a call from Ilona." He ushered Phoenix ahead of him and as she passed he bent over her shoulder to murmur, "It's not my fault if you have this effect on me."

Her narrow glare only made him grin.

"You know, W. G., I found out something very interesting last night."

He wasn't going to get the response he wanted. Phoenix kept on climbing.

"Don't you want to know what I found out?"

She shook her head.

The splendid male trainer offered a salute as she walked by. "Are you Phoenix?" When she nodded he gave her a double thumbs up and said, "Welcome to the club."

"Refreshing," Phoenix said, when they were out of earshot. "A good-looking male who doesn't come across as on the make."

"James would like to be my close friend," Roman remarked. "Very close."

She clamped her mouth shut.

"Last night I found out I've got a much better memory than I thought I had," Roman said.

"I'm glad for you."

They reached a row of doors. Roman pushed one open for her and followed her inside. Rather than the massage bed she'd expected and dreaded, she faced sheepskin-covered pillows lining a square, sunken conversation area with a large rosewood table at its center.

"Make yourself comfortable." Fiddling, he adjusted lighting recessed into fluted plaster folds edging a rose-colored ceiling. "I could remember every inch of you. Lying in my bed, with my own tent pole making sure the sheet didn't fall on me, I remembered the look and the touch and the taste of you, W. G."

"You are disgusting." Almost missing her footing, she stepped down into the conversation area and perched on the edge of a puffy, sheepskin-covered pillow. "Of course, I'm not supposed to say that, am I?"

"Nooo. I'm a partner around here, remember. You're a lowly almost-employee who made a deal she'll have to live with."

For an instant she didn't know what he meant.

"Don't tell me you've forgotten our pact?"

"Of course not," she said. "I scratch your back and you scratch mine."

Satisfied with the lighting, he dropped to arrange himself against a pillow-lined ledge. "We could do that, I suppose, but I wouldn't want to waste too much time on it."

An idea hit Phoenix. Why hadn't she thought of it before? "There hasn't been any mention of salary." She felt almost smug. He was so sure he had her under his spell, he probably thought she'd work for nothing but his favors.

"How much do you need?" His features were devoid of expression.

*Drat.* "I get seven at the Bend." She should have decided what to say first. True, she had a mission here, but she was also very close to broke. "They did say something about a raise soon."

A drawer under his seat pulled out easily. Inside, crystals

winked. "Get Ilona to show you some of these. They're fascinating if you like that sort of thing. Is that a week?"

"Excuse me?"

"Do they pay you seven hundred a week."

She swallowed. "Um—"

"Doesn't matter. We'll put you on a retainer. And you'll be
on call. Each time you come in there's a bonus on top of the
basic. You won't have any difficulty making a couple of hundred
grand a year."

Phoenix had never been good with numbers. "Thanks." Two
hundred thousand? "A year?"

"Not enough?"

Two hundred thousand a year. "Oh, I'll get by on that. If I
run into trouble I'm sure you won't mind renegotiating." As a
junior trial lawyer she'd made fifty thousand and felt like an
heiress. Not that it mattered—she was unlikely to see a penny
from the Peak Club. With a little luck, she'd get a decent lead
on April and be out of here before the first check was ever
signed.

"You're beautiful."

She covered her face.

"Don't do that. I like to look at you."

"You muddle me up."

"Shouldn't. I can't be the first man who said nice things to
you."

"Roman, no man ever came up with the kind of line you've
tossed to me."

"Maybe that means something deep," he said, without inflection. "Like we were meant for each other."

He made her squirm. "Aren't you ever serious?"

"You intrigue me. And I could look at you all day. That is
serious. Shall I go on?"

He took her mind and turned it into a replica of a muddled
Rubik's cube. She'd never been good with a Rubik's cube. When
she could speak again, she said, "Last night you could hardly
wait to get away from me."

"Lady, I was doing you a favor. About ten more seconds and

I'd have broken my word. You know, the word that said you only had to tell me to back off and I was gone."

"I didn't tell you."

He worried the side of a thumbnail. "Some things don't need words. One minute you were burning up and taking me with you. The next you were like ice. Cold and hard and telling me to get lost with every chilly inch of that lovely, satin skin of yours."

"I'm not into casual sex."

"Neither am I."

She gaped at the bulge in his jeans.

Roman shifted his position slightly. "You don't believe me?"

"Let's just say I have difficulty swallowing that one."

"You probably would have, but unless my memory isn't nearly as marvelous as I said it was, you didn't make any move to swallow it."

The door opened in time to save him from the next tart comment Phoenix had in mind. He aimed a cherub's smile at an elegant, tawny-haired woman dressed in a black caftan shot through with shimmering gold threads.

"Roman!"—Her pleasure at seeing him was no act. "Who did you bring me?" The sunny smile shone just as warmly upon Phoenix.

"This is W. G. Phoenix. She's going to work for us."

Ilona's smile slipped. Her white, long-fingered hands wound together before her. Her recovery came, but not for several seconds, several seconds too long for Phoenix to do other than wonder why the woman didn't want her here.

Roman got up. "I've got an intake session with a member. Can I leave Phoenix with you for a while?"

"Of course." Ilona nodded to him as he went to the door. "Are you following your heart these days, Roman?"

He chuckled and shook his head. "You never give up, do you?"

"You concern me. You come so close, yet never quite have the courage to be vulnerable. I should mourn the loss of your spirit."

Ilona was a stately woman. She descended fluidly to sit opposite Phoenix. "He is a good man," she said, as if he wasn't present. "A clever man. One who has learned to hide himself away in order to do what he thinks must be done."

"Ilona!" Vexation mixed with amazement in Roman's voice. "I don't know what all that crap's about, but I don't think this is the time or place, do you?"

"Yes," she told him calmly, swiveling to look up into his face. "It is exactly the time and place. Things are happening here. Things are changing. Listen to me, friend, or you may make a wrong and foolish decision. You have something very precious. I feel that. Something you would protect with your life. But a force threatens that, and you are being careless. Then there is the element that is hazy to me, but it will become clearer soon. I can see another element entering your life. It will confuse you, bring you down, perhaps. But then it may lift you up. Be open, Roman. Always be open."

He listened with his lips parted. When she'd finished, he raised one flaring brow, blew her a kiss, and left without another glance in Phoenix's direction.

"So," Ilona said when the door closed behind Roman. "You are the latest member of our happy family."

"Yes." But Phoenix noted a complete absence of cheer in the psychic's voice.

"I've been expecting you."

At first Phoenix thought she'd misheard. Then a rush of cold raised goosebumps on her arms and legs. She laughed nervously.

Ilona opened the drawer containing crystals and selected a pale green cluster that fitted in the palm of her hand. She covered it with her other hand. "Olivine," she said. "The color of your eyes. Pale, almost transparent green. Sometimes known as peridot. It is found in Egypt and Burma and Brazil. This piece came from Egypt. I had forgotten it until I discovered you were coming."

Phoenix couldn't swallow. "The countess told you."

"The countess tells me nothing." A hard, white line formed

around the woman's soft mouth. "You came to the club alone, didn't you?"

"Yes."

"But you didn't come because you want something for yourself."

This was mumbo jumbo of the worst variety. "Of course I wanted something for myself. I wanted a job. I've been—"

"Traveling," Ilona said. Weariness crept into her tone. "How unfortunate your travels could not have brought you this way much sooner."

"I don't understand." She was afraid to understand.

"Of course not. And I would be foolish to persist, wouldn't I? After all, perhaps if I continue to tell you what I feel as I hold these crystals you will gain the power to destroy me."

"No!" Phoenix got to her feet in a rush. "I'm . . . Please, I'm not into any of this stuff. It's not that I don't think it's probably fascinating, but I'm a . . ."

She'd almost said she was a lawyer, a dealer in logic. The goosebumps made a rapid return visit.

Ilona nodded and a warm glow entered her amber eyes. "You're a logical woman, yes? A woman who had a very different career from the one she supposedly has now."

It was a trick, a way for these people to find out if she was who and what she said she was. "I'm a masseuse who sometimes works in a diner. You know Round the Bend in Past Peak? Opposite the old train depot?"

Sadness entered the amber eyes. "I've frightened you. Made you cautious. I must go. Take no notice of me—unless you decide you need a friend."

"Thank you." She needed a friend. "Perhaps we could get together again. I'd like to know more about what you do. Really, I would."

Ilona smiled secretively. "I think you will come to want to know more. There was someone else who wanted to know more. She came before you."

Phoenix held her breath.

"Not now." Ilona waved a hand and stood up. "Take this,

please. It will remind you of what I've said to you. I'd like you to have it."

The olivine crystals had formed into a prismatic cluster that shot pale green lights in every direction. "I couldn't," Phoenix said.

"Nonsense." Ilona lifted Phoenix's hand and opened the palm. For several moments she simply looked into that palm before she said, "Do not make hasty decisions."

"Who did you mean when you spoke of someone else wanting to know . . . To know something?"

"The time isn't right. It's too dangerous—for all of us."

"Too dangerous for you to tell me?"

"Yes."

"Dangerous for you and me?"

"And another who is the greatest challenge. I must go now." She placed the olivine in Phoenix's hand. "You will not mention anything I've said."

"No, I—"

"I was not asking you to be silent. I was simply stating what I know. You would never betray a confidence. But there are other things that are not as clear to me."

Phoenix made to follow Ilona from the sunken area.

"Remain," Ilona said. "Someone expects to find you here. I don't know who and it may not matter."

Complete and utter crap. She'd always thought this psychic business a sop for superstitious people.

"I hope I will finally be able to do what should be done," Ilona said. "Will you allow us to be friends?"

"I'd like that," Phoenix said without any thought of refusing. "All the stuff about . . . Well, you know. I don't believe in it. But I'd like to know you better."

"Because you think I may be able to help you."

Phoenix averted her eyes.

"That's all right. First I help you, then we have a friendship that will last forever. Phoenix, I need a promise from you—a promise on the friendship we shall share."

She only hesitated briefly before saying, "I will if I can."

"You can. You're in a great deal of danger. More danger than you can possibly have guessed."

The crystals dug into Phoenix's fingers. She saw a speck of blood well on her palm. "You're frightening me."

"Good. Perhaps fear will save your life."

Phoenix gasped and almost dropped the olivine. "Don't go," she begged. "We should talk now."

"That would be a mistake." Ilona's hand was on the door handle. "What you do not know, you cannot repeat. Until there is the right moment to make plans, it's best for you to know very little."

"Very little about what?" Desperation drove her in Ilona's wake.

"About what happened," Ilona told her. "And what could also happen to you. Tell no one about this conversation. And do not be deceived by an apparent solution to your problem. Nothing worthwhile comes easily. Be very, very careful, Phoenix. You have more work to do before you die."

# ELEVEN

Sir Geoffrey Fullerton studied his reflection in mirrors that covered one wall of the observation room. He straightened his back, raised his chin.

"Do you like what you see?" Vanessa asked, slipping her arms around his waist and kissing the back of his neck. "You please me, darling. Today you look particularly . . . interesting. It has been too long for us. When we are finished here, we should get in touch with each other again, hm?"

Vanessa in a conciliatory mood made Geoffrey nervous. She never gave without wanting a great deal in return. He ran a speculative eye over her. In a black silk jumpsuit, split to the waist between her breasts, she showcased the promise of a satisfying interlude. Each time she chose to move just so, a full breast slid almost totally into view. Only a large, erect nipple held her bodice in place.

She threaded an arm through his and reached up to nip his ear. "I feel in the mood for something very special today, Geoffrey." Her left nipple gave up its chore and he was treated to a view that never failed to bring him to her heel.

"Geoffrey?"

"Your wish is my command," he said, deliberately not touching her because he knew withholding himself drove her mad—and made her even more inventive. "Cover that up, my sweet. If Chester turns around we'll have difficulty restraining him." Chester Dupree sat in the middle of the front row of seats near a one-way sheet of glass. His anticipation held him too much a captive for him to hear the conversation.

Vanessa, rarely squeamish about anything, shuddered and covered her breast. "Demanding fool," she said under her breath. "At least he can be controlled. He knows he'd be finished if he ever became a real problem."

"Too bad Parker seems determined to be a nuisance."

Vanessa pursed her lips. "That may require special attention. He called this afternoon. Wanted to bring several friends here tonight—to the Insiders—and he gave a list of those who should be on hand to greet them. When I refused, he made threats."

"Parker also has a great deal to lose. I'll remind him of that."

"Roman was with the new masseuse last night," Vanessa remarked. "Phoenix."

*"With* her?"

"At that apartment at Belle Rose."

Geoffrey spread his fingertips over his brow. "He knows the rules. He doesn't indulge himself with employees unless he clears it with us first."

"He's a maverick," Vanessa said, not lightly enough to fool him. "A maverick who's seen something he likes. Perhaps he should be warned about April."

"You fool!"

She rounded on him. "Never call me that." Her face drew so close he saw the thickness of her pale makeup over coarse pores. "Never, do you understand?"

"No one must ever know about . . . No one *else* must ever find out about April. How do you know he was with Phoenix?"

"I remembered something you once told me. Hate is a great motivator. Do you recall saying that?"

There was no need for him to respond.

"Of course you do. I simply tested your theory and found it sound. Now I have a perfect source. There will be no difficulty in dealing with Phoenix if the necessity arises. By the way—I called April's—I called the number at that apartment. Phoenix picked up. Either the bug's gone or it isn't working."

"We don't need this." Geoffrey turned to her sharply. "Is there something you're not telling me?"

"No. No, I'm merely making certain there are no surprises. Coincidences happen, but for her to be living where that other creature lived is . . . unsettling?"

"You think she's lying? You think she knows something?"

"Frankly, no. And Roman is no fool. If he senses something wrong, he'll be the first to protect his investment. Dependence is the surest way to buy loyalty, Geoffrey."

"True. We'd better join Chester. He's getting restless."

They went together to sit in the row of chairs behind Chester Dupree of The Church of the Only Saved. In front of them the sheet of one-way glass overlooked a shower room—the shower room adjoining the Jacuzzi pool. At the moment the Jacuzzi was "out of order," and locked.

"What's taking so long?" Chester asked. He overflowed his chair. Dressed entirely in light beige, his silk suit pants stretched over bulky, splayed thighs. His belly overhung his belt, all but obscuring the bulge of his private parts.

Vanessa leaned forward and placed a cool hand on Chester's fat, red neck. She smoothed the flesh where a handmade silk shirt collar dug a trough. "We weren't expecting you this afternoon, dearest," she told him. "We had to send for what you wanted."

"Bunny," he said, catching Vanessa's hand and pressing it to his damp mouth. "You did get Bunny?"

"Would we disappoint you?" Geoffrey said, casting a blank glance at Vanessa.

"I shouldn't think so, boy," Chester Dupree said. "Not for the kind of bucks I pour into this little gold mine of yours."

"You compensate us well, Chester," Geoffrey agreed. "You're our most important member."

Out of the funds Chester collected from his faithful flock, he paid vast sums to the Peak Club. The Church of the Only Saved consisted of several thousand frenzied members drooling for the opportunity to mortgage their every possession to the greater glory of their prophet, the Reverend Chester Dupree.

Fortunately for that flock, Chester had a magical talent for turning money into more money. He generated enough money to keep his followers happy with the bigger and better edifices he erected to house their elaborate ceremonies, and far more than enough to keep Chester happy in his private entertainments.

"Don't you ever forget how much I pay," Chester said. When he grew impatient, he grew childlike. "I'm going to want something to help me along today. Some of your best, Geoffrey. You know what I like."

"It's yours, Chester."

"You bet it is. A few words from me and you might not be enjoying yourselves quite so much. Never forget that, friends."

Geoffrey opened his mouth, but pressure from Vanessa's hand on his thigh stopped him from making a bad mistake. "We wouldn't forget it, would we, Geoffrey?" she said, not looking at him. "We never forget how important our friends are."

The temptation to tell the fat egomaniac that they could destroy him every bit as quickly as he could destroy them frequently came close to choking Geoffrey. Vanessa, always present when Chester was at the club, made sure those fatal words were never spoken.

"Shall I get you . . . Would you like something now, Chester?"

"Hush," he said. "Here she comes. Later, boy. When I pick something out to have a little fun with."

Chester liked having fun with small women, small in height, large on all other dimensions. On the other side of the glass the door from the Jacuzzi room had opened to admit a woman who might easily have been no more than eighteen. Geoffrey knew that Bunny would never see thirty again and that, like all the people they chose to work at the club, she regarded her work as an art. Bunny was quite an artist.

"She's the one!" Excited, Chester wiggled and pointed a pudgy, diamond-banded forefinger at the five-foot brunette who deposited her purse beside a sink and took off a nondescript tan raincoat. "I picked her out, didn't I? Can I pick 'em? Look at the tits on that girl."

"You can pick them," Geoffrey agreed, already bored. He sat back in his seat and crossed his legs.

Vanessa enjoyed these little entertainments almost as much as Chester. "There's something about a white blouse, wouldn't you say that's correct?" she said softly.

"I would indeed." Chester's hands, slapping the arms of his chair, made Geoffrey jump. "Why, I've just had a thought. All those lovely ladies in the choir would look delightful in white blouses. Pure. Saintly, just like their sainted little asses. Did I ever tell you about how I get to watch those ladies change for services?"

"You've told us."

Vanessa glowered at Geoffrey. "Tell us again, Chester."

"I got me a piece of glass like this. Right in the wall where they purify themselves. No woman comes into the presence without strippin' to the skin and putting on garments never used outside the church. And they do it right." He chuckled and his flesh moved. "I tell you, they do it *right.*"

"They do it right for Chester," Vanessa said with dutiful delight.

"Tell Bunny to turn this way."

"You know I can't do that," Geoffrey told Chester. "She doesn't know we're here, remember?"

" 'Course not. Forgot. You got some young buck lined up to surprise her with?"

"If you're going to insist on knowing the whole story we might as well not bother with the show," Geoffrey commented.

Bunny faced the glass. On her side, she looked into mirrors, mirrors all around her.

"Whooee!" Chester drummed his fists on his knees. "She doesn't have an idea inside her head except how sexy she looks. Look at that. Look at that mouth."

Bunny applied a heavy coat of coral lipstick and pouted at her reflection.

*What if this Phoenix was trouble?* Geoffrey steepled his fingertips. Vanessa was smart, but not always as smart as she thought she was. He might have to deal with this himself.

The tiny black skirt Bunny wore was made of a stretchy material that hugged her hips. When Bunny found it necessary to adjust a narrow black suspender, the skirt rose above the tops of lacy black stockings.

"Oh, yeah," Chester mumbled. "Pull it up a bit more, girl. Let Chester see what you've got."

Geoffrey's nerves jangled. He took deep, calming breaths that didn't calm him.

The door to the shower room opened again and a muscle-bound man in a white terry-cloth robe entered. Bunny's eyes widened as she watched him in the mirror. He approached and stood behind her.

"Whooeee!" Chester bounced in his chair. "Let her have it, boy. Show her what to do with it!"

The man, Mike, one of the club's trainers, reached to turn one of the showers on full. Steam rose instantly, coating the glass.

"Shit!" Chester shifted forward. "I can't see."

"You'll see," Vanessa said, consoling. "Be patient."

And the steam cleared enough to give a hazy impression of Bunny, with one of the man's hefty arms around her waist, being thrust, fully-clothed, beneath the gushing water.

The white blouse was instantly transparent.

"Yes, yes, yes," Chester chanted

Bunny scrabbled against the glass. Her feet in their high-heeled shoes went swinging off the tiled bottom of the shower. The man had shed his robe to reveal the naked, impressively defined body of a weight lifter.

Buttons popped. The white blouse parted beneath Mike's fingers and he tore it open.

Bunny flailed. She was a natural for the porno films she made—and which Chester had viewed with lascivious interest before picking her to play the lead in one of his entertainments.

"Will you look at that girl go?" On his knees now, Chester shuffled to the glass for a closer view. "Go, baby, go. Fight that nasty boy. Whooeee!"

Following instructions to the minutest detail, Mike tipped

Bunny forward, flattening her big breasts to the glass. At the same time he hiked her tiny skirt up to her waist and hooked her legs backward around his waist.

Chester whined and panted. He opened his puffy lips wide over the place where one of Bunny's impressive nipples met the mirror on her side of the wall. With both hands, he cupped the images of her breasts.

Mike stared straight ahead, his expression impassive. He didn't have to be an actor. Chester never looked at the men's faces. For him, they were Chester Dupree with the body he'd never had, exciting sexy women as he never had.

"Pathetic," Geoffrey muttered, unusually uncomfortable with the display. "Poor bastard's off his rocker."

"He insists he's going to want to spend time with someone while he's here," Vanessa said, never taking her eyes from the action. "Perhaps a massage would be just what he needs."

Geoffrey turned toward her. "That's a plan, sweetheart. Test the potential of our latest acquisition? Nothing like a session with Chester to prove how dedicated an employee's going to be. Correct?"

"Correct," Vanessa agreed.

"Ooh, I'm ready for you, girlie," Chester wailed, rocking to and fro on his knees. "I'm ready. Here I come."

Bunny parted company with her skimpy black panties and she squeezed her eyes shut in anticipation.


Phoenix checked her watch. If she didn't get away in the next few minutes she'd miss her appointment with Nellie at Cheap Cuts.

By the pool, preparations were underway for a party. A "get acquainted" party, the countess had told her. A very intimate affair for a handful of important new members. Phoenix was to wait until the guests arrived, circulate, and get the feeling for putting these people at ease. A touch here, a smile there, Vanessa instructed. And always, always give the impression there could be no one as fascinating as the member she was talking to.

She'd never make it to Cheap Cuts. Fortunately Nellie wasn't likely to get concerned. Mort and Zelda, on the other hand, would go ballistic if Phoenix didn't turn up tonight.

"There you are, Phoenix!" Countess Von Leiden, graceful in black silk, came toward Phoenix with short, rapid strides. "There's someone who's just dying to meet you, my dear. Come along."

The countess had entered the area through a door Phoenix had been told was reserved for only a very few members and for Sir Geoffrey and the countess. Apparently it was an unwritten law that the door, and what might be beyond it, were never mentioned. Now the countess held that door open for Phoenix to enter.

She hesitated on the threshold and glanced backward. The eyes she met belonged to James, the trainer. He frowned and looked quickly away.

"Hurry, my dear. This is a rare honor for you. It's rare for one of our regular staff to meet with the type of people who enjoy the most special services we have to offer."

Phoenix's stomach looped the loop and didn't quite level out. Wearing the brief halter and sarong skirt she deeply disliked, she walked along a corridor where silk Persian rugs lay upon pale wood floors with a muted sheen. The walls were the color of ripe eggplant, the artwork all original and modern—and unrecognizable to Phoenix.

"In here," the countess said, entering an open door into a room that continued the scheme from the corridor. Several plush, brocade-covered couches, a fire leaping in a white marble fireplace—and a massage bed—completed the decor. Countess Von Leiden looked around with pride. "Now, tell me if you've ever seen a massage room like this."

"Never," Phoenix said, knowing she'd given at least one answer the other woman wanted to hear. "Spectacular."

"Mm. Isn't it? Before you meet the person who is interested in you, there is something that must be made clear."

Phoenix wanted a clear escape route—immediately.

"I'm taking a chance by giving you a try here. This is not

the same as the rest of the Peak Club. Those who come here are among the most fabulously wealthy in the world. All our members expect—and get—total confidentiality. These members must have more. They must be assured that those they favor understand the serious consequences that would occur should there be any linking of their name to . . . to the specialized recreation they enjoy."

*Where was Roman?*

"Do you understand? Or have I confused you?"

"I understand."

"Are you interested?"

"I'm not sure I know what you're asking," Phoenix said with complete honesty.

"Very well." Vanessa leaned against the massage bed. "If you leave now there will be nothing you can report. There are no witnesses to our conversation here, so you will not be able to accuse me of inviting you into some situation you thought might be unsuitable, or even *wrong.*"

Phoenix's stomach repeated its aerial maneuver. "And if I decide to stay?"

"Then you will be very wise. You will enter into an agreement to occasional visits here for the purpose of bringing happiness to the discriminating few who are admitted. And in return, you will be compensated beyond your dreams. But, if you should ever attempt to speak of what happens here—even to other employees—your employment will be terminated."

"I'll be fired."

"In a manner of speaking." Vanessa's thin lips parted to show her pointed teeth. "There is no, er, comfortable alternative to giving us your absolute loyalty if you once accept the honor I'm offering you."

April had been made this offer. It took willpower for Phoenix not to wince at the thought. Phoenix's intuition suggested that April had also been brought through the private door and made an offer she couldn't refuse—or didn't want to refuse. Perhaps that's what happened, April became involved in this elite setup and withdrew from her former life.

"I'm very flattered."

"You should be, but we think you will do very well for us."

"But if I choose to do so, I can leave now?"

The countess lowered her eyelids and said, "I give you my word. We shall simply never mention this conversation again."

"May I think about it?"

"No."

Phoenix averted her face. "Very well. I accept." *Where was Roman?* She thought of him as a champion! He'd shown nothing but pure wolf, yet when she felt threatened she wanted to turn to him.

The countess's fingers, settling on her shoulder, startled Phoenix. The woman said, "You won't regret the decision."

Panic threatened to overwhelm her. "The arrangements will remain the same? I'll be called in for appointments? I don't want to interfere with—I like my apartment and the people in town."

"Nothing will change." The countess's nostrils flared. "I can't imagine what you see in those people, but that is your affair, of course. Make yourself comfortable."

Countess Von Leiden left.

Phoenix fought an urge to flee. The walls with their heavily framed paintings felt too close. This was another room without windows. Phoenix had always avoided being shut in. Elevators made her uneasy. Even crowded stores sent her dashing for the street and open air.

Choral singing, voices raised in celestial harmony, burst from hidden speakers. The eerie sound sawed at her nerves.

Had Roman set her up?

After he'd left the previous night, she'd examined every word that had passed between them and been certain she'd said nothing that could tie her to April. Had there been something?

"Phoenix." The countess spoke from the doorway. "I've brought a very dear friend of mine to meet you."

Phoenix was confronted by a man whose creased silk suit conformed to the folds of his soft, heavy body. He leaned heavily on the doorjamb and opened his eyes wide as if trying to see her more clearly.

Drunk. Phoenix recoiled at the thunder of her own heart. Or drugged.

He came into the room and the door promptly closed behind him—with the countess outside.

"Phoenix?" He massacred the name, slurring it out between bulbous lips. "Vanessa . . . she told me about you." His right index finger made several stabs in her direction.

His suit and shirt were the same color as his skin; uncooked pastry was the shade that came to mind. Hanks of straight bleached hair fell untidily over his sweat-beaded brow.

"I 'spect you recognize me, hm, girlie?"

If she said she didn't, he'd probably be offended. Phoenix smiled and while she smiled she gauged how easy it would be to draw him to the middle of the room and escape.

"Knew you would. Everybody does. Reverend Chester Dupree in the flesh. What d'you think of that, girlie?"

"An honor." The massage table. If she could get him on the table—without a disaster on the way—she'd have time to get out.

"You been saved, girlie?"

Phoenix squinted at him.

He held up a hand. "Don't you worry your pretty head 'bout that. You're saved now. I say it and it's so. Reverend Chester Dupree says you're saved. Got to be, before we have a little fun, girlie."

Phoenix warred with nausea. He stumbled toward her, pulling his already loosened tie from beneath his collar. "You wouldn't believe what I just saw." He shook his head. "Whooeee! Hot, girlie. Hot. You and me gotta get that hot."

Suppressing the desire to scream, she put the table between them.

Chester Dupree stopped. His large head jerked back on his shoulders like a retreating turtle. "Hey. Hey, don't tell me you're afraid of Chester. Lookee here." Fumbling, he searched his pockets until he located a twist of plastic film containing white powder. "Little more for me. Lot for you—so's you can catch up." He giggled.

Definitely drugged. Probably cocaine. Phoenix had seen enough of it to last a lifetime. Several of her co-workers in Oklahoma City had suffered from constant "colds."

Chester approached, weaving. "We'll just get you in the mood here."

Panic could throw her into his hands. "I don't need that," she told him, smiling so widely it hurt. "Not to be with you. Come and let me make you feel good. Did the countess tell you I'm a masseuse?"

"Sure did." He seemed unsure what to do with the coke. "Best little masseuse there is, she said." Almost dropping it, he rewound the plastic and shoved it back into his pocket.

Phoenix sighed with relief. "Isn't the music beautiful?"

"Damn fool woman," Chester muttered. "Thinks I like that stuff. Take off your clothes."

Phoenix stood absolutely still.

"C'mon." His graying brows drew together over little brown eyes buried in fleshy pouches. "I'm ready for you, girlie. Take it off, or I'll do it for you."

"You'll do no such thing." Composing her features into a disapproving scowl, Phoenix patted the bed with both hands. "Off with *your* clothes, my boy. Let's see what we've got to work with."

Swaying even more, he hesitated before a quivering grin appeared. "Well, aren't you the tease?" He staggered two steps closer. "Gonna play your own game, huh?"

"Take it off, Reverend." She began a slow hand clap. "Take it all off."

He guffawed. "Doesn't go with the damned music, does it?"

Phoenix kept on clapping.

Dupree struggled out of his jacket and dropped it on the floor.

She didn't expect his next move, a shambling dash to get to her side of the table.

Phoenix was clear-headed and quick. She took his place while he reached hers and almost fell. Purple suffused his face.

For moments he stood, propped on the table, breathing gustily. "You take my clothes off," he said. "Too much damn trouble to do it myself. What do I pay you people for, anyway?"

Whatever she did, Phoenix knew she must not get within reach of him. "Okay. So come here and let me undress you."

His tongue darted around his lips. He looked at her breasts. "Vanessa knows what I like. Guess she's decided I need to broaden my tastes."

Phoenix put her hands on her hips and waited.

"Maybe little tits will amuse me." He rolled his eyes. "You shoulda seen the tits I just saw—just *tasted.*"

She held her back very tight and straight.

Dupree raised his hands and splayed fat fingers. "Needed both of these to handle one, I can tell you." He nodded to Phoenix's chest. "Reckon suckin' two at a time will be interestin'?"

Sick bastard.

He came at her again, holding the edge of the table in one hand, reaching for her with the other.

Phoenix darted out of his reach.

"C'mon, girlie! Anybody'd think you didn't want this as much as I do."

Phoenix looked at the door.

Chester lunged and placed himself in her path. He spread wide his great arms. "You wouldn't be thinkin' of duckin' out on Chester, would you? The countess wouldn't like that. Neither would I." Ponderously, his arms still thrown wide, he came at her. "A redhead with lots of freckles. Let's see where all you've got 'em, girlie."

Caught between the table and the wall, unable to turn quickly enough to evade him again, Phoenix felt glued in place.

"That's right," Chester said, his huge face converging with hers. Gripping her by the shoulders, he pulled her toward him and plastered his lips on hers.

*Out of her depth.* The thought congealed as the man's tongue filled her mouth.

He paused for air and Phoenix cried, "No!"

Angry red flowed over his face. He grabbed for the halter

and all but bared her breasts. Squeezing her flesh, he looked closely. "Well, what d'ya know. Freckles on her tits, too. How about down here?" He grabbed at her through the sarong skirt.

The next sound Phoenix heard was the door flying open.

*Roman*. Thank God.

"Chester? Chester, you're late for our appointment and I've got a great deal to tell you." The voice belonged not to Roman, but to Ilona.

Gradually, Phoenix's heart began to slow down. Chester stopped grabbing for her and even made a clumsy attempt to straighten the halter. He turned around.

Ilona, still in black and gold, went to him with outstretched arms and troubled eyes. "Chester, my dear. I tried to call you this morning. I left a message to say I'd be here. I did mention the time. Perhaps you didn't check in?"

"Didn't get a message," Chester said. He dropped into a brocade couch and stared at Ilona as if Phoenix had ceased to exist. "What is it? Is something wrong?"

"It may be," Ilona said. "I brought you this. You must carry it with you at all times until I tell you it's safe to return it to me."

Phoenix caught the other woman's eye and saw a warning there.

Into Chester's hand, Ilona placed a small, silver-capped bottle filled with pale, silvery liquid. "Keep it with you, Chester. Promise me you will."

"What will it do?" He peered closely at the contents of the bottle.

Ilona indicated for Phoenix to leave and she slipped quickly past and through the door. When she was in the corridor she paused to make certain no one stood between her and freedom.

"It will give you peace, Chester, and the strength to do what must be done," she heard Ilona say. "Never let another soul know you have it or someone who knows its power will take it from you."

# TWELVE

Roman pressed the accelerator to the floor and prayed the famous I-90 patrol was napping.

*"You promised me. Where were you?"* Phoenix's voice on the phone had been barely recognizable. He'd walked through the door of his condo in time to snatch up the telephone and catch her call. *"I want to see you—now. I've got to get away from here."*

At first he'd intended to tell her to drive to Seattle and meet him. The wildness in her voice changed his mind. She could reach Issaquah, roughly a midpoint between Past Peak and the city, on fairly quiet roads. He'd directed her to a restaurant that was busy enough to give them a shot at being anonymous—just in case she'd been careless enough to be overheard when she'd called him.

In the distance the snow-topped peaks of the Cascades cut into a pale sky. He passed the suburban sprawl of Eastgate and, with the spring blue gleam of Lake Sammamish on his left, traveled on to take the second Issaquah exit from the freeway, at Front Street. A sharp right after the ramp took him onto Gilman Boulevard. Trendy businesses bordered both sides of the road.

Gilman Village clustered on the left of the boulevard. The village, made up mostly of turn-of-the-century houses transported to the site and renovated into boutiques and restaurants, drew customers from all the surrounding areas. Roman took the first available turn and pulled into a parking lot.

He left the Land Rover behind for brick paths and boardwalks that led past planters filled with tulips and daffodils. Shoppers wandered in the late afternoon sun. Roman slowed his pace. A man in a hurry always ran the risk of being noticed.

Phoenix sat at an oak drop-leaf table in the fragrant main room of The Boarding House. He'd miscalculated. The middle-of-the-day rush was long over and few patrons passed through the cafeteria-style line to buy sandwiches on homemade bread, or soup, or pie.

She didn't acknowledge him, but Roman saw that Phoenix had coffee in front of her, and a sandwich she had yet to touch. He bought coffee and joined her.

"Not hungry?" He reached for the sandwich.

Phoenix's hand came down on top of his with enough force to make their coffee mugs jump and overflow.

"Hey," he muttered, leaning toward her. "Calm down. Whatever's happened is over. I'm here."

"You weren't there when I needed you," she hissed. "You told me you would be, but you weren't."

"I can't follow your every step. You were with Ilona. I thought you had some sort of appointment in town after that."

"I missed my appointment." He thought she shuddered. "Your partners came up with other things for me to do."

"Phoenix? It wasn't Pierre? I told him to lay off and I thought he understood."

"Not Pierre." Her clear eyes met his. "Did I misunderstand you? Didn't you say you were going to protect me?"

She wanted it all and she didn't want to give anything back, but it was getting harder to keep up the tough front with her. "I said I'd make sure you were all right—in exchange for certain considerations." Knowing she was a good guy would be all the consideration he needed.

"I can't believe you'd say that again now!"

He reversed the position of their hands, squeezing hers instead and indicating a man who sat with his back to them at the next table.

Phoenix repeated, "I can't believe you'd say that again," in a whisper. "What kind of man are you?"

"A man who'd like a little comfort. A man with his own weaknesses." The words were out. There was no recalling them.

She screwed up her eyes. Her lips remained parted.

"Forget I said that."

"You said it. I don't forget things. Are you . . . Would you admit to needing someone or something? Would you admit to being vulnerable?"

He turned to the window and allowed the passing shoppers to become a blur.

"Are you as tough as you'd like me to believe, Roman?"

"Tougher."

"I wonder."

*Keep on wondering.* He couldn't afford to give her another glimpse of the man he'd successfully managed to lose a long time ago. He said, "Are you calm now?"

She tapped the back of his hand until he looked at her, then pushed the sandwich in front of him.

Roman took a bite and realized how hungry he was. He hadn't eaten since breakfast. "You want any of this?"

"No."

"Something happened at the club?"

"Yes. There's a lot I wasn't told when I asked for a job, wasn't there?"

He concentrated on poking sprouts back into the sandwich. "What do you mean?"

"There's another club, isn't there? A club within a club where the members have got megabucks and a lot to hide."

Carefully, he set the sandwich down. He'd expected her to say Pierre or Miles made a pass at her—or maybe a member. He knew about the Insiders, had even been shown the inner sanctum—once. The fact that only Geoffrey and Vanessa, together with a handful of members and their special "guests," were entitled to frolic there had been made clear. Apart from Ilona, employees who worked in the rest of the club never passed through the mysterious door to the underground quarters.

Roman considered his words before he said, "I think you're overwrought."

She thrust her back against the chair. "That's got to be it. Overwrought. Hysterical. Probably suffering from PMS." She gripped the edge of the table. "I was almost *raped!*"

Several heads turned.

Trembling with anger inside, Roman picked up the second half of the sandwich and studied its contents. He had to get them out of here with as little fuss as possible. Then he'd kill the bastard who'd threatened her.

A flash startled him.

He looked around but the only thing that moved—apart from the help behind the counter—was the door. It swung slowly shut.

"Did you see that?"

Phoenix said. "The flash? Yes. Probably outside the window."

"Inside," he said absently. "Someone took a picture in here."

"What does it matter?" She pushed her hair back from her pale face.

He didn't want to scare her by saying just how much it might matter. "We'd better get out of here. Go somewhere more private." Craning his neck, he studied each figure visible from the window. No one familiar. No one with a camera or behaving unusually.

"I'm not sure I can stand up."

Roman snapped his face back toward her. "What the . . . What d'you mean?" He stood and moved around to her side. With one hand on the table and the other on the back of her chair, he bent over her. "Have you been hurt? Don't bullshit me now, Phoenix. If you're hurt, I'm taking you to a hospital."

"I don't need a hospital." Her fingers went to a Band-Aid at her hairline. "But your concern is touching. Last night I thought you were going to kill me."

"God—" No, he was not going to lose his temper. Something had happened to her, something serious. And he had been too aggressive with her the previous evening. "I regret that. I mis-judged your size. And I'm not used to roughing up women."

"Only men?"

"Since you ask—yes."

Her eyes suddenly filled with tears. She sniffed and held her trembling lips tightly together.

Not everyone chose a profession that made them capable of dealing with just about anything—and almost oblivious of their own feelings. He'd done that to find an identity. Had he found an identity, or lost himself completely?

The questions felt rusty. He'd stopped asking them a long time ago.

Roman took the wooden tray she'd used to carry her food and put it on an empty table. "Phoenix," he said, turning back. "It's okay to let go sometimes."

She shook her head. "This is stupid."

"It isn't stupid. When we get out of our depth, we can't be sure we'll cope."

Two tears overflowed and she tilted up her face. "I'm not out of my depth and I'm coping just fine."

"Are you?" Her neck, beneath her hair, was warm. He ran his thumb up a delicate tendon. "I don't think so. You aren't fine and you aren't what you want me to believe you are."

When she tried to pull away, he spread his fingers on her shoulders and held her still. Dropping to his haunches, he picked up a napkin and blotted at the tears. She tried to jerk her head away.

"Sh," Roman told her. "It's all gotten to be too much, hasn't it?"

This time it was Phoenix who stared through the window.

"Hasn't it?" He eased her face toward him.

Her eyelids lowered. Moisture made spikes of her red-gold lashes.

"Want to talk about it?"

"I don't know what you mean."

Very carefully, braced for resistance, he folded her in his arms and tucked her damp face under his chin. "You cry if you need to." He patted her back and thought wryly that he hadn't known how to dry a female's tears and rock her—and enjoy the sensation—until a certain small girl came into his life.

Phoenix crumpled. She made fists against his chest and leaned on him.

He stroked her hair. Her scent was that lemon fragrance he'd begun to imagine even when she wasn't anywhere near. And she was soft. And the feelings he had were the kind most foreign to him, and the most dangerous to him—protective, possessive.

"When you play with grown up people—people who are too grown up—you've got to be grown up, as well." Folding his arms around her felt so natural, so very nice. "You aren't cut out for it, Phoenix."

She grew still.

If he did this right, he could play both sides of the fence. Avoid revealing his own hand, but try to find out exactly who and what Phoenix was. Whether he liked it or not, who she was mattered to him.

"D'you want to tell me all about it? All about you—before you came to the club?"

Phoenix raised her head and looked at him. The touch of her fingers on his mouth startled him. She watched her fingernail outline first his upper, then his lower lip.

This wasn't the place for the kind of instant reaction she aroused.

Her thumb replaced her finger. She rubbed slowly back and forth in the dip beneath his mouth. "It would be so easy to fall in and never come up for air," she said.

He frowned. "Translation?"

"I don't think so. People are watching us."

"Let 'em."

"You didn't finish the sandwich."

"The sandwich isn't what I'm hungry for right now."

She wrinkled her nose. "Lousy line."

"Best I can do. And it's true. I guess we'd better get out of here."

Once outside, he tried to hold her hand but she plunged her fists into the pockets of a baggy red sweat jacket.

"I take it your Chevy got fixed."

"Len did it."

"Good for Len. Len the champion."

"Don't be sarcastic. He's a good friend."

"He's a marginal tackle."

Phoenix made for the parking lot on the opposite side of the village from where he'd left the Land Rover.

"How long have you known Len?"

"Three—maybe four weeks."

"How come a guy can be a good friend after only three or four weeks?"

She paused and squinted against the sun to see his face. "Seems to me a lot can happen in much less time."

"Yeah." Like a man getting too interested in a woman who might be his nemesis. "You seem calmer now. What was all that about the club?"

"The countess took me into another part of the building. Underground. Even more plush than the rest. But I'm not telling you anything you don't know about, am I?"

She was telling him something that made him very uneasy. She was also telling him something he couldn't imagine her revealing if she was working for Vanessa and Geoffrey. On the other hand . . . He walked on. What better way to gain someone's confidence than to keep on telling them things they wouldn't expect you to tell them if they weren't your buddy?

"Was that what upset you? Something that happened with Vanessa?"

"She told me . . ." Without warning, she speeded up, then ran, her arms and legs pumping, her hair blowing behind her.

Roman checked his stride for an instant before breaking into a jog. He caught up with her as she wrestled to unlock the Nova.

"What was that about?"

"This is weird. It's all weird. Why are you asking me questions about things you already know?"

He swung her to face him. "Why did you come to tell me about it if you don't want to?"

"Stop." Raising her arms, turning aside her face, she pushed his hands away. "Don't touch me. Just don't touch me. You're right. I shouldn't be saying anything about it to you. I shouldn't be complaining. I've got a good job that pays better than I've ever been paid and I'm going to make the best of it."

He rested a hand each side of her on the car. "You aren't convincing me. Tell me the whole story."

"You'd like that, wouldn't you?" Her voice skated higher. "This is all part of a plan. I see it now. Make me think you're on my side, and . . ."

"And?"

"Go away, please. You have a nasty habit of pushing me around."

"I admit I may have pushed you around a little last night. I've reformed. I'm just making myself comfortable now. What plan are we talking about? And what side—or sides? Sides of what?"

"Did you know the countess intended to sic Reverend Chester Dupree on me?"

His mind went blank. The name was familiar, but not as anyone involved with the Peak Club.

"You did, didn't you? It's all part of testing me and I think it's horrible."

"Dupree?"

Her eyes grew huge again. She fumbled until she joined the two halves of the jacket zipper and closed it all the way to her neck. "You know who I'm talking about." Despite the mildness of the afternoon, she drew the sweat jacket hood over her head and clutched the pilled fabric beneath her chin. "Disgusting. A disgusting fraud who'd been told to scare me."

*Reverend Chester Dupree.* "I doubt it." The flashy evangelist with a string of big churches and enough rumors attached to his name to rival Jimmy Bakker. "Heavyset guy with bleached hair? Rings? Flashy clothes?"

Her mouth opened and she worked her jaw.

"Is that who you're talking about? He's on television?"

"Stop it!" Without warning, she erupted into a flurry of fly-ing fists, raining blows at any bit of him she could reach. "You've been playing with me. A man like you doesn't look at women like me. Did you laugh when you saw I was falling for your line?"

He made futile grabs for her wrists.

Sneakered toes joined the fists. "You'd look after me? *You* wanted me and you'd make sure no one got to me because you wanted to save me for yourself? And I fell for it!"

"You fell for the truth," he told her quietly.

A fresh barrage of pummeling was his reward. "He offered me cocaine! He tried to tear my clothes off! He—he— He *grabbed* me."

"Phoenix—"

"He was going to *rape* me. If Ilona hadn't arrived, he would have. I couldn't have stopped him."

Her nails were short and very clean.

Roman looked at his shoes. Why would he notice little things like her clean nails when he was faced with what could be the biggest judgment call of his life?

"Where did you train?"

She wiped the back of a sleeve over her face. "Train?"

"Don't you have to train to be an actress?" Even as he asked the question, he hated himself. If she wasn't for real, then every instinct he'd ever trusted was useless.

He expected anger.

She surprised him.

Her eyes lowered and she turned to the car. Crossing her arms on the top, she rested her forehead.

"Phoenix."

"Why would I pretend to be afraid? Why would I act? When you go back to the club they'll tell you I ran off like a scared kid."

"I doubt it." He wanted to touch her.

"Of course they will."

His concerns were quite different. She'd seen the inner sanctum. Geoffrey and Vanessa would be frantic to make certain she didn't become a leak that would undermine what he suspected went on at the Insiders.

"Will you come with me to see some friends of mine?" Either he was nuts, or very smart. Time would tell. "They live here in Issaquah and I'd promised to drop by."

She didn't answer.

Hell, nothing was really moving in his search for April's past—and her murderer. If he could get closer to Phoenix he might at least get to poke around among April's things at Belle Rose.

"What friends?"

Who was he kidding? Sure, he'd like a chance to look for a lead, but he wanted to get close to Phoenix because he wanted to get close to Phoenix.

"What—"

"Dusty Miller," he told her rapidly. "We met in Coronado when I first went into training for the SEALs. Dusty was an underwater demolitions expert."

She looked ahead and pressed her chin into the backs of her hands. "Sounds horribly dangerous."

"It is. He lives with his, er, granddaughter." The story had better be fast and very, very good. "Little house over by Lake Sammamish. Will you come?"

"Why do you want me to?"

"Sensible question." Too sensible. "I think we're both trying to feel our way with this thing—with us. Maybe if we do something ordinary, we'll relax a little. You may even start to trust me." He wanted to see her with Junior.

Roman blew into a fist and waited. He didn't need this complication.

"All right." She pulled open the car door. "Get in. I'll drive."

Not one, but two formidable men confronted Phoenix in an overwhelmingly yellow sitting room in a house overlooking a large lake.

Roman had used a key to let himself in and ushered her before him to the back of the house. Both strangers stood and looked directly over her head at Roman.

"This is Phoenix," he said, sounding different. "Countess Von Leiden hired her to work for us. We ran into each other in Issaquah and I invited her to come and meet Dusty and Junior."

The older of the two men sent her a laser stare that ought to have stunned her. He stuck out a hand and said, "Dusty Miller."

Phoenix smiled through a bone-crunching greeting and tried to keep her glance above his Tweetie Bird slippers.

"Ferrito," the other man said, and subsided into a chair.

As Phoenix said, "Hi," she registered that he was both extraordinarily attractive—and fearsome in some way she couldn't quite identify. Cold on the inside, and he didn't care enough to cover it. And coiled like a waiting cobra inside all that lazy grace.

Roman's chuckle wasn't particularly cheering. "Nasty," he said.

She looked at him sharply.

He indicated Ferrito of the short, sun-bleached hair, unreadable brown eyes and long, lean musculature one might associate with a Scandinavian downhill skier. "Nasty Ferrito," Roman said. "Nasty for short."

"Only to my friends," the man said. "Call me Nasty." He didn't smile, didn't look as if he'd ever smiled. He had the coldest eyes she'd ever seen.

"Dusty didn't mention you'd made contact," Roman said to Ferrito.

"Dusty didn't know I was coming."

"Bastard just—" Dusty coughed. "He just showed up. Plans to settle his lazy carcass here for a month."

The next sound Phoenix heard was Roman rubbing his hands briskly together. "Great. It'll be good to have you, buddy. That's that, then. Introductions over. Or almost. Dusty's granddaughter lives with him."

The lines on Dusty's weathered face deepened. He looked at Nasty, who looked at nothing at all as far as Phoenix could tell.

"Phoenix is a friend," Roman said. "You won't mind if I tell her you've got Junior because your daughter died, will you?"

If Dusty didn't mind, she'd rather not be around when he did mind about something. He muttered something guttural and unintelligible and turned away so sharply he walked into a lamp and had to stop it from falling.

"Sorry, Dusty," Roman said, but sorry wasn't exactly what he sounded. "Sometimes I forget it hasn't been all that long. Dusty and his daughter were very close."

"I'm very sorry," Phoenix said.

"Doesn't help that she didn't know who the kid's father was," Nasty said offhandedly.

Dusty made a choking sound.

"Hey." Nasty shrugged. "You heard Roman. Phoenix is a friend. She won't think less of you, Dust."

"Less of me?" Dusty Miller spun around. And he hit the same lamp and managed to catch it—again. "Why the hell would she think less of me because my . . . my daughter . . . Shit! Damned if I know."

Nasty produced a stainless steel knife and began flipping blades in and out.

Distressed, Phoenix went to Dusty and tentatively touched his arm. "I'm sorry you lost your daughter. How terrible it must have been for you. It sounds trite, but I'm glad you've got her little boy."

"Girl," Nasty said.

"Oh. You said Junior so I thought—"

"Dusty wanted a boy," Roman said.

"Her name's actually . . . actually . . ." Dusty's mouth remained open.

"Zinnia," Roman finished for him. "Isn't that a lovely name? Just like her mother. That's why we all call her Junior."

Nasty sighed loudly and pushed all the way up to his considerable height. "Why don't I go see if the young lady's interested in visitors?"

He left the room and Phoenix listened to his footsteps on the stairs.

Roman and Dusty pocketed their hands in similar motions, cleared their throats as a man.

"What does Nasty do?"

"Navy," Dusty said. "He's on leave. Got here today."

She checked Roman's expression. "Is that where you know him from? The navy."

"He's a SEAL."

"You got out of the service early?"

"Right."

The responses were getting shorter. Phoenix had a hunch Roman would never be loquacious when he was the subject under discussion.

Footsteps sounded again, these returning. The sitting room door swung open.

"Here she comes," Nasty said. He could smile, and wow, it was a killer smile. "Little Miss Queen of Everything."

Little Miss Queen of Everything wore—surprise, surprise—yellow sleepers. White blond hair curled softly around her face. Bright turquoise-blue eyes were still heavy with sleep. Her left thumb plugged her mouth firmly and trailed a blanket at the same time—a yellow blanket.

Roman dropped to his haunches beside Phoenix and held out his arms to the child. "Come on," he said, his voice soft. "I need a hug."

Phoenix's right hand stole to her throat.

Junior dropped her blanket. She forgot to suck her thumb. Her gait was the tottering, bouncy, headlong dash of the fearless new walker. Into Roman's arms she tumbled and he swept her up into the air over his head.

The baby shrieked.

"You'll make her sick," Dusty said gruffly.

Roman stood up and held her in one arm while he rubbed her back and nuzzled his brow against hers.

"She's only fourteen months old," Dusty said. "Smart as a whip. Been walking a month. Did you see the way she runs?"

"Until she falls flat on her face," Nasty said.

"She's lovely," Phoenix said, stunned by the force of her reaction to the sight of three big, strong men gentled by one little girl.

"Talks a blue streak, too," Dusty said.

Nasty went back to his chair. "Does a hell of a job singing the 'Star Spangled Banner,' " he said, but not without a hint of a grin.

"Was it . . . Was it an accident? What happened to your daughter?" She instantly wished she hadn't asked.

"Childbirth," Nasty said promptly. "Nothing could be done."

Phoenix's heart turned. She avoided Dusty's eyes.

"Do I get a kiss?" Roman asked the baby. "Where's my kiss?"

His ease and obvious delight with the child was magnetic.

Junior put her tiny hands to Roman's face and studied him with absorption. Roman made owl eyes and wiggled his nose.

Phoenix covered her face. Happiness, ridiculous, bubbling happiness filled her with warmth. He couldn't be a monster. Monsters didn't kiss and cuddle babies with such obvious joy.

"I want my kiss," he told Junior.

Promptly, and with a loud smacking sound, the baby planted her mouth on the corner of his.

Roman's eyes closed. He cradled the little girl and rocked her from side to side, smiling with a bittersweetness that hurt Phoenix in places she wouldn't know how to find.

Junior drew back and clapped her hands, and she chanted, "Da, Da, Da."

# THIRTEEN

Phoenix entered Belle Rose by the door into a big, airy kitchen. Evangeline, Rose's companion, hovered over a halved grapefruit, carefully separating the flesh from the rind.

"Good morning, Evangeline."

The woman raised her round, pleasant face and smiled. "You're about early, Miss Phoenix." Her rich brown hair was wound into a smooth coronet of braids atop her head.

"Phoenix. Just call me Phoenix."

"Yes," Evangeline agreed, as she had on several previous occasions. Phoenix doubted she'd ever be anything other than "Miss Phoenix," to Evangeline.

"Rose up and about yet?"

Evangeline popped one half of the grapefruit into a crystal dish, plopped a cherry in the middle of the fruit and sprinkled sugar on top. She wiped her hands on a dishtowel. "She should be down any moment now." Her expression became troubled. "Seems she hasn't been sleepin' as well as usual. What with all the fuss of that man in the driveway and the garage apartment getting broken into and the police coming out and all."

Evangeline's accent duplicated Rose's. Phoenix understood that the two women were the same age and had grown up together. Evidently Mr. Smothers had provided for orphaned Evangeline and brought her from Georgia to Washington to be company for Rose. The two were absolutely devoted to each other.

"Fortunately the disturbance seems to have calmed down,"

Phoenix said. "I could almost believe I imagined it all." A complete fib, but appropriate around Rose and Evangeline.

Evangeline pursed her lips and a single frown line creased her smooth brow. "You're much too sensible for such foolishness. It's a difficult world these days, Miss Phoenix. The best we can hope for is that whoever did such dreadful things has moved on."

"Mornin'!" Rose pushed through the swinging door into the kitchen and beamed when she saw Phoenix. "How perfectly lovely. Come and have breakfast with me."

"Well, I—"

"No, no, I absolutely *insist*." Holding wide her arms, she made a complete revolution on the toe of one short black boot. "Tell me what you think. It's the new casual approach. That Ralph Lauren is *so* clever." A red turtleneck showed above the neck of a black sweatshirt emblazoned with USA in huge white letters. On her extremely shapely legs Rose wore tight black leggings. Her black beret tilted at a rakish angle over one eye.

Phoenix shook her head in wonder. "You're marvelous. Rose, you could be a model anytime you felt like it."

Rose flapped a hand and slipped into a chair at the round oak table. "I could not. It's just easy to put these things together when they do it all for you in those wonderful catalogues. See the earrings? Australian crystal opals and diamonds. Isn't that the cutest idea to put with somethin' like this?"

"Very cute." Phoenix caught Evangeline's eye but the other woman's expression remained neutral. "I would love a cup of that coffee I smell. Don't you bother, Evangeline. I'll get it myself."

"You'll do no such thing. Will she, Evangeline? You sit right here with me. Give her the other half of my grapefruit." Rose leaned conspiratorially toward Phoenix. "I don't suppose Evangeline told you her news?" She hunched her shoulders.

Evangeline turned pink and scurried to bring Phoenix a delicate china cup of coffee and another crystal bowl containing grapefruit.

"Evangeline's steppin' out." Rose nodded smugly. "There. You didn't expect me to say that, did you?"

"Well—"

"She *is*. With Web. Have you met Web? He's our handyman and he is an absolute wonder."

"I have seen him."

"Did you ever see such red hair? And that beard?" Rose clapped her hands to her cheeks. "But he's very nice to Evangeline. Takes her drivin', doesn't he Evangeline?"

"I need to get started upstairs," Evangeline said, her face scarlet now. "All those new comforters you ordered came. I want to get them on the beds this morning."

Rose jiggled in her chair. "Oh, my, what fun. You run along, dear. I'll be up later to take a look."

When the door swung shut behind Evangeline, Phoenix took a deep, grateful breath. Since yesterday, after she'd listened to Roman explain that Junior Miller called everyone Dada, she'd decided there was far more going on in Past Peak than even she had unwillingly imagined. Today was a new beginning, the beginning of the end of what she had to do.

"Eat your grapefruit, dear," Rose said.

Phoenix did as she was told. The club was an evil place, a place where April had fallen into some dreadful trap that still held her. Phoenix intended to go back there today—in the afternoon when she was scheduled—and behave as if nothing unusual had happened yesterday. If the countess went on the attack, Phoenix would play the dumb redhead again. She was getting pretty good at that act.

The biggest dilemma of all was Roman Wilde.

She'd . . . She might actually be falling in love with the man.

Phoenix choked on a segment of grapefruit and grabbed her coffee. How could you think you loved a man you'd only met a few days earlier, a man who'd pushed you around in the woods and overwhelmed you with enough sexual wattage to fry your insides?

The grapefruit finally slipped down her throat.

She smiled slowly. Fried insides were a delicacy she could come to crave.

"Would you care for some toast, dear?"

"No, thank you."

"I didn't think so. You have such a lovely figure. We do have to be careful, don't we?"

"Mm. Yes."

She had driven Roman back to the quaint shopping village in Issaquah. After a long silence, he'd told her he was aware of the club having two levels, but that he was involved with only one, the one outside the mystery door. He advised her to behave as if nothing was amiss. Then he asked her not to mention anything about his friends in Issaquah.

Phoenix thought it all through again. *"Dada, Dada."* Junior hadn't called anyone else Dada. Yet why would Dusty Miller be so pleasant to Roman if he'd indirectly caused the death of Junior's mother?

Roman had been quietly direct after they'd left Dusty's. He'd told her he would never be far away again if she was at the club. He'd asked that she should always let him know her schedule. *No strings attached.* He'd said that, too.

Was he reaching out for intimacy? Offering a sign of trust? Or staging another test?

She pushed the grapefruit aside. She could continue to play the game as she'd played it so far. No one knew who or what she really was. And no one knew she and April were old friends.

Ilona was her key. The woman had given a warning and she'd mentioned—without naming names—someone else who had run into trouble at the club. To Phoenix, taking a psychic seriously was akin to believing in the efficacy of snake oil, but behind all the flowing robes and talk of crystals and premonitions, Ilona was the link to April. After a sleepless night of weighing the previous day's events, Phoenix had never been more sure of anything.

But first there was more to be learned here—with Rose.

"More coffee?" Phoenix asked.

"Why, no, my dear. I never indulge in more than one cup in the morning. Did Evangeline give you Nellie's message?"

Phoenix shook her head, no.

"She's getting forgetful. Let me see if I can remember." She screwed up her eyes. "Yes. Eleven o'clock this morning for a cut and . . . Bananafish? Could that be what she said? A cut and Bananafish?"

Phoenix stared at her, then grinned. "Yup. J. D. Salinger's 'Bananafish.' Nellie's expanding her culture—her words, not mine. She's started a beauty and book group. And we're only going to discuss meaningful stories. Evidently the minister at her church didn't think J. D. Salinger was particularly appropriate so Nellie's sure she's chosen wisely."

Rose cocked a questioning brow.

"Sophisticated stuff," Phoenix said. "Rose, I wanted to talk some more about April. I'm getting worried about her."

After far too long, Rose said, "Nothing to worry about. I've told you that."

"I know." Phoenix held her cup in both hands. The china was transparent. "I want to believe you're right, but . . . Do you suppose I could read her cards?"

Rose's cup clattered into its saucer. "I showed them to you."

Just as Phoenix had anticipated, this wasn't working. "I shouldn't push," she said.

"You love her." Rose blinked back tears that welled in her lovely eyes. "So do I. She was the first one who ever . . . April told me things. And she never thought I was a silly fool for—for bein' the way I am." She swallowed noisily.

"April doesn't judge people," Phoenix told her gently. "April didn't have an easy life. Growing up, I mean. We were the two musketeers. We helped each other. Only she helped me more than I helped her. April always believed in me. When no one else thought I was worth beans, April kept telling me I was as good as anyone—better, she used to say. I—" She paused, appalled at the welling up of emotion.

Rose regarded her with unwavering concentration. "You do love her. How could anyone not? She never says a bad word about a soul, and mostly she finds somethin' good to say—even about people no other body would bother with. She's comin' back, Phoenix. I just know she's comin' back."

Phoenix lowered her cup slowly and bowed her head. "I hope so."

"I *know* so, I tell you. You wait right here and I'll get those cards of April's. You take another look at them and you'll know she must be havin' such a good time on her trip she's forgotten to . . . I guess, she's just forgotten Past Peak for a while. But she'll come back. She's got her favorite things here."

"Her vase," Phoenix murmured. "Did she tell you how she saved up for that? It's Waterford. Sat in the corner of the pawnshop window covered in dust. April used to pray no one would clean it up and notice how pretty it was before she could get it."

Rose got up. "She told me. And she laughed, but it wasn't a happy laugh. Her Hopes, she called it. She saved up and bought it for her Hopes. For when she got married and had a beautiful polished table where she could set it and keep it filled with flowers. April wouldn't leave that vase behind. And her bears. Why, she adored those bears. She's comin' back for all of them."

The lump in Phoenix's throat had grown huge. She was glad when Rose left in a flurry, still chattering about April's treasures.

Of course April wouldn't leave the things she loved—not if she didn't expect to come back. But expecting to do something and actually having it happen could be very different things.

Rose returned.

Phoenix wasn't surprised to see that she didn't bring the postcards. Best not mention them again for a while. "I guess I'd better get into town. I need to talk to Mort and Zelda before I go to Cheap Cuts." She carried her dishes to the white enameled sink.

"Don't do that," Rose said.

"Oh, I'm used to cleaning up after—"

"I don't mean that." Rose's tone was sharp. "I mean, don't behave as if I'm a little crazy and you have to humor me."

Phoenix turned around.

"You think that because I . . . I don't go about too much. And some people believe I'm strange. What's wrong with choosin' to watch the world rather than be in it, anyway?"

There was no suitable reply.

"You're thinkin' I'm a silly woman who forgets and pretends and that I'm not showin' you my April's postcards because I'm selfish and don't want to share them."

"No! No, Rose, I don't think that."

"So you say. Well, it doesn't matter anymore."

Phoenix approached. "I think that as long as no one else is hurt by it, a person should live life the way they choose. Don't worry about it anymore. I'm grateful to you for allowing me to rent the apartment, and for being so kind."

"I'm more than glad to have you here." The sound Rose made shocked Phoenix all the way to her toes. A gulping sob.

"Don't cry. *Please.*"

Rose pressed the knuckles of one fist to her mouth. Tears streamed down her cheeks. "I can't show you those postcards because they're gone."

When he got back to the club he'd know if he'd blown it by opening up to Phoenix, even if he hadn't really told her anything of substance.

Roman drained a mug of coffee at the counter in Round the Bend, gave Mort a sloppy salute, and sauntered out of the place as if he didn't have anything more important on his mind than deciding what to have for lunch.

On the sidewalk in front he tossed his keys in the air and caught them before stepping off the curb and strolling across the road toward the Land Rover. Once behind the wheel, he drove off in the direction of North Bend.

A leisurely tour around the block brought him to a bright pink rambler with a sign at the end of the path proclaiming: CHEAP CUTS—BEAUTY FOR LESS—SOMETHING FOR ALMOST NOTHING—WILL NOT BE *UNDERCUT.*

On a scrub grass and gravel verge in front, Phoenix's Chevy

stood behind a camouflage-painted Volkswagen bus sporting white lace curtains drawn back from the windows.

Roman parked behind the Chevy and got out.

Pink flamingoes, duck windsocks, plaster elves and wooden tulips in red plastic pots lined the path to the front door. Santa in his sleigh, pulled by a line of reindeer, still crowned the roof of the rambler.

OPEN, a sign on the front door announced.

Once more he was gambling. Gambling on a hunch that Phoenix wasn't one of the enemy, that by infiltrating—as casually as possible—her everyday life he would find a link to April, and gambling on his own gut feeling that he'd finally found the one woman he'd like to come home to.

Roman stuck his head into the house, grimaced at the blast of perfumed odors that met him, and heard voices coming from somewhere in the rear of the building. Voices and the lilting whine of country fiddle music. He followed the sounds all the way to a room, obviously added for the purpose, where the business of CHEAP CUTS was conducted.

The four women present didn't see him arrive and lean against a wall to watch.

A voluptuous little woman in a pink and white checked shirt, tight black jeans and high-heeled white boots, paced and jabbed a finger at the open book she held. "It's all about symbolism," she said. "Her painting those toenails is pure symbolism. Pure and simple symbolism."

The woman from Round the Bend sat with her legs crossed beneath her and a hair dryer turning her face red. She also held a book.

The blond woman in jeans strutted. "See what I mean?"

"Symbolic of what, Nellie?" Phoenix's voice was muffled. Tipped backward over a washbasin, she endured a ferociously vigorous shampooing from a pale girl with hair resembling a bronzed porcupine. The girl had a silver ring in her nose.

"I already know," Nellie said. "Now I want to see if you all did your homework."

The girl with the porcupine do snapped a large green gum

bubble, chewed it back between her purple lips, and said, "What's 'symbolic' mean?" She turned off the water.

"You explain 'symbolic' to Tracy, Phoenix," Nellie said. "You're so good with words."

With a white towel enveloping her hair, Phoenix sat up, swiping at a rivulet of slightly sudsy water that trickled into her eye. "Symbolic," she said. "Easiest way to put it is it's something that's supposed to make you think of something else—it *means* something else."

Another green bubble lived its short life. Tracy tapped one Doc Martin-clad toe to the fiddle music and considered before asking, "So why not just say what it is you're talking about in the first place?"

Roman couldn't contain his smile.

That's when Nellie saw him. "Well, lookee what we've got here!" She sauntered toward him, hips swinging. "What can I do for you, cowboy?" She winked hugely, but her grin was purely friendly.

"I understand you do the hair cutting around here. Want to cut some of mine?"

"I surely do," Nellie said, threading an arm through his and urging him away from the wall. "It'll be a pleasure."

"Hi, Phoenix." He raised a hand as he was led to the basin next to hers. "I dropped by the Bend and Mort mentioned you were here. Thought I'd kill two birds with one stone."

"A *symbol*," Tracy said, pointing at him.

"Ah, he's more than a sex symbol, aren't you, cowboy?" Nellie said.

"No." Tracy rubbed Phoenix's hair with the towel. "Kill two birds with one stone. A symbol, right? He really meant he's getting two things done at the same time."

Phoenix looked at the ceiling.

"Well," Nellie said, "you can't really blame her. You said a symbol was something that meant something else."

Zelda, who had pushed the hair dryer hood up, slid to the edge of her seat. "You're Phoenix's old friend."

"Roman Wilde," he said pleasantly, trying not to stiffen while he waited to see if Phoenix would say he was no friend of hers and that he was a partner in the Peak Club.

She said nothing at all.

Nellie guided him backward and aimed a heavy jet of water over his hair. "You live around here, Roman?"

"Not too far."

"You and Phoenix"—she peeked at Phoenix—"You got something going?"

"Depends," he said, raising his brows. "I came by to ask her to dinner tonight—and to get the haircut."

Phoenix still didn't say anything.

"Perhaps you can talk some sense into her," Zelda said. "Has she told you about this job at that wretched club?"

At last Phoenix had a word to say. *"Zelda."*

"What's it mean when the man kills himself, then?" Tracy asked. "In the story."

A short silence followed, then Roman said, "Phoenix did say she had a second job. She's always been a hard worker." The tone was set. There was no way she could fail to miss the signal that he didn't want her to mention his connection to the club.

Nellie finished washing his hair. She settled him in a chair before a mirror where he could see Phoenix's reflection in a mirror behind him.

"She hasn't told you about that club, has she?" Zelda said. Tracy took out pins that had held her hair loosely on top of her head. It fell, still damp, to all but hide her small body. "If you're her friend, you should tell her to quit with that place."

"Phoenix is a determined woman," he said. "I don't think she'd appreciate being told what to do. Not by me or anybody else."

Nellie combed through his hair. "How short?"

It was already short. "Just trim the neck," he said.

Tracy had left Zelda and removed the towel from Phoenix's head. Wet red hair sprang free.

"No wonder you kept this one secret, Phoenix," Nellie said, smiling at Roman. "Threw away the mold after they made you, I'll wager."

"Another symbol!" Tracy shouted.

Nellie frowned. "Later with the symbols, Tracy, okay? You don't have it quite right. Leastwise, I don't think you do."

Tracy pushed out her purple mouth and set to work on the seemingly impossible task of brushing Phoenix's hair.

Phoenix met Roman's eyes in the mirror. She made no attempt to look away—and she didn't smile. Weighing him. Trying to figure out what he was doing here—really doing here.

"Did you know April, too?" Nellie asked the question off-handedly.

His blood stood still. He glanced up at her. "April?"

"She worked at the club. Left Past Peak well over a year ago now."

"Roman's not interested in any of that," Phoenix said, the words tumbling out. "Tracy, I think we need a different explanation of symbolism, don't you?"

"You know"—Nellie settled her weight on one foot and wiggled her comb—"You know, there's something funny about the way April just took off like that."

He ironed all expression from his face.

"Last time I saw her was in this room. She had a manicure and a pedicure."

"Did she have her nails painted?" Tracy asked.

"Sure did."

"Just like the woman in the banana story."

" 'Bananafish,' " Zelda said. "It's called 'Bananafish' and that woman painted her own nails. April was excited. Reckoned she was off on a tour or something."

Roman felt Phoenix's stillness. He glanced at her. She watched Nellie fixedly.

"I thought there was something funny about her. Something unnatural."

"Unnatural how?" Phoenix asked. She took the brush from Tracy who shrugged and returned her attention to Zelda.

Nellie rested her hands on Roman's shoulders. "Like she was saying one thing and meaning another."

"Symbol again," Tracy said.

"Not," Nellie snapped. "Like she was pretending to be happy."

"You mean she was unhappy?" Phoenix swung around in her chair. Her hair was drying in soft, springy curls.

Nellie picked up a pair of scissors and wiped them slowly on a towel. "Not unhappy. Scared, maybe." She shrugged. "But maybe I'm making something out of nothing. Do *you* think she'll come back?"

"No," Zelda said, before Phoenix could reply. "No, I don't think she'll come back. I think something's happened to her."

Roman kept his attention on his hands. Inside, he clenched up. He felt again the weight of a slender woman in his arms, and the way that weight grew heavier—heavier with death. He would find out who did that to her. He'd find out and make sure they knew how it felt to die in agony.

"Could she have been sad?" Tracy asked tentatively, finally reflecting the change in mood in the room. "If she was sad, she could have gone away to . . . Sheesh, I don't know."

"No," Nellie said, not unkindly. "You don't know. You never met April. She was lovely."

"Don't talk about her as if she's dead!"

Roman's head jerked up and he watched Phoenix. Her eyes had grown wide with what had to be terror. She tossed the brush toward the table under the mirror. The brush missed and clattered to the floor.

"Oh, Phoenix," Zelda whispered.

Roman kept on watching a face he was never going to get tired of watching. Emotions flitted, one after the other, across her features, and every one spoke of desperation.

"That's foolishness," Nellie said. "April will be all right. She's one of those women who get to do exciting things, is all. I didn't—don't always think she's as sensible as she should be. I tried to get her to tell me about this tour of hers, but she said she wasn't allowed to. Now, I ask you, not *allowed* to when you're a grown-up woman?"

"She never mentioned any tour to me," Zelda said. She drew

her hair over one shoulder and began braiding. "If it wasn't for Rose, Mort and I would have looked into it, I can tell you."

"Sin and sex," Nellie said, her voice barely audible. "That club. Sin and sex and *witchcraft.*"

Roman felt the frozen wave of shock in the room. He forced a laugh. "Sounds a bit unlikely in a little place like this."

"Not *here*," Nellie told him. "Not in Past Peak. That club. I'd stake everything I own on those people knowing where April went. We hear the stories. Sin and sex and witchcraft."

He met her eyes in the mirror, then Phoenix's.

"There's some," Nellie said, "who even talk about murder."

Phoenix drove the fingers of both hands into her hair.

"Oh, don't listen to that," Zelda said, going to her. "We're getting carried away. You'll get to give that friend of yours a piece of your mind one of these days."

*That friend of yours.* Roman pretended to doze. Even if by omission, the lady had lied. April Clark was no stranger to Phoenix.

"Hey, everybody," Nellie said, picking a bottle of green stuff from a shelf and laughing nervously. "Lighten up. Why don't we all try this new nonsurgical face-lift?"

# FOURTEEN

In the end Roman hadn't actually issued the invitation to dinner. He'd walked out of Nellie's beside Phoenix, but left her at the end of the path and gone to his Land Rover without looking back. But he'd kept his most important promise. Throughout her shift at the club, Phoenix had seen him coming and going. She'd worked on two women and a man. When she left the man, the first face she saw was Roman's. He stood facing her, talking to James and the weight-lifting lady in pink—only she wore chartreuse this time.

Phoenix had smiled at Roman.

He hadn't smiled back.

At Nellie's, Roman had showed no sign of noticing Zelda's comment about Phoenix and April. He'd noticed. And he'd probably told the countess and Sir Roger. They knew now. They all knew April wasn't just the previous tenant in Phoenix's flat. They knew she was her best friend.

When her shift was over, she hurried up to the first level of the club where she'd been provided with a comfortable changing room. In less than five minutes, she let herself out and turned toward the front entrance.

"Are you being careful?"

Phoenix recognized Ilona's soft voice behind her but didn't turn around. "Why should I be careful?"

"You are trying to do something very dangerous."

"Am I?" Her heart beat fast. She felt in the bottom of her purse for car keys. "Why would you think something like that?"

"I know. There is nowhere here that is really safe. Do you understand?"

Phoenix looked sharply over her shoulder at the psychic.

"Eyes everywhere," she said, glancing upward at a point beyond Phoenix. "Eyes but no ears—no ears in the corridors. We are having a friendly conversation. A longtime employee to a new recruit."

"Yes." Phoenix turned the corners of her mouth up and scanned the ceiling. A subtle hint of light on the lens of a camera, a white camera to match the plaster molding that held it, was easier to miss than to notice. "Do you know what I want to know?" Phoenix asked.

"I may know what will help you find out what you want to know."

This evening Ilona wore a gauze scarf over her hair, deep red gauze to match her caftan. She reached for Phoenix's hand, turned it, and pressed their palms together. "Let's see what we can divine."

"I'd rather not." But Phoenix didn't pull away.

Ilona smoothed her cool palm over Phoenix's. "I see a journey, a desperate, dangerous journey. Hope mounts, but the peril only grows. Hope makes one vulnerable in this instance."

"I'm going on a journey?" Phoenix asked, her throat dry.

"Fields of wheat. Blue skies." Ilona raised her eyes. "I wonder what month of the year it was."

*Was.* Phoenix passed her tongue over her lips. "Sometime in spring?"

"Late spring, perhaps. I would need to be certain of the month before I could continue. Otherwise the risk to . . . to my integrity might not be worthwhile."

Phoenix turned her hand and gripped Ilona's wrist. "Could it be April?"

"We cannot talk here," Ilona murmured. "But I will find a way. Be patient and do *not* be rash." She turned and walked away.

Sweat slicked Phoenix's back. She hiked her purse handles

over her shoulder, but saw Roman heading purposefully in her direction before she could get away.

They couldn't do anything to her. If they did, there were people in town who would come looking for her.

They hadn't looked for April . . .

"On your way out?" He took hold of her elbow and propelled her onward without pausing. "Perfect timing on my part."

She opened her mouth and swallowed air.

"Night, Bob," Roman said to the burly man who sat at a desk in the paneled lobby. "This is so good of you, Phoenix. I don't know what I'd have done if you hadn't volunteered."

She tried to look up at him, but had to concentrate or trip over their feet.

Outside, the evening had a crystal quality, clear, moon-bright and with a sharp, clean snap in the air.

"What are you talking about?" Phoenix gasped as Roman hurried her toward her car in the employee parking lot.

His grip on her elbow tightened painfully. "You sound as if you're starting a cold. Best not talk until we're in the car. You only need to take me as far as the service station. My Rover should be ready now. Darn nuisance throwing a belt like that."

Inside the club, Ilona hadn't been afraid of being heard. Out here, Roman evidently thought even the trees had ears.

He took her keys and opened the driver's door of the Chevy. For an instant she expected him to get behind the wheel and she contemplated trying to run. Only there was nowhere to run except into a pen with four Gladiator Dobermans. The pen was immediately inside the gates. To get that far on foot would mean outwitting electrical current at ground level designed to contain the animals—among other things.

"Hop in," Roman said, holding the door for her. But he didn't give the keys back until he was seated beside her. "Off we go."

"Roman—"

He put a finger to his lips and began running his fingers under the dash. Methodically, he skimmed one surface after another, ending with the roof. He unscrewed the dome light cover, hooked a finger around the ledge inside, nodded at her and pulled a tiny instrument into view.

"Having difficulty with your starter?" he asked, holding the device in his palm.

Phoenix turned the key in the ignition and deliberately held it long enough to cause a loud grinding noise. Roman gave her a thumbs up sign and the next time she started the car smoothly and pointed the Chevy in the direction of Past Peak's one and only service station.

When they arrived, Roman thanked her and motioned for her to get out of the car without turning it off. He placed the bug on the passenger seat and they slammed their doors.

She looked around the darkened forecourt of the station. "Where's the Rover?"

"Round back. There's nothing wrong with it. I needed an excuse to leave the club with you."

"What's happening?" Had he been told to frighten her off?

"Do you want to tell me about this April?"

She moved several steps from him. Indecision pulled her back and forth. He was part of the club. From what Ilona had said, it was obvious April was in danger and that danger had to be connected to the club.

"Phoenix?"

"She lived in the garage apartment before—"

"Cut the bullshit!"

She swallowed. There was no sane or logical reason for her to trust him. "Why did you want to leave with me?"

"So we could be alone."

*Alone.* Alone where she would be helpless to defend herself against him. "Why?"

"I never got around to inviting you to dinner. I thought we'd go into Seattle."

Go into Seattle with him—alone. Get into his vehicle—*alone.* "I'm very tired. Thanks for the offer. Can I take a rain check?"

"I'd rather you didn't."

"How did you know there was a bug in my car."

He kicked at the gravel. "A hunch."

"I would never have a hunch like that."

"Say what you mean."

"I'm confused, dammit!" She hated losing her temper. "Thanks for the invitation, but I'm going home and going to bed."

"Want company?"

She closed her eyes. "I wish you hadn't said that."

"Because you want to say yes?"

She felt him move, felt him draw close enough to press against her back and rest his chin on the top of her head. "I'm not the bad guys, W. G." He wrapped his arms around her and held her. "Tell me all about it. Believe in me."

Believe in him? She couldn't believe in anyone—not even herself when he was anywhere near, or even if he wasn't.

Roman swayed, swayed her with him—slowly, gently. He nuzzled her hair aside and rested his cheek on hers.

"They'll wonder what's going on," she said, breathless. "The bug—"

"Let them." His lips, finding the tender place beneath her ear, made her tremble. "Come home with me."

Phoenix stroked the backs of his hands, threaded her fingers between his.

"I'll make us dinner. I'm a passable cook."

She'd bet he was a passable everything. "I need time to think."

"Think if you like. But do it with me."

She laughed shortly. "Think with you? I'm only human."

He turned her, keeping her trapped in his arms. "You mean I have the same effect on you that you have on me? You scramble my brains, Phoenix. It's a great sensation."

"It's a luxury I can't afford. Not now."

"I think you're wrong." His hands spread wide on her back and he massaged slow, hypnotic circles. "I don't think you can afford to do anything else *but* be with me right now. We need each other."

His big body, layered against hers, was all male, and all ready to be male—with her. "Roman—"

His mouth cut off the rest of what she might have said, not that she had any idea what she'd intended to say. This kiss was different. This kiss slanted delicately over her lips, tickling exquisitely sensitive skin. He pulled her to her toes, crossed his arms around her and murmured nonsense.

He felt so good, so strong. Phoenix needed strength and her own was no longer enough. She was scared and needy.

Gradually, he raised his face, never taking his eyes from her mouth. "I want you."

And she wanted him. But she wasn't a silly kid. Regardless of how little time she'd had for romance, she was a grown-up woman. "The time isn't right," she told him.

"You take what you want in this world. When you can get it, Phoenix. Sometimes the chance never comes around again."

She gripped his massive, tensed biceps. "I don't do—"

"Casual sex?" His mouth jerked down. "I know. You've already told me. This doesn't feel casual to me."

Giving in to a purely physical need would be stupid, stupid when she had plenty of reasons to think he wasn't her friend. "Let's give it more time." The firmness in her voice pleased her.

"How much?"

She pushed on his chest. "I don't know."

For an instant he resisted letting her go, then he said, "Have it your way," and dropped his arms. "I'd settle for just having you with me."

Her heart felt squeezed. "Thank you. But I need to go home. I'm going to put in an hour or two at the Bend later."

"You could call in and cancel."

"I don't want to."

He raised his face to the sky. "You know how to hurt a man."

"Thanks for keeping an eye on me today."

"My pleasure, I assure you. Who was—who's April?"

Was he asking her who April was, or simply trying to find out if they had actually been friends. Playing it safe was the only option. "I told you."

"And that's all you know?"

Lying had never come easily to Phoenix. If it had, she'd have suffered fewer blows when she was growing up. "How would I know anything else. Good night, Roman. And thanks again."

"If you change your mind—"

"I won't."

"You've got my number if you do. Put the bug back and remember it's there."

She did as he instructed and drove away, seeing him standing there, but giving him no sign. How did a woman get so lucky? To finally meet a man who made her feel the way Roman made her feel, and to be almost sure he was as lethal as cyanide.

The gates swung open just as she arrived at Belle Rose. She drove cautiously forward, but her headlights picked up Len. He waved and waited for her to draw level and roll down her window.

"Just dropping off some things Rose ordered from town," he said, pointing to his blue truck. "Glad to get to see you. Everything okay?"

"Wonderful," she lied.

"Not what I heard." He gripped his knees and stared into her face. "Heard that guy who was here the other night's been dogging you around town."

"People talk too much." *She* talked too much. "Nothing to worry about, Len. Rose and Evangeline okay?"

He frowned and pushed out his mouth. "I wouldn't say so. You've scared them."

She gave him her full attention.

"You told Rose that April won't be coming back."

"No, I didn't." There were too many people involved in this now. "All I said was that I'm a little worried about her. I'll go up and talk to Rose and Evangeline."

"They're going to bed early. Web said he'd stay over—so Rose'll be able to sleep. She can't stop thinking about the man you saw here in the driveway. I'll come up with you and make sure everything's okay."

"No!" Phoenix forced a smile. "It isn't necessary, Len. Whoever did it isn't likely to come back." She wished she believed that.

His chin jutted stubbornly. "I'll watch awhile, then—just till you're in."

"Fine," she told him wearily, and drove slowly down the path to the garage with him clomping along behind.

True to his word, he stood at the bottom of the steps until she'd let herself in, walked through the apartment, and called down that everything was all right.

On her own at last, she turned the key in the lock, shot home the safety chain and leaned her back against the door.

She'd left the windows open that morning and now the apartment was chilly. Going from room to room, she slid down sashes and drew curtains. She left the ones in the living room open so she could see the sky.

The place was too silent. Phoenix had never needed a lot of company and she hated too much noise, but the stillness crept in around her, a reminder that she was by herself in an apartment, in the middle of almost nowhere. And outside was only darkness . . . She hoped that's all that was out there.

For the first time since she'd moved in, she turned on a small black and white television on top of the bookcase near April's vase. The TV belonged to April, too.

Three women on a talk show railed about the sexual inadequacy of their partners. Their partners pointed out that they weren't getting complaints from other lucky recipients of their attentions.

Phoenix switched channels. A woman on a shopping network peddled "sweet" gold bracelets. Phoenix had a weakness for gold, not that she could afford to do more than admit the fact.

She went to grab a bag of chips and a can of Coke from the kitchen and she dropped to the floor in front of the couch. An hour went by before she realized she'd eaten all the chips, drunk all the Coke, and was currently absorbed in a glowing sales pitch for a mechanical robot that could be turned into a dinosaur.

On her knees, she scooted to flip through the channels. Nothing worth watching.

*"Prepare your hearts!"*

She'd already started to depress the power button when she heard his voice. Phoenix withdrew her hand and stared.

"The time is at hand, my brothers and sisters," Chester Dupree roared, pacing before a group of women in short, glittering dresses who crooned, and cried—and swayed.

Phoenix sank to the floor with a thud. It was true, that sickening, grabbing, sweating beast was an evangelical preacher. Roman hadn't needed to tell her that. In the interests of the precious club, he *shouldn't* have told her.

Chester raised a beefy fist and starbursts of light shot from his immense diamond ring. "I'm goin' to reach out to America, my brothers and sisters. We live in a heathen land, but I'm goin' out there again. Chester Dupree, minister of God, doesn't give up. No, never, my brothers and sisters. I *never* give up."

He was horribly fascinating.

"Get ready. You don't know when you'll see my face and I'll see yours. Don't be among those who only realize they've missed salvation when it's passed them by."

She scrambled to hit the button and black out his disgusting stretched mouth. "Foul creature," she muttered, getting to her feet. Tomorrow she'd gather fresh spring flowers for April's vase. She polished it with the sleeve of her sweat jacket and almost knocked it over when the phone rang.

She'd never received a call here before. With a thudding heart, she cautiously lifted the receiver to her ear. As she did so, she noticed the time and realized it was already past time for her to be at the Bend. Everyone was worried about her. This was probably Mort or Zelda.

"Hi," she said tentatively.

Short breaths sounded.

Phoenix held the receiver in both hands. "Hello?"

"Is that you?"

She gripped the phone tightly. "Who is this?"

"Is that you, Phoenix?" The woman's voice was hoarse.

"Yes." Relief flooded through her. "This is Phoenix. Sorry

I'm late, Zelda. I didn't notice the time. Have you got a sore throat?"

"Get out of there."

Phoenix drew her spine up absolutely straight. Cold marched right along the same route, vertebra by vertebra. "Who is this?"

The woman started to sob. "Just do as I tell you. *Go.*" She coughed and choked. "Please. Don't wait. And don't call the police. They're in on it, too."

Phoenix searched every corner of the room. The door to the bedroom was open but she hadn't left a light on in there. Beyond the wedge of light from the living room lay blackness.

"I'm going to hang up now."

"Get away from there, Phoenix. Get in your car and drive. And don't go back."

A bubble of raw fear rose in Phoenix's throat. "Who *are* you?"

"Don't you know?" The woman coughed again. "It's April."

# FIFTEEN

"This is Roman Wilde. Leave a message—"

Phoenix hung up the phone.

Of all the people she might call for help, Roman should be the last, not the first.

The night had a beat. The same beat pumped inside her head, her body.

*April.*

She didn't know what to do, what to think. It should be Mort and Zelda, or Len that she called. They were friends. If people who were almost strangers could be friends.

No one was a friend, not a friend she could be sure of. These people should have tried to find April long before Phoenix showed up.

She could call the police. What if they found out that she wasn't exactly the person she said she was? *What if the police are in on it, too?*

The Peak Club could be paying off the local law. Phoenix had had her fill of similar setups.

*Get out and drive.*

Drive where? Do what? April had sounded terrified and ill— and threatening. Without naming it, she'd issued a threat: Phoenix was in danger.

Roman must have gone out again—if he'd ever gone home.

The phone rang. She snatched it up. "April! Don't hang up. Where are you?"

"This is Roman."

Phoenix rested her forehead against the wall and closed her eyes.

"Phoenix?"

"Yes."

"Did you try to call me?"

Why had she blurted out April's name like that?

"Did you?" Roman repeated.

"Yes. Where did you get this number?"

"Off your phone the other night. I've got a photographic memory."

Superman in person. "How convenient." She felt sick.

"You're in trouble, aren't you?"

A photographic memory and intuitive, too.

"Who is this April you keep talking about?"

"I don't keep talking about her."

She heard him tap the receiver. "Why didn't you wait longer before hanging up? Or leave a message."

"I shouldn't have called you."

"But you did."

He was too sure of himself. "You expected me to call."

"No. But I hoped, and when I heard someone hang up I decided to take a chance on getting bawled out if I'd hoped wrong."

Phoenix flattened her lips against her teeth. "I really need to go now."

"Why won't you trust me?"

"Because you're one of them!" *Oh, God.* "Good night."

"One of what? If you hang up on me I'll only call back. Who do you think I am?"

Caution was slipping through her fingers. "Nothing and no one. I'm tired and I'm not thinking straight."

"Tell me about April. Why did you think it would be her when I called?"

She scanned the room again. Where would anyone hide? Who was going to hurt her if she didn't leave?

"Phoenix? I want you to listen to me. You really did wander into Past Peak and come to the club looking for a job, didn't you."

"What?" Her throat hurt. "What else would I have done?"

"I believe you."

Phoenix rubbed her eyes. Her scalp was tight.

"Listen carefully. You're panicked. I can hear it."

There were guns that could shoot you right through a door—or a wall. She sat down on the floor hard enough to jar her spine.

"I can hear the way you're breathing. Speak to me, dammit! Tell me what's happened."

"I'm scared," she whispered. "I think someone's going to kill me."

He didn't answer at once, when he did, his voice was flat, flat like sheet steel. "Where are you?"

"S-sitting on the floor in the living room. April told me to get out and keep driving."

"April?"

"I can't explain. She told me the police are in on whatever's going on. I don't know what to do."

"Do not leave that room. Do you hear me?"

He was so far away. "Yes."

"Remember my friend, Nasty? I know you do. He'll be there before me. I'm leaving now."

The line went dead.

Nasty. Nasty with the too-old, empty eyes. And then Roman.

Phoenix let the receiver slip softly back into the cradle and scooted backward until she thumped to a stop against the couch.

From the table beside the bed came the faint whirring of April's old alarm clock. April wouldn't do anything to hurt her.

The whirring grew louder.

Phoenix turned her head slowly. Was the door to the bedroom opening wider?

*Get out—now.*

Mort or Len could be here before Nasty and Roman. She scrambled back to the phone and smacked the numbers for the Bend.

No ringing.

Phoenix punched in the numbers again. Then she drew back and looked at the receiver. She depressed the cradle and let it up—tapped it several times. No ringing, because there was no dial tone.

Out of order. How could the phone choose this moment to be out of order?

April had stood by her from when they were children. They'd looked after each other. They would hang together against anything.

Roman asked why she didn't trust him. She wanted to. She wanted to because she was infatuated with him.

Fool. Idiot female who hadn't learned to give up on the notion of white knights, or romance—or essential goodness.

Wrapping her arms around her drawn-up shins, she buried her face in her knees. The whirring from the bedroom marked passing seconds, passing minutes. Louder and louder. She pushed her fingers into her ears.

In her mind she heard Roman, *"Do not leave that room."*

And she was doing as he'd told her.

The whirring sound cut through her fingers, through her head. She just wanted to close it all out. She wanted to run, needed to run.

She heard a voice—from outside.

Carefully, she took her fingers from her ears. Then she heard it again, "Phoenix." A masculine voice.

April might have been trying to warn her against the very people she was waiting for, the very people she was supposed to believe would save her.

"Phoenix, can you hear me?"

Any man's voice. A thin voice, thin as if diluted by a wind. Was it familiar?

"It's okay, Phoenix. We're here."

Slowly, she stood up.

"The engine's running. Come on, Phoenix."

Her legs reacted sluggishly, covered the floor toward the front door with almost languid steps.

"Phoenix!"

What choice did she have? If whoever was out there intended

to do her harm, they'd come for her. If they wished her well, they'd take her away from this.

She unhooked the chain and took off the lock.

"Phoenix!" Louder now that she was closer.

When she opened it, the door whined. Web was going to oil the hinges.

"Jesus. *Finally!* Come on."

She stepped outside onto the small landing.

"Catch this. You may need it. Over here."

Phoenix turned toward the voice, turned away from the steps. A flashlight shone from below. She looked over the railing. The beam shone in her face.

"Here. Catch!"

Something rose in the air. A coat. Too far away. She leaned on the rail to make a grab and her fingers closed on slippery fabric.

She heard the snap too late.

Beneath her weight, the railing exploded outward. Her falling body tore it away.

The fall ended before it should have. Surely it should have taken longer—and hurt more.

She lay where she landed, winded—her arms outstretched. Above her the flashlight beam still shone, but not on her now. Instead, the light glared on the hooded face of whoever stood over her, bounced from spectacle lenses, turning them into dazzling twin circles.

"Hurt?" A distorted voice now—muffled. Not a voice she knew.

Phoenix tried to push herself up. Beneath her she felt the scratchy, formless mass of a pile of hay.

"Who are—"

A hand slammed over her mouth, and crammed her words back. She tasted the copper flavor of her own blood. She struggled, heard her own muffled scream. He kept pushing her, pushing her down into the hay. Pain screamed from the bruised and scraped skin of her face.

Phoenix lashed out. Her fingers hit a leg, closed on fabric.

Pushing, pushing. Hay piled onto her face. Hay thrust into her mouth.

"You should have done what you were told to do, *bitch.*"

She writhed sideways and her foot met solid ground, then her knee.

He let her scramble a few inches before he stopped her.

"You're going to find out what it feels like, bitch." One rough shove slammed her onto her back again. "You couldn't leave it alone, could you?"

When she opened her mouth to scream, he filled it with hay. He pushed more and more into her mouth, covered her face, ground it into her tightly shut eyes.

No air anywhere.

He rained blows on her shoulders, her breasts. It should have hurt much more, but the weight on her face deadened the pain in her body.

She would die.

Her arms flailed. Her fingers found nothing, nothing but the air that slipped over her skin.

He'd ripped off her sweat jacket, and her shirt.

Hay was in her throat, in her nose. Dry. Dry dust.

Let him beat her. She wouldn't know now.

Phoenix slid into the hay, into the earth, into nothing.


Waving his arms, Nasty walked into the beams from Roman's headlights. Above and behind him, the door to Phoenix's apartment stood open with light shining from inside.

"Oh, *shit.*" Roman cut the engine and jumped from the Land Rover. "Is she hurt?"

"Gone," Nasty said.

"Struggle?"

"Not the kind you're talking about."

Roman made to stride past him. Nasty blocked his path.

"What?" Roman said.

"Someone went through the railing at the top of the steps.

Back of the landing. She's not inside. Nothing's out of place except the phone. No dial tone."

"Wire cut?"

"Uh huh." Nasty raised his face. "He sweated like a pig. His scent's still here."

Roman ran a hand over his face. This felt different—was different. This time it was personal and personal made the stakes higher than any he'd ever played for.

"Take a look at the railing"—Nasty moved aside—"and inside. You were here before?"

"Yeah." Roman ran up the steps and made a quick visual throughout the inside of the apartment. Everything was as Nasty had reported. Phoenix had opened the door herself and walked outside. That much was obvious.

The railing jutted outward, broken jaggedly as if someone had leaned on rotten wood. He crouched and shone his high-powered miniature flashlight on first one rail, then another. Someone might make an argument for a crack caused by a knothole. He wouldn't. The wood was good.

Shuffling came from below. A flashlight beam like his own, illuminated a heap of straw. He ran down the steps and joined Nasty—who held a tattered shirt.

Roman's gut tightened. He dropped to his knees. "This wasn't here. The hay."

"Looks like a couple of bales broken open and spread. You seen this before?"

"Yeah." Roman didn't have to give the red and white checked shirt another look. Phoenix had worn it beneath her red sweat jacket. "Tire tracks?"

"Yours and hers here." He inclined his head to where Phoenix's Chevy still stood. "Another couple of sets in the main driveway. One recent enough."

"She got a call."

"So you said."

"From April."

Nasty stared at him. "What does that mean?"

"Either we're being reeled in like a couple of prize marlins, or she is."

Nasty chewed gum with his lips parted. His eyes moved away. "What d'you think?"

A smarter question might be, what did he *want* to think? "Fifty-fifty would be logical, I guess. Somehow I think she knew April—very well. I think she's trying to find her and that's why she signed on at the club."

"And they've figured it out?"

"Looks that way." He shone his flashlight around the area. "Whoever did call her said she shouldn't contact the police. Told her they were on the take."

"Your partners are covering their asses."

"Just as well for now. We'll need the cops later. Let's hope it's not too much later. Work outward from here." He studied the hay, bent and began feeling through it. "There was a struggle here."

"Hell of a struggle. I'll skirt the perimeter first."

"Wait!" He threw the hay aside, going after a flash of color. "Sonovabitch. Her jacket. Help me get through this heap fast."

Their efforts turned up one white sneaker.

"Did you go into the garage?"

"I'm on my way."

Roman searched the ground around the area. He heard the garage lock respond willingly to Nasty's entry request, followed by the scrape of one of the big doors over gravel.

In the dirt near the heap of hay, Roman found a wide expanse of freshly churned dirt. He stood back, using the flashlight. If it came to calling in the police, the less evidence tampered with, the better.

She'd been in the hay. He turned the beam back up to the broken railing. Fallen into the hay. The detachment he'd gradually grown, like a skin, was stripped away. Dread. Dread had become something ordinary men felt, not Roman Wilde and his kind. He felt it now.

Sweeping the beam in an arc, then in front of his feet, and back to the wider sphere, he searched. Piles of wooden crates behind the building yielded nothing but the scurrying exodus of a rat. A stack of tires—all unused but coated with dust and cobwebs—did not contain Phoenix, dead or alive.

His beam picked up two glittering circles. Dropping to one knee, he found a pair of glasses. Rimless and unbroken, the earpieces had been folded and the lenses shone as if freshly polished. He used the cuff of his jacket to pick them up and put them into his pocket.

When he finished his first circle of the building, he walked into a yellow glow spilling from the open garage door.

Nasty stepped out. "Damndest thing you ever saw. An old Rolls and an older Aston Martin. Aston Martin doesn't look as if it was ever used."

"It wasn't. Not according to Phoenix. Nothing, right?"

"Nothing."

"We're going to need help."

"Yeah. Police?"

"God, I don't trust them. For all I know, they may be part of the problem." A clang, metal on metal, rang from the garage. Roman didn't wait to ask questions. He stepped through the door and surveyed the space under its hanging bulbs.

Nasty passed him, crouched, weapon drawn, and headed for the far side of the gleaming Rolls. In front of Roman stood the turquoise Aston Martin. Drawing his own gun, he hunkered over and set off along the side of the car, ducking beneath the level of the windows.

With his left hand, he threw open the passenger door. Empty.

The clang vibrated again.

This time he knew where the sound came from and stood up, making the clicking noise with his tongue that guaranteed Nasty's attention. When he saw his old partner's face, he pointed the Beretta at the trunk of the Aston Martin and Nasty nodded.

With nerves leapfrogging in his jaws, he made himself wait until he and Nasty stood, one on each side of the car. In an ambush, numbers counted. Not that Roman had any doubt what he'd find in the trunk.

At Nasty's signal, he threw open the trunk.

"Oh, *shit.* It's okay, Phoenix. Okay."

Silently, Nasty took off his coat, dropped it over the end of the car, and walked away.

On her stomach, her ankles lashed to her wrists, Phoenix had managed to pick up and wedge a wrench between her bruised hands. Naked but for jeans pulled down around her thighs, she still wore one tennis shoe. The bastard had gagged her with her bra.

"Hang on." He used his knife to slit the twine that cut into her wrists and ankles and threw Nasty's coat over her before getting rid of the gag. "Take it slowly. Give the blood a chance to make its rounds again." As quickly and efficiently as possible, he tugged her jeans back into place before taking off his own coat and sweater.

She didn't move, didn't speak.

"I'm going to put my sweater on you. It's cold." With no help from Phoenix, he pulled his turtleneck over her head, stuffed her arms into the sleeves, and grimaced when she whimpered.

"Hold on," he murmured. "You're safe now." As carefully as he could, he turned and lifted her from the trunk—and brought her high against his chest until he could kiss her cheek gently.

Her scratched cheek. Phoenix's face, including her closed eyelids, was covered with scratches that oozed pinpoints of blood.

He carried her outside and found Nasty standing with his back to them. "I'm going to make Phoenix comfortable," he said. "Dusty might like to know she's okay."

"You've got it," Nasty said, his voice devoid of inflection. "Do I need to do anything else here?"

Roman looked at Phoenix. "Our friend isn't the type who'd want to party with me. Give me half an hour. If I don't make contact, you'll know we're all clear. Other arrangements will have to be made after tonight. We'll talk."

Nasty turned and his unflinching eyes went to Phoenix's face. He chewed his gum slowly, deliberately. "Whatever it takes." With that he walked away into the darkness.

She rolled toward him in his arms, spread her fingers on his bare chest. He'd been in the shower when she called. Afterwards, he'd only taken enough time to pull on sweater, jeans and jacket.

"I've got you now. Nothing is going to happen to you, Phoenix. Nothing bad, I promise." Promises were sacred to Roman. He'd grown up surrounded by broken promises. He made very few himself, but they were for keeps. "Up we go, kid. I'm going to make you comfortable."

She still didn't speak, but her breathing was regular, her pulse strong, and he knew she was conscious behind those battered eyelids. What he didn't know, was what he couldn't see.

His teeth came together hard. If this was the work of whoever had killed April, anything was possible.

Once inside the apartment, he slammed the door shut with his foot, fumbled to shoot home the lock, then carried her directly into the bedroom. When he tried to set her on the bed, she curled closer and clung to his neck.

"I'm going to put you down," he said into her tangled hair. "Then we're going to do whatever makes you feel best. Do you want me to call the police?" No response. "There's absolutely nothing to be afraid of now, Phoenix. Do you hear me?"

She only gripped him more tightly.

Finally he sat down on the bed and cradled her on his lap. He lost track of time and didn't care. This woman wasn't the enemy, she hadn't been sent to set him up. The line he walked at the club would only become finer from now on, but at least he'd found something he'd never expected to find, a woman he could . . . He'd found a woman he might be able to care about. Enveloping her, he rubbed his cheek against her hair and rocked her.

"Don't go away."

Her voice was clear and strong and Roman took a grateful breath through his mouth. "You're stuck with me, buddy. I'm not going anywhere."

"You aren't one of them? The ones at the club?"

The instinct to cover was instant. "I'm not anyone you have to be afraid of."

"He called to me. The man outside called me."

"D'you know who he was?"

She shook her head. "I fell through the railing and he beat me."

Roman studied her face. He'd seen the red marks on her back and shoulders, marks that would be bruises by the morning. "I'd like to wash your face. It got scratched a bit."

She made a sound that might have been a laugh.

"Something funny?"

"I must look ready for Halloween. He pushed me under the straw. It hurt. He kept on hurting me."

The fist in his guts made another turn. "He's never going to hurt you again."

"Be back. That's what he told me. I'll be back."

"Either you won't be here, or you won't be alone."

She didn't say anything to that.

"Let me get a cloth and some warm water."

"Don't leave me."

"Just to go to the bathroom for a cloth."

"No."

Her fingernails gouged his neck. Roman hugged her convulsively. She could stab him with her nails anytime. "Okay, here we go." Carrying her, he went to the bathroom and located a washcloth and some antiseptic cream.

A bowl of warm water came from the kitchen and, at last, she let him put her on the bed. Promptly, she curved into a tight ball on her side shaking from head to foot.

For the first time since he'd come into the apartment, he caught sight of the cat. It jumped lightly onto the bed and rubbed its sinuous body along Phoenix's back. She winced and smiled at the same time.

"How come he gets the smiles and I don't?"

"I've got a thing for blue eyes."

He glanced at the cat and was rewarded with an unblinking, very blue stare. "I've got blue eyes."

"I noticed."

Roman returned his attention to her face. Her swollen lids were open a fraction and she turned the corners of her mouth up at him. He brushed back her hair and brought one of her hands to his lips. "You are a beautiful lady. So beautiful."

"Did you forget your contact lenses?"

He grinned. "I don't wear contact lenses. It'd take more than a few scratches to spoil that face. Will you let me clean you up?" The question he knew he should ask stuck in his throat. "Should I take you to a doctor?" was the closest he could get.

"No. Not unless there's something that needs stitches."

"Should I call the cops?"

"No, I don't think so."

"Did he—"

"No."

Roman looked quickly away. "You're sure?"

"I'd know. I fainted, but he didn't start . . . The bruises are in the wrong places. He didn't rape me."

"Okay." Relief made him laugh. "Now I only have to kill the bastard once."

"I'll never understand this." She groped for his wrist and pulled him down beside her. "Evil doesn't have any meaning. This served no purpose."

"Don't think about it." With his free hand, he put the bowl on the bedside table. "Could we unravel you a bit? Just so I can get at those scratches?"

Gradually, she released his wrist and straightened.

"On your back?"

She followed his instruction but her eyes were tightly shut again. "Where's your shirt?" she asked.

Roman glanced down at himself. "You're wearing it."

"You'll get cold."

Never as long as he was with her. "Forget me. I'm fine." He dunked the washcloth and rang it out. "Once I clean this up it isn't going to be as bad as it looks now."

With one hand behind Phoenix's neck, he blotted her poor, bruised face, inch by careful inch. Several times he rinsed the cloth and reapplied it. Specks of fresh blood replaced some of the dried ones and he held gentle pressure on them.

"It is, isn't it?" she asked.

Roman paused. "It is what?"

"As bad as it looked before."

He smiled, suddenly overcome by that damned sweet emotion he'd never suffered from before he met her.

"Isn't it?" she said.

"No, it is not." Carefully, he slipped his arms around her and rested his face on her pillow, beside her head.

She touched his back, lightly at first, then spread her fingers and stroked him from shoulder to waist, again and again. "Roman?"

"Yes," he said into the pillow.

"Are you all right?"

*No.* "Terrific."

"Just tired?"

*No.* "A bit."

"Thank you."

"My pleasure."

"I'm going to be all right, too. You don't have to stay."

"The hell I don't!" He jerked upright. "Try to get rid of me, lady. As far as you're concerned, I'm glue."

"You don't need to shout."

"Sometimes shouting is appropriate."

"When something frightens you?"

He frowned. "I'm not frightened, Phoenix."

"Not even for me?"

Roman narrowed his eyes. He hadn't expected her to say anything that might draw him in deeper. "I'm concerned for your safety."

"Of course. Very honorable of you." Her smile, distorted by scratched and bruised eyes, disarmed him.

Rather than say something else he'd regret, he went to work on scrapes across the backs of her hands and beneath her chin.

"I want to tell you something, Roman."

He didn't look at her face. "Okay." An imminent confession had a certain sound. *Please let it not be a confession he didn't want to hear.*

"Could you hold me first? In here?" She patted the bed. "You said you're not leaving and you do have to sleep."

Sleep? From what he could feel—painfully—he'd have to keep some space between them and he wouldn't be doing much sleeping.

"Roman?"

"I'll lie on the couch."

"No!" She sat up and framed his face. Just as abruptly, she averted her own face. "You don't have to look at me. Just lie beside me so I know you're near."

This was the stuff medals were made of. "Okay. Can I get you something else to put on—something soft?" The sweater was heavy oiled wool.

Without a word, she swung her legs past him and stood up. With her back to him, she stripped off the sweater and slipped on a white cotton gown she took from a drawer. Her jeans joined the sweater on the bottom of the bed. Watching her spun a thread of intimate yearning between them. He felt it. She had to feel it.

Roman stood up and threw back the covers. She climbed in and lay in a rigid line while he covered her up to her chin.

He kicked off his shoes, unzipped his jeans and stepped out of them.

Roman didn't turn his back.

Phoenix didn't shut her eyes.

The double bed had never been intended for a man of his length and breadth. Beneath the covers, he put as much distance between them as possible.

Not enough distance.

He could feel her, feel her warmth.

Her fingertips slipped over the back of his hand and across his palm until their fingers twined together. Phoenix's scratched knuckles settled against his thigh.

Roman set his teeth and glared at the ceiling.

"I trust you."

He swallowed and said, "You can."

"April Clark is my friend, my oldest friend. She's the sister I never had. I'm not sure I'd even be alive today without her."

*Is? You mean, was. She's dead. I delivered her little girl. She's mine now—I made her mine, my life. I'm here to get justice for her more than for her mother. Her mother can't be hurt anymore.* He couldn't tell her, not like that. "I thought she was someone you knew."

"I came to Past Peak to see her, then found out she'd dropped out of sight. I came here to Belle Rose because this was the last address I had for her. I'd spoken to her here. She told me she worked at the club. Do you know her?"

"No." That much was true—more or less. "I only bought into the club six months ago."

"Oh." Her disappointed sigh hurt him.

"What did she say about working at the club?"

"She met someone in San Francisco. One of the partners, I think. April was working as a personal trainer and this man asked her to come and work for him. She said he was wonderful and they were going to get married."

*Roger? Pierre? Miles? Which one?* "She didn't give you any other hint. His name, maybe?"

"No. She said it was all very private and she wasn't allowed to talk about it. I wasn't to call her at the club. Next time we spoke—so she told me—she'd probably be married and then she could tell me everything. But I didn't hear from her for months and I headed here while I was trying to decide what to do about . . . What to do."

He turned to look at her. How would she react if he could tell her about Junior? He wanted to tell her.

She reached to turn off the light.

"What are you trying to decide?" he asked.

"It's boring."

"Not to me."

"I dropped out about two years ago. A bit elderly to drop out, I realize. Something unpleasant happened. I lost my job in Oklahoma City because I didn't follow the rules. Sooner or later I've got to grow up again and make something of myself."

"You seem all grown up to me."

Dumb, suggestive comment. Her silence made him wince. "You liked your job?"

"I thought I did. I was—am—a lawyer."

"Jesus."

She snorted. "Evidently that wasn't what you expected me to say."

"Hardly. What happened?"

"Doesn't matter. I couldn't defend some creep of a psychiatrist is all. At least, I defended him but my heart wasn't in it. His thing was to hypnotize attractive young girls, then rape them. I leaked incriminating evidence to the prosecution. He went to jail. I got caught. I got fired. End of story."

"An honest lawyer. The world needs you."

"I need to find April. She kept me sane, Roman. When we were kids. I'd never have made anything of myself if she hadn't pushed me."

There would be a way to tell her, but not yet. "Do you have any leads on what . . . on where she may be?"

"There's no way to know where she called from tonight. But she was in the Midwest. At least, I think she was in the Midwest early last year. She probably went there when she left here, and traveled around. There were postcards she'd sent to Rose."

He barely stopped himself from crushing the bones in her hand. "Where are they now."

She was silent a moment before she said, "Rose says someone's stolen them."

Roman held his breath while he thought.

"I was sure I'd find a clue at the club and I have."

He let the breath out in a rush.

"Ilona. The psychic. She warned me to be careful. And she spoke of someone else who hadn't been careful. She meant April."

His heart beat a little faster. "How can you be sure?"

"I'm sure. Ilona's going to help me. If someone doesn't manage to kill me first."

"No one's going to do anything to you. I'll help you, buddy.

We'll find out about April together." Please let him find the right words to break the truth when he had to.

Phoenix rolled toward him and scooted close.

With the help of another deep breath, Roman kept his hormones under some sort of control. He adjusted his position and pulled her head into the hollow of his shoulder.

"Thank you," she said.

"You're welcome," Roman told her.

"You make me feel safe." She combed the hair on his chest with her nails.

"You make me feel . . . You make me feel glad I'm here." Sainthood was in sight. "Go to sleep."

"Are you comfortable?"

"Absolutely." Absolutely not.

"I'm hoping April calls back."

Her nails followed a path downward to his belly.

Roman stopped breathing entirely.

"I'm keeping you from something, aren't I?"

"Hmm?"

"You need to be doing something else."

How had she guessed? "I need to be right here. I've got a lot of thinking to do and this is a good place to do it." Her breasts pressed his side softly. Talking, diverting his attention was the solution here. "By the morning I've got to decide exactly how to proceed."

Phoenix snuggled. One bare knee came to rest on top of his thighs.

Roman prayed for strength—of will.

"You're comfy," she murmured. "Feel comfy."

*Gee, thanks.*

Her touch on his belly shifted again. Downward.

Roman parted his lips, ran his tongue over the roof of his mouth.

"Mm. You'll help me find April?"

"I'll help you."

The end of her fingers met more hair and kept on going.

"Um, Phoenix?"

She didn't answer.

Raising his head from the pillow, he peered at her in the dim light from the living room. The mass of red hair hid her face. He could see her softly rounded shoulder and little else. "Phoenix, I don't think . . ." The trouble was, he did think. "But if you really feel up to it. Do you, sweetheart?"

Phoenix's long fingers settled at the base of that part of him most in need of attention. His hips jerked involuntarily.

She was scratched and bruised. "We don't have to do this now. I'm afraid of hurting you."

Her knee rose higher.

"Phoenix?" His voice also rose higher. He stroked her shoulder. "I want to kiss you."

A soft sound reached him.

Roman arched his neck, drove the back of his head into the pillow. Terror had exhausted her. She was snoring . . . and holding onto his penis as if she was afraid of falling out of bed.

# SIXTEEN

Quietly, Geoffrey closed and locked the door between the darkened Jacuzzi room and the main workout area. A check of the showers from the other side of the one-way glass had reassured him he would soon get what he wanted—the chance to break his news to Vanessa. She'd pushed him too far, cramped his style. The price for those mistakes would be high.

On bare feet, he slipped to sit in a corner where a black-lacquered Japanese screen cast a deep enough shadow to hide him. The huge size of the pool had been Vanessa's idea. Plenty of room for groups to move around—or energetic pairs—or even someone alone and with very special needs.

Geoffrey's patience wore thin before the door to the showers finally opened and then clicked shut again. At the edge of the Jacuzzi, Vanessa flipped the switch that cast red light from the bottom of the bubbling, steaming water, cast a hot glow over her voluptuous white body.

He was going to get the upper hand. Countess Von Leiden would learn that Sir Geoffrey Fullerton had seized the power from her greedy claws.

Vanessa stepped down into the water, descended steps at a leisurely pace, gradually sank deeper and waded through the rosy bubbles.

Geoffrey fingered the key in his pocket, a small gold key on a gold chain. He smiled as he closed his palm over it.

Timing might not matter to most men, not tonight, but it

mattered to Geoffrey. He watched Vanessa stand, waist-deep, in the water and support the weight of her breasts.

Sick bitch. Vain, sick bitch.

Her eyes were closed. The tip of her tongue went darting in and out of her thin lips. She played her thumbs over the tips of her nipples.

Women, men—they were all the same to her as long as they brought her pleasure. But this was what she enjoyed most— feeding her own insatiable body's needs herself.

Vanessa would be glad when she saw him. Even more than providing her own satisfaction, she craved an audience while she did so, preferably an audience driven to sexual frenzy by an arousal she would refuse to relieve.

She'd be glad for such a short while.

His pleasure was deep, and warm, and consuming.

Bobbing, Vanessa returned to the side of the pool. She climbed up the steps until only her feet remained under water. Then she knelt, facing him without knowing he was there. In this moment of self-worship there was no one for Vanessa, but Vanessa.

He heard her sigh, saw her head fall back while she massaged her breasts with one hand. With the other hand she delved into the folds between her thighs.

She started to shudder and abruptly withdrew her hands.

A little discipline? A last-minute decision to deprive herself of the release that was everything? Hardly likely.

Spreading her knees, Vanessa felt under the surface of the pool. A jet shot upward, a glittering spear of water adjustable to a pressure capable of turning skin as red as the lights in the pool.

Vanessa adjusted the jet.

She wouldn't notice him now. Geoffrey stood up and stripped. From now on he would decide when, where, how and for how long he and Vanessa would use each other, only the using would be all on one side—his.

The Jacuzzi jet met Vanessa's favorite button with the kind of force guaranteed to send the lady's elevator to the top floor and into space. She arched forward, dragging in her stomach. Her body was vibrating with the force of the impact.

Geoffrey curled his lip and started toward her.

This was a "When Harry Met Sally" rerun, only no one was acting. Vanessa panted and cried out and then she jerked and jerked some more before slumping to rest her brow on her crossed forearms.

Satisfaction was always short-lived for Vanessa. Tonight she would learn a new meaning for the term, letdown.

Sluggishly, she turned to sit on the step. She spread her arms along the rim behind her and slid her hips forward until she could rest the back of her head.

Geoffrey looked at her big breasts, her dark, distended nipples, and marveled that they still had the power to snap his cock to full alert. After tonight those breasts would be on view whenever he clicked his fingers, and her fingers would be wherever he wanted them, whenever he wanted them there.

Her mouth with its long, thinly voracious lips had always tantalized him with visions of seeing them suck him in. She'd never done that for him. The countess didn't deal in blow jobs.

Only the countess was about to develop a fresh and insatiable taste for Geoffrey's distinctive flavor.

He still held the chain and key—they dug into his flesh and the pain pleased him.

Swiftly, he approached the pool and dug the toes of each foot into Vanessa's elbows just hard enough to make her eyes fly open and ensure she couldn't move.

"What the *fuck* do you think you're doing?" She spat the words at him.

"Looking at you," he said, knowing her view was a direct line on his balls and erection. "Thinking about how you're going to *fuck* me."

"Get off!"

"I don't think so, Countess."

She jerked her arms.

Geoffrey increased the weight on her elbows.

Vanessa shrieked. "You're hurting me! Damn you! You'll suffer for this. I've been waiting to talk to you, you fool."

"Really? Convenient. Here I am, and I've been waiting to

talk to you. I'd have talked earlier but you seemed engrossed, darling." With the same lithe speed he used to mount a polo pony, he stepped over her and turned to sit astride her ribs. "Who goes first? You or me?"

Predictably, she landed a stinging slap across his mouth.

Geoffrey slapped her and trembled with delight at her horror—and rage.

"What's the matter with you?" she screamed. "How dare you touch me unless I tell you to. Leave. Don't come back until I contact you."

"I'm not going anywhere." He dangled the key from its chain. "Guess what this is?"

Wriggling, she struggled to push him away. Geoffrey grasped her beneath the arms and hauled her to sit on the edge of the pool. He caught her flailing hands and trapped them on her knees. With an effortless push, he opened her thighs and pressed himself between, teasing her with his rigid shaft.

Her fight against desire was rapidly lost. The hate in her eyes turned to hunger. "Push it in," she said. "We'll talk later. Maybe we both need this."

Geoffrey didn't do any pushing into Vanessa, not with what she expected. Instead he grasped one of her breasts and flattened her on the ground. What he pushed was the golden key on its long chain—he pushed it high inside her and grinned at her screeches of mixed shock and ecstasy.

"Like that, darling?"

"You come in, too. *Now.*"

Oh, yes, she'd really like that. Geoffrey played with the swollen nub between her slick folds until she made futile grabs for him. Then he slowly pulled on the chain, slowly withdrew the key.

"No! No, Geoffrey! You are such a beast. Come on. *Please.*"

"You beg so prettily, love. I asked if you recognized this key."

"I don't care about the key."

"Yes you do. Pierre got it for me—from someone in his lovely Swiss banking family."

"I don't *care* where you got the key."

"It's the key to a great big box. In that box is a huge collection of flawless, almost priceless gems, darling. They're what I bought with most of our money."

She grew still. Her eyes cleared. "What are you talking about?"

"It's simple. I withdrew most of the funds from our accounts in Switzerland and bought diamonds. I put the diamonds in a vault—also in Switzerland. Of course, those diamonds are as negotiable as money."

Vanessa struggled and he let her sit up. "How could you do that? You can't touch any of the money without me."

He trailed the key in the water. "Amazing what one can do with the right contacts. You were the one who thought Pierre would add something to the club—primarily his name and money. I don't know why it took me so long to think of asking him to help me."

"Help you?" Even in the darkness her pallor shone.

"Help me change the balance of power here. For a certain consideration, Pierre pulled certain strings and I was able to make some very lucrative transactions. Not to worry, love, I assure you I've negotiated only the most advantageous investments."

"With *my* money."

"Our money."

"The seed money was mine."

"Without me you couldn't have built what we have."

"Give me the key."

"Certainly." He handed it to her. "Unfortunately you can't use it without the number—and you don't even know which bank I've used."

She stared at the key. "Why are you doing this?"

"First I should explain Pierre's price. He's a true voluptuary, our Pierre. But he's easy to please. He only wants to spend time at the more inventive Insiders' activities."

"For God's sake! You know we have to keep things as they are. We can't afford to risk any leak."

"There will be no leak from Pierre. He has broken laws. One word in the wrong places and he would be cut off from his precious family fortune and thrown in jail—neither of which he would risk."

"I don't understand any of this."

"Simple, really. I want what I want. And I'm sick of asking you for it as if you were my mommy."

Her features twisted. "Without me there would be no Peak Club. I've given you everything you've got and you've come close to ruining the entire enterprise with your stupidity."

"But I didn't ruin it. The danger went away as I knew it would."

"I want access to those stones."

"Never. I'll toss a little one in your direction from time to time, but it wouldn't do for you to see them all. The lust for them would probably stop your black heart from beating."

"I'll destroy you."

He laughed and looped his hands around her neck. "Destroy me, and you destroy yourself. Take me down and I'll take you down with me."

Her sudden, violent scream jolted Geoffrey to his bones. Vanessa screamed again and again. She went for his face with her long, red nails and kept on screaming.

"Stop it!" Catching her hands took too long. She'd already inflicted wounds. "Shut up and listen to me."

She gave another endless shriek, then grew silent, her breasts heaving.

"Good," he said, closing his stinging left eye. "All you have to do is whatever I tell you to do, and we'll get along famously. You won't go short of anything, my lovely animal. You'll hardly notice any change—except for the fact that I have taken your place in the chain of command. Understand?"

"You poor, stupid man. The danger you caused isn't over. We're faced with the biggest crisis of our careers and you're risking everything for the sake of some crazy power play."

"The play is accomplished. And there is no crisis. We have everything under control."

"Do we? The woman Phoenix? Our new masseuse? She knew April Clark. They were friends from childhood."

Geoffrey frowned. What she said took shape slowly. "You're sure?"

"If you'd been here, giving me the support I need, instead of plotting your ridiculous revenge, you'd already know what we're facing."

"She can't know anything."

"Maybe not yet. But she intends to find out."

Bemused, he stared at her. "There's no way she can find anything out."

"My source assures me she already has a vague lead."

Geoffrey regarded Vanessa's breasts. Thoughtfully, he pinched her nipples, ignoring her attempts to stop him. "Who is your source?"

"You have your little secrets. I must now have mine. I can finish you, Geoffrey. Never forget that."

"We'll get rid of her."

"Naturally. But this time we won't be in a rush. Roman's fucking her."

Geoffrey raised a brow. "Connection?"

"Roman has certain excellent skills. He hasn't proved nearly as useful as we expected. This will be a way for him to make us happier."

He understood at once. "You intend to ask Roman to deal with Phoenix?"

"I intend to *tell* him to deal with her."

Doubt turned his stomach. "What excuse will you give?"

"She's dangerous. She's a fraud sent by a government agency to find a way to close us down. If she succeeds he'll lose everything he's invested."

"You're sure he's really involved with her?"

"He's with her now. Has been all night. He was seen through her bedroom window. Undressing."

"What if he refuses?"

"He won't." She attempted, and failed, to put distance between them. "I want to get up."

"We have to make sure she doesn't find anything out before we can deal with her."

"I've told you I've worked it all out."

"Tell me who your insider is."

She shook her head. "Get out of my way. I've got to think. The sooner I decide the best way to make sure Roman kills her, the better. She's got to disappear as completely as April did."

*As completely as April did.* Uneasiness muddled his conviction. "This is pointless. Fire the woman for incompetence and be done with it. April disappeared. End of story. There's nothing for Phoenix to find."

"I'm afraid there might be."

He drove his fingers into her shoulders. "You're trying to get back at me. There's nothing to find, I tell you."

Vanessa squirmed. "That hurts."

"There's nothing to find. You know there isn't."

"You didn't see what I saw yesterday afternoon. Phoenix spoke with a certain employee in the corridor upstairs."

"Who?"

The expression on Vanessa's face became smooth and distant. "My secret again. Let's just say it was someone I trust, someone who will give all for the cause. That's all you have to know."

Anger exploded, broke over Geoffrey in waves. "You'd do anything to take back what you've lost. It's not going to work."

She raised serene eyes to his. "Isn't it?"

"Never again. Open your mouth."

Some of the serenity faded.

"Do as I tell you."

She averted her face.

"Suck me or kiss good-bye to all those lovely diamonds."

"You know I find that disgusting," she told him.

"You don't find it disgusting when you're on the receiving end. Your mouth, Vanessa. Open up."

Her head turned toward him and she looked into his face. He stood up and brought himself closer. Vanessa opened her mouth and he crammed it full.

The next sound he heard was his own scream.

Vanessa's pointy little teeth made themselves unforgettable.

# SEVENTEEN

Dawn did great things for Roman Wilde.

Phoenix stood at the bottom of the bed and watched him sleep. He wore his life in the harshly spectacular lines of his face. At rest, those lines softened, allowed some of the boy he'd once been to show through. His mouth held her attention. The hint of laughter was there—and the promise of passion.

She'd awakened with her head on his chest, her body curled over his. He'd held her firmly enough to make slipping away without waking him a delicate operation.

Roman had an unforgettable chest. Wide, muscular, meant to be appreciated—which she did. And he had unforgettable shoulders, which she also appreciated. He felt so good.

Roman was naked.

Furious heat burst over her skin. Had he been asleep when she'd wound herself around him like that? Like ivy around a fence post?

She pressed her hands to her cheeks, felt the towel she wore slip, and secured it more firmly.

Not even the sound of the shower had awakened him. He must be exhausted. Phoenix was exhausted. She was also scared. More than scared. When Roman did wake up she was going to ask him about getting a gun.

Her hands—her entire body—shook. Would she be able to fire a gun?

She wouldn't ask him.

The dawn shone silver. Phoenix went to the window and

looked toward the roof of Belle Rose, barely visible through pewter-tinged mist. Higher, on the rise to the right of the house, stood the incongruous windmill Rose's daddy had built to fulfill one of his young daughter's whims. Rose kept it as white as the house, but the blades sported fanciful panels of painted flowers in bright shades.

None of this was real.

Nothing in Phoenix's life seemed real anymore.

She uncoiled the towel from her hair and ran her fingers through wet strands that instantly sprang into unruly curls. Her face, neck, and much of her body bore scratches from the straw. They could be worse. There were some bruises, too. Her attacker had beaten her and she didn't even know who he was.

*Bitch.*

Phoenix clutched the roots of her hair and struggled to close out the eerie voice.

*You couldn't leave it alone, could you?*

It was a warning. She was to give up her search for April.

Not possible. Just not possible.

"Please get away from the window."

At the sound of Roman's deep voice, Phoenix started so violently she felt sick.

"Sorry," he said. "Didn't mean to shock you. Just step to your left and I'll be quiet."

Phoenix stepped to her left, away from the window, and spun toward him. "You think someone's out there!" The beating in her chest grew suffocating.

"Hush." His voice was relaxed and early-morning grumbly. "Being careful is all. Just an old habit."

She was suddenly aware of being dressed in nothing but a towel. "I'll get some clothes on and make coffee."

"I wish you wouldn't."

"You don't want coffee?"

"I don't want you to put clothes on."

Once more the fire flew into her cheeks.

He held a hand toward her.

Phoenix pushed awkwardly at her wild hair.

Roman laughed. "I love the way you do that."

"You do?"

"Mm. It doesn't accomplish a thing."

She bit her lip.

"Your hair is really something."

"A mess."

"Sexy as hell."

"Thank you very much for helping last night. I don't know what I'd have done without you. I got up early and took a shower and I don't think any of these scratches is going to take too long to heal. But I am scared about that guy. D'you think he'll come back? I was wondering what you'd think about me buying a gun. I'd learn how to use it properly . . ."

The sight of his legs, and other parts, coming into view, stopped her. His feet met the floor. Phoenix backed up until she bumped into the wall.

"Am I that scary?" he said.

Her lips formed an "Oh" but no sound came out.

"Uh-huh," he said wryly. "I'm very scary."

"No! You're beautiful."

His grin broke slowly, wickedly. "Beautiful, huh? I don't believe I was ever called beautiful before."

"Oh, darn it." She buried her face in her hands. "I am so inept at this. You wouldn't believe what a dope I am when it comes to . . . to . . . well, you know."

"Do I?"

"Gabbling like an idiot. I'm so embarrassed."

"You are so sweet when you're embarrassed."

"Don't tease."

"You're sweet. And you're lovely. And you're gutsy. Don't you ever change a single thing about the way you are. Understand?"

"I'm hopeless. I've failed at everything."

"Will you scream if I come and hold you?"

Phoenix couldn't bring herself to drop her hands. "I may scream if you don't."

His laugh was low, suggestive—irresistible. She heard the fall of his footsteps and grew tense.

Rather than his touch, she felt his presence, his warmth—over and around her. "You told me you weren't into casual sex."

She lowered her hands and stared up into his face. The lines weren't softened anymore.

"Didn't you?" he prompted her.

How did she explain how little she'd been into sex, period? "Yes. I've always thought sex meant two people . . ." Geesh. If she didn't shut up, she'd say something absolutely mortifying.

"Go on," he told her softly. He placed his hands on the wall above her head and leaned on straight arms. "I like watching your mouth when you talk."

"That's it. I don't think sex should be . . . It's not like having a drink with someone, is it?"

He shook his head. "Uh-uh. Definitely not like having a drink with someone." His left arm relaxed until he propped the elbow beside her ear. His face was only inches from hers. That silvery early morning light made an etching of every tensed muscle and sinew.

"I'm not very experienced," she blurted out.

His chin rose a fraction and he looked down at her. He didn't answer.

"I understand that's a real turnoff for a man who . . . Well, for a man who expects . . ." Why couldn't she just shut up and enjoy something for once, particularly something she wanted?

Roman took far too long to say, "A man who expects what?"

Phoenix breathed so deeply she had to grab the towel and tuck it more tightly. "Well, satisfaction, I guess. After all, a man like you isn't into inept performances from—"

Mercifully, his mouth stopped her. The kiss was both gentle and thorough enough to steal not just thought, but breath—and reason. The soft touch of his lips on hers moved her face from side to side. Roman adjusted the angle, breathed into her, took back her breath, left no millimeter untouched or unchanged by his tongue and teeth.

"Inept, huh?" he said against her cheek. "You don't feel inept to me."

"Mm."

"I'd like to make love to you."

Swarms of butterflies attacked her tummy.

"There's a difference between sex and love," Roman said quietly. "I think that's what it's all about. Sometimes people have sex. Other times they make love. If you and I do this, we're going to be making love. All I'm telling you is that this is special to me."

Her heart threatened to stop beating. They were little more than strangers but she wanted what he wanted—to share love with him. Not that he actually meant *love* love. He meant loving that was special. It could be enough, couldn't it?

"There isn't anyone else in your life, is there?"

"No!"

"So emphatic? Did you get hurt?"

"Not the way you mean."

"You want to explain that?"

"Some time, maybe."

He ran a knuckle up and down the side of her neck. "You aren't used to being naked in front of a man, are you?"

Phoenix shook her head.

"You felt so good in bed."

Her face heated up yet again.

Roman nuzzled her chin up. "I'd like to make a habit of falling asleep with you doing what you were doing last night."

He *had* noticed. "I didn't mean to—"

"Ssh. Don't spoil a man's fantasies. I'd like to believe you thought through every move."

"You're stalling, aren't you?" she said. "Trying to give me time to get used to . . . You don't think . . . Oh, boy. I am making such a hash of this."

"Want me to take over? As in, how about putting this entire operation into my hands?"

In the new light, his eyes were navy blue.

Phoenix settled a hand on his beard-rough jaw. She rose to

her toes and kissed his mouth softly. "Entirely in your hands," she whispered. "Whatever you do—however you touch me—I always like it."

He pushed away from the wall and stood with his weight on one leg, his arms crossed.

Phoenix watched his face, his eyes, searched for a hint of what came next.

Roman beckoned her closer, and when she came, he backed away, backed to sit on the side of the bed and draw her between his thighs.

He framed her face as if it might break, brought her lips to his as if this kiss could have the power to wound.

And, as if he heard her thoughts, he said, "I don't want to hurt you, Phoenix. You're bruised."

"You won't hurt me." *Unless I lose you.* Somewhere a warning sounded: she could only be hurt by this in the end. Regardless of the pretty words, men like Roman Wilde didn't fall in love, or stay around long enough to see what they did to the hearts they left behind.

"I don't want to put any weight on you."

Her insides turned to white fire. "I'm not fragile."

"I'm a big man."

"I know." The fire only grew hotter. "I love how big you are."

"Take off the towel."

Phoenix clutched it to her.

"I'm in charge, remember?"

She nodded and lowered her hands—lowered her hands and encountered his solid thighs. Automatically, she pressed her fingers into muscle that didn't give.

"Nope," he said. "Nothing doing. *You* take it off. I want you to want this as much as I do."

Phoenix put her hands on his shoulders. "You do it."

"Tempting," he said. There was no smile now. "But more tempting to have you offer yourself, sweetheart. Just a little quirk of the moment. I want you to give yourself to me."

She looked down at the towel, and beyond—and shut her

mouth against an exclamation. He was huge, and so ready. This man had the kind of control—in all things—that had to be learned.

"Show me you want me, Phoenix."

Her mouth was so dry. She said, "You want me, don't you?"

His laugh was hoarse. "No kidding. You're observant."

She smiled faintly and unhitched the towel. With her eyes on his, she let it fall.

Roman took his time. While he studied her, he tilted his head. Tension drew his features tight.

She tried to cross her arms.

He caught her wrists and held them.

Phoenix laughed nervously. "I was a scrawny kid. I kept hoping I'd turn into one of those women men took a second look at, but—"

His finger, firmly applied to her mouth, cut off the rest of her babble.

His lips, firmly applied to the dip between her breasts, stole her breath.

Roman enfolded her, nuzzled her with his face, urged her so near that he pressed his penis between her thighs, pressed against her aching flesh. "There isn't a man alive who wouldn't take a second look at you. And a third, and a fourth and a fifth, and—"

"Stop!"

"Have you got the message?"

She thought about it. "Okay."

"You're driving me nuts."

"Good." Desire made her bold. "I want to touch you."

"You already are."

"All of you."

Kissing her breasts absorbed him. Kissing and caressing. Lifting, and, finally, taking a nipple into his mouth.

A sob broke from Phoenix. She was helpless not to cradle his head and hold him to her.

Gathering her strength, she drove her fingers into his hair and forced his face far enough away for her to see his glittering eyes. "I just want to find out about you," she told him. "What feels good to you. What you hate."

He let her push him backward onto the bed—with incredible results. When she stared at that part of him that was impossible to ignore, he chuckled deep in his throat.

Phoenix pretended not to hear him and started with his groin.

*"God!"*

She withdrew her hands. "What? You hate that?"

"No. Carry on. And make it fast."

This time, his long, hair-sprinkled thighs received her slow stroking, all the way from his knees, back to his groin.

He jumped again and she grinned. "Touchy there, huh?"

His lips were pressed tightly together.

Phoenix decided to save certain parts for last. His belly was drawn in like coiled steel. Rough there. His buttocks didn't even dent at her touch. His sides were smooth.

"You did kind of make this tour before."

"Test run," she told him.

"Getting forward now, are we?"

"Hush. This is my tour. Spread your arms. Resistance won't do you any good."

"Yes, ma'am. Anything you say, ma'am." He extended his arms. "Would it hurry the process if I said I was dying?"

Phoenix's response was to spread herself on top of him and open his lips with her own. She delved inside his mouth, rubbed her breasts slowly back and forth over his chest and shuddered at the electric response she sent into her own body.

"How much experience have you had, exactly?" His abrupt question, his callused hands holding her face, stunned her to silence. "You're not telling me this is your first time?"

"No! I've had—"

"Fine."

Roman moved fast enough to make her thoughts run together. One second she leaned over him, the next she sat astride his thighs.

"Roman!"

His mouth made it pointless to say anything else.

His fingers between her legs made it pointless to *try* to say anything else.

Her body wept for him, wept for what he promised. Several times he sent a finger reaching inside her and she whimpered. She also felt him reach away from her and heard him find something that crackled. A condom. She should have known he would always be ready for moments like this. His teeth, fastening lightly on a nipple, blocked her train of thought. Her back arched and Roman's response was to suck.

While his finger reached, his thumb played over the nub that had passed beyond aching. Holding her about the waist with one arm, he worked that bud of flesh until she clawed at him with her fingernails and cried out meaningless pleas.

The inferno erupted. Phoenix clung to him, consumed, only to cry his name over and over as he raised her hips and drove her down on him, drove himself into her waiting, wanting body.

There was a burning, a breaking, a sweet torture. She accepted and contracted about him, welcomed him deep within her.

For an instant he paused, breathing raggedly, his skin wet beneath her hands. "You said this wasn't the first time."

"Don't stop."

"It's the first time, sweetheart."

"No. In high school I went—"

"Oh, my God." He muttered against her lips. "You're unbelievable. Later, sweetheart."

He was unbelievable.

It was unbelievable.

The force of his thrust took her feet from the floor. His thumb returned to the slickness hidden between her legs.

Phoenix writhed.

"Now, my love?"

"Yes." She didn't know what he meant, but now was fine.

His great hands bracketed her hips and moved her. His pelvis jerked to meet each descent.

"Now?" Phoenix shouted the word and knew what it meant.

It meant the beautiful, searing, consuming flame that shot to her womb, to her breasts, to her knees.

Roman's hips rose once more. And once more. And he fell backward, clamping her against him. With one shove of his heels, he pushed them all the way onto the bed—crosswise. Phoenix didn't care what way they were anywhere as long as she didn't have to stand.

He caught hold of her hair and pressed her face into his neck.

When she could breathe again she said, "It didn't make too much difference, did it?"

"Difference?"

"That I hadn't done this. Not properly, I guess."

"Um. Difference? Yeah, yeah it did. Don't worry about it. I'm going to make your training a priority."

She frowned against his salty skin. "I'm sorry."

Roman made a weird, growling noise. He rolled her over and she was helpless to resist. "You are marvelous," he said, looking down at her. "You are perfect. You have also completely worn me out and do you know what that means?"

"No," she whispered.

"I have to rest. I have to rest right now."

"I see."

"I wonder if you do. You have to rest, too."

"I do?"

"You do." He picked her up and arranged her in the bed. Once beside her, he hauled up the covers and wrapped her to his side. "Rest fast."

"Why?"

"So we can continue your training."


He would keep her safe. Whatever happened, this woman would never be hurt, not as long as he breathed.

Roman withdrew from Phoenix for the third time. Not more than two hours could have passed since he'd first made love to her and, if he had his way, they'd make love at least that many times again in the next two hours.

"Your lips are swollen," he told her.

She opened and closed her great green eyes in sleepy sweeps. "Sorry."

"Do not tell me you're sorry about anything again. I love the way your lips look. *I* did that to them."

"And you're glad?"

"Very male reaction. Possessiveness. Primal."

"Ah."

He grinned and kissed her again, and looked at her lips again. "I intend to keep them looking like that."

"Sadist."

"Me?"

"You said you weigh a lot."

He frowned.

"You do. You weigh tons."

"And I'm on top of you!" He made to shift but she grabbed his ears and pinched. "Ouch! That's abuse."

"Sure is. I like you right where you are."

"Phoenix, I know this is kind of fast, but I'm not a kid, and—"

"And neither am I?"

He screwed up his eyes. "That isn't what I was going to say. I was going to say—"

Phoenix pressed her fingers over his mouth and shook her head. "Whatever it was, probably ought to wait until we've fed ourselves, don't you think?"

He studied her. There was something indefinable in her eyes. Fear? Was she afraid of commitment? Or just afraid in general.

Roman took her hand away. "I think we ought to let things take their course. That's what I was going to tell you. This is good—this thing between us. And we need each other."

She smiled bitterly. "You mean I need you. I'm the one who was threatened big time last night. Now you feel responsible."

*Shit.* "You aren't in my head. You don't know what I feel."

"Of course I don't. I'm . . . I apologize for being presumptuous."

He took a deep breath. "Fortunately I'm a patient man. My

advanced years have brought a certain mature ability to wait things out. Including your stupidity."

"Hey!"

"As I was saying. I can wait you out. There will be no guns. Is that understood?"

"You've got one."

"That is not a point for discussion. *You* will not have a gun. Please accept that."

"I don't want one. But I've got to have a way of protecting myself."

"You'd probably end up killing a friend, or having the gun used against you. I'm going to keep you safe, Phoenix."

"You can't—"

"Yes, I can. When you were sleeping last night—and making sure I had the biggest hard-on in history—I worked out a plan."

Her crimson cheeks made him smile. He'd never seen anyone blush as readily as W. G. Phoenix. "I'm keeping you close as much as possible. When it's not possible, Nasty will be within shouting distance."

"Nasty?"

"Nasty. Take it from me, you couldn't have a better body-guard."

"How . . . Where will he be?"

"As far as the landlady's concerned, Nasty and I are your brothers. We drop by and sleep on your couch."

"Oh, dear. Some people already think you and I are old friends. And I told Len you're my new boss."

"We'll tell 'em it's a family joke. We'll say we're afraid the people at the club will cry nepotism if they find out we're related."

"I don't think it sounds funny—or particularly convincing."

"Who's going to call us liars?"

Phoenix thought about that. "My brothers who stop by and sleep on the couch?"

"Exactly. The only difference will be that Nasty really will sleep on the couch. Or you can come to Seattle and move in with me."

"No. I've got a job to do and I'm not giving up. I will find April and to do that I know I've got to stay at the club."

He swallowed the lump in his throat. "You could be in Seattle and still work at the club."

"Someone knows I'm looking for April. It has to be someone at the club. That's why I was attacked. Somebody wanted to try to stop me."

Letting her know he was also searching for April—in a way—wouldn't be smart. "You can't be sure of that. Your April may have ducked out for some reason. She could just as well come back, right?"

"You didn't hear her voice last night. Something happened to her at the club. Before you became a partner. I don't think they should know about . . . Well, about us. Really, Roman, the gun's probably—"

"No gun. Nasty will come and go without being seen at all. That's one of his specialties. Leave the other to me. My partners. I'll tell them I'm having an affair with you. If I just lay it out, there won't be any questions. And we can't be sure the attack was anything to do with the club, can we?"

*An affair.* "I've never had an . . ."

He placed a tender kiss on the space between her eyebrows. "An affair? No, you haven't, have you? But you're having one now. Do you suppose I could persuade you to make love again?"

"Oh, thank goodness," she said, a mischievous gleam in her eyes. "I was afraid you'd worn it out."

He frowned. "Worn *it* out?"

Her fingers pushed between them and closed on his blossoming arousal. "Phew! Still something left."

Growling, he fell upon her and proved just how much of *it* was left.


The sound of someone hammering at the front door broke into Phoenix's delicious, if somewhat achy, nap. She pushed her hair out of her eyes and looked sideways at Roman. He continued to sleep deeply.

The knocking sounded again.

She crept from the bed and unhooked her robe from the back of the bedroom door. Shrugging into the old chenille wrap-around, she trod sleepily through the living room and was about to throw open the door when caution kicked in.

Taking a step backward, she said, "Who is it?"

"Phoenix?" Rose's voice. "Oh, Phoenix, please help me."

With fingers that wouldn't move fast enough, Phoenix un-hooked the chain and opened the bolt. Obviously hastily dressed, Rose stood on the landing. She wound her hands to-gether repeatedly.

"Rose? What is it?"

"What's happened to you?" Rose asked, peering at Phoenix. "Your poor face. Did you fall in a bush?"

"No . . . Yes, yes, I fell. What's the matter? Why did you come?"

Rose grasped Phoenix's arm. "A man broke into the house."

Phoenix took an instant to absorb what Rose had said. "When?"

"Oh, a while ago. Web got up and chased him, but he must have had a car waiting with the engine running. The police came, too, but besides asking questions, they didn't do any-thing."

"You were robbed?"

"No."

"What, then? Too soon to do anything about what?"

"I know they're wrong."

"Rose," Phoenix said, striving for patience. "What are they wrong about?"

"She didn't go off somewhere on her own. That man came and took her. I saw him. I saw him take my Evangeline. And he said if he didn't get what he wanted, he'd kill her."

# EIGHTEEN

"Sin, sex, and witchcraft," Mort said, his bald head aggressively jutting while he paced Rose's kitchen. "Ever since that club opened its doors, this little town's never been the same."

Phoenix deliberately avoided looking at Roman. With a mug of coffee in one hand, he propped up a corner of the room. The last time their eyes had met there'd been no doubt about how little he approved of Rose calling in Mort, Zelda, and Len. The handyman, Web, sat at the kitchen table with his shaggy red head buried in his hands.

"This may have absolutely nothing to do with the club," Phoenix said. It wouldn't do for any well-meaning soul to interfere there. "We're going to wait and hope Evangeline comes back. If she doesn't, the police will have to take us seriously and help."

Rose, her hair streaming down her back like blond satin, stood looking through the window. "I was wrong," she said softly. "Completely wrong. I should have listened to him."

"The kidnapper?" Len asked. Several times he'd tried to put an arm around Phoenix. He did so again now, and she shrugged away again. He cast her a reproachful glare. "We've all got to support Rose in this."

So put your arm around *her*. "Tell us exactly what you mean, Rose," Phoenix said. "Why were you wrong?"

"I wouldn't be quiet long enough for him to tell me what he wanted. I just kept on screamin' like a silly child. Like the silly child I am. So he left, and took my Evangeline with him."

"Not your fault," Web mumbled. He had small, bright blue eyes beneath heavy brows as red as his hair and beard. "My fault. I should have woken up sooner. Can't believe I slept through the whole thing."

"It is *not* your fault," Rose said.

"It's the fault of whoever that dreadful man was," Zelda said. "What I cannot believe is the cavalier attitude of the police."

"Can't you?" Mort raised a brow.

Zelda snorted. "This is America, not wartime Europe."

"I shoulda woken up," Web said. A shambling man, Phoenix had never seen him dressed in anything other than shapeless overalls and a denim work shirt. He pushed up from the table and hovered as if uncertain whether to go or stay.

"Let it go," Phoenix told him, sorry for the man, who was obviously miserable.

"Always did sleep too sound," he said. "I was supposed to be taking care of things."

"You hush, Web," Rose said to him, and to everyone else, "Web's become very fond of Evangeline. I can't bear it that this has happened when she finally might get some happiness for herself."

Phoenix felt, more than saw a movement and turned toward Roman. He continued to lean into the corner and drink his coffee.

"Sis! There you are!"

Phoenix—who almost spilled her coffee—was wrapped in a bear hug. "Coffee," she squeaked, craning her neck to see Nasty's dark brown eyes.

"Say the right things," he told her through teeth that didn't move.

Past his wide shoulder she saw Roman grin into his mug. "Nasty! Where did you come from? Wow, this is terrific. Why didn't you call? I'd have arranged something special. *Wow!*"

"Don't overdo it."

She smiled serenely. "Everybody, meet my other brother, Nasty. Just where did you come from, anyway?"

"Through the front door," Nasty said, facing the company.

"Nice to meet you all. Looks like I walked in on a powwow of some kind."

"Brother?" Len said, suspicion painted all over his sharp face.

"Older brother," Nasty said and hooked a thumb in Roman's direction. "But not as old as the oldest bear, here."

"Huh?" Mort stopped pacing. "He's her old friend. Isn't that what you told me, Phoenix."

Len snorted loudly. "She told me he's her new boss."

Nasty laughed. He slapped his knees, shook his head and planted his fists on his hips. "Same old, same old," he said, for all the world like the truly jolly guy-next-door. "Family jokes. We always introduce each other as very old friends. Or oldest friends. Or anything but what we are. Started when we were kids and Roman here didn't want anyone to know he had a little brother and sister. Back then, we were friends-of-friends." He burst into fresh gusts of hilarity.

Roman grinned broadly and strolled toward his two "old friends." Draping an arm around each of their shoulders, he pulled them, face-first, toward him and muttered, "Smile, dammit," to Phoenix.

Bemused, she forced a chuckle and, when she could set down the mug, she delivered a less than playful punch to Roman's midsection. She was sure the blow hurt her hand more than his gut.

More laughter ensued, more thumping of shoulders between Roman and Nasty.

"We've got a problem here," Web said, abruptly and clearly. "Nice to see a family reunion, but a lovely lady got kidnapped this morning."

Nasty was instantly serious. "Kidnapped?"

"Evangeline," Rose said indistinctly. With her arms tightly folded about her ribs, she turned from the window. "My friend and companion since we were children. My sister in all but blood. That awful man said he'd kill her if he didn't get what he wanted."

"What did he want?" Nasty asked.

Rose's lovely eyes rose to his. "I wouldn't be quiet long enough for him to tell me. Can you credit anythin' as foolish as a screamin' woman who wouldn't be quiet long enough to save her friend?"

For the first time since Phoenix had met him, Nasty appeared speechless. He moved his gum to his back teeth and stared at Rose.

"All I had to do was be quiet and let him speak."

Nasty cleared his throat. "It's not always easy to be calm in these situations, ma'am."

Phoenix realized her mouth had fallen open and closed it.

"If the situation had been reversed, Evangeline would have coped," Rose said, to no one but Nasty. "She is just the most collected person you ever met. I am truly ashamed of myself. I truly am."

"I'm sure you have no need to be," Nasty said. He shoved his hands into his pockets and rocked up onto his toes. "Why don't you sit down and start from the beginning. Tell me everything that happened, then leave things to me. To Roman and me," he added quickly, glancing at Roman.

Despite the recent difficulties, Roman appeared to be trying to reverse a grin. "Good idea."

"What did this man look like?" Nasty asked. He held Rose's arm and led her to a chair. Once she was seated, he dropped to his haunches beside her and layered an arm along the back of her chair. "Take your time. Allow the panic to settle down. Panic always gets in the way of clear thinking."

Phoenix assessed Rose with different eyes. She really was very beautiful. With her hair unbound she appeared almost ridiculously young, yet she couldn't be less than forty, could she?

So what? Nasty might be thirty-five. She was getting carried away. Nasty wasn't smitten with Rose, merely being kind to someone in trouble.

Sure. And in December he probably took a job as a mall Santa.

Nasty was smitten.

"It was awful," Rose told him. "You couldn't see his face at all. He wore this black woolen thing that covered his head and tucked into the neck of a black sweater. A thug, my daddy would have called him."

Phoenix grew quite still.

"Go on," Nasty said gently.

"Don't you push her," Web said sharply. "She's not used to all this. She's not used to anything but being quiet."

"It's all right, Web," Rose said, without looking at him. She had, in fact, not taken her attention from Nasty's face since she'd seen him. "Glasses. He wore little round glasses with the ear-pieces pushed through the woolen thing. Really horrible."

"But that's—"

Roman threw his arm around Phoenix again, effectively making her swallow the rest of what she'd been about to say. "Let Rose finish," he said, squeezing hard enough to get his message through. He didn't want Phoenix to say anything about the attack.

"There isn't much more," Rose said. She sniffed, and accepted the tissue Nasty immediately plucked from a box on a counter. "Black thing on his head. Glasses. Black sweater and trousers. Black gloves. Big rubber boots."

"You did fine," Nasty told her. "Fine. Perfectly. You can't describe what you didn't see."

Phoenix felt close to exploding. The same man who'd attacked her had broken into Belle Rose hours later and made off with Evangeline? Why hadn't she called the police then? Why hadn't she done more to stop him? Why did he have to hurt Rose? Why did he need Evangeline?

"You are so kind," Rose said to Nasty.

"We're going to start a search," Mort said. "You take your truck, Len. I'll drop Zelda back at the Bend. She can borrow Nellie's wheels. Web, meet us outside. We'll split up."

Phoenix noted that Mort didn't attempt to enlist help from Nasty or Roman.

"Oh, dear," Rose said, tears rolling down her cheeks. "I should have listened more closely. I should have told him he could have any papers he wanted."

Everyone but Roman, Nasty and Phoenix was marching purposefully from the kitchen. Phoenix didn't miss Rose's comment.

"Don't question her," Roman said quietly. "Not now. We
need to talk first."

"Do you think he'll telephone?" Rose asked.

Nasty looked over her head at Roman who nodded. "Yes.
Yes, I think that's very likely," Nasty said. He got up and came
to Roman and Phoenix. "Do you know something I don't
know?"

Roman nodded. "Yeah. But it doesn't make a whole lot of
sense. Look, I've got a visit to make. It's been too long."

Nasty studied his sneakers. "Dusty said something to that
effect. Phoenix and I can hold down the fort here."

"You and I have a lot of talking to do, buddy," Roman told
him. "We can't trust the phone. I'm taking Phoenix with me."

"I can't leave Rose."

"You can do as you're told," Roman said shortly.

Rose's soft sobbing assured she wasn't listening to the conversation. Just as well. Phoenix narrowed her eyes at Roman.
"You've been very good to me."

"Thanks," he said, oozing sarcasm.

She filled the fingers of her right hand with the front of his
sweater. "As I just said, you've been very good to me and I'm
very grateful. That doesn't mean you can tell me what to do."

"Yes, it does."

Nasty was actually humming!

"Darn you, it does *not*. I've got enough trouble, without this."

"Without this, you'll have a whole lot more trouble," Roman
said, his face as calm as if he were ordering breakfast. "You
are in danger, sweetheart."

"Don't call me—"

"Females are *so* impossible to understand sometimes."

"Sure are," Nasty agreed. "Better do what big bro' says, Sis.
Big bro' always knows best."

"This is ridiculous."

"This is deadly," Roman said. "People have already died. Do I make myself clear."

Gradually, her fingers released their hold on his sweater. "Who?" What was he saying? Who was he talking about?

"It's a long, long story," Roman said.

Nasty raised his massive shoulders. "Exceedingly long. Too long for the time we've got to give it right now. What d'you think, Roman? About this Evangeline?"

"Beats me at this point. Stay with Rose, okay?"

"You've got it."

"I'll head to Dusty's."

Nasty laughed shortly. "You'd better, friend. He's about to come and find you."

"Shit," Roman said under his breath. "Come on, Phoenix. And, please, don't argue. If you don't go, I can't go. And I've *got* to go."

She let him hurry her outside and down the drive to where he'd parked the Land Rover. Once they were both inside, she scooted sideways in her seat and slammed a hand over his on the ignition.

"Phoenix." He leaned to kiss the corner of her mouth. "I've spent my life in tight corners. Let me call the shots in this one, my love."

Despite her irritation, the sensation his caress gave her made her eyelids drift down. "I can't just follow you blindly," she told him in an unsteady voice. "I'm used to making my own decisions. Safer that way. Less chance of blaming someone else if it all goes wrong."

"You can explain where that came from later," he told her, placing another kiss on the same spot. "For now would you please let me drive us to Dusty's?"

Phoenix rested her forehead on his shoulder. "Why was it so important for me not to say the man who took Evangeline is probably the same man who attacked me?"

"They don't know you were attacked and I want to keep it that way." He stroked her hair. "How do you think *I* know it was probably the same man? You didn't describe him to me."

Her eyes snapped open. "No, I didn't."

Reaching into his pocket, he produced a pair of round-lensed glasses wrapped in a handkerchief. "I found these near the garage. I doubt if there are any prints. They'd obviously been polished and put where they'd be found."

Phoenix took several seconds to say, "He could have dropped them. But . . ."

"But not if he needed them to see where he was going."

"But he took Evangeline later. And he had glasses then."

"I know." Roman lifted her hand and kissed her fingertips. "That does have me puzzled. Maybe it's a trademark. Maybe the guy buys his specs by the van-load and leaves them at all his crime scenes."

"It's so scary," Phoenix said. "He's violent, Roman. And he's got poor Evangeline. Why didn't you call the police when he came after me?"

"We just can't trust them, love. The mess at the Peak Club has been going on for years, and the police haven't done anything. They never followed up on your break-in or Evangeline's kidnapping. We have to assume that they're being paid to look the other way. What papers d'you suppose Rose was talking about?"

"Papers she never meant to mention."

He switched on the ignition. "Or papers she forgot *he'd* mentioned. She isn't too—er—well, she isn't, is she?"

"Rose is fine. Somewhere along the way she got frightened into her shell. She probably needs someone strong to draw her back out."

Roman chuckled. "Someone like Nasty? Forget it. Nasty's got a short attention span where women are concerned."

"How . . ."

"How nasty, is Nasty?" Roman drove from the driveway of Belle Rose. "He's a great guy and he'd never hurt someone as helpless as that lady, so put your weapons away."

"What kind of name is Nasty, anyway," Phoenix grumbled. "Why doesn't he use a proper name?"

"Maybe the two of you should have a chat on that subject."

She ignored the jab, relaxed a little and allowed herself to be lulled by the lines of evergreens they passed, and the wildflowers waving in the early afternoon breeze. "Do you always have to check in with Dusty?"

"Yeah."

"You do it to be nice? Because you feel sorry for him?"

"No."

Phoenix sighed. "Why do I feel you're an iceberg and I'm the *Titanic?*"

"Because there's a lot you don't know about me. Just the way there's a lot I don't know about you."

"Not as much."

"You want to know why I have to make sure I see Dusty?" She felt pushy. "It's not my business."

"It could be. The truth is, I go to Dusty's every day."

*"Every* day?" She glanced at him. "You didn't go yesterday."

"That's why I'm in trouble."

"I don't get it."

"You will. I've got responsibilities and I take them seriously. If I ever forget them, even for a day, the way I did yesterday, Dusty reminds me. Not a pretty scene."

"I still don't get it."

"Dusty believes fathers should put their children first."

Phoenix turned completely sideways in her seat. "Dusty's your *father?*"

"No. I'm Junior's father."

# NINETEEN

Shell-shocked, but with latent hostilities about to bust out. Yeah, that about summed up Phoenix's expression.

She wouldn't even look at Roman. And she'd ignored Dusty, which was a fine idea until Roman could get his old buddy alone and run through what could and couldn't be said. If luck smiled on him, what he'd found with Phoenix wouldn't blow away, but there were hurdles to jump. Hearing about April's death from Dusty might be enough to make Phoenix quit the race altogether. What he'd found with Phoenix was special. What he owed April was sacred.

With both small hands firmly anchored in Dusty's wire-brush hair, Junior entered the yellow living room on his shoulders. Showing all of her twelve teeth, the baby eyed Roman with glee, but when she held her arms out and said, "Da, Da, Da," Dusty swung her down and held her firmly.

"Better late than never, so they say," Dusty commented to Roman. "Never did quite figure out who 'they' were and I don't put much stock in 'their' opinions, either."

"Ouch," Roman said. "Nasty warned me you were pissed."

Dusty pressed a big hand over Junior's ear. *"Not* in front of the baby." He glowered from Phoenix to Roman. "You two shacking up?"

*"Not* in front of the baby," Roman said.

Phoenix threw herself onto the love seat and placed her feet—in non-too-pristine tennis shoes—on the opposite arm. "The baby doesn't understand terms like *shacking up*. I do, Mr. Miller, and I find it offensive."

Roman grinned, and instantly knew he'd made a mistake.

"I'm glad you think this situation's funny," Phoenix told him. "Evangeline's been kidnapped by some crazed sex maniac who drops Coke-bottle glasses all over the place. I can't find my best friend. My life's probably not worth the price of a pack of Nasty's gum. And besides, everything I've ever touched has turned to shit!"

*"Not* in front of the baby," Dusty hollered, so loudly Junior gave a surprised hiccup and started to cry. "Now look what you've done," Dusty said to Roman, rocking the baby.

Phoenix was instantly on her feet, patting Junior's back and murmuring soothing sounds. She and Dusty aimed matching glares at Roman.

"You been having a rough time?" Dusty asked Phoenix gruffly. "You're pretty beaten up."

She curled wisps of Junior's fine hair around a finger. "Rough," she said, rolling in her lips and nodding. "Really rough, actually."

"Nasty said something like that. Said he'd like to get his hands on the . . . He'd like to have a chat with whoever did that to you."

"He's a good guy," Phoenix said. "My landlady—Rose Smothers—Rose is very reclusive. She doesn't open up to new people easily. Nasty was so nice to her this morning. He won her over."

"He can be like that." Dusty held one of Junior's little fists inside his own. He bobbed up and down in his ridiculous cartoon slippers and said, "Gentle when you don't expect it."

"I noticed. She was angry with herself because Evangeline— that's the woman her daddy brought with them from Georgia— Evangeline was kidnapped this morning."

Dusty swung Junior from side to side. "I thought Nasty went up there because of you."

Roman caught his eye and sent the appropriate "clam-up" signals.

Junior peeked at Phoenix, who made circles on a pink cheek with her thumb. "She's the prettiest baby." She brought her nose close to Junior's. "Aren't you the prettiest baby?"

Junior's nose wrinkled to a pink button and her teeth made another appearance.

"Nasty did come to Belle Rose because of me. This creep— the guy who took Evangeline—he attacked me last night and shoved me in the trunk of a car in the garage."

"Son-of-a—"

*"Not* in front of the baby," Roman said softly.

Dusty whistled soundlessly, then said, "That's bad, Phoenix. Real bad. Da . . . Darn it, we're going to have to make sure nothing like that *can* happen again."

Roman crossed his arms.

"The police haven't helped with Evangeline yet," Phoenix told Dusty earnestly. "You know they wait—"

"Yeah. I know. Kind of like the way someone has to be killed before you can get a stop sign put up. I don't want you to worry. Understand?"

Roman tapped a toe. When had he become invisible?

"I think you're a very kind man," Phoenix said. "And you are so sweet with Junior."

Dusty shrugged and, unbelievably, turned faintly pink. "You've got to do what you've got to do."

"Not everyone would be so generous." She stroked Junior's hair away from her face. "About me. And Roman. Considering your daughter, and everything."

"My . . ." Dusty frowned.

Roman cleared his throat and removed Junior firmly. He held her above his head and slowly brought her face down to his. "Phoenix knows Junior's mine," he said, praying Dusty wouldn't give the whole show away. "I guess she's saying that under the circumstances, she'd understand if you didn't roll out the red carpet for any woman I might be involved with."

"Ah," Dusty said promptly. "Because of Junior's mother. Mm. A true sign of maturity is learning to forgive. If I'm anything, I'm a mature man."

Roman sent up silent thanks for Dusty's agile recovery. "You sure are. Is there any hot coffee, Dust? Phoenix didn't get much sleep last night."

"I got as much as you did," Phoenix retorted.

"That a fact?" Dusty sounded serene. "Long night, was it?"

Roman didn't have to look at Phoenix to know what color her face would be. "Phoenix can't be left on her own from now on. I stayed with her last night."

After just enough pause to ensure awkwardness, Dusty said, "This guy who attacked Phoenix throws Coke bottles around?"

Junior grabbed Roman's ears. He grimaced and said, "Glasses with thick lenses. He left a pair where they could be found. Near the place where he jumped Phoenix. He was wearing another pair when he snatched Evangeline. We can go over this later, Dust. How about that coffee?"

"Where's Nasty now?"

"Still with Phoenix's landlady. To keep her company."

"Huh?"

"This isn't your average landlady. She's one of those cool, sexy pieces. And she's a nut, but I'm not sure Nasty's noticed that part yet."

"Roman!"

He smiled reassuringly at Phoenix. "Just joking. Nasty's going to bunk up there for a while. When I can't be with Phoenix overnight, he will be."

"Cozy," Dusty said.

Roman paused in the act of tucking Junior inside his jean jacket. He screwed up his eyes at Dusty. "Nasty will be sleeping on the couch."

"Rather than where you'll be sleeping when you're there?"

"None of your Goddamn business!"

"*Not* in front of the baby," Dusty said, keeping his voice down this time. "Seems to me this is one time it is my business where you dip your wick."

Roman shook his head in disgust. "You are out of line, friend. I'll try to forget you said that in front of Phoenix."

"Oh, dear," Phoenix said.

Stella Cameron

Efficiently, Roman put Junior inside his jacket and pulled up the zip. She'd loved being close to him that way for as long as they'd been together. He cuddled her. She'd loved it from the moment of her birth.

"Mr. Miller," Phoenix said seriously. "If I'd had any idea what the situation was here, I'd . . . Roman being Junior's daddy. Well, I would have . . ."

"What would you have done?" Roman asked, deliberately menacing.

"You don't have to worry that there'll be another, well"—she indicated Junior—"there won't be. Roman's very responsible."

He couldn't believe she'd said it.

Dusty backed away. He didn't say a word until he reached the door to the hall. Then all he did say was, "Responsible," very faintly, before all but jogging from the room.

"He is such a nice man," Phoenix said, winding her fingers together. "Very understanding under the circumstances."

Some people would find this situation funny. Roman wasn't one of them. "Dusty's the best." After all, how was she supposed to know she'd been told nothing but lies until he'd finally confessed to being Junior's father.

At that instant, his blood felt as if it had stopped circulating. "Come on, baby," he said to his little girl. "Let's you and me sit and hug." She was his little girl. He might not be her father in the biological, or even the legal sense—if anyone ever found a reason to dispute his claim—but she was his and he was hers.

Cross-legged in an armchair, he kissed Junior's eyes and nose, nibbled her chin and blew over her ears, until she squealed and placed one of her big wet kisses on his mouth.

Roman closed his eyes and held her. She smelled of baby powder and clean clothes, and . . . and just sweet, sweet baby.

"Da, Da." She straightened her legs and bounced, and clapped her palms against his cheeks. "Wow!"

Phoenix laughed. "Wow? Is that what she said?"

"Latest, favorite word."

Playing to her audience, Junior repeated, "Wow," with gusto.

"I love you," Roman told her, resisting the urge to squeeze

her too tightly. "You are the best, baby. The best." And, whatever else happened, he would do his damnedest to make sure she never as much as sniffed the dark, destructive side of life that had become her mother's lot.

"What was her mother like?"

His attention shifted slowly. He hadn't noticed that Phoenix had stretched out on her stomach on the yellow rug. She rested her chin on the heel of a hand and watched him seriously.

"Her mother"—Roman said, remembering to breathe again—"was a wonderful person. She was courageous and unselfish. Her last thoughts were for her daughter."

Phoenix's eyes glistened. She blinked. "Why didn't you marry her?"

Hadn't his sainted father always warned against the evils of being less than "forthright?" This was the kind of mess lies landed you in. "She didn't want to marry me," he said, ridiculously grateful for an inspiration that was true.

Dusty slammed noisily back into the room—without coffee. "Someone on the blower for you, Roman. In the kitchen. Important."

Once more he was grateful. He might not be so lucky with her next question. "Coming," he said, getting up. He took Junior from his jacket and held her out to Phoenix. "Think you can handle her for a few minutes?"

"She doesn't go to strangers," Dusty said.

With all the fingers and the thumb of one hand stuffed into her mouth, Junior went silently into Phoenix's hands. Roman motioned for Dusty to follow, and crept from the room.

In the hall, Dusty stopped to listen.

No wild wails reached them from the living room.

Roman pointed to the kitchen and led the way.

Once the door closed behind them, Dusty turned on Roman. "What the fuck do you think you're doing with that girl?"

"She's not a girl. She's thirty. And what I do with her is my business."

"The hell it is. We're all here because of you. We're here

because you say you can't rest till you find whoever killed April. You have to have your revenge."

"I have to have it for Junior," Roman ground out. "And for April. Now drop it. Just don't say anything critical in front of Phoenix until I say it's okay."

"Okay?" Dusty picked up a pack of Camels and knocked one out. "One minute this female's a member of the enemy camp. The next minute you're sleeping with her."

"She wouldn't be the first enemy someone slept with."

"Ah!"—Dusty lit his cigarette and squinted through the smoke—"So you admit you're sleeping with her?"

"Stuff it, buddy. The little lady already gave her charming testimonial about how responsible I am."

Dusty inhaled all the way to his toenails. "Glad you still remember not to go out without your rubbers."

"That's not cute. She's special. Or I want her to be."

Twin streams of smoke shot from Dusty's nostrils. "I like her."

Roman raised one brow. "I didn't think you liked any women anymore."

"I don't. But, for a woman, she might be okay. This is different for you, isn't it?"

"Yeah."

"I knew it. I *felt* it. I haven't completely forgotten the signs. You love her."

Roman wasn't ready to talk about this. He might never be ready. "I didn't say anything about love."

"You saying, *no,* you don't love her?"

Roman thought about it. "I'm saying, I'm not saying. But I am hoping."

Dusty dragged on the cigarette. "What if she's . . . If she turns out to *be* the enemy? What then?"

"She's not."

"You didn't answer the question."

Roman fixed him with a flat stare. "If she is, she won't be a problem to us. I'll make sure of it."

Dusty nodded.

"Damn it!" Roman snatched the cigarette. "What are you doing?"

"Stress," Dusty said sheepishly.

"You promised me you wouldn't. Not with Junior around."

"I don't smoke around Junior. And you're not my father. You're not anybody's father."

"Neither are you, dammit."

Dusty took back the cigarette, went to the sink and stubbed it out deliberately. "I choose to be as close to a father as you want me to be to you, okay?"

Chastened, Roman said, "Okay. I shouldn't have said that."

"We're even. You're the best father Junior's going to get. And she's a lucky kid. Now, can we get on with the business of getting out of this shit hole? With or without your Phoenix, I want to see that baby as far away from Past Peak as we can take her."

"So do I." But, God help him, he wanted it to be *with* Phoenix. "I made it back into the viewing room and went through a bunch more files."

"And?"

"Nothing. There isn't going to be anything. They're useless. They read like a boys' and girls' club mailing list."

"Too bad," Dusty said.

Roman took the pot of cold coffee from the coffeemaker and put it into the microwave—and remembered how Dusty had got him out here. "I didn't hear the phone ring."

"It didn't."

"You said . . . Dusty, if Phoenix asks, you'd better make up some story about a phone that only rings in the kitchen so it doesn't wake Junior."

"Thanks." Dusty grinned. "That's exactly what I'll tell her."

The phone rang.

"So much for that excuse," Dusty said, and picked up the wall phone. "Yeah?" He listened, then handed it to Roman.

"Just stripped your messages from Seattle," Nasty said. "Thought you'd like to know, the lovely countess is looking for you. Sounds desperate."

"She wants me back at the club?"

"Make contact. That's all she said."

"Okay. Any sign of Evangeline?"

Nasty lowered his voice. "Nothing. But Rose is calm. Playing the piano seems to relax her."

"Good." Roman's eyes lost focus. "What are you doing?"

"Listening. She likes that. Plays fantastically. You know *Pachelbel's Canon?*"

Roman pinched the bridge of his nose. "I know it. Thanks for the call. I'll be in touch."

"You know what?" Dusty asked when Roman had cut off the connection.

*"Pachelbel's Canon,"* Roman said. "It's a piece of music. My mother liked it."

"Uh-huh."

Roman didn't bother to explain further before tapping in Vanessa's private number at the club. She said, "Yes," after one ring.

"Roman here."

"Where are you?"

"In a Seattle call box." This number could not be traced.

"We've found out something very troublesome."

"We? You and Geoffrey?"

"Billy Wilberton called from London. You know the kind of contacts he has. Someone dropped a comment. We may have to take certain steps to protect ourselves."

"Protect ourselves from what?"

"Your friend, Phoenix."

The tiny hairs on his spine prickled. *"My* friend?"

"We make it our business to take a deep interest in anyone closely connected with us, darling. I know you're sleeping with her."

He stared at the door to the hallway. "I'd give a great deal to know *how* you know. Not that I'm denying it. The lady's quite something and I'm not one to pass up a good thing."

"I don't blame you one teensy bit, darling. And you could not possibly know she might be dangerous."

Roman grabbed Dusty's arm and held on. "How might Phoenix be dangerous?"

"I can't talk about it over the phone. Billy's in Italy with one of the Insiders. I might as well tell you who. It's the evangelist, Chester Dupree? One of our very best members—not that he has anything to do with this issue. It's something that was said at a party that's so frightening. And I do mean, *frightening*, darling."

"I'll get there as soon as I can."

"We can't risk contamination. You do understand, darling?"

*Darling* couldn't be more fucking confused if he'd worked at it. "Of course I understand. Do you have any ideas about what we should do about this?"

"First we've got to make sure the danger exists, rather than being a rumor. Although I really can't imagine how such a rumor would be circulating about a *masseuse* if she was only a masseuse."

"What—"

"I'd rather wait until I see you. Let's just say that if what Billy was told is right, we'll need some of your special skills."

He passed his tongue along the edges of his teeth. "Such as?"

"We'll go over it, but it won't be anything you haven't done many times before. First you must keep the problem in sight at all times. You'll enjoy that. Then, when we give the word, you'll act. I understand men like you are very good at arranging for people to—relocate? Permanently?"

A death sentence.

Countess Von Leiden was suggesting she and Geoffrey might ask Roman to kill Phoenix.

He met Dusty's frown and took his own hand from the other man's arm.

"Roman! Roman, are you still there, darling?"

"Here and ready, Vanessa. As you say, we'll talk as soon as I see you." He looked at Dusty again and realized what he had almost failed to notice. "Miles," he said. "Miles told you about this rumor?"

"Yes. He heard it in Rome."

"But you didn't call him Miles."

She hesitated before laughing. "Oh. Sorry. Sometimes I forget. Miles William Wilberton. The Honorable. To his closest friends, he's Billy."

From the shadow of the doorway, he watched her for a long time.

Stretched on her side, her back toward the door, sleepiness had caught up with her and she played languidly with Junior. Buttery light made its way through the blinds to bathe the woman and the child. Phoenix's hair was fire—Junior's pale gold.

The baby had hauled her stuffed green snake from the toy box and lay on her back with her head on Phoenix's arm.

"Ssss," Phoenix hissed.

Junior copied her. "Ss. Ss." She held the snake's droopy black tongue to Phoenix's face, jerked it away again and clutched it close. "Wow!"

"Aren't you going to let me have your snake?" Phoenix asked.

Junior looked solemnly into Phoenix's eyes.

"Oh, you'll share him, won't you?"

Once more she received a quick thrust from the snake's nose.

Roman saw Dusty approaching from the kitchen and signaled for him not to interrupt the scene. Making a face, Dusty retreated.

Junior rolled toward Phoenix. One plump hand found springy red curls and patted.

Roman's heart did things that weren't entirely unpleasant. One night mission that went awry and his whole life had changed. Before there had been just him—and the unwritten law that was his responsibility to the other members of his team—afterward he'd known it would never be just him again. He didn't want it to be.

*"Tell Billy."*

Like hell, he'd tell Billy. Kill Billy, maybe. Give a lovely, innocent little girl to him?—even if he wanted her, which was unlikely. Giving Junior to Wilberton was too disgusting to contemplate.

No, what he would do was fulfill his promise to look after April Clark's baby—forever.

"Ooh, you feel so good, baby," Phoenix said. "If I ever had a baby, I'd like her to feel just like you."

Junior found that funny.

Roman found he needed to open his mouth to breathe. Children needed two parents. Two parents who really cared what happened to those children. He knew personally what it was like when that didn't happen.

And he was getting fanciful. Phoenix was hardly mommy material. Was she?

"So soft," Phoenix said indistinctly. "You a sleepy baby?"

Junior rewarded her with one of the sloppy kisses that could always make Roman smile.

Phoenix giggled and scooted onto her back, taking Junior with her. Junior did exactly what she always did with Roman in similar moments; she stretched out on Phoenix's chest, found a pillow for her face beneath Phoenix's chin, and sucked her thumb.

Tender baby, green snake, and lovely woman.

Phoenix folded her arms around Junior and pressed her cheek to the top of the baby's head.

Treading softly, Roman went into the room and dropped to sit beside them. Phoenix's green eyes flickered to his face and she smiled. He swung out to his full length, propped his head on an elbow and surrounded them both with his free arm.

"Sh," Phoenix whispered. "She's sleeping."

Roman kissed her forehead. "Ever feel like stopping the clock?"

There could be no mistaking the tears that sprang into her eyes. "Like now? Yes, Roman."

"Me, too." He sighed. "We're going to have to think about us, aren't we?"

"Are we?"

He glanced at Junior. "I won't do anything unless it's good for her."

"Like getting involved with a bad woman?"

"Are you a bad woman?"

"You tell me."

If her good soul wasn't in her face, in her clear eyes, and her trembling mouth, he wasn't the sterling character judge his reputation claimed he was. "You're the best, kid. I'm never going to forget last night."

"*Not* in front of the baby," she murmured. "It wasn't real, was it?"

Roman frowned. "Felt real enough to me." ∗

"But it was . . . Just one of those things? Circumstances? Opportunity? Need?"

He stroked her hip. "Maybe bits of all the above. But for me the first word that jumps to mind is, desire. I desired you, Phoenix. I could even have lusted after you." Showing his teeth, he pretended to snarl. "I lust after you now."

She found his thigh and smoothed her way to the hard evidence that he told the truth. Her smile disappeared. "I lust after you, too, Roman. I'm a late starter and I've obviously been missing a great deal. I hope I get to catch up. Real lust is . . . it's interesting."

He swallowed a laugh. "Interesting? I think that's an interesting way of describing it. I need to go back to the club. I'm going to take you to Nasty. He'll look after you till I can come to you."

"I'm not another baby, Roman."

"Who said you were?"

"You're telling me what to do. Telling me what's going to happen to me. I don't like—"

"I don't care what you don't like." He snapped back without thinking. The frozen look on her face made him think. "Scratch that. I do care. The problem is that you're in danger. The guy said he was coming back."

"I'm more worried about Evangeline."

"Yeah. Of course you are. For the moment. But it's my job to worry about you, too."

"Who made it your job?"

"I did," he told her shortly. "I care what happens to you. What happened with us mattered to me."

Her chin came up. "It mattered to me, too."

"You don't have to tell me that. I haven't forgotten how much it must have mattered. And don't think I'm too thick-skinned to be affected by what you gave me. You aren't just a body, Phoenix. Not even, just a woman. What you are to me and what I am to you is going to have to be discussed. But not now. Will you please do what I ask?"

She cradled the back of Junior's head and looked away.

"Please? I can't make you"—he could, and he would if he had to—"but I'll only do what's best for you. Right now you need me."

"I know I do," she said quietly. "I'll probably regret saying this, but I'm afraid it may be hard to stop needing you."

She had to be for real. If she wasn't, he'd be changed one more time—forever, one more time. "We're going to talk as soon as I get through at the club."

"Why do you have to go there?"

*To be told why I'm supposed to kill you.* "The countess wants to see me."

"And when she snaps her fingers, you run?"

"Something like that."

Phoenix looked at him again and smiled very faintly. "Oh, dear. I sounded jealous then, didn't I?"

He returned her smile. Her hand, resting lightly against his bulging crotch, made concentration a feat. "Perhaps I'd like to think you were jealous." He covered her hand and pressed. "In this case, possessive is good. You can possess me anytime the mood strikes."

"It's struck."

"You learn so fast."

"I've got an irresistible teacher."

The phone shattered the mood. He muttered, "Damn," and waited to see if Dusty would pick up in the kitchen.

Only seconds passed before a voice thundered, "For you, Roman. Nasty."

Roman got up and came face-to-face with Dusty who promptly reached down and lifted Junior out of Phoenix's arms.

"I'll take the call in the kitchen," Roman said.

"He hung up."

Roman swallowed his irritation. "I'd better call him back. Is he still at Belle Rose?"

"The blonde's house? Uh-huh. He said for you and Phoenix to get there."

"What's happened?" Scrambling, Phoenix gained her feet. "Is it about Evangeline?"

"That's the name. Guess they found her."

# TWENTY

Babbling voices burst in gusts from Rose's kitchen.

Phoenix squared her shoulders and walked in. The smell of strong liquor made her catch her breath.

Mort and Zelda were the only occupants of the room, but they were shouting streams of their native German at each other with red-faced fury.

"Little domestic argument," Roman said mildly. "As my dear father used to say, when the wine's in, the wit's out. Only it looks like bourbon's the poison of choice here."

Mort glared at Roman. "I suppose you *old* friends never argue?" He rolled onto his heels and took a backward step to regain his balance. "According to Len, it would not be natural for brother and sister to be the kind of old friends you are."

Embarrassment numbed Phoenix's tongue.

"Do not listen to him," Zelda ordered, going to put an arm around Phoenix. "He is a pig. A *pig*. For hours he is gone. They are all gone. *I* am gone. The difference is I was indeed searching. As was Nellie. Web has yet to return, poor man."

"Is there a problem here?" Roman asked.

Phoenix felt him march innocently into big trouble. Zelda's dark eyes narrowed to slits. "All men are the same. Not to be trusted. You should not trust this one, Phoenix. Sleep with him, but do not trust him."

Roman laughed.

Phoenix practiced being a fish.

Zelda pointed a long finger at Roman. "You, I thought were

different. But you are like the rest. Only interested in one thing—or two. Fucking and drinking."

*"Zelda!"* Phoenix said, taking the woman by her shoulders. "What is the matter with you?"

"Now you see what I put up with," Mort said. "Just because Len and I were cold and in need of a little warmth."

"Drunk," Zelda said. "They sat by the road and got *drunk.* Then they drove here in such a condition."

"They're in shock," Phoenix told Roman sharply: "It has to be that. They would never . . . Zelda, where's Rose?"

"Playing the piano."

"But—"

"Where's the piano?" Roman asked grimly. "You've hit it. We've got a major case of shock around here."

She led him from the kitchen, through a corridor papered with rose-colored grass cloth, toward the sound of Rose's white piano.

Upon entering the room, the first person she noticed was not her musician landlady, but Evangeline.

Phoenix halted so abruptly that Roman stepped on her heels. She hissed with pain.

"Sorry," he said, not sounding particularly sorry. "You shouldn't have stopped like that."

Fighting back tears, she flapped a hand at Evangeline. "You—you're all right. Evangeline, you're back and you're all right."

*Pachelbel's Canon* droned on and on.

Evangeline, her thick brown hair loose about her shoulders, sat on one of Rose's floral couches. "You wouldn't say you were all right if you'd suffered the way I have," she told Phoenix. "If I hadn't used my wits, I wouldn't be here at all."

Phoenix looked at Rose who sat at the piano as if nothing had happened. Nasty stood behind her and avoided meeting anyone's eyes.

Len, a foolish grin crumpling his thin face, stared adoringly at Phoenix.

"Evangeline's only reacting, Phoenix." Dressed completely

in tight denim, Nellie leaned over the back of the couch. "Don't take anything she says seriously."

"Shock," Roman said. "She's angry and shocked."

"You don't know what I am," Evangeline announced. "Any of you. To you I'm just a silly creature dependent upon charity."

The music ceased abruptly. "You are not, Evangeline," Rose stated. "What would make you say such a terrible thing? Why, I can't manage without you."

"Then stop playin' that damn piano."

"Oh!" Rose popped to her feet. "You know you shouldn't swear, Evangeline."

"There are a whole lot of things I've never done that I may just start doin' now. Life's capricious. Here today and gone tomorrow. That's what we are. *Carpe diem.* You know what that means, Rose?"

Rose's brow puckered with worry.

"Seize the day," Evangeline announced. "Get on with it while you can. Make hay while the sun shines. Don't let the grass grow under your feet."

"The grass is always greener on the other side," Len said and hiccuped."

"Shut *up,* Len Kelly," Evangeline said. "You are a drunk. Keepin' warm while you searched for me, my foot. It isn't cold. And you can go away any time you can get your skinny carcass through the door."

*"Evangeline!"* Rose sat down on the piano bench with a plop.

Nasty massaged her shoulders, but amusement warmed his cold eyes.

"I was kidnapped," Evangeline said, glowering around. "Hours. For hours, that mad man drove me around."

Roman squeezed Phoenix's elbow and went to sit beside Evangeline. "Did he take his mask off?"

"Yes."

Phoenix put a fist to her mouth.

"What does he look like?" Roman asked.

Evangeline drew herself up. "How are you, Evangeline?" she

said primly. "How are you feelin'? Did that mad man hurt you? Did he—*touch* you? Did he do *things* to you?"

Rose cried out.

"Did he, honey?" Nellie lifted a handful of Evageline's heavy hair aside. "Should we get you to a doctor? Or have a doctor come here?"

"That's what we'll do," Rose said in a rush. "We'll send for Dr. Percy. He'll come right on over."

"I do not need Dr. Percy. I need a little lovin' care and compassion. A little consideration for what I've been through."

"Evangeline," Phoenix said, feeling guilty. "I'm not going to pretend. I was afraid I was going to be told you'd been found dead, and—"

"Don't!" Rose covered her face.

"Behave yourself, Rose," Evangeline said brusquely. "You're such a child."

"I thought you might be dead," Phoenix continued. "Roman did too. We're all in a state of shock. Would you please explain what happened?"

Evangeline's gaze settled on Phoenix with piercing intensity. "You ought to want to know."

Phoenix pressed a hand to her stomach. "I do."

"It was your fault. He threatened all of us, but it was you who brought him here."

Sickness overwhelmed Phoenix.

"Hours of driving around and not knowin' if I would live or die. *Carpe diem.* Never again will I put off till tomorrow what I ought to do today."

Phoenix shook her head.

"Regular walking cliché," Len chuckled. "Should say, sitting cliché."

"You should shut up," Nellie said, her mouth pursed.

"Goin' to get even," Evangeline said, pulling her hair from Nellie's fingers. "He's goin' to get even with all of us, but he's savin' Phoenix for last. That's what he said. We're goin' to be sorry, but not as sorry as her. He said that, too. Over and over, he said it. He said he's goin' to make you wish you were never born. He said horrible things I don't even want to mention."

"*Don't* mention them," Roman said quietly. "Nasty, I think it's time for the police."

"Couldn't agree more."

"Not till I'm finished," Evangeline spat. "And I'll say whatever I want to say. If he hadn't had to go to the men's room he might be doin' some of those things he talked about to me. He went to a gas station and tied my wrists to the shift." She held up her arms to show red marks. "I waited till he went inside and managed to pull the knot over the top. I started runnin' and I thumbed a ride in a truck. Can you imagine that? Evangeline Jones thumbin' a ride in a truck like some common tramp?"

No one attempted a response.

Evangeline dabbed at her eyes with a wrinkled handkerchief, then flicked the cloth toward Phoenix. "He's goin' to take his time with you. That's what he kept sayin'. He's goin' to make you undress for him and go down on your knees—"

"That's it," Roman snapped. "Why don't you help Evangeline to her room, Nellie."

"He's going to make you do things to him, then he's goin' to tie you up—"

*"Be quiet!"*

Evangeline started and closed her mouth. Color fled her face.

"I'm sorry," Roman said. "You aren't yourself. Nasty, could you find the lady a little brandy?"

"I don't touch strong liquor," Evangeline almost whispered. "I'm calm now. That—that *creature*. He's a kind of pleasant lookin' man, I guess. Average height. Dark hair. Thin. Brown eyes. And those awful glasses."

"Did he mention papers again?" Nasty asked.

Evangeline appeared disoriented. "Papers?"

"The ones he asked Rose for."

Rose answered quickly, "I wasn't asked for any papers."

"No," Evangeline said. "No papers."

"But you said—"

Roman's shake of the head stopped Phoenix.

"I took this," Evangeline said, pulling a rolled brown envelope from a pocket in her voluminous skirt. "He kept looking in here and talking about Phoenix."

She let Roman take the envelope. "Fingerprints will be lost from this by now," he said, dumping the contents in his lap. "Did you open this, Evangeline?"

"Yes, of course. The truck driver didn't know what to make of them."

"The truck driver touched these things, too?"

"He did. And his partner in the back."

"Great," Roman said, sending a significant glance in Nasty's direction. "Would you put in a call to the police, please, Miss Smothers?"

"Well—"

"We have to call in the police at this point."

She got up and meekly left the room.

Roman stared at three photographs and turned them for Phoenix to see.

Two shots of Phoenix in the sitting room of her apartment. In one she was by the window and in the act of catching the Waterford vase. In the other she was sitting with her back against the couch.

The third picture was of Roman and Phoenix at the Boarding House in Gilman Village. Phoenix tapped it. "We saw the flash."

"Yeah." Roman looked at the other two photographs. "These were taken with a telephoto from somewhere outside. Somewhere high."

"Had to be from the windmill." Phoenix stared fixedly at the photographs. "Before I got . . . Before I got my friend's call."

"And before you went outside. About fifteen or twenty minutes?"

"I guess."

A pair of thick-lensed glasses and a small brown pill bottle were the other items from inside the envelope. Roman set the glasses aside and opened the bottle.

"Ground glass," Evageline announced. "I know because I checked."

Roman checked, too, and nodded. "Little pieces. I don't get the connection."

"He said Phoenix would. He said if she didn't, he'd remind her—when he cut up her insides."

# TWENTY-ONE

Nasty's hand bore down solidly on Phoenix's right shoulder. He walked beside her into the Bend. The only sound he made was an occasional pop of his gum.

She stood still in the middle of the diner and pried his fingers loose. "I'm visiting friends, okay? You don't have to shadow me like this."

The gum made its trip from one side of his mouth to the other. Roman hadn't returned from the club the previous evening and, as threatened, Nasty had slept on Phoenix's couch. She had listened to a lot of gum popping—and lost Mel's loyal company behind her knees. Evidently her cat preferred sleeping on Nasty's stomach.

"Look. I'm grateful. You're being kind. But it's broad daylight and I'm among friends. I'm going to be fine."

"Yup. You're going to be fine."

How could such a gorgeous man be so . . . so unapproachable? "Why do you have to be with me now?"

"Roman's orders."

She faced him. "He's not your commanding officer, is he?"

"Let's get this over with and get you back where you're supposed to be."

"Supposed to be?" Sometimes one had to give up. "Excuse me." She stalked past empty tables to sit at the counter.

Zelda came from the bar into the diner, with a cleaning rag and can of polish in one hand. "I'm so embarrassed," she wailed when she saw Phoenix. "What an exhibition! And from people old enough to know better."

"Forget it," Phoenix told her, grinning. "It's kind of nice to be around people with passion." She didn't disguise the incline of her head toward Nasty.

Zelda eyed her silent visitor and said, "Good morning to you, Mr. Nasty. Can I get you coffee?"

"It's just, Nasty. No coffee, thanks."

"As you wish." Zelda shrugged. "Mort isn't feeling too good. If he was, he'd be apologizing to you for what he said yesterday."

"No need."

"What can I get you. Lunch rush is going to start in an hour. Till then, I'm all yours."

Phoenix wasn't hungry but she said, "I'll have a sugar donut and coffee."

"You going to have some time to come around and help us tonight?"

"No," Nasty announced, stealing Phoenix's voice and leaving Zelda with her mouth open. "Phoenix is busy tonight. She just came by to say hi."

Phoenix made up her mind. "Will you please excuse me? I have to go to the bathroom."

"You went before we left your apartment."

"I have to go again!"

"Better have the coffee first. Cut down on trips."

He was unbelievable. Phoenix raised her eyebrows at Zelda who smothered a grin and poured coffee—two cups. She pushed the second in front of Nasty.

Zelda picked up a pair of serving tongs and placed two sugared donuts on a plate. She put the plate between Nasty and Phoenix and instantly slapped her brow with the heel of one hand. "I was going to call Rose and get a message to you. Mort's complaining made me forget. Someone came in asking for you."

Nasty's hand slid beneath his leather jacket. He turned, looking in all directions.

"A woman," Zelda said. "Early this morning."

"Relax," Phoenix told Nasty, irritated with the constant vigil. "Not a pair of Coke bottle specs in sight."

Fortunately Zelda didn't ask for an explanation of that. She said, "Beautiful woman. Tall. Dark haired. Very mysterious-looking."

Phoenix frowned. "Foreign? Straight, black hair. Sort of a Morticia Addams look-alike? Did she say she was Countess Von Leiden?"

"No, nothing like that."

"Then I don't know her."

"She knows you," Zelda said, leaning across the counter. "I'd have given her your address, but with things being the way they are . . ." She raised both palms.

"You don't give anyone Phoenix's address," Nasty said without inflection. "Got that?"

"I just said I didn't, didn't I?" Zelda stretched upward to her full height, almost five feet. "Rudeness isn't tolerated here."

Nasty picked up his coffee and stared into it.

"The lady wouldn't give her name. She said you'd figure out who she is. She needs to see you. Wore one of those caftan things. Black and gold."

"Ilona," Phoenix breathed, suddenly excited. She slipped from her stool. "I've got to go to the club."

"No," Nasty said. "You heard Roman. You are not to go near that place. You've got an excuse to be away from work. You fell."

"I've got to see Ilona."

"You called in and said you couldn't go. You can't."

She would go. She would go the instant she figured out how to give Nasty the slip.

Zelda excused herself and went into the kitchens.

Phoenix nibbled all around the outside of her donut and searched for a brilliant way out.

Nasty produced a fresh stick of gum. While he unwrapped it, he studied the mutilated rim of her food.

Phoenix repeated the process, this time with her thumb through the hole, while she twirled the donut.

He looked at his watch and drummed the counter.

"I need to go to the bathroom," Phoenix said, extricating her sticky fingers.

"No."

"What do you mean, no?"

"No."

"This is ridiculous. I'm going."

"I'll come with you."

"What's the matter with you, Nasty?"

"You plan to go in there and get out of here without me seeing you."

She made a face. "How would I do that?"

He took her elbow and marched her toward the ladies' room. After knocking on the door, he opened it wide and they looked in at a washbasin, a toilet and, high on the wall, a window to the outside.

Phoenix sniffed.

"I rest my case," Nasty told her.

"Are you suggesting I could climb through that?"

"Yup. You ready to go home?"

Phoenix didn't get a chance to answer. Pointing through the front windows of the diner, Zelda rushed from the kitchen. "Fire!" She made for the door. "Call the station from the kitchen, Phoenix. Quick. Tell them it could be gasoline!"

Whirling about, Phoenix saw flames shooting from the roof of a sleek camper parked out front. She shrieked and dashed for the phone.

"Son-of-a-bitch," Nasty said succinctly, striding after Zelda. "My camper."

Phoenix made the call to the fire station.

She found Nellie waiting for her in the alley behind the building, with the engine of her pickup running. The route to the Peak Club was circuitous, but rapid enough. Bristling with disapproval, Nellie followed the instructions she said Zelda had given and dropped Phoenix outside the main gates. Phoenix was admitted as soon as she gave her name.

* * *

Something had changed, and the signs weren't subtle.

Roman studied Geoffrey across Vanessa's glass desk. "She told me she wanted to see me. Urgent, she said. Where is she? You've been putting me off since last night."

Geoffrey tented his fingers. "Aren't you supposed to be watching our friend, Phoenix?"

"I can't watch Phoenix and talk to Vanessa *about* Phoenix at the same time. The sooner someone tells me what's going on around here, the sooner I can get back."

"Where is she now?"

"Asleep," he lied. "She fell through the railing outside her apartment. Got hurt pretty badly." If Geoffrey and Vanessa had had something to do with Phoenix's "fall," Roman's best approach was honesty. He didn't think they had instigated the attack—which puzzled him even more.

Geoffrey pushed Vanessa's chair back and swung his Ferragamos onto the untouched surface of the desk. "We're waiting for something," he said. "But there's no harm in my telling you that we've made a very important decision. We want you in on all phases of the club. You'll give us new dimension. So will Pierre and Miles."

*Why?* "Sounds interesting. I thought you and Vanessa were adamant about the Insiders being your special baby."

"We were. We aren't now. Vanessa and I have negotiated a slightly different arrangement. I am now the senior partner. I prefer that all of my partners bear equal responsibility here. Do you have a problem with that?"

Only a sense of urgent need to find out the reason for the shift. "Mm—no. Absolutely not. I'll do anything I can to help maximize our success."

Geoffrey smiled his wolfish smile. "I knew I could count on you. Why don't you go back and watch over our little problem. I'd feel better if you were there. Call in every few hours and we'll let you know when to meet with us. All right?"

Roman stuffed down his irritation. "Sure. Any idea how long it's likely to be?"

"Not really." Geoffrey pulled out his glasses and perched

them on his nose. He took a leatherbound notebook from an inside pocket of his jacket and began to read.

Dismissed.

Roman let himself out of the office and closed the door. Going back to Phoenix was no hardship. Awaiting the pleasure of these assholes was a pain. Maybe he should get Dust, Junior and Phoenix out—now.

Phoenix wouldn't go.

Unless he told her April was dead.

He strolled aimlessly along the corridor leading to the lower floors.

If he told Phoenix April was dead he'd have to decide exactly what to say—how much.

Hell, who was he kidding? She'd refuse to leave Past Peak until justice was done.

He smiled bitterly. He'd fallen in love, dammit. After a lifetime of never letting a woman get close enough to make him want to stay in one place, he'd been helpless to stop this one. She'd climbed into his mind, into whatever his heart was, and taken over. And part of the reason was her spirit. If she knew what had happened to April, she'd never quit this place without tracking down the killer.

In the main workout room a dozen or more members sweated on various pieces of equipment. Swimmers made methodical laps of the pool. People with reasons to need better-looking bodies. Roman eyed them all with dislike. Self-indulgent empties with too much money. Their emptiness made them targets for the worst empties of all—the worst empties in the world. He had no doubt that, despite everything he'd seen and done, in this place he had come into the company of evil with as much devastating potential as any he'd known.

Trainers strolled between members, touching, chuckling, whispering in ears.

Roman turned around—and saw Phoenix slip into a room and close the door.

* * *

"Lock it," Ilona said. "Lock it and come here. Quickly." She rubbed her neck with rapid, agitated strokes.

Phoenix locked the door and jumped when the handle immediately turned, this way and that.

Ilona said, "I am in session," in an imperious voice.

"It's Roman. Let me in, please."

Phoenix shook her head sharply. Her heart clamored.

"Soon," Ilona told Roman. "We cannot be interrupted now. Should I call Sir Geoffrey? Perhaps he will explain how these things are."

The handle ceased its turning.

Only the muted sounds from the workout room penetrated the walls.

Ilona pointed upward. "I have made sure we are not seen or overheard. But I do not know how long it will be before someone comes."

A metal cylinder on a wire hung unevenly from a hole in the ceiling. "Is it broken?" Phoenix asked.

Ilona arranged herself on an ottoman. "Forget it. Where is the crystal I gave you?"

Phoenix continued to look at the wounded electronic eye.

"The crystal? You do not have it, do you?"

A sense of urgency struck at Phoenix. "Please. Tell me what you went to the Bend to say. Have you heard from April?"

"Answer my question."

"The crystal? The peridot? It's somewhere."

"Somewhere?" Ilona stretched her neck from side to side, producing a snapping sound. "I feel great danger. I told you to keep the crystal with you. You have not taken me seriously. That was a mistake."

"I don't believe in this type of stuff," Phoenix said. "I'm not being insulting, or rude. It's just not my thing."

"What is or is not your *thing* cannot always be of your choosing."

"Perhaps not. The crystal is very pretty. Thank you. I think I put it near April's vase."

Ilona closed her eyes. "The Waterford vase from the pawnshop. The vase she called her Hopes? You keep fresh flowers in it?"

Goosebumps whipped over Phoenix's skin. "You visited April in her apartment?"

"Something terrible happened to you. Not last night. The night before. Something fearsome."

Phoenix rubbed her arms.

"You are being watched. You know you are being watched because you have seen the evidence."

"Stop it."

"Why? Do I say anything that is not true?"

"You're helping him, aren't you? You're helping him victimize me."

"I do not know who he is." Ilona rose. She massaged her temples. "It is the one thing I cannot see. His face. But it will come. I know it will come. You should not have set the crystal aside."

"I've got to go."

"If you had not set aside the crystal, you might have paused a moment, perhaps to decide which pocket you should place it in."

Phoenix shook steadily. "Paused a moment when? What are you talking about?"

"Before you went outside. If you had treasured the crystal—and trusted me—you might never have opened your door and walked into a trap."

A cry escaped Phoenix. She swallowed and tried to moisten dry lips. "I've got to get out of here," she told Ilona. "Please don't try to stop me."

Ilona dropped back onto the ottoman and supported her face in her hands. "Go. Ignore me if you must."

Phoenix unlocked the door and opened it.

"There is no time now," Ilona muttered. "They will be here soon. Expect me to come to you."

She must talk to Roman, but not at the club. She must get away and reevaluate everything she'd set out to do. "What do you people hope to accomplish?" she said quietly. "If I'm a threat, why play with me? Why not just get rid of me?"

Ilona's eyes met hers. "Never speak of such things again. Go to your home and stay there. I do not know when I shall see you again. I must make preparations. When I do, I am going to tell you everything you need to know."

Running was pointless. Phoenix ran anyway. And Roman ran after her.

Her slick-soled shoes slipped on rocks and fine dirt at the edge of the trees lining the Snoqualmie River.

"Phoenix! Stop it. Stop it, now."

She saved her breath for running. In the moment when she'd seen his face—through the windshield of the Rover when he'd steered across the road to where she walked along the opposite shoulder—his rage had turned him into a stranger she didn't want to confront.

When she'd left Ilona and seen Roman talking with Geoffrey, she'd seized the opportunity to get away and return to Belle Rose. Perhaps that hadn't been such a good idea.

Willows overhung the river, and the gnarled red roots of madrona trees poked through between trickles of treacherously loose scree.

Phoenix could hear Roman breathing.

A scream bubbled free and she was helpless to swallow the sound. "Go away!" Her left foot hooked under a root and she sprawled, slashing her knees on jagged rocks.

His hand came down on the back of her calf.

"No!" Rolling away, she leaped to her feet and half-hobbled, half-ran. "I've had it with this craziness. Go away and leave me alone." A sharp turn to the right took her to a thick stand of Douglas firs.

Phoenix glanced behind her.

Roman had stopped following. He stood, his hands on his hips, staring after her.

Sobbing with relief, she plunged into the trees—and narrowly missed slamming into a sheer rockface. "Oh, darn it." Phoenix leaned on the craggy surface. "Darn, darn, darn!"

The trees had closed behind her, closed her in against the cliff. Those trees parted again, and Roman stood only feet from her.

Phoenix sniffed and crossed her arms.

"Darn it?" he muttered. "You deliberately arrange to have Nasty's van set on fire—or to have it seem as if it has been. You countermand my orders. Orders made with your welfare in mind. Then you slip away and start walking along the highway where you can be picked off like a can on a fence. And all you can think of to say is *darn it?*"

"I don't have to say anything at all to you."

"You see me following you. You see me stopping the Rover to pick you up. And you *run?* Have you completely lost it?"

Phoenix searched for an escape route.

"Don't even think about it," Roman said. He folded one big hand around her two crossed arms and lifted her skirt high enough to display her knees. "Was it worth falling on your already punished face and ruining your knees?"

"They're my knees."

"They're *my* knees, Goddamit." His face came so close she could see chips of black in his blue eyes. *"You* are mine. Every bit of you. *Mine!* Do you understand me?"

She flinched at each word and began to tremble.

"What happens to you, happens to me," he told her, his breath warm on her lips. "I'm never going to let you go. I can't. I didn't ask for this to happen, but it has and I can't help it. I have to have you, Phoenix."

The trembling changed to convulsive shaking.

"Say something, dammit!"

Phoenix tried to toss the hair away from her face. "You're so angry."

"I'm so in love."

The ground seemed a very long way below her.

"Say something. I love you. I love you. Doesn't that *mean* anything to you?"

"Wh-why?"

"Why should it mean anything to you?" His free hand slid around her neck.

"Why do you love me?"

He stared at her. "I can't believe you're asking that. A hundred men must have loved you . . . not that it got them far."

She failed to stop tears from welling. "No one loved me. No one but April."

His eyes darkened. "You think no one has loved you? Unbelievable."

"M-my mother and father were never sober. They hated me. My mother didn't speak to me. My dad said I was ugly and he wished I'd never been born." Why was she telling him all this dead history? "It doesn't matter now."

He grimaced bitterly. "Sure it does. Some time I'll tell you about my cheery childhood. It can mess you up. Nothing's going to mess up Junior's life like that."

Phoenix shook her head. "You wouldn't let it."

"I wouldn't let any of my children's lives be messed up."

A wave of lightheadedness made her sway.

Roman released her crossed arms and held her shoulders.

"You have other children?" Her voice sounded distant.

"Not yet. But we will, won't we?"

Other women heard these things. Other women heard men like Roman tell them they were loved, tell them they would have children together. Such things didn't happen to Phoenix.

He shook her gently. "Phoenix? Can you love me?"

Adrenaline, the flooding of reaction after all the fear, exploded in Phoenix. "Don't," she told him. "Don't you play with me."

"I'm not—"

"Do you think I'm a fool? Do you think I don't know you can have your pick of women—any women you want? Why are you doing this to me? Let me go! Get away!"

For an instant she thought he would. His arms dropped to his sides and he stepped back.

Fighting with branches, Phoenix slapped her way into the trees.

She never made it to the riverbank.

"That's it." Roman's arm shot around her waist and her feet left the ground. "I don't know what your trouble is, W. G., but I'm going to find out and fix it. Starting now."

He hauled her back to the wall of rock. "Look at me," he told her. "Look closely."

She looked.

"What do you see?"

"You're angry," she breathed. "I don't want you to be angry."

His eyes glittered. "Anger? That's all you see?"

Her mind refused to work properly.

Holding her head between his hands, Roman kissed her—hard and long and demanding. By the time he lifted his head she was clawing at his chest.

"Now tell me what you see?"

"I don't know what you want from me."

His features twisted. He rested his brow on hers.

"Tell me what I'm supposed to say," she begged.

"Damn you," he said through his teeth. "Damn you for letting them do this to you. I want you, Phoenix. I want to love you."

She touched his mouth with shaky fingers.

He covered her breasts with hands that weren't gentle anymore. "I want to make love to you in every way there is. There are a lot of ways, sweetheart, and we haven't even put a dent in the list."

Phoenix undid a button on his shirt, and another, and another. She felt as if she watched herself, watched both of them, from outside her own head.

"Undo your blouse," Roman told her gruffly. "And take off your bra. I want you naked."

"Here?"

"Here. The trees won't tell anyone."

Phoenix slipped a hand inside his shirt and stroked the soft hair on his chest. She leaned into him and kissed the hollow beneath a collarbone. With her thumb, she flicked a flat nipple.

Cool air hit her legs. Roman pulled her blue cotton skirt up to her hips and pushed a massive thigh between hers. She wrapped both arms around him beneath the shirt and hung on, straddling his thigh, already shuddering at the mounting pressure in her core.

Roman eased her away from him, leaned her against the rock. "Do as I asked. Take it off." He indicated her blouse.

Phoenix's fingers went to the top button. It resisted, but he made no attempt to help her. One by one, the buttons parted from their holes. Inch by inch, the same cool breeze that stroked her legs slipped across the bared tops of her breasts, her shoulders, her ribs. She had to arch her back to take the blouse off.

With his eyes on her exposed flesh, Roman spanned her waist and rocked her slowly back and forth. She drew in a hissing breath. Sensation mounted between dampening folds. Too little fabric separated her from his skin—or too much.

The blouse fell.

Roman bent. He traced the lacy edge of her bra with his tongue. "Take it off."

She hesitated.

"Do it, Phoenix."

The front fastener slid undone and the cups sprang apart. She tried to cover herself but he stopped her.

His teeth and tongue fastened on a nipple and he sucked.

Phoenix panted. She gripped his hair.

Roman supported her breasts. He lavished them with attention, murmuring, licking decreasing circles until she moaned with her need for satisfaction. Only then did he capture a pouting tip again.

"I love you." She heard her own words and squeezed her eyes shut. "I . . ." *Never make a fool of yourself for a man,* April had warned her, when they were teenagers.

"Say it again," Roman demanded. He found the wet place between her legs and tore at her already ruined pantyhose. "I want to hear you."

If she was a fool, so be it. "I love you."

The thin nylon shredded, and her silk panties. "Then we're even, my love. Oh, sweetheart, we are going to make one hell of a team."

She wanted him, needed to feel him. Her awkward fingers fumbled with his belt, and then his zipper. He let her feet slip to the ground and she released his straining penis. His chest rose and fell. His belly drew rigid. Phoenix sank her hands under the weight inside his shorts and stroked the satiny length of him to the bulging tip.

"That's it," he said, his voice cracking. "I'm losing control here."

He whipped her to face the cliff. "Rest your forearms and hold on."

Phoenix felt him dip, and then he filled her, drove past her tattered underclothes.

"But you're—" What was she saying? She knew the ways he'd talked about—the ways of making love. She'd read plenty.

"I'm what?" he asked raggedly, holding her breasts to anchor himself against her back. "I'm dying from feeling so good? You're right. Phoenix, you've got to kill me this way over and over again."

"Roman!"

"Promise you will."

"Roman! I feel . . ." Each thrust jerked her to her toes. "I *feel* you so much."

"Too much?"

"Never too much."

He gave a keening cry.

"Roman! Oh, Roman." She couldn't think of anything but his name, couldn't feel anything but the places where they touched. "Don't stop."

"I'm not stopping, sweetheart."

Her teeth snapped together. With one hand and wrist he covered her breasts. With the other hand he reached down to massage the bud so close to his own pumping flesh.

Phoenix grew stiff. She straightened her arms and forced herself backward against him. Then, when her legs would have failed her, Roman took her with him to the place they wanted to be.

In the first clamoring seconds of satisfaction, Phoenix threw her arms back to grip his neck. Roman's laugh shocked, then thrilled her. He laughed and possessed her breasts once more.

He supported her like that, her arms twined around his neck, her breasts in his hands, her legs splayed across his hips—their bodies joined—for a long time.

"I didn't use anything," he said at last.

Phoenix slowly realized what he'd said. She stretched luxuriously. "You weren't planning this."

"Wasn't I? I wonder."

She opened her eyes. "I'm not sure what you're telling me, Roman."

"Seems pretty clear." Slowly, he withdrew and turned her toward him until he could place a leisurely kiss on her mouth. "Mm. I love you. You love me. We didn't just find that out."

"We haven't known each other very long."

"We've known each other as long as it takes."

"You mean that, don't you?"

He kissed her again, smoothing her back from shoulder to waist and back. "I mean it. Don't ask me exactly how these things work, but if you're pregnant, then I'm going to die of happiness."

She grew warm, then giggly. "Don't get ahead of yourself. This isn't a soap opera. People don't get pregnant the first time."

"This isn't the first time."

"You know what I mean."

He knelt before her so suddenly, she dropped to join him without thinking.

"If I don't lie down, I'm going to fall down," he told her.

"Me, too."

Roman stretched her out on the thick bed of fir needles. He leaned over her and it all began again. And somewhere in the heat and haze of loving, he said, "Will you marry me," and Phoenix said, "This sounds so corny, but, yes. *Yes.*" And Roman said, "I'm crazy about corny."

# TWENTY-TWO

The royal summons had finally come. After three days of waiting, Roman was to meet with Vanessa.

Using the gold key Geoffrey had given him, he let himself into the Insiders Club.

He reached an elevator, used his key again, and traveled deeper into the bedrock beneath what most of the world believed was all there was of the Peak Club.

The doors slid open. He stepped out, collided with Ilona, and automatically caught her elbow.

Phoenix didn't know if Ilona was a friend or a foe. Neither did Roman. He met the psychic's eyes, searching for some clue. He found none. The woman passed him and was swept away by the elevator. Her silence felt wrong, but what could possibly feel right in this disguised pleasure house?

The room he finally entered was circular, with a circular white divan at its center, and an array of cylindrical, mirrored tables glittering beneath a crystal light shaped like a woman's body. White carpet and white walls. White everything, except for Vanessa's black sheath, Geoffrey's impeccable gray, Savile Row suit, and the green sweats worn by Miles Wilberton. The heavyset man Roman recognized as the Reverend Chester Dupree wore a white terrycloth robe.

"Come on in," Geoffrey said, too heartily. "This is Roman Wilde, Reverend. Our fifth partner."

Dupree looked Roman over. "You anyone I ought to know?"

"He's a man who prides himself on being known by very

few," Geoffrey said quickly. "Ex-SEAL. You name a decoration for valor and he's got it."

"That so?" If Dupree was impressed he must play great poker. "Gotta have money to be a partner here, right? Where'd you make your money?"

Roman rarely hated on sight. He hated this man. "I didn't," he said with total honesty.

Dupree sat on the divan and splayed his legs. He was naked beneath the robe. "I'm waitin' boy. I like to know who I'm dealin' with."

"Roman will have his little joke," Vanessa said. "His father is—or was—Arthur Wilde." Sheer black silk encased her legs. She sat down beside Dupree, revealing a long slit in her skirt— and very white skin above the lace top of a stocking.

The reverend went straight for the skin. "Arthur Wilde?" He pulled Vanessa's skirt aside. "Not the Wilde who killed his wife?" Diamonds sparkled on his thick fingers.

Long practice kept Roman's face impassive. "He was cleared of that. They'll never know if she was murdered, or if she committed suicide."

Vanessa, who showed no reaction to Dupree's intimate delving, rested a wrist on his shoulder and said, "The Wilde who turned his wife's considerable fortune into a massive fortune. The world's most successful manufacturer of toys."

The Arthur Wilde who was also dead now. No more chances for Roman to try to know the man who had brought laughter to millions of children, and misery to his only son and heir.

"Bit of a mystery about the way your father went, too, wasn't there, Wilde?"

"No, sir. No mystery. He stopped breathing and left everything he had to me." To Roman, who had never wanted any part of the Wilde financial empire. "Which is how I come to be part of this fine establishment. Vanessa, you and I need to talk."

She flashed him a silencing look. "Chester and Miles just got back from Europe."

"That's right." Dupree squeezed her thigh. "Miles knows everybody. Got me a private audience with the Pope. What d'you say to that?"

"Lucky you."

"Aren't I though? Close to him as I am to you now. Closer. All Miles had to do was say I wanted to see him and I was in. Went to a party near Paris, too. That Bridget Bardot. Fund-raiser for endangered species." He guffawed. "Everyone's got their thing, right? Different toys for different boys—and girls. How about that? Should appeal to a toy boy—right?"

Fascinated, appalled, Roman stared at the man.

Miles, who had been engrossed in a stack of photos, tossed one to the reverend and strolled forward. "Roman's got the money but not the business," he remarked, as if bored. "Sold out. Isn't that right, Roman?"

"Yes." For the first time since he'd come into the room, Roman looked directly at Miles Wilberton. *Billy.* A good-looking man. Blond—like Junior. Blue eyes, but not the heart-stopping turquoise-blue of Junior's—or April's.

Miles wrinkled his brow. "Vanessa wants me in on this. You know, the little problem?"

Roman nodded briefly.

"Duchess of York was at the party we went to in London," Dupree said, importance spilling from his shiny, pouting mouth. "Shouldn't mind helping her out of a bikini top myself, I can tell you." He lost interest in Vanessa's thighs and concentrated on the photograph Miles had passed. The lady depicted might just be in the running for a mention in some record book. The reverend said, "Whooee. Look at them apples. Get her for me, Billy."

"Will do," *Billy* said.

Three sibilant rings sounded. Vanessa got up. "There's a special treat waiting for the reverend in the showers. Why don't you take him up, Geoffrey?"

"I don't think so," Geoffrey said. "I know Chester would rather be with you, love. Run along. I'll take care of things here."

Vanessa's eyes narrowed. "Billy and I have spoken at length on this matter."

"Hey," the reverend said. "Am I going to be let in on this little secret of yours?"

Geoffrey slapped his back indulgently. "No secret. Just housekeeping. Boring stuff. Vanessa's going to stay with you through your entertainment, aren't you, Vanessa? She's been working too hard. Make sure she has a good time."

Dupree hauled himself off the divan. "My pleasure," he said, settling a hand on the back of Vanessa's neck. "Lead the way, Countess. I'm going to make sure you have the time of your life."

They left, but not before Vanessa turned a venomously tight-lipped face on Geoffrey. "Take care of business," she told him. "Later, you and I will take care of some business."

"Finally," Geoffrey said when the door closed again. "Tell him, Miles."

"The party that asshole talked about. The one in London. I heard someone talking about this female the FBI uses on certain kinds of cases."

"I thought Vanessa said it was in Italy."

Miles appeared momentarily confused. "Italy. Yes, it was Italy. We did so much in a few days. That old bastard's voracious, I can tell you. If he's not doing it, he's watching it and begging for it."

"You heard something in Italy?" Roman asked.

"Yes, yes," Miles agreed. "This chap said something about how he'd run into trouble with a certain operation. Providing diversions for certain Middle Eastern clients. American diversions. Caucasian. Ordinary stuff, but some little intelligence fart picked up on it and decided to make a name for himself."

Roman shoved his hands into his pockets. At least while they were there they couldn't grab the man's throat. "Is this going somewhere?"

"No reason to be shirty, old man," Geoffrey said. "Have a little patience."

"Anyway," Miles went on, sounding aggrieved. "The intelligence fart planted a female who blew the whole thing wide open. Something about her carrying a camera in some unmentionable place and taking pictures inside the tent, so to speak. Cut a long story short—the female was known as Phoenix. Redhead with green eyes. Played the naive young thing to a tee. Fooled the gentleman I was talking to, I can tell you."

"And you think our masseuse is one and the same Phoenix? That's asinine. She'd hardly run around using the identical name, would she?"

"We know you're inside the lady's knickers," Geoffrey said, the corners of his mouth jerking down. "If you weren't, you'd probably think more clearly. Maybe we should all find out what's so bloody irresistible there. She must have screwed your brains out through your ears, old chap."

"And I repeat, according to this story, she used the same name for two covert operations," Roman said, no longer having difficulty holding his temper. Cold reason had taken over his emotions. "Explain that, please."

Miles make a sputtering sound. "The chap in Italy got the name from a source he couldn't mention. She wasn't actually calling herself Phoenix on the job."

"So, why is she using the name here?"

Geoffrey pushed out his lips. "Probably doesn't intend to use it again. We've got to protect ourselves. You do see that, Roman?"

Every step must be calculated and calculated as quickly as possible. "Naturally. How should we proceed? Should I ask some careful questions?"

"Absolutely not!" Geoffrey pushed his jacket aside and laced his hands behind his back. He stalked across the room and hooked the stopper off a decanter on top of one of the mirrored tables. "I can't believe you'd suggest such a thing. You'd tip our hand and she'd be in touch with her people before we could regroup."

"Phoenix needs to go away, Roman," Miles said. "Far, far away. We'd like you to arrange that."

Roman studied his fingernails. "Where do you want her to go?"

"Don't be bloody obtuse," Geoffrey snapped. He poured himself a hefty scotch and didn't offer drinks to Miles and Roman.

"In other words, you want me to murder her."

"For God's sake!" Miles made the mistake of grabbing Roman's arm.

Roman threw him off with enough force to send the man staggering against the divan. "I say." He overbalanced and sprawled on the white velvet.

"I don't like being touched by men," Roman told him dispassionately. "No problem. We must make sure nothing jeopardizes the integrity of this club. Consider the business taken care of."

Looking deeply wounded, Miles gathered himself and stood up again. "When? And how?"

Roman addressed Geoffrey alone. "We don't know if she's got another operative in the vicinity. I haven't noticed anything, but it's always possible. I want to take enough time to make sure she's working alone."

Geoffrey nodded.

"That means we should allow her to continue working—coming and going—as if nothing's been noticed. Are we agreed?"

"Look here, Vanessa wants—"

"Stuff it, Miles," Geoffrey said. "Agreed. Business as usual until she's lulled into believing we don't suspect her of anything?"

"We think alike," Roman said.

"Vanessa wants her dead now." Miles's chin jutted. He glared at Geoffrey. "Tell him to get on with it."

"Vanessa's not in charge anymore. I am. Proceed however you feel most comfortable, Roman."

"I'll do that."

"What the fuck happened between you and Vanessa?" Miles asked, his face red. "Pierre knows, doesn't he?"

"Pierre helped Vanessa and me come to an agreement we can both live with. That's all as far as you're concerned. Now, if you'll both excuse me?"

"Ciao," Roman said, slouching on one leg. The temptation to beat the shit out of both of them, right here and now, was titillating but under control—barely. "I'll let you know when it's time to view the body."

If he touched her, she'd probably attack. "I told you I've got everything worked out, sweetheart. Relax, will you? Come here and let me hold you."

Phoenix broke her stride to send him an amazed stare. "Let you hold me? You agreed to bump me off."

"For an FBI operative, you use remarkably unprofessional lingo."

"I'm not amused."

"Neither am I. I came here as soon as I could to discuss this with you because we've got to work out a plan."

An old, pale green T-shirt didn't quite cover her black panties. When he'd arrived to relieve Nasty, she'd been fast asleep. Her return to snapping awareness was admirable. Her elegant bare feet and long bare legs—and the soft sway of her unrestrained breasts—were equally captivating.

"Phoenix, we know exactly what they're planning. That's good news."

"They're planning to kill me. Great news."

"But *I'm* supposed to do it! And they're convinced I'll choose exactly the right moment. We're in the driver's seat."

"One thing goes wrong, and *I'm* in a hearse."

He'd misjudged what her reaction would be. He'd scared her, dammit. "Sweetheart, I will not let anything happen to you."

"How did they find out what I'm trying to do?"

Roman captured one of her hands and pulled her against him. "I have absolutely no idea how they know. They didn't tell me. They haven't told me they know anything about you looking for April. All they've said is that you work for the FBI and that you're investigating the club."

"That's stupid." Her eyes gleamed. "How could they think you'd be dumb enough to swallow that bunk?"

"Possibly because they think I am dumb? They didn't take me on for my brains, kiddo. They took me on as a killer with bucks who could provide a few thrills for anyone willing to pay for them."

"The FBI stuff's a cover," she muttered. "They know about April."

*No kidding?* "If they do—and I agree with you that it seems likely—but if they do, we're going to turn this on them and use it to get the information we want."

"How could they find out?" Her teeth dug into her lower lip and the gleam in her eyes turned to a sheen. "How could they even suspect I was anything to do with April unless someone told them?"

He shook his head, then, slowly, released her hand. "Are you suggesting I told them?"

Phoenix put a hand over her mouth.

"Are you?"

"Someone did. That's all I know."

"And you think it could have been me?"

She took a step toward him.

"No," he told her, backing away. "No. I don't believe this."

"Can't you put yourself in my place? Can't you imagine where I'm coming from?"

"I'm going into Seattle," he told her. "I'll get Nasty to come back. You'd better go to bed before it's time to get up again."

"Roman, don't leave until we've talked this out."

"Talked it out? If I don't get out of here I'm going to do something I'll regret?"

"What?" She advanced again. "Hit me? Kill me now and get it over with?"

"Hit you?" he said softly. *"Kill* you? Can you even ask questions like that?"

When she pushed at her hair, her hands shook. "I don't know

what I'm saying or doing. I'm frightened, darn it." Tears slipped down her cheeks. "I'm frightened out of my wits."

"I'd noticed. Isn't this the perfect time for you to turn on me? The perfect time to suggest the man who loves you—the man you've agreed to marry—could hurt you?" He took his mini-radio from his jacket pocket and asked Nasty to come back.

"Roman—"

He cut her off. "We need to do a lot of talking. But not before you decide whether we're friends or enemies. Friends and lovers, or enemies. I'll let you be the one to decide. Do it quickly."

"Don't go."

Turning away when she sounded so broken all but destroyed him. "You've already sent me away, Phoenix."

# TWENTY-THREE

Climbing out of the bedroom window hadn't been the cinch Phoenix had expected. Slivers from the sill, embedded in her palms, made holding the steering wheel painful.

At the gas station in town she pulled in and ran to use the phone. Roman's answering machine picked up. Listening to his voice, she felt as if she'd been punched. How could she have been such a fool? She loved him. He loved her. She knew it with her heart and soul. Why had she allowed her brain to interfere with instinct? Her brain and the old patterning from times she should have learned to forget?

The message finished. "Just Phoenix," she said, hardly able to breathe. "I'm sorry. I'll reach you—"

"Don't hang up." He came on the line and she knew he must be screening his calls. "Where are you?"

"Past Peak. The gas station."

"Where's Nasty?"

"Asleep. I waited till he stopped popping his gum."

Silence.

"I climbed out of the bedroom window."

More silence.

"I am so scared, Roman. But I love you more than I'm scared. I can't stand it if you're upset with me."

"If I told you I thought you'd be prepared to kill me, would you be upset?"

"Don't be silly."

"Mm."

"Can we talk?"

"Look around you very carefully."

The hair on her neck prickled. "You're frightening me."

"Do as I tell you."

At a little after eight in the morning, the area was deserted except for a boy filling containers with blue paper towels to clean windshields. "There's nobody."

"You shouldn't have left your apartment like that."

It was Phoenix's turn to say nothing.

"Drive into Seattle. It should take you—an hour at the most, maybe. I want to meet you away from my place. I've got to be sure you aren't followed."

She was close to tears. "Just tell me where." He mustn't hear her cry again. Already she'd shown how weak she was.

"You know the Westlake Center?"

"I can find it."

"Get there. Ride the escalators up. If you don't see me by the time you get to the food court, walk around. Buy coffee. People watch. Then ride down. Repeat the process if necessary."

"Then what?"

"Just do it." The line clicked off.

Phoenix left the phone booth. It was going to be a pretty day, warm. She glanced about her again and hurried to the Chevy.

She drove fast. The road out of the Cascade foothills wound sharply in places, but she couldn't make herself slow down. All that mattered was getting to Roman and making him believe she hadn't been herself when she'd closed him out.

Few vehicles were on the road. Phoenix hadn't made the drive into Seattle before. When she'd arrived in the area she'd spent one night in the city, then gone straight to Past Peak. Issaquah was the farthest she'd driven in the return direction.

She remembered the area in front of the Westlake Center. Steel bands and flower stalls, hellfire preachers and a fountain you could walk through. There should be no difficulty finding the place.

A black car pulled out of a logging road and fell in behind

her. Phoenix noted the darkly tinted windows and knew a moment of fresh panic.

This morning she'd panic at the sound of her own voice.

The radio would only crackle. She turned it off.

On a straight stretch of road, a white Camry overtook the black car, and Phoenix.

The black sports car was low, and shiny new—fast.

Why didn't it overtake, too?

She traveled on toward the Carnation turnoff.

The black car stayed where it was—close enough to make Phoenix hope she didn't have to brake unexpectedly.

Ahead lay the right turn leading to Redmond. Phoenix deliberately drove onto the shoulder at the side of the road, left her engine running, and pretended to search her glove compartment.

She felt the black car draw level.

It also stopped.

Her engine started to miss.

Phoenix slammed the glove compartment shut and glanced to her left.

The passenger window on the black car slid smoothly down and she looked at a man wearing thick glasses over a dark woolen ski mask.

The window slid up again and the car turned right in front of her—toward Redmond.


He was gone. Really gone. Every second, all the way from the Redmond turnoff, Phoenix had checked her rear-view mirror. She'd been certain the car would appear again. It hadn't.

By the time she left I-90 for I-5 and Seattle, traffic was dense and she began to feel safe again. The object had been to scare her and that object had been achieved, but at least for a while, the danger was behind her. Soon she'd see Roman.

Phoenix took the Madison Street exit and swung over the freeway toward the heart of the city. Sun sparkled off mirrored office buildings—blue, rose, black, steel gray. She made the first right she came to, on Sixth Avenue, and knew she should have asked Roman for directions.

Flowers caught her attention. Plantings along walls outside the Seattle Sheraton Hotel. She entered the drive-through and waited for a green-liveried valet to jog around to her window.

The Westlake Center was on Pine, he told her, giving directions to get there. She could drive around the block, park under the Pacific Center, and easily walk the rest of the way.

People teemed across every intersection. When Phoenix finally drove into the garage under the Pacific Center she no longer cared that gripping the steering wheel hurt. She had to get to Roman before he decided she wasn't coming.

Row after row of parking spaces was full.

She drove slowly around ramps, looking left and right, and found a spot opposite the elevators.

Patience was the key. Patience, not panic. Roman wouldn't leave before she got there.

Making a mental note of the parking floor, Phoenix headed for the elevator, tucking her keys away as she went. Once inside, she punched the button for the street level.

The doors began to close.

Phoenix stared toward her car. A man leaned against the trunk. He wore dark clothes, and thick glasses threaded into a black ski mask.


Roman rested his forearms on the third floor railings inside the Westlake Center. He held a bus schedule open before him. Workers and shoppers choked the escalators. He watched every fresh rider who stepped on at the floor below. Behind him he heard the rush of monorail cars arriving from the Seattle Center. The elevated tracks terminated at Westlake.

Phoenix had called well over an hour earlier.

Anger had faded. He'd walked in and told her he was supposed to be her executioner and she'd freaked. Reasonable enough. She wasn't used to moving in circles where people threatened her life. He was. Maybe if he hadn't been, he wouldn't have been so quick to lose his temper and leave.

A stream of passengers from the monorail poured through glass doors and into the center.

Even if the traffic was heavy, she should be here by now.

Roman saw a flash of red hair two floors below. Red hair and a red sweat jacket. Relief made him smile. Relief and the anticipation that came whenever he knew she'd soon be close enough to touch.

Still holding the schedule open, he turned his back to the escalators, and watched reflections in shop windows. She got off the escalator, hesitated, and walked toward the busy food court counters. He waited a few seconds before setting off in the direction that would bring him behind her.

She didn't buy coffee.

On the second lap of the floor, he fell in with a crowd and made an opportunity to slip a hand under her arm. "I thought we'd take the bus," he said pleasantly. "Shall we?"

Her eyes, turned up to his face, were huge. "Yes."

They rode down the escalators until he could guide her onto the mezzanine above the bus tunnel.

"I was followed."

He gripped her arm tighter. "You're sure?"

"Sure. He's mad. Completely mad."

"Who?"

"Ski mask. Thick glasses."

"Shit."

"He drove behind me from just outside Past Peak." She sounded breathless. They ran down a flight of steps to the bus level. "Then he turned off toward Redmond. I thought I'd seen the last of him, but after I parked my car he was watching me when I got on the elevator."

Roman walked them rapidly to the right bus stop and maneuvered into the middle of a group of waiting passengers.

"So he got on the elevator with you?"

Phoenix leaned against him. "No. He just watched. It doesn't make any sense, but I think all he wants to do is keep scaring me."

Roman considered that. "Because he could have got at you by now?"

"He already did get at me. He could have killed me that first night, or raped me, but he didn't do either. Today it would have been easy to follow me onto that elevator. I was alone."

He couldn't argue with her logic. "You may be right. I think the next bus should be ours." Lowering his voice further, he said, "We'll get off in the International District and double back to my place by cab."

A bus sporting a flying-pigs paint job rumbled into view. People jostled forward and Roman put his arm around Phoenix's shoulders.

"Do we need change for the fare?" she asked.

He shook his head. "It's free downtown."

The shove came without warning. A shove that caught him off guard and made him stagger sideways.

Roman swung around.

A woman screamed.

*Phoenix!*

The collective cry of a dozen people arose, a giant gusting gasp. The colors of their clothing, their bodies, swayed and merged and jerked.

Roman pushed forward, launched himself after a falling splash of red.

Between shining headlights yawned the wide grin of the lead pink pig. The howling squeal was not the pig's, but that of the brakes.

Phoenix hit the ground in front of the bus and rolled. She hadn't stopped rolling when Roman reached her. "Let me do the work," he breathed.

Praying a second bus wouldn't overtake the first, he scooped her up in one arm and threw them both past the skidding vehicle.

Phoenix wrapped her arms around his head.

They came to a thudding stop against the hard tiles of the opposite wall and slumped there, gasping.

Her wrists were still looped over his head. Trying to protect him. Roman gripped her so tightly, she moaned. Still he squeezed.

"Someone deliberately pushed me out of the way to get to you," he said into her hair.

Phoenix nodded against his chest. "You saved me. He wanted me dead this time. And he wanted you to see it happen."

Slowly Roman became aware of an excited babble. The bus driver arrived, followed by a stream of gabbling passengers.

"You could have been killed," the driver shouted. "What the hell did you think you were doing?"

"I was—"

"She tripped," Roman said brusquely. "Calm down. We're sorry you got a scare."

The driver swiped at his sweating face. "You must have been too close to the edge."

"She probably was," Roman agreed. "We're all shaken up. Can we get on with it now?"

It took several minutes before they were seated on the bus with Phoenix next to the window. She leaned against Roman and clung to his arm.

"It was deliberate," he muttered.

"He hit me behind the knees and they buckled." Phoenix glanced up at him. "Did you see him?"

"No. But I probably wouldn't know him, would I?"

She frowned.

The bus rolled forward. "He wouldn't be likely to trip around in an April crowd wearing a ski mask, would he?"

"Of course not. I wasn't thinking."

Roman was thinking. There was another element in all of this, an element potentially more dangerous than the one presented by the Peak Club. He had been ordered to find a way to kill Phoenix. One death was all that was required, so why were there two hit men?

Ahead lay the tunnel.

Roman smiled tightly at Phoenix and they both looked out of the window.

Time was running out.

In the instant before the bus shot into the dark underpass, a lone man waved from the platform. He wore a stocking cap pulled down to his ears, and a muffler over his nose and mouth. His eyes were blurred pinpricks behind thick-lensed glasses.

The cab dropped them at an entrance to Pike Place Market— beside the bronze statue of a large pig. Phoenix eyed the statue with distaste and made a wide circle to avoid getting too near.

Roman paid the cab driver and caught up. He inclined his head to the pig. "That's Rachel," he said. "Most people think she's cute. You look as if you think she's going to bite."

"Or run me over," she told him loudly. "From now on I'm not going to think pigs are cute." Stall owners hawked fruit and vegetables, held up great fresh fish, shouted to prospective customers. The din and the crush agitated Phoenix.

"Come in here." Roman yanked her into a shop, all but pulled her from her feet. "We're going to buy something for Junior."

Phoenix stared at him. "Now?"

He picked up a toy set of brightly painted false teeth and turned a key in one metal jaw hinge. His reward was an explosion of clacking.

"They're awful," Phoenix said. "Junior would cry."

He wasn't listening. Instead, he concentrated intently on the ebb and flow of shoppers outside the windows.

"Junior's too young for this stuff," Phoenix said, hearing the shake in her own voice. "You're not sure we've lost him, are you?"

"Yes, I am. I just want to make absolutely certain."

She touched a black plastic beetle and leaped away when it hopped, and hopped, and hopped until it collided with a stuffed chicken that looked too real.

The chicken squawked and tipped onto her nose. An egg rolled out.

"There's a back way," Roman said, taking her hand. "Let's use it."

The emaciated young man behind a counter didn't even look up when Roman took Phoenix into a storeroom and unlocked a door leading to an alley. The door latched behind them and he moved swiftly, looking back from time to time.

When they finally passed through green metal gates into a lushly planted courtyard, Phoenix realized they'd been criss-crossing the same ground. She remembered passing the gates several times before. They only opened after Roman keyed in a code.

He lived on the top floor of the four-story, red brick building—the entire top floor.

Roman let her into a huge, almost unfurnished apartment. She walked across pale, highly polished wooden floors that formed a semicircular platform around a sunken room. Dark green carpet covered a lower level banded on its opposite, bowed wall, with undraped floor to ceiling windows. A single navy blue leather wing chair faced the outside panorama.

"What a beautiful place," Phoenix murmured, stepping down to the carpet. No buildings impeded his view of a great bay that glittered beneath the sun. "Puget Sound?"

"Elliott Bay."

She shuddered at the gleaming beauty of snow-capped peaks sharply defined against a pale blue sky. "Growing up in New York I only saw pictures of mountains. The first time I saw the Alps I was amazed, but the Cascades are gorgeous."

"Those are the Olympics," he told her. "The Cascades are behind us. I've got wine and beer and pop. Or I could make coffee."

Phoenix turned to look at him. In a vaguely rumpled and dust-streaked white cotton shirt, and well-washed jeans with oily marks on the knees, he still managed to make his spectacular surroundings pale. His hair had grown longer and become curlier. The late spring sunshine had already raised a sheen on his tanned skin, making his eyes impossibly blue—his square teeth very white.

The churning within Phoenix, brought a flush to her body. Desire.

She'd always assumed that women didn't lust after men. After all, she'd never lusted—until Roman.

He cocked his head, returned her direct stare.

Phoenix lusted for Roman Wilde.

"Oh God." She faced the windows again. This time she didn't see the scenery.

His hands settled on her shoulders. "Still frightened?"

"Not the way you mean."

He chafed her upper arms. "Tell me, my love. Let me help you."

Phoenix slowly closed her eyes. "I'm frightened of what you make me feel."

His hands grew still.

"All I have to do is see you and I want you," she told him. "Frosty Phoenix has turned into a sex maniac."

He didn't laugh.

Neither did Phoenix.

Very gently, he tipped her to rest against his chest and folded his arms around her. "I am one lucky man—to have you. I could have gone through life without meeting you. *That* thought frightens me."

"I may come to regret telling you this," she said, "but I never wanted a man before I met you. I mean I never met a man who could make me feel I wanted to share all of myself. Does that make sense?"

He slid his hands beneath her jacket to cover her breasts. "I already know you never gave yourself to a man before me."

"That's not what I said, I said—"

"That you hadn't met someone you wanted to share yourself with. Thank God for that. I wouldn't have met you if you had."

"Maybe not."

"Definitely not, sweetheart. You'd still be with him."

She hung onto his wrists. "We've got to decide what to do next, haven't we?"

"Uh-huh. You hungry?"

"No."

"Neither am I. Wine?"

"A little. If it's white."

"Come and help me."

The kitchen—all granite and steel—appeared unused. From an almost empty refrigerator he produced an unopened bottle of Chardonnay and used a corkscrew on a pocket knife to pull the cork. He had only one glass—red plastic with a band of Santa faces at the rim.

"There's a mug," he said, opening the dishwasher to reveal the mug and very little else.

"We'll share Santa," Phoenix told him, smiling a little. "Do you intend to turn this lovely place into a home?"

He filled the glass and set down the bottle. Looking into her eyes, he said, "Do you like it here?"

Phoenix spread her arms. "Who wouldn't?"

"Then we'll turn it into a home. There are four bedrooms and three bathrooms. The floors below me have two units apiece. The builder intended this one for himself then changed his mind."

*They would turn it into a home.* "I wish we could just forget everything that's happening." Instantly she was overcome with guilt for not wanting to think about finding April. "But we can't yet."

"No." He passed her on his way back to the living room. "Follow me, madam. This way for the next tour."

Phoenix followed him but the tour terminated at the first bedroom he reached. There he'd accumulated a few items supposedly designed to bring him some comfort.

"You haven't unpacked anything"—she eyed a heap of cardboard packing boxes and an open hide-a-bed precisely covered with a khaki blanket, a turned down white sheet, and topped by two pillows—"Do you sleep on that?"

"I haven't had time to shop for anything much." Setting the wine on a packing box that served as his bedside table and bore a telephone, he moved to close the hide-a-bed.

"Don't," Phoenix insisted. She shrugged out of her sweat jacket, kicked off her sneakers, and climbed to sit against the pillows. Grinning, she patted the space beside her. "Come on. It's like camping out. Fun."

Roman appeared uncertain.

"Come *on*," Phoenix said, teasing gently. "It'll be easier to share the wine this way."

Shedding his own shoes, Roman lowered himself beside her and stretched out his long legs. "Sun's decided to hide," he said. More undraped windows covered the side of the room that faced the bay. "It could even rain."

"Fine with me." Phoenix snuggled against him. "I like rain."

As if the skies heard her and approved, gray clouds drifted to cast shifting shadows over the water, and a few huge raindrops spattered the glass.

Roman offered Phoenix the red glass and didn't take his hand away while she drank. She put her fingers over his and watched him watching her.

Their hands remained entwined when he swallowed some of the dry wine.

"Go away, world," Phoenix sighed.

He grimaced. "It's not going to. There are some things I need to tell you. Some of them aren't going to be easy."

"You don't have to tell me anything that doesn't feel good."

"We can't have secrets, Phoenix. Not if we're going to make it work—make you and me work."

She touched his mouth, played her fingertips over his lower lip. He caught her forefinger between his teeth and flicked it with his tongue.

Phoenix drew her tummy tight. He made it hard to think at all. "Why do you have Junior in Issaquah rather than here with you? Dusty doesn't have custody, does he?"

"No. But she might not be safe with me at the moment. I'm not one of them, Phoenix. Not one of the Peak Club group."

"You're a partner."

"Only to get what I want."

She couldn't bring herself to ask what that was. "I'm there to find April. No other reason. I think I might like to practice law again—public prosecution, probably."

"Sounds like you"—he tipped the wine to her lips once more—"I can't imagine you in some sleek and sleazy defense lawyers' outfit."

"Why did you join the SEALs?"

"To infuriate my father."

She took the glass from him and drank deeply. "You didn't like your father?"

"I hated him."

"Something we have in common."

"My father made a huge fortune out of toys. My mother was rich before they married. Her money gave him his financial start, but it was his own inventions that got Arthur Wilde off the ground and into the big time."

"Arthur Wilde." She screwed up her eyes. "Not the Wilde of—yes, of course. Wilde Toys. That's your father?"

"Was my father. He died several years ago. He never liked me, either. My mother did, but she liked the bottle better. You see before you an orphan. Pitiful, ain't it?"

Making fun of the things that hurt most was a familiar ploy to Phoenix. "It is pitiful. It's horrible and sad. No child should be abandoned. And you don't have to be alone to be abandoned—just ignored, or used when it's convenient, then pushed away again."

He held up an arm. "That was me, ma'am. Used for convenience, then pushed away again. 'This is our son, Roman. Meet Mr. and Mrs. Blah, Blah, Roman. Shake hands nicely. Don't bang the door when you leave the room.' I still remember the night when I did bang the door. My genteel father beat the crap out of me. I had to stay home from school and lie facedown on my bed for three days."

Phoenix balled her fists. "Why didn't your mother stop him?"

"Don't ask me. She never did, that's all. She just drank more and more gin and tonics. More gin. Less tonic."

"We really do have a lot in common," she told him bitterly. "Except my mother drank the same beer as my father and neither of them ever had a nickel."

"Father wanted me in the business. I cut out right after college and joined the navy. Then went into the SEALs."

"Why did you decide to get out of the navy?"

He took the glass from her, drained it and placed it beside the phone. "Things happened. Things I hadn't expected."

Of course. "Junior?"

"In a way." He turned his searingly blue eyes on her. "It was time for a career move."

"But you didn't want to go into your father's business?"

"I'd already sold it. I sold it right after his death. He drove off a bridge and drowned. My mother died two years before him. At first he was accused of shooting her. Later he was exonerated. You never heard about the case?"

"It rings a bell." She wanted to hold him. "They couldn't decide whether or not it was suicide, could they?"

"No. I think it was. I also think that if my father hadn't felt like a bloodsucker for using my mother's money, he wouldn't have been such an angry man. And I believe he loved her. End of subject."

End of subject. He must be the one to decide when and if to discuss his life. Phoenix knew how that went. "What made you decide to buy into the Peak Club?"

"It was the right thing to do at the time. I didn't get to mention Ilona. I saw her yesterday afternoon."

Phoenix drew her feet beneath her and gave him her complete attention. "At the club?"

"Getting onto an elevator in the Insiders."

"What did she say?"

He gave her an assessing look. "Nothing. That's what bothers me. There was something about the way she avoided seeing me. Seeing me, not looking at me. She looked at me. It was as if she was afraid I might be dangerous to her." He pulled her into his arms. "Hell, I don't know. I'm probably getting fanciful. But I do believe we need to be careful of her. The only reason she could have for taking you aside was to pump you for any leads about your connection to April. She'd do that for Geoffrey and Vanessa, I suppose."

Phoenix tucked her head under his chin. "I guess it could have been Ilona who told them I was trying to find out where April is."

He stroked her hair. "I found a way to buy into the club for the same reason as you. For the same reason you went there supposedly looking for a job."

Phoenix splayed the fingers of her left hand on his chest. "The same reason? I didn't go there because I wanted a career change."

"Neither did I."

"What then?" Pushing away a little, she studied his face. "What are you trying to tell me?"

"I'm there because of April, too."

Phoenix swallowed and coughed. She took several seconds to catch her breath and say, "I don't understand."

"This isn't easy. I met April in Mexico. Not far from Tijuana. In the desert."

A violent rattle of rain on the windows momentarily startled Phoenix. She looked over her shoulder at panes awash with driving, almost horizontal rivulets.

"Early last year," Roman continued. "That's when I met her."

"In Mexico?" Phoenix said quietly. "But you lost track of her."

He pulled the khaki blanket from beneath them and settled it over their jean-clad legs. "Seems chilly," he remarked distantly.

"You lost track of April and went to Past Peak looking for her."

"I went to Past Peak to find out about her."

He was making a distinction but she wasn't sure what it was. "Why? Did you . . . Every man who ever saw April wanted her." As soon as she'd uttered the words she was horrified.

"I didn't want April—not in that way. There wasn't time."

Phoenix scooted to kneel beside him "You're at the club to find out about April. Why? To find out what about her?"

His gaze settled on her mouth, then lowered. He didn't reply.

"Roman." Phoenix framed his jaw and waited for him to look

at her again. "Why did you follow her to Past Peak and what did you want to find out about her."

He removed her hands carefully and held them between his. "I went to Past Peak because I wanted to know where it had all started. What happened before she left for wherever it was and went on her way to Mexico."

Phoenix's heart did strange things. Fear swelled, made her breath harder and faster. "Do you know where she is now?"

"In a way." His eyelids squeezed shut. "She's dead."

# TWENTY-FOUR

The two girlish faces in the photo smiled at a world they were sure they could beat. At sixteen, Phoenix had been a stick waif, but already beautiful. And her hair hadn't changed. Even then she'd walked through life with a mad red halo.

April Clark's face and figure could have been her fortune. Roman looked at her image and knew it had played a part in killing her. Shining honey blond hair. Eyes the color of deep tropical waters over blue coral. A full, laughing mouth bracketed by twin dimples. And, even at sixteen, April had been no stick.

Roman turned the picture over and read, "April and me. Coney Island."

The door to the ladies' room at Round the Bend opened and Phoenix came out. Roman returned the picture she'd given him to the inside pocket of his jacket.

Twenty-four hours had passed since he'd broken the news of April's death to Phoenix. First she'd cried—until there were no more tears. Then she'd slept. The hours he spent holding her in his spartan bedroom at the condo had been the sweetest he remembered. The sweetest and the most bitter. As yet he'd evaded her questions about exactly how April had died, and he hadn't admitted that Junior was her child. He'd have to find the courage and the inspiration. Most of all the inspiration that would allow him to lessen the shock.

Some of the signs of grief had faded from her face, but not from her shadowed eyes. She slid onto the stool beside his at the bar.

"How are you doing?" he whispered, holding her hand on his thigh.

"I'm beginning to feel mad. Maybe that's good."

Maybe it was damned dangerous. "Mad about what?"

She snorted. "You know about what. Those people had something to do with April dying, didn't they? That's why you're here and that's why they want to get rid of me. They're afraid I'm going to get them into trouble and spoil their nasty, lucrative setup."

"I guess that about sums it up." Worry gnawed at him. "Promise me you won't make a move we don't plan together first."

She picked up the mug of coffee Zelda had brought and drank. "Tell me what happened to her."

"She didn't . . . She wasn't alone when she died."

"You were with her?"

"I've already said I was."

"Why won't you tell me the rest?"

He kissed her cheek. "She wasn't thinking about herself. She was very special."

"I know. You're not going to tell me, are you?"

"Give me some time, Phoenix." Not that time would make the truth any prettier.

"I need to break it to Rose."

"Not yet!" He lowered his voice. "Under no circumstances must you tell anyone yet. Okay?"

"Okay." Her mug smacked the bar. "They're going to have good reason to wish me dead."

Roman flexed his tense shoulders. "Give me that promise, Phoenix. Not one step without me."

"I don't plan to do anything foolish."

"*Promise* me."

"I promise."

Relieved, he sighed. "Thank you. Your friends seem in high spirits."

Len, who hardly took his eyes from Phoenix, had already been at the Bend when they arrived. Holding up the bar, he'd ordered drinks all around and insisted Phoenix and Roman be included.

"Hey, Mort," Phoenix said, beckoning to him. "What's all the fuss about?"

"Len," Mort said, shrugging, but grinning. "He didn't tell us, but he almost lost his place."

"He owns Up the Creek," Phoenix told Roman.

"Yeah. I know. The truck stop out of town."

"Seems business has really picked up," Mort explained. "And they're going to use Up the Creek in a movie. The movie company paid Len so much money he may even get out of the business altogether and invest in something new. What d'you think about that?"

"Great, I guess," Phoenix said. She raised her mug and shouted, "Congratulations, Len."

His grin slipped a little but he called back, "Thanks, honey. You'll have to let me buy you dinner. And your brother, if he wants to come." The look he sent Roman was anything but friendly.

A familiar voice drew Roman's attention to the TV mounted above one end of the bar.

"Chester Dupree," he said to Phoenix. "That guy is pure slime."

"Slime deserves better press," Phoenix commented.

"The Pope was interested in what I had to say," Chester announced. "We were together for more than an hour, my brothers and sisters. This troubled world is bringing together the old and the new. The old is worn out and worried. The old is looking to the new for inspiration and advice. *I* am the new. The Reverend Chester Dupree and The Church of the Only Saved, are the new wave and we invite all of you to ride on that heavenly wave. We invite you to travel all the way to the shores of paradise with us."

"Crap," Roman muttered.

"Bridget Bardot? You remember that little lady? Her concern is for the animals, the weak animals who can't look out for themselves. She's fighting for their rights and I take my hat off to her. But I'm fighting for the weak among my own brothers and sisters." Dupree pointed straight at the camera. "You and you and you. I want your souls for the Lord."

"Snake," Phoenix said. "Lying, phony, sacrilegious snake."

"I'm goin' on another crusade. Last year proved how the folks at the heart of this fine country haven't lost their roots in the Lord. Simple, honest people who want a chance to join hands for the good of the world."

Len, who had an arm draped around Nellie, sent up a whoop. "Another round on me, everybody!"

"I do believe our Leonard is becoming looped," Zelda said in her charmingly accented English. "No doubt we shall have an overnight guest."

"You'd better," Phoenix said lightly.

The reverend continued to rail, "I'm comin' back. I'm comin' back to the roots of this great country. The heartland is where I must seek my inspiration to continue. And I know you'll all help me find what I need to continue my work. The lines are open, brethren. Call with your pledges. Call from Iowa. Call from Nebraska. Call from Kansas. Help bring me back to you, my brothers and sisters. Bring me and I'll bring your salvation. Bring—"

The channel clicked to a boxing match.

"Thank goodness," Phoenix said. "What a horrible man he is."

"Well," Mort said, rising to his toes to see past Roman. "Look who's here. Twice in one night. I don't believe it. Never came in at all before."

Roman and Phoenix turned together.

Web was making his way between crowded tables to the bar. To the bar and to Phoenix.

"Rose said you told her you were coming here," he said when he arrived at her side. He nodded to Roman but his bright blue eyes quickly returned to Phoenix's face. "The police came to Belle Rose. We thought you'd want to know what they've found out."

Roman leaned across Phoenix. "Thanks for coming. What did they say?"

"They found out what was in the bottle. You know, the bottle Evangeline brought back with the photos of Phoenix?"

"We know the bottle you're talking about."

"Doesn't mean anything, I guess," Web said, passing a hand over his mop of carrot-colored hair. "Hard contact lenses. Ground up hard contact lenses. That's what was in the bottle."

Roman looked at Phoenix. She frowned and shook her head slowly. "Contact lenses. Doesn't mean a thing to me."

"And the thick glasses," Roman said, mostly to himself. "If it's some sort of trademark, it's damned obscure."

"Uh-huh, weird, huh?" Web said. "Evangeline and me think it's weird. But I'd like to get my hands on the guy who took her off like that. She's still shook up."

"Of course she is," Phoenix said. "Would you like something to drink?"

Web appeared surprised. His brow puckered. "Well, I guess I could have a lemonade. If that's okay?"

Roman hailed Mort. "Lemonade, please."

"Police say someone was in the old windmill all right," Web said in confidential tones. "Must have taken the photos of Phoenix in her apartment from there."

"Makes sense," Roman agreed.

"Did anyone find out who it was that went off the road earlier tonight?" Web asked. He made no attempt to sit down. "Nasty crash, I guess."

Mort put a tall glass of lemonade on the counter. "Went off the road where?" he asked.

Web pointed. "Not far out of town. That sharp bend on the other side of that club place everyone talks about. They said it took an hour to get 'em out."

"D'you suppose it was someone local?" Len said. He'd moved closer to Phoenix. "Who did you talk to, Web?"

"Police. The one who came to Belle Rose."

Mort picked up the phone behind the bar and dialed. "If it's a local we need to know. Might need some help."

Zelda set two beers on the bar and joined Mort. She turned down the volume on the TV. Gradually the conversation in the room faded to a low hum.

"Steve?" Mort said. "Mort here. Understand there was an accident earlier."

Nellie and a group of men from the other end of the bar drew closer. Nellie's assistant, Tracy, came with them, dragging a gangly man with a shaved head and numerous rings in numerous holes.

Mort listened and said, "Yes," from time to time.

"Who's he talking to?" Tracy asked.

"Steve Oker," Len said. "Volunteer firefighter forever. Knows everything that happens for miles around."

When he hooked the phone back on the wall, Mort's expression was grim. "Not a local," he told the cluster at the bar. "Went off the road and rolled. Dropped a couple of hundred feet and caught fire."

"Oh, my God," Nellie murmured, pressing her hands to her cheeks. "How many people."

"One."

Roman said, "One too many." He'd seen what fire could do.

"They think someone swerved into the victim's vehicle," Mort said. "Skid marks and so on."

"But they didn't stop?" Phoenix asked.

"Steve says it looks like it might not have been an accident." Absolute quiet fell.

Phoenix groped for Roman's hand and twined their fingers together. Her face was ashen. "No one we know?" he asked, as lightly as possible.

"A woman who worked at the Peak Club. Psychic or something. Ilona?"

Roman felt Phoenix's grip slacken. He shot an arm around her waist and stood up beside her. "It's okay," he told her softly. "Hold on. Just hold on."

*"Ilona!"* Zelda slapped her brow. She appeared close to tears. "What's the matter with me? Oh, that poor woman. So gracious and beautiful. She was here again. I forgot to tell you, Phoenix."

"When was she here?" Roman asked.

"Oh, not so long ago." Zelda swallowed audibly. "A little over an hour ago, perhaps. Maybe longer, but not so much."

Phoenix gripped the edge of the bar with both hands. "She came in for a drink, or something to eat?"

"Nothing like that. She came to see if you were here. Such troubled eyes—and strange. She asked me to tell you not to let them send you on any trips. That's all she said. Then she left."

Dusty let them in and went straight to the living room where Nasty sat on a straight-backed chair with a sandwich on one hand. "Got my message?" he said. "We gotta do some thinking, right, Dust?"

"Right," Dusty agreed. He looked at Phoenix. "Sit down before you fall down, girlie."

She let Roman steer her onto the couch. Nasty had left a note at her apartment telling Roman to bring her to Dusty's. Suddenly exhausted, she asked, "Where's Junior?"

"Asleep."

The baby. For Phoenix, thinking about her sleeping peacefully upstairs, felt like the one normal thing in a wild world. "Ilona died because of me, didn't she?" She'd thought it over and over since they'd left the Bend. "We made a mistake. She wasn't on their side. They got rid of her because they were afraid of what she might say to me about April."

"We're not sure of that," Roman told her.

Phoenix leaned against the couch and closed her eyes. "Yes, we are. And we're going to stop them."

A thin yowl made sure she opened her eyes fast. Mel leapt onto the couch and high-stepped his way onto Phoenix's lap. She looked from the cat to Nasty, who shrugged and said, "I brought him down for Junior to see. She likes animals."

Phoenix stroked the cat. *"You* like animals. You like animals and babies and helpless females. You're not nearly as tough as you'd like everyone to think."

"I'm a marshmallow," Nasty said, completely without expression. "Ask Roman."

"Sure," Roman said. "A marshmallow. Dusty, I'm going to leave Phoenix with you until I can get her away."

Her head snapped up. "I'm not going anywhere."

"Yes you—"

Nasty didn't let Roman finish. "You sure are. This place is bad for your health. And it shows signs of becoming terminal real soon."

"I'm going back to the club in the morning."

"No you're not, girlie," Dusty told her. "You aren't playing a kiddy game. This is the big leagues. Roman knows what's best."

"Roman's not my keeper."

"He's bigger than you," Nasty said casually.

She glared at each of them in turn. "You all know April Clark was my best friend. And you all know she's dead because of these people. Do you honestly think I'm going to run away without making sure justice is done?"

"Leave the heroics to people who can deal with these clowns," Dusty said.

"I don't think the lady's listening," Roman said quietly. "It isn't safe for you here, Phoenix."

"It isn't safe for anyone who isn't homicidal," she responded. "I'm going back as if it's business as usual. I'm going to pretend I don't have any idea there's something wrong. If I don't keep after them, they'll find a way to make all this seem as if it never happened."

"Phoenix—"

She cut in on Nasty, "You can't change my mind. Give it up, all of you. Now I've got a debt to settle for Ilona as well. I know she was forced off the road. I know it."

"Have it your way." Nasty took a huge bite of his sandwich. "Someone called your place from Oklahoma City," he mumbled. "Wants you to call him back. Doesn't matter how late. Dusty's got the number."

Dusty, half-glasses on the end of his nose, was already pressing numbers. He handed the receiver to Phoenix.

"Who—" she began, then heard a familiar voice say, "Silius here. What d'you want?"

She couldn't help grinning. "Silius! It's Phoenix. You called me?"

"Yup. Live-in boyfriend, huh? Something new for you, my frosty, fragile flower."

Phoenix glanced at Nasty. "Just a—friend. What's up?"

"I wanted to let you know someone finally followed up on your phony references."

She stopped breathing.

"Female. She called me and said you'd given her my name. I told her you were a fabulous masseuse. Said you worked me over better than any woman I'd ever had."

"Silius!"

"Just joking. I backed you up all the way. Unfortunately she didn't stop with me."

"What do you mean?"

"She must have checked me out, too, and found out where I work."

Phoenix stood up and flipped the cord. "Is that a problem?"

"Maybe not. The woman called the firm. Wondered if the receptionist knew someone called Phoenix. Unfortunately Bernie said she did but that you didn't work there anymore. Then he told her why. In other words, your present boss knows giving massages is strictly moonlighting to you, love. She found out you're a lawyer."

"Darn it!"

Roman caught her arm and frowned.

She shook her head. "Thanks for warning me, Silius. You're a dear."

"I know. Think nothing of it. One other thing. Remember Rupert Saxton?"

She patted Roman's wrist with her free hand. "How could I forget him? Did someone finish him off in jail?"

"Unfortunately not. He's out.

*"Out?"* Phoenix tipped her face up to the ceiling. "A man hypnotizes patients and rapes them and he gets out of jail that quickly?"

"Time off and all that," Silius said. "He's been out several months. I wouldn't mention it except he's evidently been making threats against you."

She hesitated.

"His wife called me. Said she remembered you and I were friends. He told her he was going to make you suffer the way he suffered."

"He blamed me, didn't he? I was supposed to make sure he got away with it."

"Point is, he's skipped parole."

Phoenix's skin turned icy. "How long ago?"

"Weeks. Months, maybe. Thought you might like to know."

She didn't like knowing. "I need to know. Thanks, Silius."

Their good-byes were brief. Phoenix handed the receiver back to Dusty and sat down again. "Rupert Saxton, the psychiatrist I failed to represent to his satisfaction? He's out of jail and threatening me."

Roman pulled a chair close in front of her. "Threatening you with what?"

"Oh, yes." How could she have forgotten? *"Yes!* Thank goodness. I feel in control of *something* again."

"Share the good news," Roman said.

Phoenix pressed his knees. "I forgot. At least, I didn't forget, I just didn't think about it. Right after Saxton was sentenced, he tried to escape. He broke his contact lenses and swallowed them, then told a guard what he'd done. He wangled a trip to a hospital and ducked out of an examining room. They caught him."

"Contact lenses," was all Roman said.

"Exactly. Contact lenses. Then he had to wear thick plastic lenses because they wouldn't give him another pair of contacts. He's a vain man. He hated the glasses and made sure we all knew he did."

"Is this supposed to be good news?" Roman asked.

"Of course. It's Saxton. He's been following me. He attacked me and kidnapped Evangeline. We don't have to try to figure out who he is anymore. We'll tell the police and they'll get him."

"Will they?"

"Yes. Or they'll scare him away. That gets rid of our second so-called killer."

"Probably."

"And you're the other killer." She laughed, feeling slightly hysterical. "So I'm okay, aren't I?"

Nasty plucked Mel from the couch and draped the cat around his neck. "Not unless you think this Saxton ran Ilona off the road."

"Saxton wouldn't have any reason to do that," she told him.

"No, he wouldn't. Which means you won't be driving alone any time soon."

# TWENTY-FIVE

Vanessa slapped Geoffrey's face.

"Damn you," he growled, touching his lip and looking at blood on his fingers. "What the hell do you think you're doing?"

"You are a fool. An imbecile. A stupid, irresponsible—"

"Have you forgotten who calls the shots here these days?"

Her contempt for him sickened her. "You call nothing—nothing but more and more mistakes that could cost us everything we've worked for. You are so drunk on your petty power play. You can do nothing without me. Do you hear me? *Nothing*. You and I are bound together. We live or *die* together. We succeed or fail together. If I do not curb your stupidity, we will fail and that may be the least of our troubles."

He sneered. "You exaggerate everything. You dramatize everything. Get out of my way. Parker's demanding our attention."

She deliberately stood between him and the room where Parker and his latest obsession waited. "Parker will get our attention as soon as I get your word that you won't repeat the foolishness of last night."

"She went to the Bend," Geoffrey said, sounding petulant now. "I followed her."

"Yes, I know you did."

He produced a very white handkerchief and dabbed at his mouth. "You've cut me."

"Too bad. There is no excuse for what you did. Have you got rid of the car?"

"It's in a Seattle body shop. By now it's as good as new."

"Do not bring it back. Buy a new one."

"You're overreacting."

"You have drawn attention to us. We already have enough trouble. Ilona was with us for years."

Geoffrey shrugged. "You agreed with me that she was behaving strangely. She was definitely shut away with Phoenix. The camera had been deliberately broken."

"We cannot be certain it was tampered with."

"*I* am certain. And you saw her with Phoenix in the corridor that time."

"I don't know what they were saying. Good morning, for all I know. Why shouldn't she go to that bar?"

"Why *should* she. One reason. To find Phoenix and tell her things we can't risk her knowing. Ilona could have passed on information."

"But you don't know that she passed on anything. Enough. You now understand that I will no longer suffer your insolent foolishness. We must deal with Parker. He is becoming an annoyance."

Every day had become filled with annoyances. Dear Geoffrey was the biggest annoyance of all. She fashioned a smile and entered the gold room.

"At last!" Parker, as Vanessa had expected, was making good use of his time. The latest well-endowed, not-quite-forgotten movie actress, sat astride his hips. She bounced—a moving sight—and Parker lifted up from his seat with every one of those bounces. With a high-pitched squeal, he climaxed. The actress made enough noise to suggest she wasn't entirely lying about her profession.

"Touching," Geoffrey muttered.

"Helen and I want to talk to you," Parker said, his voice slurred. He held Helen's rounded white bottom. "Something we want, isn't there, baby?"

*Baby* flipped back her shoulder-length black hair and looked over her shoulder at Vanessa and Geoffrey. Her eyes didn't hold focus.

"I see someone made sure you were both happy," Vanessa said, vaguely irritated. Parker was beginning to cost far too much. "Good stuff?"

"Pass—able," Parker mumbled. "Lousy scotch, though. Got good old Roman to thank for that. He brought it. Lousy, right, baby?"

Helen giggled. "The other was fine." She nodded hugely. "Just fine. So's that lovely Roman. Tell them what we want, Parker."

"A big party," Parker said. "A bi-ig party. Invites to the Tony Awards, too. For us and for our friends."

"Stop," Vanessa demanded.

"*Tell* her," Helen said, beginning to bounce again.

Parker transferred his tethers to her breasts. "Helen wants a change of scene. She wants Broadway. And she's going to get it. I can pay for her to get it. All you have to do is the leg work. That's what I pay you for, isn't it?"

Geoffrey went to stand behind Parker. "That's what you pay us for," he said, looking at Vanessa. He joined Parker's exploration of Helen's assets. "Spell out exactly what you want us to do."

Vanessa decided she would have to find a way to curb Geoffrey. If she didn't, he would finish them.

"The Tony Awards," Parker said. "For Helen and me and our friends. Then a big party. We're going to have the party everyone goes to. Angela Lansbury. Tommy Tune. Jeremy Irons. All of 'em. Helen needs to be seen and taken seriously. Emma Thompson and Kenneth Brannagh. The whole scene. Nothing but the top. You got that?"

"We've got it," Vanessa said softly, narrowing her gaze at Geoffrey. "Anything else?"

"Yeah," Parker said, evidently having difficulty meeting Helen's fresh demands. He grunted and strained. "I told Roman I'd better get everything I want from now on. I told him I'm pissed as hell with *not* getting everything I want around here."

Vanessa deliberately breathed more slowly. "What exactly did you tell Roman?"

"That I'll close the goddamn place down if I have to. I'll tell the world what goes on underneath your little club."

"And ruin yourself?" Vanessa said sweetly. But Parker was dangerous. He used excessive quantities of coke, and had begun experimenting with heroin. The man popped ludes like candy. There had to be a way to make sure he only got high at the club. "The Tony Awards? That's it?"

"No." He stretched his eyes wide open. "I want Sharon Stone. An hour alone with Sharon Stone."

Roman watched Phoenix move around her apartment. Keeping her away from the club was proving increasingly difficult. After they'd told the story of Rupert Saxton to the police—and received little assurance of quick action—she'd wanted to go directly to confront Vanessa and Geoffrey.

The more Phoenix thought about April's death, the more she became convinced it had been the work of someone at the Peak Club and the more she wanted to take risks to find out who that someone was.

She rearranged the white daisies in April's Hopes vase. Phoenix had fiddled with the daisies repeatedly since she'd brought them in from Rose's cutting garden earlier in the day.

"It's late," Roman said. He spread his arms along the back of the couch. "You must be tired. Come and sit with me."

"I've got to fix these."

"You've fixed them. After you cut them. And a dozen or so times since I arrived. They're great."

Her hands grew still on the vase. "Hopes," she said indistinctly. "She had lots of them. None of them came true—not for long. If I knew where she was buried, I'd put flowers there. Do you know?"

This was how she did it—tried to pry bits and pieces of information out of him. The sudden offhand questions had netted her nothing so far. "I don't know," he told her. And he didn't want to think about that.

"Why won't you tell me what happened?"

"I thought we agreed I would when the time was right."

"When will that be? I invent one story after another until I'm physically sick! Was she in an accident? Was she . . ." Her next breath hissed out through her teeth. "Did they murder her?"

If he told her the truth, he couldn't be sure she wouldn't do something impetuous—and dangerous. "I was with her. She was peaceful at the end."

"Darn it, I can't stand this."

"It's getting late, Phoenix."

She rubbed the rim of the vase. "When's Nasty coming?"

In other words, she wanted Roman to leave so she could try to get out of her apartment without being seen. "I don't know. He's with Rose."

She checked her watch. "At this time of night? Rose goes to bed early."

"Evidently Rose doesn't get tired if she's got Nasty to talk to."

"I hope she isn't going to get hurt. He'll go away again soon, won't he?"

He glanced at her. "Nasty likes Rose, too. He'll make sure she's okay. He's going to find a way to bring up the postcards. We don't think they were taken."

"You think Rose lied?"

"Don't you?"

"Maybe. I'm not sure what I think about anything anymore."

Roman knew what he thought about Phoenix. He wanted her and he wanted her safe, safely away from Past Peak. "Have you changed your mind yet?"

Phoenix turned toward him. She kept the drapes closed at night now but moonlight pierced the thin fabric to burnish the edges of her hair. "Changed my mind?"

He longed to gather her to him, to take her to bed and blot out the ugliness. "About us. We've got an agreement, remember?"

After an instant she said, "Yes, I remember. And, no, I haven't changed my mind. I want to be happy. I want to shout to the world how happy I am. More than anything else I want to be your wife and Junior's mom."

Roman smiled and held a hand toward her, but uneasiness nettled him. "Let's concentrate on the marriage bit for a while." He hadn't told her everything. Some of it would devastate her, but surely she'd be happy to know a part of April would still be with her.

Phoenix picked up a green crystal from beside the vase and approached Roman. Instead of taking his hand, she curled up on the floor beside his feet and rested her head on his thigh. "Ilona gave me this," she said. "Peridot."

"The color of your eyes."

She looked up at him. "You're supposed to be rough and tough, not tender and poetic."

"I am rough and tough." He bared his teeth. "I'm a beast."

Phoenix didn't smile. "You're complex. What we have is complex, isn't it?"

"Yes."

"I'm sad, but I'm turned on, too." Without taking her eyes from his, she massaged the inside of his leg. "We late bloomers are a challenge. All that saved-up sexual energy."

He was instantly hard. "I'd say that makes me a lucky man."

"I shouldn't be thinking about sex, should I?"

"You expect me to say no?"

She set the crystal aside and scooted around between his knees. "You're sure you didn't find out anything at the club tonight?"

"Not a thing." Concentration wasn't easy. "Parker Nash— he's one of the Insider members—was shooting his mouth off about not getting his money's worth and what he'll do about it if he doesn't start getting it."

"I don't know him."

"I don't want you to." He wanted her naked. He wanted to be naked with her.

Rising to her knees, she crossed her arms on his chest and studied his mouth. "I read a lot, you know."

Roman raised his brows. "What does that mean?"

She closed the distance between them and trailed her tongue along his bottom lip.

Roman closed his eyes and received her kiss, a full, slow, provocative kiss. He deliberately didn't allow himself to hold her.

"I've read about things men like," she murmured.

"Different men like different things," he told her.

"Do you like . . ." She buried her face in his neck.

He'd like to do something about the pressure inside his pants. "Do I like what?" A rapid, raw sense of being ripped open shot upward into his belly.

"I can't say it."

He liked what he felt. "Sure you can. I want you to."

"Am I unnatural?"

He was dying—quickly. "Unnatural, how?"

"This fixation on sex?"

He chuckled. "If you are, I am, too, kiddo. Let's keep it up."

"Blow jobs."

He opened his eyes. "Huh?"

"D'you like them?" Fire suffused her freckled skin.

Roman managed a noncommittal expression. "That probably depends."

"On what?"

He shrugged and closed his eyes again.

Her fingers, settling on his crotch, stole his breath. She opened his jeans hesitantly, fumbling with the buttoned fly, moving so slowly Roman experienced his lovely living death in exquisite detail.

Her abrupt withdrawal stopped his breath altogether.

"You don't like it, do you?" Anxiety loaded her voice.

"What makes you say that?"

"Your face. Have I hurt you?"

He slitted his eyes and grinned. "Only in the best possible way. You'll hurt me in the worst possible way if you stop now."

Frowning, concentrating, she returned her attention to lower regions. With tentative care, she scooped him into blessed freedom.

He watched her hair fall forward over his stomach, felt her breath pass over his distended tip, contracted at the uncertain contact of her tongue.

"God!" He couldn't stop himself from gripping her shoulders. "That feels so good."

If she heard, she gave no sign. As far as Roman was concerned, she'd read all the very best books.

*"Phoenix!"*

She worked hard and she'd learned well.

Roman bowed over her back. He pulled up her T-shirt and slid his hands around to support her breasts. "Satin," he mumbled. "Beautiful. I want you." He slid forward on the couch and the wave broke.

When he eased her away, Phoenix rested her face on his chest. She wrapped her arms around him. Her breasts settled softly on the part of him she could rouse all too easily.

"You do like it," she said. "Roman Wilde, I love pleasing you."

"And I love it when you please me. Give me about a minute and we'll continue your education."

"Too long," she murmured.

"Gotta get my strength back."

"Wimp."

*"Wimp?"* He hauled her up until he could see her face. "You dare call this beast a wimp?"

"Well—"

The rest of what she might have said disappeared on a gasp when he found a nipple and set about a little pleasing of his own.

"Bed," she said. "Come on."

They were both on their feet when the phone rang.

Roman held her close. "We don't have to get that, do we?"

"I don't know. Do we?"

"Get it. Be quick."

Holding his hand, she picked up the phone. "Hello." All expression slipped from her features. She looked at him. "Yes, he's here."

Roman took the receiver and said his name shortly.

"Vanessa here, darling. Sorry to interrupt your fun."

"What do you want?"

"Shocking news. I wanted you to hear it from me rather than on the television."

He waited in silence. Phoenix pulled away and went to sit on the couch.

"It's about Parker Nash," Vanessa said. "Do you know who I mean?"

She knew damn well he knew. "Yeah. What about him?"

Phoenix lifted her cat onto her lap and stroked him absent-mindedly.

"He's dead," Vanessa said after a dramatic pause. "In his car in his garage. Carbon monoxide. Evidently he'd had a little too much to drink and fell asleep."

Roman snapped to attention. "Dead?" He'd seen the man only a couple of hours earlier. At that point Parker Nash couldn't have climbed into a car, much less driven the thing. "At the club, you mean?"

"I said in his garage," Vanessa snapped. "At his home. I wanted to let you know in case the police ask you any questions."

"He was paralytically drunk and blasted out of his mind when I last saw him. He's got to be the only man who can get it up after that much coke and booze."

After a short silence, Vanessa said, "You last saw him the night before last, correct?"

He thought before saying, "The night before last?" So that was the way it was. "Exactly. That's exactly when I saw him."

"So we understand each other?"

"I understand," Roman said and hung up.

Phoenix still held Mel. "What is it?"

"We'll see. I think I just got some ammunition to use against our friends at the club."

"What do you want to do to them? I mean, what . . . What ammunition?"

"Don't worry about it tonight."

Running footsteps sounded on the stairs outside, followed by a solid rap on the door.

Roman did a rapid buttoning job on his jeans and let Nasty in.

"Yo," Nasty said. If he had any thoughts about Roman and Phoenix's disheveled appearance, those thoughts didn't show. "Brought you a present."

Mel leaped from Phoenix's arms to land at Nasty's feet.

"You've alienated my cat's affections," Phoenix said.

The cat proved her point by rubbing around Nasty's legs and purring loudly enough to be heard.

"Glad someone appreciates me." Nasty thrust a handful of postcards at Phoenix. "Rose didn't mean any harm. She was afraid you'd keep pressing for information about April then tell her she wasn't coming back. She says the guy who took Evangeline asked for these, not papers. At least, that's what she thinks."

Distress twisted Phoenix's features. "I can't imagine how Saxton would even know about them."

Roman took the cards and shuffled through them. "Wish you were here," he said, turning over each one. "Nothing remarkable. Did you read them, Nasty?"

"Quickly. They don't mean anything to me." Nasty cast a regretful glance at Phoenix. "I wish there was something useful. Actually, you've got Evangeline to thank for getting these at all. She persuaded Rose to give them up."

"Evangeline's down-to-earth," Phoenix said.

"All the big vacation spots," Roman commented sarcastically, looking at the front of each card. "Nebraska, Iowa . . . Kansas?"

Phoenix's brow puckered. She held out her hand for the cards and began looking at one after another. "The heartland," she said slowly. "The roots of this country. Home of Chester's good brothers and sisters."

"Am I missing something?" Nasty asked.

Roman stood behind Phoenix and read over her shoulder.

"We'll have to check dates," she said. "Then see if we can find out if she was with him."

He felt Phoenix sway and turned her toward him. "Someone will know if she went on that crusade," he told her.

"She did go," Phoenix said. "I'm sure of it. And at least one person around here knew."

"Ilona?"

"Yes." The corners of her mouth jerked down. " 'Tell Phoenix not to let them send her on any trips.' Isn't that what she said to Mort?"

He nodded. "I think we're getting closer."

# TWENTY-SIX

"Investment banker," Dusty read aloud from the *Seattle Times*. "Apparent accident but investigation has revealed Nash's involvement in a scheme to defraud investors of huge sums of money via deposits in Japanese banks. Those banks exist only on paper."

"Wasn't an accident," Roman said. "Someone drove him home from the club last night and left him in his garage with the engine running."

Phoenix spread dry Cheerios on the tray of Junior's highchair. "Why would they do that?"

"I don't know. I'll find out, though."

"Listen to this," Dusty said without raising his head. "A spokesperson, who asked not to be identified, said the money had definitely been deposited and there were signs that it had passed into Nash's hands. But there is now no trace of it—not the kind of sums in question."

"I'll bet," Roman said.

Dusty cleared his throat and continued, "Nash and his wife of twenty-two years divorced last year. When questioned, Mrs. Nash would only refer to certain irreconcilable differences and say she hasn't been in touch with her ex-husband recently."

"Imagine that," Roman said. "The lady wouldn't stand still for Parker's movie bimbos. Women can be so unreasonable." He picked up a piece of Junior's cereal and pretended to eat it. "Can I have this? You don't want it, do you?"

Junior scrunched up her face and giggled.

"Don't tease her," Phoenix told him. "Daddy's a tease, isn't he, sweetheart."

Junior's eyes became round. "Uh oh," she said, pointing at her father. "Uh oh."

Phoenix laughed. "She thinks you're a mess-up."

"No respect," Roman said, contriving to settle one arm around Phoenix and the other around Junior.

Phoenix stopped laughing. "Walking away from all of it would feel so good." She meant it.

"Yeah. For a while." His serious blue eyes told her what she already knew. He added, "Then you'd feel guilty for being happy."

"So would you," she observed. "You wouldn't be able to stand knowing they were getting away with it, would you?"

"Probably not." His gaze met Dusty's. "We don't have the option of finding out. Not yet. They want to know you're out of the way Phoenix, and they'd try to come after me anyway. The second I dropped out of sight they'd figure out I was dangerous to them."

"Why don't you stay here, Phoenix?" Dusty said. "What d'you think, Roman?"

"Wouldn't work. We've got to keep going as if we're still in the dark. And I won't risk drawing attention to Junior."

Phoenix wished she didn't agree with him. "I'm going to the club today."

"No you're not," Roman said shortly. "I'm going to join Nasty. He's looking for some of Chester's disgruntled parishioners—you can bet your life he's got plenty of them around. I don't want you at the club unless I'm there. We'll go later."

The radio Roman always carried beeped. He pulled it out and depressed a switch. "Yeah?"

"Pay dirt," Nasty said, his voice uncannily clear. "Mrs. Beatrice Delahide. Never got her money's worth."

"Come on in and talk."

"I'm going to keep going here. I'll find more. Mrs. Delahide was one of the reverend's right-hand women. She was on the crusade with him last year. For the last five months of it."

Phoenix held her breath.

"She gave a hefty sum to the reverend and she expected a return. He told her she'd get her return in heaven. She doesn't want to wait that long."

Dusty laughed, and promptly turned the laugh into a cough. Phoenix smothered her own smile.

"Anything about April?" Roman asked.

"A lovely girl with blond hair," Nasty said. "Dupree said she'd been ill and was traveling with him looking for healing. Evidently serving him was supposed to do the job. The girl was known as Sunshine. She was kept away from the rest of the entourage and Mrs. Delahide is of the opinion there was more to the relationship between Dupree and Sunshine than met the eye."

"April wouldn't go near that man," Phoenix protested.

Roman held out a silencing hand. "Did you show April's picture?"

"Sure did. 'Why, that's Sunshine.' Those were the lady's words. And, according to my source, Sunshine seemed confused much of the time, or worried maybe. But then, given her—given her situation, that wasn't so surprising."

"What would she hope to gain—the woman who talked— what would she hope to gain from spilling her guts to you?"

Nasty sniffed. "She asked to remain anonymous. Said if I quoted her she'd deny it. Not admissible evidence, that's what she said."

"Too much television," Roman said darkly. "That's where they all pick up this jargon."

Despite the tension, Phoenix snickered—and earned herself a glare from Roman.

"She wants back at your reverend gentleman," Nasty continued. "If she didn't, I wouldn't have learned a thing. It's that simple."

"Sounds logical." Roman turned his back on Phoenix. "Did she say anything else useful?"

"Yep. I saved the most useful for last. Sunshine disappeared from a motel room in the middle of the night. After the reverend decided on a crusade detour. The detour was pretty drastic—to San Diego."

Vanessa leaned into the slope. She walked slowly uphill between silent firs. The afternoon was still, warm, airless. If he'd followed instructions, Geoffrey had climbed this trail ahead of her. What she had to say to him must not be overheard by anyone, and must be acted on as quickly as possible.

She saw him before he saw her. Sitting on a fallen tree trunk, his trousers carefully hitched up at the knees, Geoffrey stared suspiciously into the trees surrounding the clearing she'd picked for their meeting.

From the far side of the clearing, beyond the dense firs, came the muted sound of water roaring over Snoqualmie Falls. Geoffrey didn't like the sound of water. He detested the falls. Vanessa knew he had a fear of getting too close to the crashing cascade.

He would be unsettled here. Another element to her advantage.

"Geoffrey?"

He leaped to his feet and faced her.

"There you are." Vanessa smiled warmly. "And right on time. Thank you for not questioning my request."

Geoffrey looked sullen. "You hardly gave me a choice."

"Because I said we may be about to lose everything? I didn't say we *would* lose everything, darling. Don't be so dramatic."

He pushed his hands into the pockets of his beautifully tailored gray flannels and hunched his shoulders. "Wouldn't you say this meeting—in this Godforsaken spot—was dramatic?"

"Some might say this is exactly where they might expect to find God," she told him, well aware that pseudo-pious nonsense would irritate him further. "I wanted to be certain we were very much alone. We have serious planning to do."

"Even if there were trouble," Geoffrey said, "I'd be in the clear, my dear. I've got the money, remember?"

The fool actually thought he could control her. "I realize that. I only want what's best for both of us. Miles has gone ahead to

Switzerland to wait for us. Pierre is here and will help with what I have in mind."

"Why is Miles in Switzerland?"

She walked past him and tilted her head as if entranced by the sound of the falls. "When we're finished here. And we will have to finish, I'm afraid. The potential for disaster has become too high. But afterward we'll have to start again elsewhere and we'll need funds. So Switzerland is the obvious rendezvous point, isn't it? Chester's in a panic."

Geoffrey frowned. "What does Chester have to do with anything?"

"You did a nice job with Parker. The papers have reported exactly the story we designed."

"It was easy. He never woke up after we left the club. I asked you about Chester."

The more she could set him on edge, the better—the more likely he was to go along with everything she suggested. "Someone's been asking questions about last year's crusade. To be more accurate, they showed a picture of April and asked if she was with Chester."

Dropping slowly, Geoffrey sat on the fallen tree again and whispered, "Who? Who asked? And who did they ask?"

"Don't know." Walking behind him, she leaned against his back and massaged his temples. "Relax, darling. We will manage this together."

"If you don't know who told Chester about this, how do we know he's not just dreaming the whole thing up?"

"He's not. He got an anonymous call. All the details were accurate, right down to his detour to San Diego." She pulled Geoffrey's rigid body against her. "There was no mention of Mexico."

"Oh, my, *God!*"

"They *didn't* mention it." She felt waves of shuddering pass through him and bent to kiss his ear. "Trust me, Geoffrey. I have this under control. You need to relax. Why don't you take off your clothes?

"For *God's* sake, Vanessa! How can you think of such things now?"

Laughing lightly, trailing her fingertips along the skin beneath the open neck of his shirt, she circled to stand in front of him. "I've always believed that what you call 'such things' are very helpful in stressful times." She began unbuttoning the jacket of her black linen suit. "They certainly are to me." It was no accident that she wore nothing beneath the jacket.

Predictably, Geoffrey squirmed at the sight of her breasts. They always excited him. Any female flesh excited him. Vanessa clamped her teeth together. No other woman would ever equal the power she held over him.

Geoffrey turned his face away.

"You're going to have to help me." Vanessa pulled her short, tight skirt up to her hips. Apart from the flat shoes she'd kicked off, her black, lace-topped stockings, were her final items of clothing. "You're going to have to do exactly what I tell you to do."

Geoffrey said nothing.

She raised his clenched right hand to her crotch and ground his fingers into the moistness.

Finally he looked at her, at the slick black hair between her thighs. "You never get enough," he said, his gaze traveling up to her swaying breasts.

"In that, we are very alike." Her voice came in husky gasps. "Finish this. Finish it now," she demanded, her knees growing weak.

When he didn't respond, she thrust her breasts at his face. He rubbed her sluggishly. Vanessa grew desperate. She grabbed his fingers and thrust them inside her. Her release was instant.

As she'd known he would, Geoffrey surged up, tearing at his clothes, shoving her down on the grass. In seconds he sat astride her shoulders with his cock in her mouth. She endured long enough to satisfy him.

Almost immediately he was upon her again, grunting noisily, forcing himself between her legs.

She would always be able to subdue him.

"We will have to work together and work fast," she said, arching upward against him.

"Yes," he agreed.

"Phoenix isn't a masseuse. She's a lawyer." When he grew still, she told him the rest. When she spoke of the crazy shrink, Geoffrey's eyes narrowed. Then she made her announcement: "We're going to use him. He's the answer to our prayers."

Geoffrey gave a final pumping shove and fell on her. "How? Have you found him? Can we get him to finish her for us?"

"No. On all counts. But the police will think he's killed her."

"How will we make them do that?"

"All I want you to do is give me the go ahead to arrange things with Pierre."

"What things?" He was drowsy. Sex made Geoffrey drowsy to the point of seeming drugged.

"If you agree—and you give me the number to the Swiss vault—I'll make sure we're both safe."

His eyes, when he looked at her, held a mixture of confusion and cunning. "Why would I do that?"

"Because, if you don't, I'm going to make sure everyone finds out exactly what happened to April Clark."

"But—"

"Don't try to threaten me, Geoffrey. Chester Dupree is my man. He'll help me make sure you go down. Save us both a lot of irritation—just agree to my request."

He shook his head.

"You will give me the number. Then I will deal with what must be done. Afterward, we will join Miles and Pierre in Switzerland. I already have plans for our future."

"What about Roman?"

She smiled. "So you agree. Good. Roman will not be there. I am convinced he is not on our side now. He is too besotted with Phoenix. No. We will be in Switzerland. Roman will be on the bottom of Elliott Bay."

Geoffrey's eyes cleared. She saw him moisten his mouth. Just imagining death in the water was guaranteed to terrify him.

"Roman will drown and Phoenix will drown with him.

Thanks to Roman and Phoenix going to the police with their little stories about Rupert Saxton, everything will work beautifully. We'll be in the clear, and Saxton will be blamed."

Rose leaned on her white piano and idly shuffled through an array of catalogues scattered before her. "What do you think about this?" she asked Phoenix, who had come into the room several minutes earlier.

Phoenix went obediently to look at a picture of a model dressed for a tropical resort evening. "Elegant," she said.

"You think the salmon color is appropriate for my skin tone? They also have the set in aqua."

"The salmon's perfect." Phoenix could hardly keep her voice calm. "What did you want to talk to me about?"

"You don't think the aqua would be better?"

"You're already wearing the salmon." Until that instant, she hadn't noticed that Rose's gauze shirt—tied at the waist over a halter top—and matching, wide-legged pants, were exactly as depicted in the catalogue. "You must like it. You bought it."

"Did I?" Rose looked vaguely down at herself. "Why, so I did. I declare, I am so preoccupied these days I can hardly remember my own name. My Ferry says I worry too much about things."

Phoenix pursed her lips before asking, "Fairy?" Surely Rose wasn't completely losing her grip. "What fairy would that be?"

Rose blinked, then giggled. "Oh, my. Nasty, to you. He has me call him Ferry. Short for Ferrito. That's his last name. Isn't that a fine name?"

"Very fine." How many wounded hearts would hobble along in the wake of what was happening in Past Peak?

"Anyway, Ferry says I worry too much," Rose repeated. "Maybe he's right."

"What are you worrying about now?"

Rose smoothed her hair. She wore it down and Phoenix couldn't help admiring its sleek beauty. "Here comes Evangeline," Rose said with a fluttering wave. "Hello, sweet thing. You're all that keeps me together sometimes."

"Hush," Evangeline said. Worry lines creased her brow. She turned to Phoenix. "Rose has been waiting for you all day. Did she give you something? A . . . Rose, did you give what you've got to Phoenix?"

Rose slapped the catalog shut and moved around the piano with quick, agitated steps.

"You didn't, did you?" Evangeline pressed. "Really, Rose, it's the only thing. It's right."

"I don't think I should. I don't think it's necessary. Anyway, I haven't said I've got anything to give her."

Evangeline went to Rose and folded her in big, strong arms. "You do. You know you do. You as good as admitted it. But it's goin' to be all right. I'm here and I'll look after you just like I always have."

Rose began to cry softly.

"Do it now," Evangeline coaxed. "You know you should. Where is it? I'll come with you to get it."

"There's nowhere we have to go." Sniffing, Rose pulled away from Evangeline and turned to Phoenix. "I promised her."

Deep cold settled on Phoenix. "Who?"

"April. I promised her I would. If she didn't come back within six months."

Buzzing inside Phoenix's head joined the icy coldness on her skin. "What did you promise her?"

Rose reached into a pocket in the loose pants and withdrew a pristine white envelope. "I promised her I'd contact you in Oklahoma City and arrange to send you this. She left me your number there."

"You knew who I was when I came looking for a place to stay?" Phoenix stared at the envelope.

"I surely did." Rose swayed jerkily.

"But you didn't say anything. And you never tried to get me by phone." Not that she'd been in Oklahoma City at the time.

"No." Very deliberately, Rose shook her head. "April said

that if she didn't call within six months, it would mean she couldn't. But the postcards—"

"She didn't mean postcards," Evangeline said. "They didn't have anything to do with it. She meant that if she didn't contact you by telephone you should do something. Anyway, those postcards stopped coming a few weeks after she left Past Peak."

"Do you like the earrings?" Rose lifted her hair. "Ceramic seashells of exquisite detail. Fourteen-karat gold posts. Hand detail. And the matching pendant."

"Yes, they're beautiful," Phoenix said.

"The sandals? I thought the gold trim set the braided leather off just right. What do you think?"

Phoenix rubbed her eyes. "Perfect, Rose."

"I may even redo this room like this." Rose ran her fingers over the salmon and aqua drapes pictured. "I got the idea for all the roses from this catalogue. An earlier copy, of course. From the catalogue and because of my name." She smiled. "My daddy said I should be surrounded with roses."

*Please*, stop this." Being harsh with this soft woman felt wrong, but time was running out. "Please may I have what April left for me?"

Rose passed her tongue over her lips. "I'm sorry. I'm bein' silly." Her eyes held a haunted expression, but she gave up the envelope.

Without allowing herself time to think, Phoenix passed the end of a forefinger beneath the flap and ripped it open. She withdrew several sheets of paper. A handwritten letter and a legal document.

"Will you tell me what it says?" Rose asked plaintively.

"Yes," Phoenix said, although she knew she wouldn't, not yet, and then, not exactly. "Give me a little time to think, please."

"Dear Billy," the letter began. "Don't even think about crying."

# TWENTY-SEVEN

Of all the damn fool things to do!

Roman started to run down Broad Street toward Pier 70 and the waterfront.

According to Nasty, Phoenix was upset. She needed a quiet place to be—to think. A good long walk by the water. *That park by Elliott Bay,* she'd said. Phoenix didn't know Seattle, but she had seen Myrtle Edwards Park. Shit, she better have meant Myrtle Edwards. If she was in some other park near the water he could only pray she hadn't been followed there from Belle Rose.

Railroad crossing bells sounded and red lights flashed. Red and white barriers began their descent to block off Broad Street for an oncoming train.

Roman speeded up.

Too late.

He couldn't make it past in time.

Damn. Damn. *Damn!*

Roman cut to the right on Elliott Avenue and sprinted. He dodged between idling vehicles and dashed down Bay Street, beside the green glass Elliott Building, to the cinder verge beside the railroad tracks.

Nasty had called from Rose's, Nasty sounding more ruffled than Roman ever remembered. Something about Rose giving Phoenix a letter from April. Then it all got even more garbled. Phoenix took off without showing the letter to anyone. Nasty said she'd seemed disoriented and preoccupied at the same time.

Why hadn't Nasty insisted on going with her? Because Phoenix said she'd go to Roman after she'd had some time alone.

Alone at sundown in a deserted park while Roman knew of at least two people who wanted her dead.

Containers destined for ships in the bay, rumbled by on flatbed cars. Roman jogged beside them. A dusky film coated the light. The falling sun cast a russet glow.

The cars curved around the bend toward him and, blessedly, the caboose came into sight.

The instant the last green car passed, Roman leaped over the first set of tracks. Rocks between the railroad crossties rolled under the soles of his sneakers. A second rail line separated him from the park. He crossed the shiny tracks in two bounds, reached the grass, then a bicycle path.

No cyclists. No walkers.

Nothing.

Not a soul in any direction.

Roman searched the area leading back toward the piers. No one. He strode over a grassy rise to a deserted joggers' path near the water. To his right lay a group of artfully arranged flat rocks. He knew they meant something but couldn't remember what. Right now he didn't care.

He had no choice but to make the trip as far as the grain elevators and the warehouses at the far end of the park.

An unfamiliar burning tore at his throat. He was scared, dammit. Scared something might happen to her—might already have happened to her. What if they'd taken her out. Forced her off the road out of Past Peak the way they did Ilona?

*Check it out. Check it out, then check out every other goddamn park if you have to.* Nasty was already driving on the road from Past Peak.

A thin line of surf curled about driftwood heaped on the rocky beach to his left. The smooth water glowed beneath the warm, old-day sunlight.

Phoenix's hair glowed.

Roman skidded to a halt.

Sitting in a fork where two weathered logs crossed, Phoenix

rested her head and back on one piece of wood, crossed her ankles high on the other. With her arms wrapped around her middle, she was absolutely still—except for her breeze-mussed curls through which the sunlight glinted.

"Shit!" Like a runner out of the blocks, Roman started from the pathway and bolted, slipping and sliding, down the bank toward her. *"Damn* you," he yelled.

She didn't even look up.

The tumbled mass of wood got in his way. He scrambled over log after log until he could reach her. "What the *fuck* do you think you're doing?"

Phoenix lost her balance and fell onto the sand and pebbles.

"Did you hear me?" Roman hauled her to her feet. "You stupid little idiot! Look at it here. Totally vulnerable."

She bowed her head.

Roman shook her. "Look at me, dammit! You have a problem, you come to me. Got it? You don't take off to some deserted beach where anyone can pick you off and walk away."

Phoenix didn't raise her face.

*"Look at me!* We're walking a tightrope about the thickness of fishing line here. And we're wearing hiking boots. Do you get it? One tiny wrong move and someone is very *dead."*

"Stop it."

He worked the muscles in his jaw and fought for control. "Did you tell me to stop it? Is that what you said?"

"That's what I said." At last she looked at him. She grabbed handfuls of his shirt, rose as high on her toes as possible and whispered, *"Stop* it. Go away and leave me alone. I'm not your problem. Go away. D'you understand?"

"Not my problem?" He had to calm down. "You are going to be my wife. I think that makes you my problem."

"A smart man doesn't willingly marry a problem. Not that you want to marry me."

"What? What did you say? Shit! Back when I made up my mind to steer clear of commitments with women, I was a smart man."

"Right." She made to shove away from him. Roman rewarded

her with another shake and a more solid grasp on her shoulders. "Go back to avoiding commitment," she told him.

"What's happened? Why are you behaving like this?"

The sunlight turned her eyes to clear crystal green. "It's all blown up in my face. My friend is dead. I should have come a long time ago when she needed me. I could have helped her then. If she hadn't been so alone, she wouldn't have made such bad choices."

"April?"

"Who else?"

This time he let her tear herself away. Turning from him, she all but tripped. Roman didn't go to her. She climbed to the water's edge and stared toward the shadowy hulks of the Olympic mountains.

Roman took out his Beretta and checked the clip. Pushing the gun away again, he made a slow visual in all directions. His instincts told him they didn't have any company.

He approached her slowly and stood a few feet distant, looking over the water—just as she looked over the water. "Sorry if I came on too strong."

"I need to be by myself."

"You need to be taken care of."

"I'm not a helpless little female."

"And I'm not a chauvinistic male. I'm realistic, that's all. You are in danger, Phoenix. You are also my fiancée." A strange little nerve jumped. He'd never even thought that word, let alone spoken it aloud. "We're a team, kiddo. Wherever you go, I shall go. Know that verse?"

"Yes. But you may not want to go where I go and live where I live. My life is going to change. And I'm not going to be able to stay in one place until I do what I've been asked to do."

Roman looked at her profile. "Asked to do?"

"I'm going to have to find someone, Roman. I don't even know where to start, but I'll have to do it. There isn't any choice."

He extended a hand. "Talk to me, Phoenix. I know Rose gave you a letter from April. She told Nasty it upset you and that's why you took off down here. You said you intended to come to me when you'd had time to think."

She looked at his hand, then grasped it with both of hers. "That's what I said."

"So I came to you instead. The end result's the same. Here we are, together." He pulled her toward him. "We can't have secrets. Tell me what's going on. Whatever it is you feel you have to do—I'll help you."

"April was desperate." When Phoenix gazed into his face he saw desolation. "She'd fallen in love with a man she met in San Francisco. He was a partner in the Peak Club. He took her to Past Peak and gave her a job. They became lovers. She wanted to marry him."

Roman pulled her against him and pressed her face into his chest. "This was all in the letter?"

She nodded. "When she wrote the letter she was four months pregnant."

His heart missed, then beat so hard he was afraid she'd hear it.

"She was sure he'd marry her if he had time to get used to the idea. But she was afraid he'd suggest an abortion if she told him before it was too late to get one, so she went away."

"With Dupree?"

"Yes. On the crusade. The man she was involved with said they needed a break from each other. She let herself be convinced to go with Chester"

"On a trip, huh?" *April had told Phoenix about the baby.*

"April said Chester planned a long crusade. Months. He needed money, a lot of it."

"He's got a lot of habits to feed."

Her arms stole around him. "She told me not to cry for her." Roman closed his eyes. *April would say that.*

"She said that when the time was right she'd tell the man she loved about his baby. Roman, she was convinced he'd marry her then. At least, she was almost convinced. But she did leave me a letter telling me what to do if he didn't."

"I'm not sure I understand."

"Neither am I. April's instructions to Rose were that if she didn't hear from her by the time six months had passed, she was to contact me and make sure I got the letter."

"Why would she do that?"

"Because—and she wrote this—she thought it would mean she had died."

"And she did die."

Phoenix raised her face. "You're going to have to tell me all of it now. You know that, don't you?"

He returned her gaze unflinchingly.

"April wanted me to find her baby—if there is a baby."

Roman's mouth dried out. "How are you supposed . . ." He could not keep up the lie. Not anymore.

"When . . . When she died. Was there a baby with her? Do you know anything about him?"

He rested his brow on hers. "Yes. Yes, her baby was with her. A girl."

"A girl." The tears she wasn't supposed to cry filled her eyes. "Well, I've got to find her. April and I had a pact. If either of us ever had children and something happened, the other one would take over. I've got to find April's little girl and look after her."

Roman couldn't speak.

"April actually made a will. I get the vase, the books, everything she had. Including her savings. And her baby."

"Lucky baby."

Phoenix wasn't listening. Her eyes glazed and she said, "In the event of my death, and if she agrees, I, April Clark, appoint Wilhelmina G. Phoenix to be the legal guardian of any children born to me, including any children born to me after the date of this will."

"Phoenix—"

"And if Wilhelmina G. Phoenix so wishes, she will adopt any offspring of April Clark."

For the first time in his adult life Roman knew the agony of uncontrollable fear. "Wilhelmina," he whispered. She was talking about Junior. He had no right to his baby. Phoenix did.

"Billy," Phoenix said. "April called me Billy. I hate Wilhelmina. Everyone else always called me Phoenix. After I got away from New York."

*Tell Billy.* "April told me to tell you. She sent me to Past Peak—to the club. And she said I was to . . . They killed her."

Phoenix stiffened. "Who?"

"I'm not sure. But I know Vanessa and Geoffrey had something to do with it. I thought Miles was Billy. It's his nickname, too. When April asked me to tell Billy, I thought she meant a man."

"No. She meant me." Her face was white and stark. "Tell me what happened."

He had to make the words. "I was on a mission. With Nasty."

She didn't comment.

Roman tipped his face up to the sky. "Night mission. Into Mexico by chopper under the radar. I was expecting someone— a man. The someone I got was April. A camper came. They . . . Someone dropped her off."

"Where."

"I told you. Not far from the Mexican border."

"The baby was with her?"

"Yes."

"But you just said April was killed. Before, you said you were with her when she died."

The nightmare played before him like a movie. "She was dying when I . . . She was dying then."

He barely stopped Phoenix from slipping to the beach.

Lifting her into his arms, he carried her to a protected hollow beneath the bank and sat down. He held her on his lap.

They were silent a long time before she said, "What had they done to her?"

Roman pushed a finger and thumb into the corners of his eyes.

"Tell me, please."

"They had beaten her. And stabbed her."

The sound Phoenix made was awful. A choking, keening

sound. She jerked toward him. "The baby? They didn't stab the baby?"

"Phoenix, listen to me, please. I can't do this . . . I can't stand reliving this. April had been beaten and stabbed and wrapped in a tarp. Someone drove her into the desert and tipped her into a ditch. She wasn't dead then. I tried to save her, but I failed." His own voice caught and broke. "She gave birth there. She lost so much blood. I couldn't stop it. April was brave, Phoenix. All she cared about was the baby."

The woman in his arms had given up on bravery. She sobbed, each sob a retching, tearing sound—and her body convulsed repeatedly.

Roman blinked against stinging in his own eyes. "April was quiet when the time came. She went softly, my love, gently."

"Beaten and stabbed?" Phoenix choked and struggled from his arms to kneel on the pebbles. "She was beaten and stabbed. Then she gave birth and bled to death. But she died quietly and softly? Oh, my God. Oh, please, no. Not April. The baby?"

"I put her inside my shirt and carried her out."

Phoenix stumbled to her feet and stood over him. "And? Did she live? Where did you . . ." In the failing light, he saw suspicion dawn.

"She lived," he said.

"Junior," Phoenix murmured.

"Junior," he echoed. "Her name's not Zinnia. It's April, like her mom."

April had told Roman to find Phoenix.

She listened to him moving about behind her. He'd persuaded her to spend the night at his condo and work through their plans. Tomorrow, so he said, they would go to the club together to make sure Vanessa and Geoffrey continued to believe Roman was on their team.

Beyond the bedroom windows, moonlight spread a coat of silvered polish on Elliott Bay. Phoenix's gaze moved from the water to luminous swaths of cloud. There was no way to confirm or disprove the story Roman had told her—except through her own intuition. Her intuition told her to accept every word. She loved him. Her stomach turned. Doubt and horror were a destructive concoction. Roman could not be the man April had fallen in love with. He could not be Junior's real father.

"Let down, sweetheart," Roman said. "Come on. We both need to be sharp in the morning."

"Yes."

Every word he'd told her was possible. Fantastic, but possible. He'd happened to be on a rock waiting for something or other when April—pregnant, dying, and about to give birth—had been dumped in a ditch. He'd delivered the baby. April had died and Roman had followed her few directions to Past Peak where he'd found a way to get close to the people he believed were responsible for atrocities to a dear, sweet woman.

He was a partner in the Peak Club.

Phoenix didn't know for sure how long he'd been a partner. Tomorrow she'd find out—if it killed her. She flinched. Death walked in the wake of people who got in the way of the Peak Club. Why should she think she could outwit those people?

Those people.

Roman was one of those people.

"Phoenix?"

If he hadn't been any part of the operation before April left Past Peak, then his version of what happened must be true.

"Phoenix, honey?" His hands settled at her waist. "Please let it go for a little while."

"I can't."

He nuzzled her hair aside and kissed the back of her neck.

Phoenix let her head fall forward. She wanted to forget. She wanted to believe. She wanted to love and be loved. She wanted this man.

"You're cold."

"All the way to my soul."

"We can't bring April back. We can look after her baby. Doesn't that make you feel better—just a little?"

"Just a little," Phoenix told him. Her throat closed and she swallowed repeatedly. "A beautiful baby."

"The most beautiful baby in the world."

"And you decided to look after her."

"I didn't intend to. I was going to give her up to the first appropriate agency I came to. Then I couldn't do it."

A big, rough, tough Navy SEAL couldn't give up a newborn infant. "You lied to me."

He turned her in his arms and pressed her to his body. He was aroused.

"You lied to me," Phoenix repeated. Even while she mourned, she responded to him.

"I didn't tell the truth."

"Semantics. Dusty lied, too. And Nasty."

Slowly, deliberately, he rubbed his jutting penis against her belly. "Mostly by omission."

She couldn't resist cupping him. "At the beginning I would have understood. But after we . . . Later, you could have told me."

"I didn't know how. Just telling you April had died tore you apart. I had to wait for the rest—for the details. For me as well as you. Sweetheart, I need to make love to you."

Phoenix found his hands and pressed them over her breasts. The room behind him seemed to revolve. "Are you . . . Oh, *darn.*"

He laughed a little. "Your shocking expletive always means I should beware."

"Is Junior yours?"

Roman froze. Gradually, his fingertips dug into her breasts. Phoenix held his gaze, saw it change. Urgent passion took on a feverish glitter. His lips drew back from his teeth.

"Roman—"

"Don't say anything else." His chest rose and fell rapidly. Very deliberately, he settled the pads of his thumbs on her nipples and curled his big hands around her rib cage. "Am I Junior's father? Is that what you want to know?"

Unable to speak, she nodded.

Roman's fingers stung her flesh. He moved so abruptly, she would have fallen if he hadn't lifted her from her feet.

The backs of her legs connected with the edge of his make-shift bed and she buckled. They fell together.

"Not like this," she whispered.

"Not like what? What don't you want?"

"We can't love in anger, Roman."

*"Love?"* His laugh was ugly, frighteningly ugly. "Is that what we have together?"

None of it mattered anymore—except the truth. "Were you the man April fell in love with in San Francisco?"

His face hit the bed beside her head. The sound he made was an animal moan.

"Roman?"

He covered her mouth, cutting off sound—and air. She fought to breathe through her nose.

"Am I capable of killing a helpless, pregnant woman? That's what you want to know. You said you loved me. I love you. Isn't that a joke? I still love you. Do you think you could fall for a murderer?"

She mumbled against his hand.

"Do you think I . . . If I murdered April, why? . . . *Why* would I murder her? Because she was having my baby? If that was it, why did I keep the baby?"

Phoenix struggled to drag his hand away.

"Doesn't make much sense, does it? And when you came along, why would I get involved with you if I'd killed your friend and you were trying to find out what happened to her?"

She managed to free her mouth. "Because she told you about the letter. Because you couldn't help loving Junior and you were afraid I'd find a way to take her from you."

His full weight came down on top of her. "I didn't know about any letter. But who the fuck cares? Who cares about anything? If I was afraid of any of that, I could have killed you a dozen times over."

Tension broke over Phoenix. Uncontrollable trembling shook her, rattled her teeth together. Everything he said made perfect sense. But he should have told her about Junior. He shouldn't have lied.

"Trust isn't built on lies," she told him.

"I can't stand this!" He began to move over her, began ripping at her blouse, bursting buttons. "If I don't get inside you, I'm going to die here."

Phoenix cried out. She pushed at him. "No, Roman. We won't have a chance if you . . . If you . . ."

"Rape you? I don't want to rape you. I want to *feel* you. I want to feel you alive with me. I want you to give yourself to me because you believe in me."

The blouse shredded beneath his hands. Her jeans scraped downward over her hips and legs. "Tell me you want me, Phoenix. Please tell me you want me."

He frightened her.

Her wisp of a pink lace bra parted between her breasts and fell open. His lips and teeth fastened on a nipple and he suckled, flipped the tensed crest with the tip of his tongue until her stomach arched off the bed.

Sex. All they had here was sex. Phoenix craved sex with Roman.

He stood up and stared down at her. "Tell me to stop and I will." Even as he spoke he pulled his sweater over his head, unsnapped his jeans. The black hair on his chest glistened. A fine film of moisture shone on his tanned skin. The muscles over his belly lay flat, tensed where his navel showed at the open waist of his jeans.

"Phoenix, tell me."

She couldn't.

In one motion, he ripped her panties away.

*"Tell me."*

Her mouth opened. She passed her tongue over her lips.

Roman groaned and fell to his knees. He fastened his mouth between her legs and his tongue darted around the aching nub of flesh he found there. Phoenix shrieked and clawed at his hair. He sucked her, performed a sweet, tormenting magic.

"Stop it. Don't." It couldn't be right this way.

He paused long enough to say, "Surely you read about this, too. Things women like?"

She formed another protest in her mind. It never made it past her lips. A burning climax burst from the spot beneath his mouth, into the deep, convulsing places that would not be satisfied yet.

Phoenix drew up her knees.

Roman pushed them higher, folded her legs around his neck and reached his clever tongue deeper inside her.

She jerked her hips away.

"What do you want?" he muttered.

"You."

His jeans joined hers.

Roman joined Phoenix.

With her ankles locked behind his neck, he braced himself and drove his massively engorged shaft into her softness. He drove deep—to the hilt.

Breath shuddered from Phoenix's lungs. She uttered high, jarring cries—and Roman shouted her name.

"Roman!"

"I love you!"

"Yes." Her body was coming apart.

He reared up, and unbelievably penetrated her even more deeply. "I *love* you, Phoenix."

"I love you," she gasped. "I trust you, Roman"

In the sweet, tiptoeing light of early morning Phoenix rolled onto her side to watch Roman sleep. They had used each other's bodies for hours. Used, and loved and used again. Most of all, Phoenix had loved Roman. He had tasted every inch of her skin, done things she blushed to remember—things she longed to blush over again. He'd entered her in ways no book had mentioned, sometimes with a force close to violence. Then he'd caressed her as if she were made of glass.

In his sleep, his hair curled away from his broad brow. The stubble on his jaw and cheeks showed dark and thick. Between slightly parted lips, the edges of his straight teeth rested together. His black brows arched over vaguely shifting, sweeping black lashes that ought to look feminine. Nothing about the man could possibly look feminine.

Amid the steaming darkness of their passion there had been moments to plan. Later the club. Roman would isolate Geoffrey and make him talk. Phoenix hadn't asked how he would do that. She just believed he could. And while he dealt with Geoffrey, Phoenix would make sure there was no interruption.

And she had told him she trusted him.

Carefully, she stretched out on top of him and rested her face in the hollow of his shoulder. At the grazing of his chest hair, her nipples instantly quickened.

His arms enfolded her but he didn't awaken.

He'd told her he loved her.

She'd told him she trusted him. Today she would put her life in his hands.

She had no choice but to trust him.

"What's your name?"

Phoenix started and raised her head. His eyes were slitted open. "Huh?"

"What's your name, W. G.?"

"I told you. I don't want to say it again."

"The G. Not the W."

Phoenix let her head fall to his shoulder again. "I've never told another soul this. Not even April. Gunhilda."

"Oh."

"Yes." At least he hadn't laughed. "Oh, about covers it."

A rumbling moved his chest beneath her breasts.

"You *are* laughing at me."

"With you, kiddo," he sputtered. "I'm laughing with you, Wilhelmina Gunhilda."

She *had* to trust him.

# TWENTY-EIGHT

Roman listened to Vanessa's voice on his answering machine. "Are you there, Roman?" He met Phoenix's eyes. She lay atop him once more—he'd prefer her in that position at all times. "Roman? If you're there, please pick up."

He saw Phoenix hold her breath.

"Okay," Vanessa continued. "This is urgent. We've got to keep one of our Insider clients happy. He's threatening to make things sticky for us if he doesn't get to fulfill his lifelong ambition."

Phoenix reached to pick up the receiver and hand it to Roman. He sighed and said, "I'm here, Vanessa."

"What took you so long? Otherwise engaged?"

He closed his eyes. "You might say that." Phoenix massaged him to full alert. He grimaced and covered her hand on top of his penis.

"Phoenix?" Vanessa asked.

"I'm human, countess. I have to take a leak from time to time like any other man. I was doing just that."

Phoenix's head shot up and she made an "ooh," shape with her lips.

"No need to be crude," Vanessa remarked.

"Who is this client?"

"Otto Perkins. He's in software."

"Software, huh?" He saw Phoenix grin. She squeezed him and he pretended to snarl. "What does he want?"

"A diving expedition. He wants to be a SEAL for a night. Tonight."

Alarms sizzled in every one of Roman's nerves. "Not possible. I'll have to meet the guy first."

"Why?"

He snorted convincingly. "Because I'm not risking a dead client, that's why. I need to take a look at him, and he needs a clean bill of health first."

"He's already got it. Geoffrey and I thought about that. The man was checked over by a doctor this morning."

They thought of everything. "I don't dive with anyone who isn't checked out on the equipment first."

"Sure you do." Vanessa's voice was silky. "You took three other members down without ever meeting them beforehand. You checked them out in the boat. What's different about poor Otto?"

Vanessa was too eager. That's what was wrong with "poor Otto."

"Roman? I asked you a question."

"Tonight?"

"Tonight. He wants to place explosives on a big ship in the harbor, or whatever."

"Bay," Roman said automatically. "What else is new? They all want to place explosives. Crazy to a man."

"Rich to a man, darling. We don't care about the condition of their psyches."

Arguing wasn't going to change her mind. "If you say so. I'll be in in an hour or so."

"Don't bother. Geoffrey and I are just leaving."

He wrapped an arm around Phoenix's smooth shoulders and held her tightly.

"We'll call you later and tell you where to meet Otto. Pierre will bring him down. He's a new member. You don't know him."

Honesty might just fool Vanessa. Roman said, "I don't like this."

She only hesitated an instant before saying, "Don't be foolish, darling. I wouldn't have you do anything I didn't think would be good for all of us, would I?"

*Oh, no, baby.*

"Would I, Roman?"

"I'm sure you wouldn't."

"Phoenix isn't at Belle Rose."

Another moment to try honesty. "She's here."

Silence lasted longer this time. "Be careful, Roman. I know you enjoy her, but she's dangerous."

"Don't worry about a thing. I can handle it."

"I'm sure you can. Does she have freckles on her breasts."

He brought his teeth together before saying, "Yes."

"Mm. Redheads are interesting. Are her nipples pale? Pale pink?"

The woman sickened him. "Yeah."

"Is her skin salty?"

"Uh-huh."

"How is she with her mouth?"

"Vanessa, where is this going?"

She laughed. "Just curious, darling. We must consider an evening together—the three of us."

He narrowed his eyes. "Sounds stimulating." And it sounded as if tonight's diving expedition might not be a setup after all.

"Oh, it will be stimulating," Vanessa said huskily. "We'll arrange it for tomorrow."

Not if he could help it.

"Take her along tonight. We'll make sure there's enough equipment for three."

"That's a lousy idea."

"Rubbish. Tell her you want to share everything with her. She'll be touched. The more she trusts you, the better. The easier it will be to do what must be done. After we've had some fun."

"I still don't like it."

"But you'll do it, won't you, darling? After all, I know best in these things. Did you ever kill a woman while you were fucking her?"

He turned his face on the pillow.

"Did you, Roman?"

"No, I didn't."

She snickered. "Then that's how we'll do it. Tomorrow night

we'll have a good time together. Some for you. Some for me. Some for her, too. Then I'll watch."

Roman felt Phoenix looking at him. He couldn't look back. "I'll wait to hear from you."

"I've got a better idea. You can do it while I'm making her come."

"Later." Roman hung up. He turned over, taking Phoenix with him.

"Ouch!" She wiggled against his grip. "You're hurting me."

He relaxed his arm and looked down into her face. "Do you really trust me?"

She frowned a little. "Yes."

"Good." Roman kissed her.

Phoenix kissed him back. This time it was her arms around his neck that hurt. He didn't complain.

"UDT." Otto Perkins giggled. "Bet you know what that is."

Roman blessed the darkness under the pier. "Tell me." Their rubber craft rocked gently. He'd already run through the routine with both Otto and Phoenix.

Otto made a disbelieving sound. "You don't know? Underwater Demolition Team! You sure you were a SEAL?"

"Sure, I'm sure."

"What about her?"

Roman glanced at Phoenix in her wet suit. "She wasn't a SEAL."

Otto uttered another explosive noise. *"Revelation.* What's she here for? To warm up any cold parts afterward?"

"You've got it." Roman shone a flashlight on the tanks to check gauges. Pierre had dumped Otto, and the equipment and taken off.

"IBS!" This time Otto's delight with himself was huge.

"What's that?" Roman couldn't resist asking.

"Damn it all! You don't know anything. We're sitting in one. Inflatable Boat Small. Maybe you're so long out of the service you've forgotten."

"Nah," Roman said. "I just wanted to test you. Bet you've been watching too many movies."

Otto guffawed. "Reading books. Hell, you're a cold-hearted bunch, aren't you? I read all about the kinds of things you did in Nam. No nerves. Wading about in all that slime. Silent killers."

Roman didn't point out that he hadn't been in Viet Nam. "Everything that was done was done to speed up the end of a war, Otto. At least in theory. You ready?"

"Ready!" Otto announced.

Phoenix didn't say anything. When he'd told her where they were going, she'd made no complaint, but he'd felt her grow wary.

Otto pulled his mask over his face and Roman didn't bother to tell him he could wait. "We gotta *row?*" the stocky man said when he saw Roman position rowlocks.

"Yeah, row," Roman told him, pulling out from the shelter of the pier. "Pick up the oars, seaman. Do what I tell you to do."

To his credit, Otto didn't protest. He rowed efficiently enough, quickly matching Roman's pace and following directions without question. They covered the dark waters rapidly, passing the elegant geometric shapes of booms—bright orange by day—booms used for loading container ships. Vessels sat at anchor. With the aid of his night glasses, Roman saw these clearly.

"We got a flashlight?" Otto whispered—loudly enough to raise complaints from snoozing sea birds.

"Don't need one," Roman said, sighting the hulk of a derelict tanker probably bound for either refit or demolition. "You'll be using your headlamps in the water. Target dead ahead."

As the IBS drew alongside a rusted hull, Otto's excitement grew. He giggled repeatedly, but donned his tank exactly as instructed. Phoenix readied herself, too. Roman didn't want to take her down, but neither would he risk leaving her here. If he hadn't feared raising suspicions about his loyalty to the cause, he'd have insisted upon her staying behind at his place.

"Now," he said quietly. "Remember everything I've told you.

Watch what I do and stay close. First of all, there's a right way to get into the water."

"Don't I know it!" Otto caroled. "You grab the stuff. I'll lead the way."

Roman already had his hands full of the dummy explosives. Before he could attempt to stop him, Otto had hoisted himself to the side of the IBS and tucked backward into the bay.

The next giggle he heard belonged to Phoenix.

"What?" he asked.

"He's unbelievable," she said. "We'd better make sure he doesn't kill himself." With that, she followed Otto's lead.

Rolling sideways from the boat, Roman slipped after them with the smooth, pleasant sensation that always came when he returned to what he knew best. He turned on his headlamp. Below him shone the lamps of the other two. The ship's hull wavered eerily behind the sucking curtain of water that surrounded it.

Working his fins, Roman speared downward, quickly catching up with Phoenix, who swam as if she'd done this a thousand times. He'd have to find out if she'd been down before, or if she was just a natural. Roman had met naturals before—one or two, anyway.

Together, they joined Otto. Roman tapped the other man's shoulder and pointed to the ship's side. Eager, even in the depths and with the shapes of sea life slithering past, Otto motioned for Roman to give him the dummy explosive device.

For an instant Roman hesitated, then he handed the pack over. Otto had already been shown how the magnets were attached and the adhesive putty packed to stop shifting, and deaden any sound.

Rather than heading directly for the spot Roman indicated, Otto took off, swimming strongly toward the bow.

With Phoenix beside him, Roman trod water.

Otto reached the point of the bow and flipped from sight.

Roman waited. He shone his headlamp on his watch—and waited. The stupid little shit was taking too long. Phoenix's hand settled on Roman's arm. She squeezed, transmitting her anxiety.

Roman nodded, motioned for her to go to the surface, and swam after Otto.

The billowing shape of an octopus burst into the beam of Roman's light. He drove nearer to the ship and watched the creature's fearsome grace as it propelled past.

About to set off again, Roman saw Otto return around the bow and head toward him. He felt more relief than the moment was worth. Most of all, he wanted to get Phoenix out of the water and back to the condo. With this piece of compliance behind him, he'd find it easier to isolate Geoffrey—tomorrow, if all went according to plan.

Pointing upward, he waited for Otto to draw almost level before beginning to rise.

He didn't expect the whiplike pressure around his body. His first thought was that the octopus had returned. Roman squirmed, failed to turn around, but reached for the knife strapped to his thigh.

His hand never found the hilt.

The second grinding blow was to his throat. He bucked. Not an octopus, but another wet-suited swimmer. Not Otto. Taller and more lithe than Otto. Stronger.

Roman brought his legs arching backward.

His assailant anticipated the move and mounted him, gripped his waist between iron-hard thighs. At the same time a searing pain shot into Roman's shoulder. He drew in a breath—a breath that wasn't a breath.

One jaggedly cut end of air hose whipped around his face. His air hose.

An inky cloud wafted about him. Red ink. Blood. His blood. The nameless swimmer had gashed open Roman's air supply and slashed his back at the same time. His arms didn't want to move.

He sank several feet. Twirled, and sank. In the cold airlessness, shock dulled his brain and his reflexes.

A spiral of light shone above him. He looked hazily up and saw the swimmer making for the surface. For the surface and for Phoenix.

Blanketed by the agony within his lungs, Roman raised his

leaden arms over his head and made his feet move. With rapid efficiency bought with long practice, he unstrapped his tanks and let them fall away. With the loss of extra weight, he shot upward.

Blood roared in his ears.

Bubbles spewed before his eyes. Air bubbles.

The last of his air.

His last breath.

"Roman! Roman!" He heard his name and knew he'd broken the surface.

"Roman! Here. Over here."

Phoenix's voice came from close by. His head bounced against the IBS and he realized Phoenix was already hanging onto the side.

"You're injured," Phoenix gasped. "I saw something happening but I couldn't get back in time."

A few yards away, another head broke the surface.

*"Darn,"* Phoenix muttered. "We're under attack. He already got you, didn't he?"

Roman gathered his strength. "Be quiet and prepare to board." With that he contrived to propel her into the IBS. "Lie on the bottom, Phoenix." The swimmer drew closer with every second.

"Like hell," she said, straddling the side of the boat. "I'll teach the bastard to touch you."

"Get—" Roman never finished.

A shot rang out. And another.

With his headlamp still on, Roman stared from the swimmer, to Phoenix, and back.

The swimmer's curse reached them before he flipped over and dove out of sight.

Phoenix held Roman's Beretta in both hands. He could see how the black weapon shook—and where the nose pointed.

"Holy shit," he said softly. "You scared the son of a bitch off. I only hope there weren't any birds overhead."

"B-birds?" Her teeth chattered like multiple picks on ice.

"The ones you were firing at."

# TWENTY-NINE

"You're enjoying this."

Nasty spared Roman a dispassionate glance and went back to unwrapping ready-threaded suture material.

Roman, facedown on Dusty's not-nearly-long-enough kitchen table, curled his bare toes over the back of a low, over-stuffed chair borrowed from the sitting room.

"Swab that again," Nasty told Phoenix, who obediently applied antiseptic solution to a deep, but clean gash between Roman's spine and his left shoulder. Nasty flexed his hands inside rubber gloves and said, "I don't think the guy intended to cut you—only the hose. He'd have kept you down long enough to finish you, then gone after Phoenix, I guess. Later it would have been an accident."

"With a slashed hose?" Roman sounded ugly.

Phoenix smoothed his hair. "It doesn't matter right now," she told him. "Just relax."

"Relax?" His voice rose to a squeak. "You and I nearly got snuffed in Elliott Bay. *Elliott Bay.* Imagine the laughs that would have generated among my ex-buddies. Geez, I'd never have lived it down."

Phoenix struggled to swallow a laugh.

Dusty didn't bother. "Wouldn't have been in a position to live it down, would you boy?" he said, guffawing. "But you didn't get snuffed. And, thanks to the presence of a lady who can think on her feet—or not on her feet—you're here making a nuisance of yourself. Put a sock in it and let Nasty sew."

Roman's brow puckered and he gritted his teeth.

"Smart to leave the IBS where it was and swim out," Dusty commented, bending over to study Roman's wound. "With any luck the guy who attacked you will think you went under. And maybe Phoenix tried to go after you. You've bought us some time."

Nasty held a syringe up to the light, then placed several small shots under the skin lining the laceration. With each puncture, Roman hissed through his teeth.

"It wasn't any fun driving here in a wet suit," Phoenix said in an attempt to lessen the tension. She shouldn't want to smile at the sight of Roman being not-so-tough.

"A wet suit and a knife wound," he said, vaguely petulant.

Dusty snapped open a small sterile drape—positioning the opening over the flesh wound—and Nasty went to work with his little crescent-shaped needle.

"Quit kicking yourself for being human," Dusty said to Roman. "I remember the way you dragged Bill Compton out of a burning hangar when the smoke took him out."

"Yeah," Nasty said, concentrating on his task. "And you had a broken leg. Never heard you carry on like this then."

"I was careless this time," Roman said. "I should have made sure who the swimmer was. If I'd been thinking straight I'd have known he wasn't Otto. Phoenix could have paid for that mistake."

"Otto who never returned, no, he never returned," Phoenix sang, deftly sidestepping his last remark. "And his fate is yet unlearned . . . Seriously, this was Vanessa and Geoffrey's work again, Roman. They set the whole thing up. Otto was a plant to get us into the water. He looked klutzy enough to be the real thing so we were both caught off guard. He must have swum around the hull of that tanker and kept on going so the other guy could come back for us."

"Makes sense," Nasty said. He dealt with the wound quickly, taking several internal stitches, and beginning to close the surface. "We've got to hope he didn't see the two of you swim away."

"We didn't use lights," Roman said. "And if he knows I drive the Rover, he'll have found it on the dock because we deliberately took Phoenix's Chevy. I wish I knew who he was."

"Geoffrey?" Dusty asked.

Roman shrugged and promptly yowled.

Phoenix stood beside him and held his hand. "I don't think it was Geoffrey. Geoffrey's big—strong—but not the athletic kind, if you know what I mean. He looks soft."

"Done," Nasty announced. He applied a dressing and stood back to admire his work. "I'm damned good at this."

"Humble, too." Roman pushed to sit on the edge of the table. He punched Nasty's arm lightly. "Thanks, buddy. Good job you keep in practice. Going to an emergency room might have cramped our style. They'd have asked too many questions."

"What now?" Dusty put a kettle on and took a bottle of liquor from a cupboard over the refrigerator. "Do we hide Phoenix's car and see what happens?"

"I'm moving on the Peak Club ASAP," Roman said grimly. "Before they get wind of the possibility we may have something concrete on them. If that happens before I'm in position, they'll take off and we may never get them."

"Eleven o'clock news," Dusty said, turning on a small, black and white TV on a counter. He made four mugs of instant coffee and liberally laced each one with rum. "Medicinal," he said when he gave one to Phoenix.

She wrinkled her nose, but drank.

Roman downed his in several gulps and handed his mug back for a refill. He took advantage of the easy chair and settled in, looking none too comfortable.

The national news progressed.

Phoenix felt an altogether pleasant warmth spreading in the wake of the rum.

"There won't be anything," Nasty said, watching the screen and voicing what was on all of their minds. "Too soon and no reason—unless there's something we really don't know."

The top local story was about three people missing and feared drowned in Elliott Bay.

Roman jerked forward.

"Holy *shit*," Dusty muttered.

"Don't swear," Roman said absently, his attention riveted on the screen.

"Someone else," Nasty said. "Gotta be. There's only two of you."

"I bet it's us," Phoenix said, groping her way to sit on a white wood kitchen chair. "I feel it coming."

"Countess Von Leiden of the exclusive Peak Club in the tiny Cascade town of Past Peak has reported that one of her partners and an employee, together with a club member, are overdue following a diving expedition into Elliott Bay."

A shot of the waterfront showed searchlights trained on the water in the area where Roman and Phoenix had entered the bay with Otto. A female reporter, her blond hair blowing across her face, stood in the foreground with police swarming behind her.

The next shot was of Vanessa, looking dramatically overwrought in black, sitting behind the desk in her office. "Well," she told the interviewer, "I haven't exactly been told not to say anything. There have been some disturbing events recently. Mostly involving a masseuse who works here. I really can't give her name at this time. She was attacked once already."

"And you think that episode had something to do with what may have happened tonight?"

"She was with my partner tonight," Vanessa responded, pressing a fist to her brow. "The boat they used was abandoned. The police say they can't rule out foul play. Particularly since they found a clue—the same type of clue that was left after Phoenix— Oh, dear. I'm so upset."

The reporter made sympathetic sounds before saying, "Clue, Countess?"

"I really can't be more specific. There was a clue after the first attack—and a subsequent episode with another female who lives in this area. The same, er, sort of object was found tonight in the bottom of my partner's boat."

Roman reached for the rum bottle and dumped a healthy

measure into the mug of coffee Dusty gave him. Before setting the rum down, he took a long swallow directly from the bottle.

"You'll get drunk," Phoenix told him. "You're probably already in shock and—"

"Just a minute," Roman said, holding up a hand. The news coverage had returned to the studio. "Will you look at that? Photographs. Who the hell is it supposed to be?"

"We think this is the man we may be looking for," a police spokesperson said of two photos, one full-face and one profile, of a blond man. "We have reason to believe he's dangerous. Please call the number on your screen if you think you've seen this man."

Phoenix set her mug carefully on the nearest counter. She trembled from the inside out.

"Where did they dredge him up from?" Roman said, frowning. "You remember anyone like him, Nasty?"

"Nope."

"He may be using an alias," the policeperson continued. "His real name is Rupert Saxton. He was a psychiatrist convicted of sex crimes in Oklahoma City two years ago. A few months ago he was released from prison. He skipped parole and his current whereabouts are uncertain. However, we have reason to believe he may be in the Seattle area."

"I've got to get away from here," Phoenix said. She stood up. The dark green sweat suit she wore belonged to Dusty. The shirtsleeves covered her hands and the pants fell in folds over her feet. "I've got to go now."

"Calm down," Roman said. "He can't get at you while you're with us."

"Who—"

Roman cut Nasty off. "Later. The guy's someone Phoenix had a brush with once."

She grabbed her car keys from a chair. "He's lost his mind. If he has followed us, he could do something we don't expect. I can't put Junior in danger by staying here. Roman, all of April's things are for Junior. Especially the Hopes vase. If I—"

*"Listen,"* Dusty commanded, indicating the TV. "This is new now."

"We've got a caller on the line," the news anchor said, her smile firmly affixed. "She says she has important information on the Elliott Bay case and she'll only give it on the air."

"What's this world coming to?" Dusty grumbled. "Scratch yourself and the whole world knows it before you do."

"We can't vouch for what you're about to hear, but in the interests of doing whatever we can to help, we'll put the lady on."

"In the interests of any piece of sensationalism you can get, you mean," Dusty said, but he plunked himself on the chair closest to the TV.

"Hello," the caller said, her voice high and nervous.

The newswoman settled a serious expression over the smile. "Hello. We understand you've got something you think will help with the police's investigations into the possible disappearance of two Past Peak residents and a third person?"

"Rupert Saxton couldn't have been involved," the voice said breathlessly. "That's all I've got to say."

"The police are going to be climbing the walls about now," Roman remarked.

"I know all about the glasses the police probably found, but they don't belong to Dr. Saxton."

The anchor leaned encouragingly forward and said, "How can you be so sure?"

"Because he was with me."

Even the anchorwoman was silenced.

"Shee-it," Dusty remarked, kicking off his Tweetie slippers.

Roman shook his head. "Don't swear."

"Junior's upstairs asleep."

"You might forget when she's not."

"Zip it," Nasty said. "Both of you."

"With you?" the newswoman finally said. "And where exactly would that have been, ma'am?"

"In Past Peak."

Phoenix passed a hand over her brow and felt cold sweat. She shuddered. "I don't know what's going on here," she said.

Roman reached for her and pulled her onto his lap.

"I'll hurt you," she told him.

He gripped her waist. "You'll hurt me if you sit there looking as if you're going to pass out. We've got things under control here."

"He came to see me tonight," the woman caller said. "He came to apologize."

The anchorwoman's smile took on a sharklike quality. "Would you like to share the reason with us?" She put her hand over her ear as if listening to someone else speaking to her. "My producer tells me we can't—"

"He wanted to say he was sorry for kidnappin' me," the woman on the phone said. "He said he never would have done such a thing if he hadn't been upset about tryin' to clear his good name."

"Ma'am—"

"He kidnapped me for most of a day. Frightened me out of my wits, I can tell you. But he was a gentleman the whole time. And he's sorry. He was with me—"

"Ma-am—"

"He was with me all evenin'. Why he's only just gone on his way and he wouldn't have done that at all if we hadn't seen the photographs on the television."

Triumph and determination glittered in the newswoman's face. "You're doing your duty," she said. "Stay on the line, please, so that we can have you give your evidence to the police and help your friend."

Roman's fingers had tightened around Phoenix's waist.

She looked into his face and said, "Evangeline?"

Using Dusty's Peugeot station wagon, Roman drove Phoenix to Belle Rose. Persuading Nasty to stay behind hadn't been easy. It had taken Phoenix's white-lipped appeal for him to guard Junior, and Roman's assurance that Rose would be okay.

"We're going to have to move fast." Roman feared they'd arrive to find the estate teeming with police. "Fast and invisibly. If the cops are there, we can't go in."

"I want to talk to Evangeline as soon as possible," Phoenix told him. "Something's all wrong with what she said. Something's wrong with the fact that she said it at all. She's not the type to blab about her life on television."

"She may have been taken in for questioning by now."

He felt Phoenix glance sideways at him. Could he keep her safe? Both Phoenix and Junior? Not unless he dealt with the club. Saxton and Evangeline were a curve they didn't need. They muddied everything.

He turned onto Mill Pond Road, saw approaching headlights, and steered into the first driveway he came to. "Stay put." Jumping from the Peugeot and keeping low, he hurried to the fence to peer over. A car had already drawn level. He saw police markings, then saw them again on a second car that passed.

When silence had fallen again, he returned to the station wagon. "Police," he told Phoenix. "We can't be sure there aren't more of them. When we get there we'll park by the garages and go in on foot."

"You make it sound like a military maneuver."

"It is like a military maneuver."

Belle Rose exuded dreamy calm. Once they'd left the Peugeot, Roman and Phoenix kept to a path through bushes leading to the house. No more police vehicles were in evidence.

Light showed through a crack in an upstairs room.

"Rose's bedroom," Phoenix whispered. "I've got a key to the house. Should I use it?"

"Yes," he told her shortly. "You are to stay with me from here on. Understand?"

He didn't like the hesitation before she said, "If you say so."

"I do say so. I don't expect Saxton to jump out of a cupboard. The police will have made a thorough search. But something's way out of line. If I didn't think we need to know exactly why Evangeline told the hokey story, we wouldn't be here."

"Maybe she was telling the truth."

"And maybe she wasn't. First we ask some questions here. Then I do my damndest to persuade the police to give me backup while I go into the club."

"While *we* go into the club."

He stopped himself from arguing. If he had to, he'd take her back to Issaquah and leave her with two very capable babysitters. "I shouldn't have let you come here with me at all," he said, thinking aloud.

"Evangeline wouldn't open up to you. She might to me."

Phoenix pushed the front door open softly and entered the rose-scented house. She shut the door carefully behind Roman. No lights showed on the main floor. Putting a finger to her lips and motioning for him to stay where he was, she started up the stairs.

Roman climbed right behind her.

"You can't come up," she whispered.

"Try to stop me."

She raised her arms and let them drop to her sides. Mumbling, she continued on to a wide gallery above the entrance hall. Rose Smothers's room faced the front of the house.

Phoenix tapped on the door. "Rose? Rose, it's me, Phoenix."

A cry came from inside and Phoenix threw the door open. "Rose? Are you all right?"

"Phoenix! Oh, Phoenix. The woman at that dreadful place mentioned your name on television. I thought you'd drowned in that nasty bay. Oh, my dear, I have been terrified." Rose, in a flowing pink cotton robe and matching slippers, surged up from a crimson satin chaise and flew to enfold Phoenix in a bone-crushing hug.

Roman entered the room and stood just inside the door. Evangeline wasn't present. Len Kelly was. Len, whose thin face shone faintly pink and shiny, and whose eyes shifted anywhere rather than meet Roman's.

"Come and sit with me," Rose insisted to Phoenix. "The police have taken Evangeline to some horrible place. They're going to ask her questions about that Saxton person she says was here tonight. I don't know what I would have done if Len hadn't stopped by. Mort and Zelda called, but I told them I was just fine. I can't have them losing business because of my troubles."

Len approached Roman and hovered in the doorway. "I need to tell you something," he said in low tones. He glanced back at the two women. Their heads were close together while Rose talked in an endless stream. "It's all my fault," Len told Roman. "I was in trouble so I took money from him."

Roman studied the man. "Who did you take money from?"

"Saxton," Len whispered. "At least, I know he was Saxton now. He came to my place and showed a picture of Phoenix. Said he was some sort of investigator who looks for missing persons. She'd just moved in here. He offered money for information and I gave it to him. I felt uneasy, but I swear I didn't know what he intended to do. Never heard from him again until last week."

Roman cocked his head in question.

Len's pink cheeks turned deep red. "There isn't any movie deal. Saxton sent more money—big money—to help me forget I ever met him. I was supposed to take the money and get out, only I can't do it. These are my people. Can't sell 'em out—not any of them. And I can't do it to Phoenix—not to Phoenix of all people. She doesn't know I'm alive, but she's special."

"I know." Roman made a rapid decision. "I want you to go to ground. For your own safety. D'you understand?"

Len swallowed. "I think so."

"Go to Mort and Zelda and have them give you a room there. Will you do that?"

"Yeah. It wasn't Saxton who took off with Evangeline, y'know."

Roman pulled Len closer. "How do you know that?"

"I saw it happen. She was snatched, okay—not that she seemed to mind. It was Web. I don't know what happened to Saxton after he broke in and threatened Rose and Evangeline. They were the only ones here. He must have taken off, I reckon. But Evangeline ran out back and got into Web's truck. Drove away with her."

"And you didn't say a thing?" Roman grappled with his own rage. "You *searched,* damn it. You pretended you were out hunting the kidnapper with Mort."

"That's why I took the bottle. Figured if I kept Mort busy with liquor, he wouldn't notice I wasn't interested in trying to find Evangeline and Web."

"What are you two boys chatterin' about?" Rose said suddenly. "For all they'd have us believe otherwise, I do have a notion men gossip more than women. What d'you think, Phoenix?"

Phoenix turned her intensely green gaze on Roman. "I don't think I could generalize," she said. "I find I need a lot of time with a man to know exactly what he's like."

Dammit. He was either a miserable man, or a very happy one. He was fighting for lives—his own and this woman's—yet a few words from her soft mouth, a hot-ice stare from her eyes, and he was the proud possessor of an instant, spectacular, and potentially embarrassing erection.


Phoenix edged along a narrow stone parapet below the second-story windows. Speed was everything if she was to do what she wanted to do before Roman realized she'd been in the bathroom a long time.

Looking straight ahead, she worked her way toward the balcony above the front door of Belle Rose. Her left hand connected with the stone balustrade. In a blessedly few seconds she was on the balcony and tugging at the doors to the upstairs gallery.

Sticky from not having been opened in far too long, when the handle finally turned, it did so abruptly and Phoenix almost fell backward with the opening door.

She regained her balance, left the door open, and sped through the house.

There was one person who hadn't had his say in all of this. Web was Evangeline's friend and—unless Phoenix was very wrong—they shared almost everything. Roman would probably alarm timid Web into silence. Phoenix knew how to question shy people.

Len had slipped away shortly after Phoenix and Roman arrived and they'd been unable to simply leave Rose alone. With a little luck, Web would open up to Phoenix quickly and she'd be able to return to Rose's room before Roman got too edgy.

Web's quarters behind the kitchen stood empty.

Phoenix slipped outside and along the path skirting the house. She drew to a halt when she saw the potting shed and workroom lights were off.

Clouds drifted over the moon, sending waves of white light rippling over the gardens. Phoenix smelled the faint scent of narcissus on the wind, a scent at odds with the ominous night.

She held her hair away from her face.

Coming out here was a mistake. Sometimes following the directions of someone with more experience was the best course.

She spun back in the direction from which she'd come—and caught sight of a different light. A yellow glow spread from the far corner of the house.

The conservatory.

Phoenix hesitated. Roman would be missing her by now.

Running once more, she made a dash for the conservatory and didn't slow down until she could look through the glass window in the structure's white wooden door. She expelled a grateful breath. Web sat on an old iron lawn chair sorting tools in a box at his feet.

She let herself in and hurried toward him. "Hi, Web!" She said. "Boy, am I glad to see you. What's going on with Evangeline? Did the police question you?"

Rather than answer, he continued to push things together in the box.

Phoenix approached more slowly. "I'm sorry, Web. I didn't mean to just burst in on you, but I suddenly realized you're the one who would know."

"Know what?" His voice cracked out the question. He made no attempt to raise his head.

"About Evangeline?" Phoenix said tentatively. She was close enough to look down on the back of his hair.

"What about her?"

Her muscles refused to move. All she could concentrate on was Web's hair. He dyed it red. Where it parted at the crown, paler hair showed. Not gray, or white, but nondescript blond.

She became conscious of his stillness. They were both still, both waiting . . .

Phoenix's attention moved to the box at Web's feet. Not a box, a big case—a case filled with expensive camera equipment.

"I asked you a question," Web said. His voice had lost the uncertain quality Phoenix had come to expect. "What about Evangeline?"

He closed a compartment inside the case, but not before she saw what was in it.

Web turned sharply and looked up at Phoenix. "Not so glib now, *Phoenix?*"

She took a step backward.

"Don't bother," he told her, rising. "You won't get out of here unless I decide to let you go."

Beneath the shaggy red brows, his little blue eyes fixed her. Solid blue eyes with no variation in color—blue disks with black dots where the pupils showed.

"Colored contacts," Phoenix said, her voice failing. She glanced back at the case and the compartment—the compartment containing several pairs of glasses with heavy lenses. "Why didn't I see it? I feel such a fool."

"You didn't see it because you didn't expect to see it," Rupert Saxton said. "If that idiot Evangeline hadn't decided to defend me to the whole world, you wouldn't be seeing it now. Never mind. I've been looking forward to this meeting. We're going for a ride in my nice black sports car. Remember the one? It's going to be fun."

"Lots of fun," an unpleasantly familiar man's voice agreed. "So Otto was right, Vanessa. Our little Phoenix isn't feeding the fish in Elliott Bay."

Sir Geoffrey Fullerton looped a heavy arm around Phoenix's shoulders and smiled down at her. She felt faint. Beside him stood Countess Von Leiden, still in the black dress she'd worn on television but no longer elegantly exotic. Her lipstick had worn off, leaving her mouth a pale, thin gash in her drawn face, and her hair was drawn back into an untidy tail at her nape.

"You're the woman from that club," Saxton said. "The one whose been paying Evangeline for information on *her.*" He inclined his head toward Phoenix.

"No need to give all our little secrets away, Rupert," Vanessa said. "I assume you are Rupert Saxton. Not that it matters what you say now, does it, Geoffrey?"

He shook his head. "I'd say this was very convenient. All we have to do is wait quietly for Roman to turn up. Too bad Pierre didn't pull things off in Seattle. That would have been so much cleaner. Thank God Otto had the sense not to get on his plane without letting us know he didn't believe Pierre had managed to kill the two of you."

Vanessa advanced upon Phoenix. "Evangeline told me about *Web*. We thought you might come here if you'd escaped Pierre and seen the TV debacle."

Phoenix shrugged violently away from Fullerton. Her heart beat too fast and too hard. Hate swelled to obliterate her fear. "Killing people is what you two are good at," she said, clenching and unclenching her hands. "You had April killed, didn't you?"

A short, electric pause followed, then Vanessa laughed loudly, her mouth and eyes stretched wide open.

"Shut up!" Phoenix searched wildly for a way to escape, a way to warn Roman. "Shut *up!*"

"We don't know any April, do we love?" Fullerton said. He enfolded one of Vanessa's wrists in a jerking grip that pulled her toward him. *"Do* we love?"

"What does it matter?"

"We don't, do we?" Fullerton repeated.

Vanessa sobered and shook her head. "Not anymore. We're going to get Roman here and the three of you are going to die." She grinned from Phoenix to Rupert Saxton, who studied Vanessa narrowly and without any visible sign of fear.

He bent to fasten the catches on the case.

"Geoffrey!" Vanessa shrieked. "Stop him!"

Fullerton slammed both fists down on the back of Saxton's neck.

Phoenix didn't wait to watch. She burst from a standstill to a sprint. The conservatory door still stood open and she made for the garden and freedom. In the dim predawn light she could see bushes and shrubs wound about by streamers of thin mist.

The door, the garden, and freedom—and Roman.

She saw Chester Dupree a second before his knuckles connected with her belly. "Where you goin', little lady?"

Phoenix heard what he said, as she fell.

Dupree picked her up by the front of Dusty's sweatshirt and flung her backward. "Good job I decided I was tired of waitin' in the car."

"Careful," Geoffrey ordered. "We've got—"

The crash of splintering glass drowned out the rest of what he said.

Phoenix smashed through a stored vegetable frame.

A dozen needles of torment shot into her hands, pierced her clothes to spear her body. The back of her head connected with a metal rim and she groaned.

Racked with throbbing pain, she peered up at shapes that wouldn't stay still.

*Roman.* She must warn Roman.

Scrambling, crying out with every fresh stab of glass, Phoenix fought her way up and staggered for the door once more.

"Git your ass where we tell it to be." Chester Dupree spoke as if his mouth was full and Phoenix braced herself. His shoe, driven by the weight of his thick leg, rammed into her back, just above her hip. "Down, and *stay* down, bitch."

A brick path ran through the conservatory. Phoenix's forehead hit those bricks. She saw the sand between the bricks, damp gray grains, gray grains that coated her lips and slipped inside to scrunch between her teeth.

Dupree kicked her again.

Phoenix vomited. She vomited and crawled.

And Dupree kicked her once more.

Dimly, she heard Fullerton exclaim, "I say. Bit much," before motion and sound exploded around her.

The voice she heard, calling her name, was the only voice she ever wanted to hear again.

She rolled onto her back but couldn't get up.

"A party." Roman's voice held no inflection. In one hand he held his Beretta, in the other a knife with a long, thin blade.

Vanessa shouted, pleaded that she was an innocent.

"You, Reverend," Roman said, "are a fat, disgusting bastard. I'm going to kill you and I'm going to enjoy it."

"Roman," Phoenix whispered, wiping her mouth on the back of a hand. "Don't."

If he heard her, he gave no sign. His right foot shot up, heel first, and slammed into Dupree's sternum. The man buckled instantly, grabbed his chest and opened his mouth to emit a strangled gurgle.

Roman leaped, and this time his heel broke Dupree's nose. Phoenix saw the tissue rupture, the blood spurt.

"Stop him!" Vanessa begged, while Roman knocked Geoffrey onto a stack of upturned flower pots. "*Stop,* I tell you. We'll make sure everything works out for all of us. Stop, now!"

Saxton landed on top of Geoffrey.

"Any bits you're particularly attached to?" Roman asked Saxton, tossing his weapons from hand to hand like a juggler and settling the glinting blade of his knife on the man's crotch. "This bit, for instance? I heard you like to use this—especially on women too out of it to know what you're doing."

Saxton swore and tried to scoot out of reach.

"You *are* attached to it," Roman said calmly, moving smoothly after his quarry. "At the moment."

"Get away from me!" The flash of silver in Saxton's hand was unmistakable.

"He's got a gun." Phoenix coughed with every word. Blood covered her hands. "A gun."

Saxton never got off a shot. Roman's knife blade came down and Phoenix heard Saxton screech. The gun flew from Saxton's helpless fingers and slithered between wooden crates. Roman had slashed the back of the man's hand, severing tendons and veins. Saxton hunched over, clutching one hand with the other to stem the flow of blood.

Phoenix saw a pair of shiny black shoes and some sharply creased light blue uniform trousers. Another pair of black shoes clicked into view, and another. The scene revolved before her. She closed her eyes.

"Police," a woman announced. "Nobody move."

Vanessa sobbed and began babbling that she was a bystander, that she was a victim here. Phoenix sat up and wiped her palms on her sweatpants.

"Yes, ma'am." The policewoman said to Vanessa, sounding patient. "I'm going to make sure everyone remains calm. Call for more backup," she told the third officer to arrive.

Her partner bent beside Phoenix. "How badly are you hurt?"

She tried to smile. "Not badly. It looks worse than it is."

"What do you mean by bursting in here?" Geoffrey said, regaining his feet and facing the armed policewoman. "This is a private affair."

"We're looking for principals in the Peak Club, sir," the policewoman said. "Would that be you?"

Geoffrey looked from one officer's gun to the other. "I'm Sir Geoffrey Fullerton. This is my partner, Countess Von Leiden." He glared at Roman, but said nothing more.

"And you own the Peak Club, sir."

"Sir Geoffrey," Fullerton said, smoothing his hair. "Yes, we own the club."

"And Mr. Parker Nash was known to you as a member in that club?"

Phoenix managed to push her head between her knees and take several deep breaths.

"What about it?" Geoffrey asked. "We have a great many members."

"Yes, sir," the woman said. "We've got a Helen McNair assisting us with our inquiries. The actress Helen McNair. She was attempting to cash a large check supposedly written by Mr. Nash."

"Good God," Geoffrey muttered.

"Don't say anything," Vanessa told him clearly. "This is nothing to do with us, officers. We've had a little domestic dispute here. Nothing we can't—"

Saxton, laughing madly, cut her off. When the laughter slowly subsided, the second police officer took up business as if there'd been no interruption. "Ms. McNair claims she was with Mr. Nash at the Peak Club only hours before his death. She claims he was under the influence of both alcohol and drugs and that driving his car would have been out of the question."

"Don't you say a word, Geoffrey," Vanessa said, driving her fingers into his arm. "They're trying to trick us."

"Would you take the countess into the house?" the policewoman asked her partner. She indicated Chester's heaving bulk. "Mr. Dupree, too. Kitchen will do until we get reinforcements."

"No! They want to separate us," Vanessa yelled. "Don't—" The second officer's gun, waved in her direction, silenced her.

Minutes of effort proved that Chester Dupree couldn't move from his crumpled heap on the ground. Vanessa was led away alone.

Dupree began to blubber. Tears mixed with blood and mucus from his unrecognizable nose. "I did the Godly thing," he said through swollen lips. "I took care of your little mistake, Fullerton."

"Shut up," Geoffrey hissed. "Don't say anything. That's what they want."

Roman continued to stand over Saxton, and the policewoman showed no sign of telling him to do otherwise.

"Didn't even know she *was* your mistake until she'd been with me weeks. Then it showed."

"Shut *up*," Geoffrey ordered.

Dupree was beyond caution. "Pregnant. I had plenty of explaining to do to my flock, I can tell you. A pregnant girl in my care and no sign of the father."

"I wasn't the father," Geoffrey broke out. "No one can say I was the father."

"She said you were," Dupree said. "And I looked after her for you. I did everything you asked me to do. Now you've got to make sure I'm all right, Fullerton."

"I didn't know she was pregnant," Geoffrey whined. "She thought it was a good idea to go with you. Probably to hide the kid she was having."

They were talking about April. Phoenix turned her aching head toward Roman and found him looking back at her, a deep sadness softening the anger in his face.

"I think you should bring the countess back," he said to the policewoman. "You can get exactly what you need now."

She nodded at him, "If you think so, Commander."

"Not a commander anymore," Roman said. "I take it you spoke to Dusty Miller?"

"Among others." She used her radio to ask for the countess's return. "You've got quite a record, sir."

Roman didn't comment.

Footsteps sounded on the path outside. Daylight filtered into the conservatory. The countess, when she was ushered back, appeared haggard in the new light.

"May I say a few words to the countess?" Roman asked the officers. Receiving a nod, he continued, "According to Sir Geoffrey, you were involved in the murder of Parker Nash."

Vanessa's face contorted. She pointed at Geoffrey. "He killed him. He killed him because Parker was asking for too much—pushing for things we couldn't deliver. Geoffrey made sure he could be rid of Parker and still keep his money. Geoffrey stole my money, too."

"No—"

Roman interrupted Geoffrey quietly. "Did he also kill April Clark?"

Vanessa recoiled. She wrapped her arms around her ribs.

"They had me drive her to Mexico," Chester Dupree moaned. "I didn't want to. Fullerton said he was going to marry the girl there."

"She threatened me." Geoffrey's voice rose. "She said I had to marry her or she'd tell the papers about what goes on at the . . . I said I'd marry her. It was all Vanessa's fault."

"Explain," Roman said.

"He killed her," Vanessa mumbled, rocking jerkily from side to side. "He had Chester drive her over the border, then Geoffrey killed April and left her there."

"It wasn't like that," Geoffrey protested. "Chester, tell them it wasn't like that."

Chester's head nodded as if on a spring. "Not like that," he intoned. "I drove. Geoffrey beside me. The countess hated that little girl. She hated that Geoffrey enjoyed her. She was the one who killed the girl. Beat her while she was tied up. Then she cut her—cut her to pieces." His battered face changed, crumpled. Fresh tears poured. Jerkily, he took a small bottle from his pocket, unscrewed the cap and emptied the contents into his mouth. A bead of silver slipped from the corner of his mouth.

"Stop him," one policeman said. "What is that?"

"To keep me safe," Chester said, coughing. "Ilona said it would keep me safe."

The officer dropped to kneel beside Dupree. "Mercury," he said, visibly amazed. "Call an ambulance. He's downed a bottle of mercury."

Phoenix smiled thinly. Apparently Ilona hadn't quite left them.

"Her," Chester burbled, gagging. "Killed that little baby, too, God help us all. She did it."

He pointed at Countess Von Leiden.

# THIRTY

Leaving again.

Phoenix refused help from the medics who arrived. "The reverend needs you," she said. "I'll be fine." Her hands would require some attention, but not here—not now.

She was no stranger to leaving. The only difference was that this time she didn't want to go.

"We'll need to ask you some questions," one of the policemen told her. "Make sure we know where to contact you." He was pleasant enough, but his interest, like that of the rest of the officials present, lay with Roman. Imposing, magnetic Roman who stood amid the debris like a lithe, dark demon who had conquered everything in his path. He *had* conquered everything in his path. Including Phoenix. Foolish, fanciful, Phoenix.

She mumbled assent to the policeman and backed away, not that she need be cautious to avoid attracting attention.

Handcuffs were in evidence.

Justice began its slow, but inevitable trudge.

And it was time for Phoenix to leave.

At the door she stood still to watch him. He had dismissed Saxton to the care of a policeman. Vanessa claimed his full attention. He stood over her, listening intently while she heard her rights read.

Roman didn't notice when Phoenix slipped from the conservatory.

Self-pity would cost too much, more than she could afford

to waste. She moved as quickly as she could. A visit to a hospital would be essential, but not until she'd found a place to think. To think and to plan where to go from here.

First she needed a vehicle. Then she would gather Mel and a few of her own and April's things.

Rose came from the kitchen door. When she saw Phoenix she picked up the hem of her robe and ran. "My dear, dear, girl. They've explained some of it to me. April, dead!" The pain in her eyes was too deep for tears. "Did you know?"

"For a while," Phoenix told her, glancing back.

No one had followed her.

"You're bleeding."

"It's nothing," Phoenix lied. "Just some slivers in my hands. I got blood on my face. I'll take care of it."

"I want to talk about April."

Phoenix couldn't stop her mouth from trembling. "Later, Rose. I can't now. I need you. Will you help me?"

"Anything. Just ask. I'll do anything you want me to. Oh, *April*. I knew, really, but I tried to pretend it couldn't be true. Phoenix—"

"We'll talk about April. I'll tell you everything. Some of it is happy stuff. But not now, okay? I've got to get away."

"No!"

*"Please,* Rose." She reached for the woman's hand and, when she took it, led her quickly back into the kitchen. "I can't talk about reasons yet, but I have to make some space for myself. My car isn't here, so I need to call a cab."

"Why? Why do you have to go? I thought you and that nice Roman were—"

"We aren't. Not really. I mean . . . What we've had has been a sort of convenience and it isn't necessary anymore." Not necessary to Roman. He might even think it was, but she couldn't let him continue to deceive himself. "Do you know if there's a cab company in Past Peak?"

"You're determined, aren't you?"

Phoenix nodded, yes.

"If I help you, will you promise to keep in touch with me?"

"You know I will."

"And you'll be safe?" Rose's doubts pinched her face. "There's no one who'll try to do anything to you?"

Like they had to April. "No one. I'm very safe. But I need a promise from you. I will contact the police to make myself available for questioning. There'll be other things later. But I don't want anyone else to know where I am. Do you understand?"

Rose pushed her hands into the pockets of her robe. "Not anyone?"

"Not anyone. The time will come when I'll be able to talk to all of you here in Past Peak. Not now, that's all."

"Do you drive a stick?"

For a moment Phoenix didn't understand. Then she realized what Rose meant. "Yes. I learned on a stick shift."

Rose took two keys from a board by the door. "You're sure you want to do this?"

"It's what I have to do—for everyone."

"I can't persuade you to wait? To talk to . . . Can I?"

Phoenix said, "No," and wished it could be *yes*.

"That Aston Martin my daddy gave me is ready to go." Rose handed over the keys. "The garage man makes sure of that."

"But—"

"It's all gassed up and it's yours for as long as you need it. Now go, if you're goin'. Before I make a fool of myself and cry again."

"Thank you, Rose."

"Shoo. *Now.*"

Phoenix left her, running through the house to the front door rather than risking being seen by anyone entering or leaving the conservatory.

"Be careful!" Rose called after her.

"I will." Her throat ached.

"Come back, you hear me?"

She barely did. "I hear you."

* * *

A week already and no word. And no clue as to where Phoenix had gone. Robin's egg blue Aston Martins weren't common. "No trace?" Roman asked Nasty on the phone.

"Zilch. The lady's done a big-time bunk. And—in case you've forgotten—she's got a right to do what she likes."

"No, she doesn't," Roman snapped.

Nasty said, very softly, "Yes, she does, buddy. I don't know exactly what happened between the two of you and I don't want to know—Dusty does—but I'd rather say I think you should be patient. I saw the way she looked at you and what I saw wasn't indifference."

He was too angry to be placated. "She'll have to show up in court eventually. They'll call her."

"Sure. But that may not be for some time. She can answer any questions the police have without you ever knowing where she is."

Roman thought about that. He didn't like hearing the truth. "Maybe she didn't take the Aston Martin."

"You aren't listening to me. She did take it. Rose isn't talking because she's obviously promised Phoenix she won't. Honor runs bone-deep with Rose, so she isn't going to break a trust. But she was the one who made a point of mentioning that she'd *loaned* her car to a friend. Come on, Roman. Loaned it to a friend. What friend—other than Phoenix? Find that car and you'll find your lady. Maybe you'll find her without the car. Maybe she'll find you."

Roman glanced around the apartment that had been Phoenix's—after it had been April's. Very little was missing; just enough to let him know Phoenix had been here before she left. "Thank you Pollyanna," he told Nasty. "One way or the other I *will* find her. I'm never going to stop looking until I do."


The last place Roman would think to check for her was close to his own condo.

Phoenix huddled in a beanbag chair in the apartment she'd

rented only blocks from where Roman lived—if he still lived there.

People told themselves lies.

She wished, more than she'd ever wished for anything, that Roman would walk through the door.

The wisest course would be to leave Seattle. She could make herself available as the court cases progressed, without having to live here.

Learning of Pierre Borges's drowning had been a shock. For a while she'd felt guilty but she was over that now. He'd hit his head on the side of the tanker. Accidental death had been the coroner's verdict.

Phoenix got up, pulled on a denim sun hat, grabbed her dark glasses and went out into the bright sunshine of the late July afternoon. She never went through the market. Instead she took her walks along First Avenue all the way to Broad Street. There she cut down past Western and Elliott and crossed the railroad tracks to Myrtle Edwards Park.

Always the same route. On the lone occasion when Roman had gone there, it had been because she'd told Nasty that's where she'd be. Roman wasn't a walk-in-the-park kind of guy—was he? There was a lot she didn't know about him, a lot she never would know now.

Chester Dupree was dead, too. Mercury poisoning. The man had died in a lot of pain. Perhaps that's what Ilona, with her second sight, had expected.

Phoenix kept her pretty piece of peridot, but only to look at and remind her of the lovely woman who had given it to her.

She walked on. Day after day—for weeks—she'd returned to the park. She continued to come for the sad-sweet memories that lingered.

Today tourists thronged the grass and the pathways. One large knoll teemed with members of a Hare Krishna wedding party, their orange robes brilliant, their canopy drooping beneath the weight of flower garlands.

Phoenix crammed her hat lower over her eyes and walked on. Then she saw him.

Leaning against one of the flat rocks that made up a sculpture, Roman looked toward the bay. Dressed in a white T-shirt and jeans, with one heel hooked into a rock crevice, his skin was darkly tanned. If he'd had a haircut since she'd last seen him, it hadn't been recent.

He turned his head away from her.

Phoenix took a step toward him, and another.

His hair reached the neck of the T-shirt, a T-shirt she now saw was worn, and frayed where the short sleeves stretched around his biceps. He appeared thinner, thinner in a way that accentuated every lean, powerful muscle.

He pushed away from the rocks and began walking—toward Phoenix. With his hands shoved in his jeans pockets, he watched the toes of his sneakers rather than where he was going.

Phoenix opened her mouth to call his name, and quickly closed it again.

She spun away and ran.

She didn't stop running until she reached her apartment.


Unbelievable, Roman decided, as Phoenix's white cotton dress disappeared into an apartment on the third floor of a building only minutes from his own condo.

He could have caught her anywhere along the way. But that would have made it possible for her to lose him again if she chose. This way he knew where she called home. At least, he assumed this was where she currently called home.

A couple of weeks after its disappearance, the Aston Martin had showed up in Rose's garage again. Rose—who was now called "best buddy" by Nasty—donned her vague mask whenever Roman tried to find out where the car had been. The Chevy remained in Issaquah.

Dusty had suggested telling the police he wanted the car removed, then waiting to see if Phoenix claimed it once it had been impounded. Roman couldn't bring himself to cause her any more trouble. She'd suffered enough.

*He'd suffered enough, dammit!*

One moment he was at the bottom of the stairs, looking up—
the next he was on Phoenix's floor staring at her peeling brown
door.

*Hi, how are you?*

What could be so threatening about that?

*What the hell d'you think you're doing to me, lady?*

That would be threatening.

Wilhelmina Phoenix deserved to be threatened. She deserved
to be shaken up. She deserved to know exactly what she'd put
him through in all these weeks.

Roman rapped on the door.

He'd rapped twice more before he heard slow footsteps approaching.

She left the chain on and looked at him through the crack.
He couldn't miss how pale she was, or that she grew even paler
when she saw him.

"Hi," he said. A whirling darkness started somewhere deep
inside him and grew. "How have you been?"

Roman felt her start to shut him out. His toe put a stop to
that. Muscles twitched by his eyes. "Reflexes are still good,"
he told her. "Something they teach you in training."

"I need to shut my door," she whispered.

"And I need to talk to you." The darkness gained force. Rage.
She'd ducked out on him just when they could have had everything, and he didn't understand why. He didn't understand one
goddamn bit.

"Please take your foot away."

"Stand back." Rather than do as she'd asked, he applied the
heel of his right hand to the edge of the door. One straight-
armed jab and the chain screws flew. So did the door—all the
way to hit the wall inside.

"Damn . . . *Why?*" He didn't expect a simple answer.

As he advanced, Phoenix retreated. Then she pivoted away
and dropped to sit in a red beanbag chair in the middle of a
room where the only other furnishings were a bookcase, and a
single bed against one wall. Mel was a black ball on the white

bedspread. April's vase—filled with sprigs cut from a curly willow tree—stood on top of the bookcase.

Roman stood beside Phoenix. "Why did you leave me like that? Why have you been hiding all this time?"

"It was best. As soon as it's feasible, I'm going back to Oklahoma City."

He dropped to his haunches. She'd taken off her glasses. "You're pale. Even paler than usual."

"I've been sick. Colds, flu, that sort of thing."

"Colds, plural? You mean you've had lots of colds, and the flu?"

"That's what I said."

Roman reached for the hat she still wore. "I'm not going to hit you," he said when she flinched. "We had that discussion once before, remember?"

Phoenix said nothing. She crossed her arms and held still when he took off the hat.

"Have you seen a doctor?"

"Leave me alone."

Roman felt a deep, gnawing fear. The fear almost overwhelmed the fury—but not quite. "You are making me angry, Phoenix. Angry and scared. How long ago did you see the doctor?"

"A few weeks. Two. Three."

"And you're still sick?"

"I'm getting better."

Roman studied her. "You could have gone to Oklahoma City before now if you'd wanted to."

She lowered her eyelids.

"Couldn't you?"

"I didn't want to."

He could barely hear her. "Did you say you didn't want to go?"

Her eyes met his and he felt weak with longing. She said, "Yes. I shouldn't want to be near you, but I do."

Roman knew better than to try to hold her. He stood up and

held out a hand. After a moment she allowed him to pull her to her feet.

"I've missed you." He held her hand tightly.

Phoenix averted her face, but not before he saw a tear slide down her cheek.

"What is it? What happened? I thought we had everything going for us."

She shook her head.

Roman reached for her other hand and stopped. The only windows in the room were high on one wall. Sunlight slanted in, turning her hair the color of fire, turning her white gauze dress to the texture of cobwebs.

His gaze settled on her stomach and his heart did things it had never done before. He touched her lightly with his free hand.

She bowed her head.

"You're pregnant."

"It happens."

"It *happens?*" He spread his fingers over her rounded belly. "Not to me it doesn't just *happen*. This is my baby."

"I guess it wouldn't do any good to tell you otherwise."

"Why would you want to?"

"Because it *happened* for all the wrong reasons."

He couldn't take his hand from her body. "Explain the wrong reasons." When he put his arm around her, she leaned on him. "What reasons, my love?"

"I'm tired."

"My God! You *look* tired. You should have been with me all this time, not in this hole. You belong with me, Phoenix. Come on, lie down while I make arrangements to get you out of here."

"I don't need to lie down. Stop worrying. Stop doing the right thing, for once. You're not to blame for this."

He made a fist against her back. "Who else is to blame, if I'm not? You've already said it's my baby." *His baby.* All he wanted was to grab her up and take her away, to know she was safe and well and happy—and his.

"I've had a lot of time to sort things out, Roman." She raised her chin. "You knew I was April's friend. I think you knew I was Billy."

"No—"

"You never pushed for my first name. I said I didn't like to use it and you let it go. We became lovers and you never tried to insist on knowing my name."

Habits of a lifetime didn't evaporate. How could he make her understand in moments, what he'd learned in years? "I spent a childhood being grilled," he told her. "I never had a private thought. I mean, I was constantly asked what I was thinking and why. And who had I spoken to and why. Phoenix, I don't believe in pushing for what people don't want to share so I didn't push you. I thought you'd tell me when you were ready. And you did."

She tilted her face, studying him so closely it was difficult not to look away. "I only have your word for it that you didn't ask because you were protecting my privacy."

Pregnant women could be a little odd, a little obsessive. He'd never spent time around a pregnant woman, but he'd heard all about how difficult they could be. "You have my word, Phoenix. You can trust my word."

"Can I?"

Understanding was soon going to be in short supply. "You'll only believe my word if you trust me, won't you? Why would I play games?"

"Because April told you she wanted me to look after her baby."

He drew a deep breath and expelled it slowly. "She didn't. But what if she had?"

"Maybe nothing at the time. But maybe after you'd had Junior for a while you didn't want to give her up. Maybe you loved April. Maybe you knew her before—"

"No!"

She clung to his T-shirt. "Maybe you want me because of Junior."

"For . . . I do want Junior. I love my little girl more than I know how to explain. But I never saw April before I found her in that ditch. I didn't even find out her last name until the day you were interviewed by Vanessa. I saw that interview on film in a room I'd found after hunting for weeks. You gave me my first lead on who Junior's mother really was."

The expression on her face changed, slipped.

"Phoenix, I want you for *you*. I've wanted you for who you are almost since I first met you." He rubbed her tummy gently. "And now I want you and whoever's in here."

She flattened her palms on his chest. "You need a haircut."

"Don't change the subject."

"And a shave."

"So what?"

"This T-shirt belongs in the garbage."

"Dusty wants it for a polishing cloth."

"Give it to him."

He smoothed the sides of her face and kissed her forehead. "I've been through hell, kiddo."

"I'm sorry."

"Don't be."

"I've been through hell, too, Roman."

"I want a promise out of you. I want you to promise that if you feel insecure you'll tell me. You won't dash off somewhere to suffer on your own—and leave me to suffer—you'll just come and tell me how worthless you are."

"Worthless?" Her face jerked up and her lips remained parted.

Roman couldn't hide his smile. "Got your attention, huh? For some reason you don't believe anyone could love you for yourself."

Phoenix wrapped her arms around his neck. He felt the solid bump between them and grinned broadly.

"Grin away," she told him. "I hope you'll keep on grinning when you've got a two-year-old and a newborn."

He opened his mouth to answer but she pressed a finger to his lips. "I do believe someone would love me for myself. You do. Now kiss me."